Private Acts

April 8, 1991

For Dad and Peg,

    Two great parents
and friends. Have
fun with this latest
read.

       Much love,

       Linda

Books by Linda Gray Sexton

FICTION

    RITUALS

    MIRROR IMAGES

    POINTS OF LIGHT

    PRIVATE ACTS

NONFICTION

    ANNE SEXTON: A Self-Portrait in Letters

    BETWEEN TWO WORLDS: Young Women in Crisis

A NOVEL BY

LINDA GRAY SEXTON

Private Acts

LITTLE, BROWN AND COMPANY

BOSTON   TORONTO   LONDON

Excerpt from "Little Gidding" in *Four Quartets*. Copyright 1943
by T. S. Eliot and renewed 1971 by Esme Valerie Eliot.
Reprinted by permission of Harcourt Brace Jovanovich, Inc.

Excerpt from *Out of This World* by Graham Swift.
Copyright © 1988 by Graham Swift. Reprinted by permission
of Poseidon Press, a division of Simon & Schuster, Inc.

Excerpt from *Couples* by John Updike.
Copyright © 1968 by John Updike. Reprinted
by permission of Alfred A. Knopf, Inc.

Library of Congress Cataloging-in-Publication Data

Sexton, Linda Gray, 1953–
    Private acts: a novel / by Linda Gray Sexton. — 1st ed.
       p.   cm.
    ISBN 0-316-78203-3
    I. Title.
PS3569.E886P75   1991
813'.54 — dc20   90-42557

HC

*Published simultaneously in Canada
by Little, Brown & Company (Canada) Limited*

Printed in the United States of America

For John . . .
in celebration

"No act is so private it does not seek applause."

— John Updike,
Couples

"Life is a tug of war between memory and forgetting.
The answer to the problem is to learn how to tell.
It's telling that reconciles memory and forgetting."

— Graham Swift,
Out of This World

Contents

ONE	*Mixed Doubles*	3
TWO	*Acts of Balance*	20
THREE	*Margins of Error*	34
FOUR	*Flight Patterns*	57
FIVE	*Gamesmanship*	74
SIX	*Comfortable Deceptions*	89
SEVEN	*The Mien of Love*	113
EIGHT	*Hurricanes and Women*	140
NINE	*Fantasies*	161
TEN	*Rumors*	180
ELEVEN	*Ascension, Declension*	194
TWELVE	*In Name Only*	213
THIRTEEN	*The Scorekeeper*	233
FOURTEEN	*An Impossible Standard*	257
FIFTEEN	*Just Business*	276
SIXTEEN	*Loyalties*	286
SEVENTEEN	*A Christmas Party*	300
EIGHTEEN	*Talking in the Dark*	313

Private Acts

ONE

Mixed Doubles

In Scarsdale, the men do not tinker beneath their car hoods on hot summer Saturdays or spend winter mornings doing small fix-it jobs in their basement shops, and the women do not clean their own houses or do their own nails. They all take their free time seriously — on the tennis court or golf course. They work hard, they play hard, and they pay someone else to manage everything that falls in between.

Scarsdale is a sixth borough of Manhattan — a suburb for those who work in the city but want fresh air at night and green on weekends. The three couples meet here for the first time, by accident, on Maggie and Sy Whitten's tennis court.

The Whittens' house on Mardon Road has a wide foyer, old dentil moldings, and hardwood floors. It is clear, immediately, that this is Maggie Whitten's home: her quiet taste — refreshing after all the chintzed-out decorators in the city — lights up each room. It is also clear, immediately, that this is Sy Whitten's tennis court, which he crammed onto their acre last summer as a way of avoiding the claustrophobic country club scene. In the New York suburbs there are at least twenty elite clubs, many with initiation fees starting at twenty thousand dollars; as a principal in mergers and acquisitions for the First Boston Corporation, Sy could easily afford to pay such a sum.

This is a game of mixed doubles: Sy is partnered with his colleague Christa Brooke, an institutional bond salesman at First Boston; Maggie is serving, teamed with Christa's friend

Jonathan Stratton. The score (2–5) brings determination to Maggie's face (she took up tennis last year as a way of spending more time with Sy). At thirty-six, she is a woman of energy, with a tall, slender frame. A blaze of long, wavy red hair, eyes of changeable hazel, and her well-defined bone structure make for a demeanor of quiet tenacity. She lifts her chin, tosses the ball, and double-faults her serve. She crosses to the ad court, sets herself to serve again, and then halts, elbow hooked skyward. Her face brightens as she looks up across the lawn.

A man and a woman stroll around the end of the house into the backyard: the woman, small, with a gloss of black hair wound up on top of her head; the man, tall and blond. Total opposites. As they get closer, he gives Maggie a slow grin (undependable, but very sexy); his legs are long beneath tennis shorts, his hair bronzed by the sun. He has a prominent nose, which gives his face an air of arrogance. Maggie kisses them both hello and begins to make introductions. As is often the case in such a gathering, it develops that they all have something in common beyond the Whittens: Wall Street.

M&A is *the* place to be in investment banking in 1986, stepping into the breach created in the spring of 1975, when the New York Stock Exchange deregulated commission rates and the bottom began to drop out on the big brokerage houses. It is a prestigious club whose prerequisites have changed from a proper pedigree to a love of fanatically hard work. To manage these deals (whose profits often climb into the eight-figure range) more and more bright young people are needed. They hold M.B.A.s from one of the top business schools — Harvard and Stanford, or Harvard and Stanford. For the men, it is all about money and power. For the women, it is all about money and power. There is no top to any market, not the financial or the personal; everything is possible.

The woman looks vaguely familiar to Christa and she realizes with a start that this is Alexis Somers, a principal in mergers and acquisitions over at Hewett Lowell — which, along with Morgan Stanley, First Boston, and Goldman, Sachs, is considered to be one of the premier M&A firms on the Street. Christa has never met Alexis before, but she knows her well by reputation. Alexis is considered by many to be the most "major" female on the Street, a real contender for partnership in

M&A — something which, in early 1986, no woman has yet managed at a top-tier firm.

As the introductions and explanations extend themselves, it also turns out that Alexis was Maggie's college roommate at Harvard, as well as being two years behind Sy at the Business School. Her husband, Nicolas Linden, who stands smiling in a rather aloof manner, is a boyhood friend of Sy's.

The shaking of hands is cordial enough, but a certain wariness emanates from Alexis, despite her smile. Apparently she feels threatened at having discovered Maggie and Sy busy with another couple. To be treated as an interloper annoys Christa because Alexis and Nicolas are the ones who have intruded.

As Alexis is introduced to Jon, she smiles and her gray eyes deepen: she becomes beautiful. Seeing his reaction to her, she sizes him up covertly. From the thick strands of silver threading through his black hair, she judges him to be older than Nicolas, near to forty; his eyes are so dark they appear to have no pupil at all; he sports a stubble. He is only about five inches taller than Alexis, with a wiry, compact frame. Hair curls through the opened neck of his white knit shirt. He catches her staring and she blushes.

"Alexis — take my spot?" Maggie offers, extending her racquet.

"Are you sure? I can wait until you're finished."

"Please don't. My two left sneakers need a rest."

They all laugh.

"You're sure?" Alexis repeats.

Maggie gives her a hug and retires to the sidelines to watch.

Alexis assumes Maggie's position as Jon's partner, and begins with a nice hard serve. The other three are keen competitors, and this will not be the sort of match where the men shunt the women aside to play a disguised game of singles.

Christa, watching Alexis and Jon discuss strategy, feels a flash of jealousy as Jon smiles at Alexis, who returns his smile, and dips her head in a rather sly manner. Her stomach tightens. She instinctively hates this sort of picture-perfect woman.

Alexis serves again, and this time, from Christa's net position, she can see her foot fault, an entire sneaker length over the baseline. She hesitates, but then does not call it. While footfaulting is not an obvious sort of cheating, it is cheating nevertheless — especially in a player so clearly schooled as Alexis. It is probably just a momentary sloppiness, Christa decides; after all, she doesn't want to look like a nasty stickler for the rules (though it bothers her, especially when Alexis wins the point).

When Alexis does it again on the next serve, if anything even more blatantly, Christa calls it before the ball lands in the service box. "Foot fault!" She makes no attempt to return the serve.

"Seriously?" Alexis asks, the dark wings of her eyebrows lifting in an arc (much too innocently puzzled).

"Seriously." Christa turns on her heel and returns to the service line, getting down and set for the next serve.

But Alexis takes her time, walking around the baseline and eyeing it. She measures with her foot in a slow and irritating manner (as if to indicate that she can't believe the pettiness, but that etiquette prevents her from objecting).

Christa's face gets hotter and hotter as the minute lengthens. How can it be that she is the one who feels embarrassed? she mutters to herself. Distracted, not concentrating well, she then fails to block the next serve, which Alexis drills into the box; Christa loses both point and game.

But now it is her turn. She has worked a long time to perfect her serve: it begins as a hard ball that flies straight at the receiver, then slices away in a weird curve as it hits the ground, skimming toward the sideline. Serving to Alexis, she balances herself: poised on the balls of her feet, she tosses the ball; her arm whips back; she stretches high, and then, with a snap of her wrist, slams into the small yellow circle at the apex of its climb.

Alexis races for it but stops short as it skids away from her, a sharp half-moon toward the sideline. Shaking her head, she sends Christa a look of grudging respect and then shrugs at Jon, who sends her a reassuring smile. Alexis smiles back, bolstered. She watches the shape of his body as he walks away from her to pick up the ball. With his back to her she can see the beige lines of his jockstrap criss-crossing beneath the white shorts. He underhands the ball back to Christa, who traps it neatly on the face of her racquet, flipping it up into her hand.

Christa shoots Sy a look of triumph. "Fifteen–love," she sings out, feeling smug as a cat in the sun and yet knowing that to be so emotionally engaged in a game is silly. She glances over to the side lawn, where Maggie and Nicolas sit: on Maggie's lap is Cash, Christa's Abyssinian, and Maggie scratches him right beneath his ears, his favorite spot; it is not surprising that Maggie (as intuitive with animals as she is with people) already knows his secret places. He looks like a tawny mountain lion cub with oversize ears. Christa never leaves him behind on weekends.

In the winter, Christa plays squash every day; in the summer, tennis — as much as time and opportunity allow. She has become a specialist in odd angles. Sports are the backbone of her life away from First Boston, and at the DAC (Downtown Athletic Club) she has made many friends, including Jon, who is also in the business — a defense-industry analyst at the research boutique of Keufel Ross. This last year, she and Jon had progressed from occasional games to a weekly match, followed by a home-cooked meal at her place.

Today, Christa's serve proves nearly unstoppable, and it is only when Jon, who has had considerable experience against it, intervenes and takes Alexis aside for a quick conference that Alexis is able to return it at all.

By the third ad in of the last game of the third set, Christa's muscles are aching with the strain. When she reaches set point for the fourth time, she bites the end of her tongue to help her focus. She looks across to the set of the other woman's body, balanced so tensely behind the baseline, and knows that Alexis is waiting for another of her hard slice serves. Christa bends, bounces the ball several times on the service line, and concentrates on its fuzzy outline. She tosses it into the sun, trying to look as fierce as possible, but at the last minute hits an American Twist, a quick, high-bouncing shot that lands just over the net on the very outside edge of the service box. Alexis, taken completely by surprise, rushes but swings late. The ball goes wide off her racquet.

Sy and Christa cheer, throwing their arms around each other. Jon and Alexis stand for a minute in dismay. Christa congratulates Sy, but over his shoulder she sees Jon cross the court to console Alexis, putting his hand on her arm again.

Christa reminds herself that Alexis is married to the handsome guy sitting with Maggie under the oak tree. Nicolas appears not to notice.

"Mommy!" screams Mikey Whitten, five years old, as he hurls himself into his mother's lap.

"Hey, Dad," Kate calls, running out onto the court and sidling up to Sy. He bends down to give her a kiss.

Maggie looks over at her seven-year-old daughter with a start: it is the first time she's heard Kate abandon the childlike appellation "Daddy." Even as she smiles, a peculiar melancholy descends over Maggie for a moment, dimming the day with a mist through which everything around her looks cloudy. The children are her timepieces: against their growth she measures her own.

Kate is smiling at her father with an expression of rapture; Maggie watches them hug and rests her chin on top of her son's head, warmed with the pleasure of him on her lap.

"Mom, can I talk to you?" Mikey's voice is earnest, serious.

"Uh-huh." She is listening and watching the conversation on the court simultaneously.

"Josh says he won't come over to play anymore if we don't get Nintendo."

Nintendo has been an argument at the Whittens for several months now. Sy is convinced that all TV computer games were designed by foreigners plotting to numb the minds of American youth. "I'm sure Josh will still come over," she says, comfortingly.

"Not for long he won't," he answers darkly. "He says I've only got a week or two left."

She kisses the top of his head again, tenderly, understanding further reassurances to be useless — around such thorny questions a small boy's world revolves. "How about if we set up your army tent in the backyard?"

He looks up suspiciously. "You think he'd come for that?"

"He might." She hugs him again and rubs her cheek against the silk of his hair, watching Alexis and Jon, still on the court, deep in conversation, even though Sy and Christa and Kate now walk over to join the group under the tree. Maggie knows her old friend well enough to interpret a great deal simply from the way she is standing — one hip cocked slightly to the side, hand on waist — and the dramatic gesture she makes as she undoes her hair from its clip and shakes it loose across her shoulders.

"Can I play with you, Dad?" Kate begs. They have just bought her her first racquet. A good athlete, she practices in the afternoons with her best friend and next-door neighbor, Samantha Kirchenbaum. She and Samantha are inseparable — sharing clothes, Barbie dolls, and secrets.

"Maybe later. How come you're home so soon?" Sy asks his daughter, keeping his arms wrapped around Kate, bearlike. Both Mikey and Kate have spent the morning next door, for a play date that will be repeated in reverse tomorrow; such swapping of baby-sitting affords the adults a little freedom. Jan takes the Whitten kids more frequently, because when Maggie takes the Kirchenbaums she is getting a houseful: Samantha, Joshua, as well as the twins, Ben and Sammy.

"So soon?" Kate repeats, indignant, throwing her head back and up to look him in the eye. She shoves her glasses higher on her nose and her lips move silently as (with the know-it-all air so characteristic of seven-year-olds) she consults the Swatch her parents have given her for her birthday. "It's practically twelve fifty-*eight* — Mom said be home for lunch."

Maggie sees that Kate's adoration is a balm to Sy, and that her daughter has already acquired the knack of a certain sort of flattery. "Can I have a kiss, too?" she asks Kate.

"Mom," Kate groans, rolling her eyes.

Maggie shoots Sy a look.

"I want hot dogs!" Mikey bounces up and down on Maggie's knees, pulling hard on her hands, one arm after the other, as if they are sparring. With a kiss, she disentangles herself, ruffles his hair, and slides him off her lap so that she can stand up.

"The baby wants dead moo-moo. Gross." Kate's upper lip curls back, just a bit, in an expression of disgust. The adults all smother smiles.

"I am not a *baby!*" Mikey says, inflamed. "I am a *boy!*"

"Babyfacebabyfacenevercouldwintherace!" Kate taunts; enraged, Mikey comes after her and she whirls away over the grass, arms pumping, her sneakered feet a blur as she runs, her skinny body already long-legged.

"Kids!" Maggie interjects, but they ignore her, disappearing around the edge of the house to the front yard. Maggie smiles at Christa. "I assume you came out here for the peace and quiet."

Christa laughs. "I could use more of this kind of peace and quiet."

"Who'll stay for lunch if I promise not to make hot dogs?" Maggie calls.

Jon and Alexis walk over. Christa and Maggie look to them for an indication of whether or not they want to stay to lunch, but Jon is engrossed in explaining something, using his hands to illustrate the words in the air. Maggie turns back to Christa, who still follows Jon with her eyes, and after a second's hesitation, Christa nods, evidently deciding that to answer for both of them is the simplest. "I'll give you a hand in the kitchen."

"Squeeze in another game before we eat?" Jon asks Alexis.

She smiles at him. "You're not too tired?"

With the look she gives him, Maggie thinks, *he'd be a fool to admit it if he were.*

"I never get tired," he says, his black eyes challenging her. Maggie sees Christa stiffen at his tone; she wants to reach over and pat the other woman on the arm; she wants to reassure her that during her years as Alexis's friend she has learned that flirtation is an integral part of Alexis's nature. A way of establishing power. Alexis sees an attractive man; she flirts; it comes to nothing. (In the end, Maggie believes that Alexis will not upset that fine act of balance called marriage.)

"You guys up for it?" Jon asks Sy and Nicolas.

"I want to pick Sy's brain awhile," Nicolas says. "Why don't you two play some singles."

Alexis's black eyebrows shrug upward and then she walks back onto the court; Sy and Nicolas, hunched forward in the lawn chairs, begin to talk shop about Linden's, Nicolas's sportswear company; Jon follows Alexis; Maggie and Christa cross the backyard into the house. There are shrieks coming from the front yard now, a little louder and more intense than before.

From the kitchen door, Christa can see through the dining room and beyond that to the large foyer and winding staircase. Everywhere she looks there are flowers from Maggie's garden, arranged haphazardly, lilac flowing over the edges of glass bowls, freesia and tulips crammed into pitchers, violet iris sprouting from a copper kettle. And because it's all slightly imperfect, it's obvious that Maggie has done it herself — which is the way she does everything, her stamp on each endeavor. She left her job as an editor at *Esquire* magazine to make this home and raise her two children. (Some people say she wasted her talents. Of course, as you get to know her better you realize those other people are just plain jealous.)

The shouting continues, distant but audible, from the front yard. "Want me to check it out?" Christa asks, hesitating at the door to the kitchen. She reaches down to pick up Cash, who has trailed in the door after them.

"The kids?" Maggie goes over to the sink and blots her face with a wet paper towel before washing her hands, sure that her nose has bloomed a whole season's worth of freckles from just these few hours in the sun. She shakes her head. "Probably more noise than action." She grins. "It's when they're *not* making noise that I worry."

Christa laughs, and — as if on cue — Mikey bursts in the back door, brandishing a stick, face scratched. Katie follows, sobbing, nose bloodied.

"She scratched me," Mikey accuses, angry and defiant, waving the stick through the air in a dangerous arc.

"He hit me!" Katie sobs. "With that!" She points dramatically and howls a little harder.

"Let's all calm down," Maggie says, drawing herself to full crisis height. She extracts the stick from her son's grasp, unperturbed by the corresponding escalation in noise, and quickly wrings out a cloth with which to sponge her daughter's face. As she works, keeping her touch gentle, she catches her breath against the surge of worry, irritation, and love she holds for each child. She wants her children to get along, especially when there is company.

Christa, leaning against the refrigerator, hands Maggie a fresh cloth and hovers helpfully nearby; Maggie peers at Kate's nose to see if the wound has stopped bleeding, making her hands light as she probes for the source of the blood. Now she sees the small gouge just inside the left nostril and pushes down against it with the new cold cloth. Kate holds very still, trembling. "Mom, it hurts."

"I know, honey. It'll stop soon, though." With her free hand, Maggie strokes her daughter's arm. One of Maggie's strengths is knowing how to comfort, and it gives her enormous satisfaction to put this strength to use. As a child she spent considerable time caring for her mother, a woman totally incapable of comforting herself, and now she finds other people gravitate to her for this sort of succor. Never does she feel more fulfilled than when she is making someone else feel better. After a few minutes more of pressure — minutes in which Mikey is silent, simply standing there with a hangdog expression, guilty over the bloody scene his stick has created — the flow abates.

Kate puts her arms around her mother and kisses her cheek. Maggie hugs her hard, glad that even precocious seven-year-olds can relent and be children once in a while. "Have a time-out until lunch is ready, Kate," Maggie says, as she releases her and takes the Bactine down from the cabinet over the oven that houses Band-Aids and coffee filters and Worcestershire sauce. Kate still looks shaken, but her chin has stopped quivering (she is certain, at this point, that she won't die of hemorrhage) and she walks carefully from the room, giving Mikey another hostile look as she holds the cloth against her face and sighs loudly.

"Your turn now." Maggie gestures with her chin. "Hop up here, big guy." Christa lifts Mikey up onto the counter so that Maggie can spray the disinfectant over the scratch on his cheek. He closes his eyes, grimaces, but says nothing. Maggie grins inwardly. This is Mikey's attraction for her: he can always charm a smile out of her, even when she is trying to remain stern.

"Mo — om," he wheedles.

"Ye-es," she replies, trying to keep a straight face.

"Can I have a hot dog?" he sing-songs hopefully.

"Mr. Irrepressible." She ruffles his hair and bends to kiss the top of his head. "Tuna fish today. A hot dog tomorrow."

Mikey subsides into a grumble, and slides down.

"I *told* you it'd be tuna fish," Kate hisses from the hall. "*In*-fant!"

"Don't push the limit, Kate Whitten!" Maggie flushes with exasperation, hands on hips. Her voice leaves no possibility of argument this time and her daughter's resentment at having been banished is now audible — sneakers squeaking and stamping over the stairs. Maggie shoos Mikey from the kitchen into the backyard, and then turns with a smile back to Christa, who marvels at her aplomb. "And where were *we?*"

"Tuna fish?"

"Right." Maggie bends and pulls out four cans, a metal mixing bowl, and a jar of mayonnaise. "Celery, onion, and dill are in the frig. Want to chop for me?"

"You got it." Christa sets Cash down on a kitchen chair where he curls up in a spot of sun and starts his motor running. She opens the refrigerator door and stops short. "Whoa!"

"What's that?" Maggie says, pausing, the fork in her hand.

Christa, laughing, begins very gingerly to pull the ingredients from shelves so stuffed with food it is hard to reach anything. "It's just" — she pauses, stretching toward the mayonnaise at the back — "well, my own refrigerator looks downright naked up against yours."

Maggie laughs. "That refrigerator will undoubtedly fall prey to my next anxiety attack." She smiles sheepishly. Some women tell other women not to peek into their closets or the medicine chest, but Maggie warns people off her refrigerator. The end of the meat loaf, the gluey clump of spaghetti, the lettuce weeping in a sea of vinaigrette — all those snips and snaps she cannot bear to churn up in the disposal because she is convinced that for lunch, or dinner, or snack, *someone* will eat them.

"I'm glad to hear you get anxious too."

"Who, me? Old Steady Eddie? No," she shakes her head, "*I* never have anxiety!"

They laugh together, and Christa pulls a sharp knife from the block. "And cleaning the frig helps?" She begins to chop the ends off the celery.

"Refrigerator, closets — anything!" Maggie laughs again (perhaps a bit more shortly this time). Talking about her anxiety always brings back the anxious sensation: pound, pound, pound from the heart, a long, slow squeeze at the bottom of the belly. She handles anxiety and depression both by scrubbing the tiles in the bathroom with a stiff brush, by washing sticky handprints off the glass windows of the pantry cabinets, by sorting through the endless mixed-up boxes of the children's toys. Any sort of dirt-under-the-fingernails activity that is difficult or smelly, neglected and postponeable until that very instant will do; to see immediate and visible improvement — to restore order, control — eases the ache within. Now she takes the can opener and starts on the tuna.

Cash immediately scents the air and hops down from his perch on the kitchen chair to come and twine himself through Maggie's legs.

"Cash, give it a rest, will you?" Christa glares at him. The cat stops, stares back, and saunters over to his chair.

Maggie watches, fascinated by the interaction. "What about you?"

Christa shrugs. "I work longer hours. Play squash. Or tennis. Cry sometimes. Take Cash for a long stroll." She smiles at Maggie, but there is sadness across her plump face. "It's all the same, isn't it?" She looks out the window and remembers the first time they met, just this past January, at one of those boring dinners for the firm where wives make stilted conversation with anyone who will talk to them. Maggie had been describing the difficulty she'd had that morning, trying to shovel out from a mini-blizzard by herself and still get the car pool to school by eight-thirty. She had joked that Sy always managed to be out of town at just the right time, making the story quite funny as a way of passing off her anger. She had seemed almost bewildered that night — as though something had knocked her over from behind but she didn't yet know what it was.

"What part of North Carolina are you from?" Maggie dumps the tuna into the bowl.

"Near Chapel Hill."

"Your parents still live there?"

"My dad does. My mother died when I was thirteen."

Maggie stops and looks at her, taken aback. "Christ."

"Breast cancer. It was awful." She smiles and Maggie smiles back, not knowing what else to say.

They work for a while in silence. Alexis and Jon are still playing singles; Mikey hangs upside down on the jungle gym and yells at his father to watch; Sy and Nicolas talk intently.

"So what's with you and Jon?" Maggie asks casually, after a minute, hoping the question is general enough not to be nosy, but will elicit a specific response nevertheless.

"Those two? Oh, theyya jes' frenz," comments Cash quickly in his deep Southern growl. The cat has been talking, with some help from Christa, since he was three months old.

Startled, Maggie laughs. Though this is Cash's second visit to Scarsdale, she still isn't used to having an articulate cat in her kitchen.

"Does he always answer for you?" she asks, nodding at the big Aby.

"He has an I.Q. higher than mine," Christa says with a smile. "No, really — seriously — Jon and I have known each other a couple years and see each other a lot, but . . ." her voice trails off.

"Theyya jes' *reel* good frenz," Cash continues again, while Christa stares off in the direction of the tennis court. Jon and Alexis stop playing. All four adults converge on the net to confer.

Maggie nods, itching to ask more but not daring to pry.

"Looks like they're switching," Christa observes.

Maggie comes to the window and sees that the men are setting up for a game of Canadian doubles, while Alexis is heading back toward the house.

"Heyuh comes trouble," mutters Cash.

"What's that?" Maggie asks in surprise.

"On'y thinkin' out loud," he answers secretively. From his spot in the sun, Cash stares at her and twitches his tail. Maggie gets the eerie idea that the cat knows what Christa says in his name.

Alexis bangs in through the screen door and grabs a soda from the refrigerator. "It's too hot," she announces. She stands in front of the window, swigging from the can. "Jon's a terrific player," she says, after she catches her breath. She and Christa are both watching the men. "He's very competitive."

Christa frowns and doesn't answer.

Maggie tenses a little, despite the fact that this is her kitchen, and only friends talking. She begins to mix the mayonnaise into the tuna, and shoves the bread in the toaster.

Alexis continues to watch the game out the window. "I keep stumbling over Jon's name in the *Journal*," she says, turning to Maggie now so that her back is turned, but not quite totally, to Christa. "But his press doesn't do him justice. We were talking about this NavCon deal I'm working on, and it's amazing how much he knows about avionics —"

"Not really," interrupts Christa, as she walks right around Alexis to Maggie, the cutting board, heaped with celery and onion, in her hand. "When you know his background."

"Excuse me?" Alexis says.

"He was an electrical engineer for Hughes Aircraft, in L.A., before he came to New York and started on the Street." (She lays the facts out as though they, and thus he, belong to her.) Her voice softens with admiration. "Six years in a row he's been the number-one aerospace analyst on the *Institutional Investor* All-American team."

The screen door bangs again. All three look up to see Jan Kirchenbaum standing in the doorway. She is a large woman with masculine shoulders and a wide face. "Hey, there." She grins and lifts her hand in greeting. "Sorry to interrupt," she says to Maggie, "but I ran out of mayonnaise."

"Here," Christa says. "We just finished with it."

"Thanks." She extends her hand and takes the jar. "I'm Jan Kirchenbaum."

"Sorry," Maggie says, from the other side of the kitchen, where she is standing on tiptoe to reach for extra glasses. "Christa — this is my next-door neighbor to the left."

"I'm Christa Brooke. I work with Sy at First Boston."

Jan nods. "Your name sounds familiar. You're the one in sales, aren't you?"

Christa nods. "Ooo, I love it — someone's been talking about me," she chides Maggie. "Or are you in the business, too, Jan?"

Jan laughs. "I *live* the business, but I work as a pediatric R.N. at Babies Hospital. My husband, Jerry, is a merger attorney with Wachtell."

Christa nods. "Another down-to-the-ground Street widow."

"Want to stay for a sandwich?" Maggie asks.

Jan shakes her head. "I left Jerry home with all four Indians, a grillful of hot dogs, and some unexpected extra mouths."

"Now I know why Mikey's so obsessed with hot dogs today! Who dropped in?"

"Who else drops in for lunch on a Saturday and expects a five-course meal, served on silver platters poolside?"

Maggie raises an eyebrow. "You mean Gertie decided to go slumming?"

"They were over at Metropolis for the day," Jan says, "and just *'happened'* to be driving by."

"So what's with the mayonnaise?" Maggie asks. "Even George McGovern wouldn't put mayo on a hot dog."

"Can you see Gertie eating wieners?" Jan shakes her head. "No, I'm making them a nice crab salad." Her tone, one of mimicry, starts them all hooting with laughter.

"Why make them a separate lunch?" Maggie asks, shaking her finger at her friend. "That'll just encourage them to come again next week."

"I think I'll say that you didn't have any mayonnaise," Jan replies cheerfully, handing the jar over to Christa. "Maybe they'll go back to Metropolis to escape my greasy grill."

"The latest weapon in family warfare —" Maggie comments dryly, "the frankfurter."

Everyone starts to laugh again.

"I'm going to scoot," Jan says, after a minute. "Maggie, I'll send the kids your way around two o'clock tomorrow. O.K.?"

Maggie nods and takes out a stack of paper napkins as the door slams behind Jan.

"*Mah-gee,*" Cash interrupts, "Ah have duhn wuhn superior job heyuh." Christa dumps the celery and onion into the bowl of tuna. "Wuhn superior job," the cat continues.

Alexis's mouth snaps shut with a click as Cash speaks; she looks startled, confused, and mostly, pissed.

"That's Cash talking," Maggie explains, wishing she could somehow defuse their hostility: it distresses her when her guests disagree.

"Cash?"

"Her cat," she elucidates, pointing at the kitchen chair with a well-mayonnaised middle finger.

"I see," Alexis says, although from the expression on her face she clearly does not. "Do you always bring your cat with you when you go places?"

"Ah neva get lef' behind on a weekend," Cash reassures

her with confidence, his drawl dipping deeper. "Ah'ze a travelin' man."

Maggie sputters into laughter over this; Alexis smiles, faintly, her expression rife with disbelief and distaste. "I take it you and Cash and Jon all live together in the city?" Her tone is pointed.

Alexis knows damned well that Christa is single, and living alone, thinks Maggie. *How mean.*

Christa flushes, and walks over to pick up the cat. "Not at all." She buries her face in the fur on his neck.

Alexis turns and raises her eyebrows at Maggie, who now pops the toast from the toaster and begins to spread the tuna fish. Alexis sips her Pepsi again and watches out the window. "Will you look at that," she says with disgust.

"What?" Maggie looks up from the assembly line of tuna and lettuce and bread and mayo.

"Jon's winning their 'friendly little game' because Nico is poaching on all of Sy's shots and screwing them up." She snorts. "Sy always brings that out in Nico."

They stand for a minute then, watching the two men snipe at each other about whom the shot belonged to, and the scene refocuses their attention.

"Boy," Alexis says, "if we were out there bickering like that they'd be smirking and chalking it up to our hormones."

Nodding, Christa agrees.

"Why don't you go break it up," Maggie suggests. "Tell them lunch is ready and they should wash up."

Christa goes out the back door. Alexis watches her cross the lawn. "She's weird."

"A bit eccentric, maybe." Maggie looks up from balancing the stack of sandwiches on the plate. "But it's a relief after all the business nerds we meet."

Alexis snorts and puts her arm around Mikey, who has come back into the kitchen looking for lunch. She laughs abruptly. "Porter says she's the opinion that counts when you're pricing a tricky new bond issue at First Boston. Of course, he doesn't know about her loud-mouthed cat."

"How are you and Porter doing these days?"

Alexis makes a face. She doesn't get along well with Chase

Porter, her immediate superior, who is not as smart as she and twice as arrogant. "Let's not get into it."

Mikey sits down to eat, stuffing the food in while making simultaneous demands for more potato chips, pickles, and milk.

"Katie," Maggie hollers up the back stairs, "come on, sweetie — lunchtime." She begins to scurry about, while Alexis returns to stand in front of the window pensively. As Maggie tries to finish up lunch for six adults as well as two kids, she wonders with a bit of irritation why Alexis can't pitch in more. "Here." She shoves the plate of sandwiches into her friend's hands, balancing a stack of napkins on top. "Take it out onto the porch for me."

"I'm worried about Linden's," Alexis says, heading toward the door as Maggie shoos her along, carrying a tray weighted with six cans of beer, two bags of chips, and a jar of kosher pickles. "I think our husbands have got us in some real deep shit." She can tell Maggie doesn't want to hear about it from the set expression on her face.

Jon holds the door open for them as they come out onto the porch and Alexis smiles up at him as she comes over the threshold. In a motion that looks companionable (concern for her top-heavy load), he puts his hand in the small of her back and guides her toward the table. And it is just that motion, and the warmth created by his palm, that Alexis will recall a month later, in June, as she steps out of the car on her way to the office that morning, trying to decide whether or not to accept his invitation for a drink.

✑ TWO

Acts of Balance

Nicolas can see her body, white against the black tiles of the shower wall, through the clear glass door. A cloud of steam obscures her for a minute, as she turns the water temperature even higher, but then she emerges again, the side of her thigh smudged up against the glass like a fingerprint. She is shaving her legs.

Even as he stands in front of the toilet, Nicolas keeps watching her and the long, careful rise of the razor, from ankle to crotch. She switches legs, raises the other, and bends again so that her buttocks bump against the glass; the ascending knobs of her spine lead the eye upward, a staircase, to the nape of her neck, which she keeps hidden under the wealth of her hair. In that instant he drops his robe and abandons all thought of returning to bed. His wife's luxurious renovation of this bathroom had seemed a ridiculous extravagance when they bought the apartment in the Seventies on Fifth, but it has proved remarkably useful: they always have their best, most innovative sex in this stall shower and in the deep, double Jacuzzi tub.

He enters the shower with a rush of cold air as Alexis turns to put the razor away: she stands, arms raised to the marble shelf, about to soap herself with foaming bath oil. Her gray eyes narrow at the sight of him, but before she can say a word, he takes the large bottle from her hand and inverts it, squirting a long lemony dribble down into her cleavage. Using the flat of his palm, he lathers the oil over her breasts, stroking, a circular motion that begins at the horizontal wings of her collarbone and ends in a near pinch at the very tips of her pale pink nipples. Alexis nude is all pinks and creams, and as he plays with her breasts she closes her eyes, her mouth tipping open to make an O of surprised pleasure, her tongue flickering out over her bottom lip. She wants to kiss him.

He squirts more of the bath gel across her flat belly and begins to stroke downward, watching a vulnerable expression cross her face. She is covered in the thick sudsy lather, her body slippery, bubbles hanging from the ends of her breasts, her throat catching at each breath. He knows how to make her feel good, and that empowers him. He feels himself rise against the curving gleam of her wet and smoothly shaved thigh, and rubs against her there, eyes closing — but the sensation almost makes him lose control, so he stops; he brings himself back by focusing on Alexis.

She sags beneath his hands, her own lax by her sides, as if she will be pulled under by the weight that tugs at the bottom of her belly, a blood-suffused ache; she is getting as wet on the inside as she already is on the outside. It has been over a month since they last had sex and so she doesn't let herself think about how late it is getting (or how much she hates the way he likes to control her reactions: the entire act). Shower water streams into her eyes, so she closes them. The sensations brought by his hand descending and stroking, working the slippery oil into lather, intensify and she remembers a porn movie in college, at a party, where she and Maggie were the only girls, present on a dare: a bound girl had been basted inside and out with oil and then fucked successively by five different men. Mortified to be present, Maggie had been disgusted, embarrassed, and even upset; Alexis, pretending to be embarrassed and disdainful, had, unwillingly, been aroused.

Nicolas moves his hand in ever-lower circles, so slow it seems he will never get there, until finally he is tangling his fingers through her pubic hair, rubbing up and down, very lightly, in just the right spot; the heat spreads up inside her until she thinks she will ignite, and she jerks her hips forward to bring his finger up inside.

She moans and, still standing, spreads her legs, arches herself forward onto his hand as she reaches for him, but he swings away from her, not willing to give in yet. Pulling her around to face him, he sits on the shower bench, tiled in the same black ceramic as the rest of the stall; as he sits, the shower plasters his hair down. His ears — perfect, whorled shells — stick out from the sides of his head; as he moves his long fingers in and out of her, probing every inner fold and curve, she traces the circuitry of the only exposed piece of flesh he will allow her to touch. He sucks her breasts, his cheeks hollowing with the suction, his tongue flickering against the tips, lizardlike, drinking in the shower water running off. She sticks her tongue deep into his ear, and, caught by surprise, at last he releases her.

She drops in front of him to fit her mouth, a soft glove, down over the length of his penis; she slides him slowly, bit by bit, deep inside until he rests against the soft palate at the back of her throat. She begins to suck, feeling him throb and thrust against her; at that he quickly pulls on her head and she moves up beside him, continuing to caress him with her hand. When he groans, she straddles his lap and lowers herself slowly onto him, as slowly as if she were unfolding a flower, petal by petal, holding herself back from the urge to impale herself, to stop the ache; and then she just can't wait any longer, and drops down.

Finally he gives her his mouth, covering her lips in a wide wet circle, his tongue pushing deep into her while the hot water beats over their backs and faces. He loves to watch her, her eyes glazed, face lost, hair plastered into black streaks down over her breasts as she whips herself up and down over him. She begins to move more quickly, the sweet pad of muscle on her inner thigh growing tenser as she gets closer; their skin slaps in the wetness, and her spiral of contractions begins, a small wave at first, widening out into strong concentric circles, like a stone thrown into a pond, each clearer and more intense than the last, until she puts her head back and screams, a high-pitched, sorrowing cry of relief, and the prickly heat rolls up and over her, her nipples go hard, her inner thighs quiver and release, and she collapses against him, grinding herself against his pubic bone. Lifting her body, he stands up and puts her against the wall, shoves harder into her, into that pink, sluiced, accordioned tunnel at the apex of which is her very center. Satisfied noises come from her stretched throat as with each stroke of his penis he extends her pleasure and creates his own, his climax building as he feels her warmth tightening again; the heat spilling from his entire body is concentrated, a raw nerve ending, and then he hurls himself up into that wet rhythmic stomping which is her body.

They slump against each other, and the water, lukewarm now, continues to wash them down. Their pulses slow, blood pressures drop, and Nicolas lowers his wife back to the ground as he fades from her body.

Her sense of time returns quickly, and she looks at her Rolex even as her breathing slows to normal. "Late," she says, turning the water off, but still leaning against him. "What are you doing awake so early, anyway?"

"Had to pee," he says, kissing her neck, trying to entice her into another round, preferably in their warm, dry bed. "Your ass was too delectable to pass up." He keeps stroking her, his hand tracing slow circles over her buttocks.

Recovered, she can think only of the time. Hastily, she gets out and towels down. They keep different schedules: she, up at the buzz of an alarm set for six o'clock and out of the house by seven; he, in bed till eight, not behind his desk at the Bronx office of Linden's till nine o'clock or so.

"It's been a long time," he goes on, following her out and nuzzling the back of her neck as she bends to dry her calves. "Let's take the weekend off, go someplace, be alone."

Alexis finds his closeness faintly irritating now when she is in such a rush; she looks at her watch and begins to use the towel more vigorously. "All right," she agrees absentmindedly, smiling at him in a distracted way while deciding that her navy linen suit would be good for today's meetings.

"How about this Saturday?" He picks his robe up off the floor and belts it tightly around his waist. "We could fly to Barbados for the weekend —"

"Fly? What?" Alexis interrupts, looking at him, startled. She begins stroking her moisturizer onto her cheeks with an upward motion. "*This* weekend?"

"Anywhere you want."

"I have to be *here* this weekend — NavCon's about to close. I told you on Monday that I'd be working through the weekend with the lawyers and the C.F.O." She begins to blow her hair dry, raising her voice. He never listens anymore when she tells him her schedule, and it makes her mad.

"You told me on Monday?" His face is set, his eyes reflect, stubborn, in the mirror. She does not turn to look at him directly; they are talking to each other through the glass.

"At bedtime. You were going over the loan reports, and you said 'fine.' "

He hates it when she can remember something in such exact detail: it makes it impossible to argue with her successfully. "I would never have said 'fine,' " he returns, mimicking her tone. "I must not have heard you."

"Maybe you weren't really *listening*." She switches off the blow dryer.

"Look —"

"No, you look!" She's pissed off now. "You don't pay attention, so stop trying to make me feel guilty!"

"We haven't had a weekend alone in months." His voice drops as hers rises.

She hears the entreaty, and her voice softens in response. "You knew what we were getting into when I joined the department." She feels as if she is beseeching him to touch back into the past, a time when they had thought as one. She wants so much to make him understand, to stitch up the distances that the past few years have put between them. "We spent that whole week talking it over to make sure it was right. Remember how excited we were?" She puts her hand on his shoulder.

He just looks at her.

She isn't reaching him, and she knows it, so she turns back to the mirror and speaks to him through the glass again. "Can't you remember when your work was this important to you?"

He watches her and still does not answer. He does indeed remember, but the truth of what she says does not ameliorate his fatigue or his boredom with being home alone on the weekends and in the evenings; he hates the distances between them. "Just this once, couldn't Porter handle it?" he asks at last.

She coils her hair into a twist and puts it up against the back of her head. "Why would I *want* him to?" she asks, opening the mirrored cabinet. Quickly she begins to put on her makeup. Mascara, liner, blush, a quick tap with the powder brush under her cheekbones — it is only a quick sketch. There's no time for anything more elaborate this morning. "This" — she pauses a minute as she stretches her mouth tight over her teeth and traces the pink lipstick across her lips in replication of their full bow — "is a fucking big deal — *my* deal."

Nicolas just stands there as she walks back into the bedroom, reaches into her jewelry box, and clips on two heavy gold earrings. She is still naked. She fastens a narrow choker around her throat. He feels his penis thicken and begin to climb against his thigh under the robe. (How he would like to push her backward onto the bed and make her late; make her moan with pleasure, his pleasure; make her lose control again and abandon herself to him.) "Just this once," he says, his voice hard and angry now, choked with everything he cannot say to her.

"Don't you realize how unfair you're being?" She turns to face him. "If I'm going to make partner early I've got to show them I'm worth it. This is an incredibly macho business. If I walk on a deal right before we close for a little R&R they'll think I can't cut it. And they'll be right, too."

"When was the last time we spent an entire weekend together?"

"I don't know," she says, with exasperation. "I'm not saying we don't need time alone, I'm just saying I can't do it right now."

"You could think about someone besides yourself," he answers bitterly. "A minute ago we were close as ever — and I was the one made you happy!"

"You can't control me like that, Nicolas." She shrugs, concealing her hurt. "I'm not a pet you stroke to placate."

"I always thought it was the best part of us."

"It's only an interlude now, once a month." She shrugs again. "Can't you remember when we were as close as that every day? You'd never have asked me to blow off an important deal in those days, because you understood me too well. My power excited you. You respected the part of me that *I* respected."

He stares back at her (he remembers when the connection between them was so finely tuned that they didn't need a word or even a look). Now she knows nothing and asks nothing.

There had been a time — he turns from her abruptly. What is the point of mourning it, or even thinking about it: it's gone now, and they have become two bodies — cohabitants — nothing more, nothing less. Sucking this deep inside his gut and holding it there like smoke, he puts his back to Alexis and walks out of the room.

She watches Nicolas move away from her, then crosses to her closet and snaps on the light. No matter what he wants she will not walk on the NavCon deal now. Successful completion (to say nothing of the $4.7 million fee) will win her enormous recognition within the firm, opening the possibility of making partner an entire year earlier than the rest of her class. (And, more importantly, to be the first female M&A partner.) She is just too close to screw it up. There had been a time when Nicolas intuited everything she must do and sacrifice to succeed in a department whose officers expected — perhaps even unconsciously encouraged — a woman to fail. She missed (mourned really) the man who had pushed her to go after whatever she wanted, and who had been delighted by the idea of hanging on for her ride to the top. Lately he asks for things she is incapable of (unwilling to give); the wild spark that had made him unique has gone dark.

Standing in her large closet, Alexis pushes these thoughts aside to dress, quickly, in a linen suit and a silk blouse. She steps into her shoes, pulls on the suit jacket, and tucks a scarf around the neck as Nicolas comes back into the room and gets into bed again, snapping open the *Journal* with a crackle and beginning to read intently.

"When are you going to make a decision about the branches in Peekskill, Nyack, and White Plains?" she asks, her voice not masking the edge she feels.

"It'll keep," he answers, without looking up.

"Procrastinating about this would be a major mistake."

"You're riled about nothing," he says, flicking the page with a moistened index finger. "It's all going to be fine."

"When are you going to stop acting like a baby?"

"When are you going to stop being a bitch?"

They stare at each other. Then she walks past him and goes down the hall, the sound of her heels clicking out into the silence.

In the breakfast room she settles back in her chair, pours herself a cup of coffee. She sighs, tries to calm herself. The small circular nook catches the early-morning sunlight — a commodity rare and precious in Manhattan — and looks out over the green of Central Park; the fourteenth floor of the building affords a bird's-eye view of trees, lawns, joggers, the Boat Pond. This room makes her feel alive, awake, part of the world — unlike the shuttered-in home she had grown up in, where the drapes were always drawn and the darkened rooms were lit solely by electricity. Her feeling as she surveys the scene below is not unlike the sensation of standing on the ten-meter diving board at the pool, with her toes curled over the edge, looking down into the clear water below. A sense of being above everything, in control, poised and ready to execute.

She and Nicolas had waited and saved until they could afford *exactly* what they wanted (they did not splurge on expensive cars and a house in the Hamptons when others did) and so when Alexis's salary and bonus at Hewett had moved close to the seven-figure range they had reached out and bought it: nine rooms in a prewar building overlooking Central Park. They left behind, with a feeling of nostalgia but not regret, the three-room rental on Third Avenue in which they had bided the first six years of their marriage.

They spent a half million on renovation and decoration alone (and while such a figure might have seemed astronomical to someone living west of the Hudson, it would have sounded perfectly reasonable to one living in Manhattan and working in the upper echelons of a Wall Street investment bank in 1986). She loves entertaining her colleagues here, loves having the opportunity to watch their faces — and their wives' faces — drop, when, as they stand in front of the sweep of the living-room windows, they make the inevitable offhand remark as to how well Nicolas's business must be doing, and she is able to joke, in all seriousness, that Nicolas bought the view, but *she* bought the apartment.

The decorator wanted to do the breakfast room in an elegant rose silk, but Alexis prevailed and hired an unknown artist she'd stumbled upon at an East Village sidewalk festival to come and draw a startling mural of jungle animals with human faces. The colors are bright and primary. Often they eat in here with friends, rather than in the formal dining room, especially at night, when the view of the park and its lights from the windows is equally startling.

Around the glass and iron table are six Summer Hill armchairs, deep with down and upholstered in a soft cotton stripe. Again, the decorator had protested — having had something more polished and formal in mind — but Alexis had insisted on buying these chairs, and several pieces for the library and bedroom as well, discovered on one of her many trips to San Francisco, designed and manufactured by a woman who had just launched her line. Alexis has an eye for spotting talent: when she sees it, she goes for it — be it in furniture or an investment deal.

She picks up a croissant and spreads it with butter and jam. Her exercise schedule at the firm's in-house facility, complete with a personal trainer (principals and partners only) enables her to eat whatever she pleases. As she drinks her coffee, she flips rapidly through her copy of the *Journal*. Soolei, the housekeeper, comes in and sits across from her, pad and pencil ready for instructions.

"Let's go over our lists," Alexis says. Soolei is a wisp of a woman: no matter how much Alexis urges her to eat she never gains any weight, and her bones seem to shine right out through her face. Soolei moves with barely a rustle, and her unobtrusive nature is one of the qualities Alexis and Nicolas most prize.

"Dry cleaning first," Alexis begins, consulting the notebook she always brings with her to breakfast, as Soolei starts making one-word notes. "The black wool suit, my silk blouse, the black camisole. Mr. Linden's suits — you'll find two on his side of the bed. His shirts to Wu's, and remind them about the starch again — the damned things are practically standing up by themselves."

"Dinner?" Her accent is still quite pronounced, so that the word has two clearly accented, delicate syllables and no ending consonant: *dee-nah?*

"Something for Mr. Linden — I won't be home. You decide." She flips the pages of the notebook. "And on Sunday night we've got a dinner party I'll try to get to."

Soolei nods and her pen moves again.

"Send some flowers for me, will you? Call and tell Phillip it's for Sunday — the invitation's on my desk in the library."

Alexis closes her notebook; Soolei slips from the room. Alexis glances at her watch and stands up to go back to the library to get her briefcase. As she walks through the hall, a small pain forks across her abdomen. She stops and takes a deep breath, but it grows. Forcing herself to stay erect, she gets to the den and sits down in the chair in front of her desk; she waits, takes deep even breaths, and gradually, it begins to ease off. With a sigh of relief, she gathers a few things from her desk, but before she finishes another sharp pain begins.

Since she was a young girl, Alexis has had bad menstrual cramps when her period starts, but this is something different, not a background ache to dull out with an aspirin. As she sits rigidly, fighting it, she considers calling her gynecologist, Lia Bates — but then tells herself not to be silly. When the pain passes, she walks quickly down to the master bath, tiptoeing past Nicolas, who is still reading the paper, and she wonders briefly (but only briefly) if he won't be late to work. She opens the medicine cabinet and reaches for the large brown bottle of codeine at the back of the shelf. Palming the tablet and swallowing it dry, she sits on the toilet, inserts a tampon, grits her teeth at another wave of cramps, and reassures herself that in fifteen minutes or so the codeine will take care of the problem. She stands, pulls her skirt down, shakes several tablets into the pill case she uses in her purse, and looks at her watch again. She is now ten minutes late.

Despite this, she pauses upon emerging from the building and stops before getting into the town car, which has been waiting for a quarter hour by now, to sniff at the air, take in the daylight and the sounds of traffic. It is a magnificent city, filled with the best of everything (and yes, she acknowledges, also the worst, but she can afford to look past the worst): from the lofts of the young artists in SoHo to the Metropolitan Museum, the Guggenheim, the MOMA; from the small bistros with fragrant, homey meals to the elaborate cuisines of Lutece, the Quilted Giraffe, and Parioli; from the Joffrey Ballet to the Metropolitan Opera; from the strange garb of the Chasidim who run the diamond district to the polished couture of the ladies who dominate Cartier's. Since she was a young child she has stepped over winos on street corners and beggars on grates, making her way from the fortress of private school to the fortress of home without so much as a glance sideways. Manhattan children learn early to make themselves blind. All the good buildings are guarded by that elite police force — the doormen; the city is armed against itself. Even so, the eccentric population of the city's rich makes it possible to sell a two-million-dollar co-op with an exercise room instead of a kitchen because everyone eats out anyway.

But it is a particular attitude that makes Alexis know that this city is her home and always will be: intelligence, creativity, daring — all coalesce here with uncanny force under the name of opportunity. Nowhere else is there such a large cluster of bright young people. New York has a rare air of freedom: come in, it says, make whatever you can here. Some are able and some are not, but those who manage produce something vast, important, and exciting. Alexis knows she will be one of these.

Overhead, the sky stretches, a thin triangular pennant, cerulean, between the tops of the tall buildings; the sun makes her squint as, faintly dizzy now, she tilts her head farther back. It is the sort of day that makes her want to play hooky and go sail a boat instead of going into the office, the sort of day that makes her feel like a little girl again: there is something about the blue above that reminds her of summers at camp, pine woods, and sunburnt fields, days suffused with warmth, sweat beneath kelly green shorts and logoed T-shirt; a time when games of capture the flag and diving off the dock took up all the time, and, as she stands there on Fifth Avenue, the dry dust of the softball diamond fills her nose, redolent of earth baking in the sun.

As the driver opens the car door for her, she gets in slowly, all this passing through her, quick as a flicker of the eye — yet lived again in that flicker, rediscovered through the single color, cerulean. The sky now, the sky then (memory: cupped within the mind, tipped in an instant by a small sensory trigger).

Alexis settles in, puts her briefcase up beside her, and lifts the car phone from its cradle. She dials overseas, direct to the firm's desk in London to get an update about trades that took place off the Exchange while New York slept. A glance at FNN (Financial News Network) over breakfast revealed a strong surge in both the Tokyo and Hong Kong markets, but Alexis needs details if she is to enter the office fully armed. She doesn't like to come in uninformed of any event, either singular or merely germane: she would feel vulnerable, as if she were sitting behind her desk in a nightgown. She waits for the call to go through as the car begins a series of stop-and-start, side-winding maneuvers through the heavy traffic; the driver's back does not waver and he does not once lean on his horn, although they are caught between streets and between lights in the lower Fifties now.

She looks at her watch and swears: even on a good day it can take forty-five minutes to get down to the financial district. Traffic is the reason her father — though a head partner at Bear Stearns — took the subway to Wall Street every morning; something as variable and frustrating as Manhattan gridlock would not detain him.

Her father had ordered his life in a certain fashion and expected it to unfold just so. As it did. Every morning during her childhood from the time she was four, she sat catercorner to the square of his placemat at breakfast, watching the shadow of his elbow rise and fall over the dining-room table — she the only family member up as early as he. They sat together in total silence, a grown man and a little girl who perched on the edge of her brocaded chair and never spilled or made a fuss. The maid served them: soft-boiled eggs, fresh juice, herring in sour cream, pumpernickel toast. Parallel silences. Alexis wanted him to put his newspaper down and talk to her, but the only break in the silence was the tap tap tap of his spoon against the brown Humpty Dumpty in his egg cup.

She followed him to the door, a softcover picture book under her arm to simulate a newspaper, a child-sized umbrella over her wrist in case of rain, and, most important, the square brown lunch box in her hand as a substitute for a briefcase; every day she put her face up to be kissed on the cheek and asked when she could come with him to the office.

Gradually, into this scene, her younger brother, David, began to intrude: first as a sleepy infant, carried by her mother (in a waft of scent and the hiss of her taffeta robe), to be kissed and pinched as Martin Somers went out the door, seven A.M. on the mark. Beginning on Davey's fourth birthday, Martin allowed him the regular privilege of dragging the leather case down from the hall table and handing it to his father before he went out the door.

To Marie and Martin Somers, well established in New York German-Jewish society, there were codes of behavior they did not care to breach; these codes were the safety lines upon which their entire world depended, and no reason existed sufficient to justify a failure to observe them. Everything — from the color suit appropriate for work, to the correct charities for Marie to chair, to the right people to mix and match for elegant dinner parties, to the number of maids one employed and the gracious but slightly condescending way in which they were treated, to the schools the children attended, to the feelings one had but never voiced — all of it was undiscussed but nevertheless clear.

They expected their daughter to be well mannered, well educated, alert, and charming; generally they were both too busy with their own events to attend Alexis's piano recitals, or ballet performances, or school plays. Never once did they suggest she should not pursue an activity or interest of which they did not approve. They simply ignored it. As Alexis rounded the corner into puberty, Marie taught her everything she needed to know about the external trappings of womanhood — from pedicure to coiffure — and was baffled when Alexis ran off afternoons to the debating club rather than accompany her shopping at Bergdorf's.

Even Martin, who tried fruitlessly to interest his son in the business section of the newspaper each morning over breakfast, was a bit unsettled by the avid answers his daughter could provide. To the relief of Alexis, her brother grew scientificminded with time, building intricate anatomical models and molecular studies in his bedroom; eventually, over his father's silence, he went to medical school and then into cancer research.

Her father remains as distant as he was during her childhood, while her mother complains more with each year about her fatigue (a disease Alexis is more afraid of catching than herpes or cancer), although now Marie does little other than go to the beauty parlor four times a week or shop.

Finishing up with London now, Alexis makes a few notes and does several calculations, still thinking and jotting in preparation for the meetings that await her. The car has proceeded far enough at this point to get trapped on FDR Drive, caught between the never-ending construction and the never-ending traffic. She stares out at the gray water of the East River, watches a garbage barge slowly pass, and then, impatient, dials again to check her voice-mail system at the office. There are three messages since she left last night; the third is a vaguely unfamiliar male voice; the sound of it nags at her for a second as she tries to identify it, and then it clicks into place: Jon Stratton. Like to get together for a drink? She has run into him several times now on the street, as their firms are directly across Broad from each other, and twice they have bumped into each other at the DAC — once coming, once going, clients in tow for lunch, a drink.

As she steps from her town car at last, with relief, she can still close her eyes and recollect the feeling of his hand, pressing into the small of her back, that afternoon a month ago when the sky was equally as cerulean as today's. She looks across the street at the building that houses Keufel Ross and wonders whether or not she can afford to meet him for even a drink. At one time her intense relationship with Nicolas would have insulated her from the attraction she feels toward this other man. Now she is not sure that she would be able (would want) to control herself if they were alone together. She believes that it is always safer to cheat with a married man — someone who has his own territory to guard and who will, in the long run, expect nothing. But Jonathan Stratton is single, notoriously single, and therefore probably quite dangerous. On the other hand, he is powerful and the smell of that power is an aphrodisiac to a woman looking to establish her own kingdom. And he has a reputation for staying single, for making sure he never gets involved for any length of time with just one woman. In a way, Alexis decides, punching the elevator button and nodding at a colleague to whom she does not want to speak, his determination to remain unattached is her insurance policy if she decides to call him back. On the other hand, it is also an outright challenge.

THREE

Margins of Error

"Wake-up time!" Mikey crows, bouncing on the bed as he pulls the sheet all the way down to Maggie's toes. Still under the weight of her dream, she reaches out for Sy (second nature, they have been together so long). She shivers as the air hits her skin. Mikey continues to bounce. She doesn't move or respond to him — hoping he will let her sleep a little longer — and then, instinctively, reaches again for Sy.

But she is alone in the bed; she remembers then that Sy is gone, to L.A. again; sometimes (but only occasionally and just for an instant), she allows herself to wonder how much longer they can keep stretching across all this distance. Waking up to an empty bed fills her with a loneliness that lasts all day. Whenever she tells Sy about this, he gets upset and defensive. Anytime she complains to Alexis, her friend points out how grateful Maggie ought to be to have a husband who is still so in love with her after all these years.

Even so, right now Maggie really wants a hug, a strong one, from her husband, and so she keeps her eyes closed, hoping Mikey will give up and go away. If she could just have a few minutes of peace. But he traces a line down her back with his finger, while simultaneously prodding and poking to try and wake her, and finally, her mouth thick with sleep, she can't help but smile and cracks one eye to peer at her watch.

"Six-thirty," she moans, turning her face back down into the heap of pillows in the middle of their king-sized bed. Deep as she burrows, Mikey pushes in after her. A series of Bronx cheers buzzes from her wrist up to her shoulder.

As her son turns her arm into a raucous musical instrument, Maggie represses the urge to laugh. He catches her watching.

"I see you!" he announces triumphantly, his small, naked body beginning a new war dance on the mattress. He stops suddenly and bounces down within a foot of her head. "Mom, I'm hungry."

Maggie flops over onto her back in defeat and puts her arms around this mischievous intruder. How she loves the smell of him in the morning, something sweet, between peaches and warm milk. "Did you ever consider sleeping until seven?" she asks, giving him a tickle, but distracted then by the ceiling, where there is both a cobweb and a crack in the plaster. *Can the roof be leaking again?* "The camp bus doesn't come till eight, Mike. You know," she says, tickling a little in his armpit this time, letting him know with her tone that she doesn't mind being awakened when it is her boy who is doing the waking.

"I don't *like* sleeping," he informs her, squirming away and turning his small freckled nose up in the air, searching for whatever had held her attention skyward. "And tonight it's definite that I'm only going to sleep a teensy-weensy bit." He looks back at her and holds up forefinger and thumb, pinched down to a quarter inch gap. "Where's Daddy?"

"On the red-eye."

He considers this for a moment, bends to pick the scab on his knee, scratches his bare bottom, and yawns.

"Why is it called a red eye?"

"Because the people who fly on it are always tired. And tired people get red eyes."

"Like Daddy?"

"Like Daddy," Maggie confirms, with a rueful nod.

"Why does he want to live in an airplane? Doesn't he like it here?" A fleeting expression of unhappiness skids across his face.

Maggie ruffles the spikes of his hair with her hand, gently. "It just seems that way, honey. Today he'll be home for breakfast." She gets out of bed and goes to pull the curtains: it is a typical day in June, cool to start but hot by noon. She looks out into the front yard, where, as yet, there is no sign of Sy. The red-eye generally gets into JFK by six-thirty; from there to Scarsdale is a forty-five-minute trip. Most of Sy's colleagues go directly to their offices if they don't live in Manhattan (and some even if they do), but Sy always comes home for breakfast with the kids and then takes a train into the city. Maggie blinks against the sun coming through the thick green of the Chinese elm and rubs her eyes as she heads toward the bathroom, where she washes her face, brushes Mikey's teeth, flushes the john after he finishes, and then sits herself. "Go wake your sister," she says, planting this idea as an excuse to buy herself a little privacy.

Flushing once more, she pulls the blind up and stands looking out as she brushes her teeth, slower and slower, absorbing the sight of her front perennial border in the early morning. English lavender and baby's breath, lilies, spirea, astilbe. Daisies. Sturdy plants, hardy and wild. But no roses — she doesn't like the elegant fussiness of roses, except at Christmastime. She spends several hours a week weeding and working the soil, and often sits on the front porch with a book, or making a silly card for one of the kids, or scribbling in her journal. Writing in her journal is one of her greatest pleasures: like writing a letter in the third person, it gives her perspective, and an opportunity to examine those private thoughts and actions of which she cannot (or will not) speak, but which nevertheless nudge her toward revelation and repetition.

When Maggie moved onto Mardon Road six years ago and met Jan, one of the first things she'd admired about the Kirchenbaums' house were the large herbaceous beds; Jan taught Maggie a great deal of what she knew, and now they spend hours browsing through seed catalogs and nurseries, drawing up plans for gardens they might someday sow. Maggie has never before lived in a house with a garden. This house is their very first home, really, and the garden — whose offerings dress her tables, windowsills, and mantel — seems as important as living-room furniture.

The curlicued white-frame Victorian had been built at the turn of the century and slowly refurbished over the history of its five owners. When Sy and Maggie left Manhattan to look for their first house, they'd turned resolutely from large lots with ranch houses. Instead (and with delight that they could afford the asking price of $450,000) they chose a big ramshackle house with strong architectural detail, a paneled library, bookshelves in nearly every room, and three fireplaces. Never mind that the bathrooms were all like closets, and the closets were nonexistent. The gravel drive, the old six-over-six windows, and the gingerbreading along the porch were all original and persistently maintained by the Whittens, even when practicality was in doubt. Buying the house together, pooling every available dollar the two of them possessed — saved and inherited — united Maggie and Sy.

It was only five years ago that they moved in, but this morning it seems much further away than that. Their first night in the house, they stopped unpacking the eighty-three cardboard boxes at midnight and went to sit on their front porch. In the wicker glider they creaked back and forth in the dark, holding hands. They were sweaty, Sy's T-shirt clinging damply to the broad muscles of his sturdy shoulders and back, but they sat close together anyway, the skin of their thighs and upper arms adhering like tape in the humid June night. Sy stroked her hair; she filled with contentment; that was all it took back then.

None of the house's drawbacks mattered to Sy and Maggie because they loved Fifteen Mardon Road from the first minute they walked through its wide front door. Part of their zeal for the house was a reflection of the way they felt about each other and about their marriage: there was nothing more important to them then. Any argument could be solved, any difficulty overcome; they were naive and trusting plumbers, certain every leaky faucet could be patched.

Now Maggie's daydream is interrupted by a flurry of protest coming through the wall, as Kate objects in a grumpy voice to her little brother's gymnastics on her bed. Kate never wakes quickly, as do Mikey and Sy; she is more like her mother, who needs a morsel of peaceful time with which to fortify herself before pushing back the cocoon of sheet and blanket.

"Mikey!" Maggie calls, hurrying from the bathroom to round the corner into her eldest's bedroom. The blue-and-white room is dark, and Maggie crosses to put up the shades.

With his mother's entrance, Mikey bounces to a standstill; as soon as Maggie's back is turned he begins to tickle his sister's feet through the cotton blanket.

"Mommy, he's *bothering* me!" Kate says indignantly, sitting up at last and peering out through a wild tangle of curls.

"She's a class-five phantasm!" Mikey screams, spraying his sister with an imaginary neutrona blaster as he leaps up and down on the bed. "Trap out, Janeen!"

Maggie tackles him and starts to tickle. Giggling, wriggling, he is momentarily distracted from his original purpose of torturing Kate. Maggie stops for a moment to catch her breath and smiles at her daughter, who still sits stunned with sleep, clutching her pillow. Mikey scrambles to his feet and resumes the attack.

"Now you look, Mr. Ghostbuster," Maggie says, catching him by the back of his pajama-shirt top. As she opens her mouth for a lecture, she sees herself in the mirror and is instantly reminded of her own mother (whom she has vowed never to imitate). Instead, keeping one arm around Mikey, she hands Kate her glasses and gives her a kiss on the top of her head. "Morning, honey. You look *so* sleepy — Mikey, go get dressed, will you please?"

She follows him down the hall to his room, forced to weave a pattern of complicated footwork over the scatter of train wrecks, trucks, bridges, cities, and farms. The Legos and Construx are all carefully joined to form the weapons his parents still refuse to buy him. She wonders sometimes if this is the early profile of a terrorist. How can it be that she and Sy, leftover pacifists from the sixties, now have a son whose main recreational interest is building bombs, guns, swords, and spears? She sighs and steps around the munitions factory. Maggie loves walking into the orderly peace of her daughter's room, where dolls from baby to Barbie keep watch in a neat line of painted faces, where row after row of My Little Ponies preside, where crayons are sorted and boxed by color.

"I'm not wearing that shirt," Mikey says now with defiance, his arms karate-chopping through the air. Keeping her frustration contained, Maggie reminds herself that every five-year-old is argumentative.

"It's a camp day. You have to wear a camp shirt."

"I want to stay home with you."

Maggie smiles, tempted for a moment by the thought of Mikey to herself for an entire day. They could go to the zoo, have lunch. . . . She snaps herself back to reality, knowing that such a break in routine would be a disaster: she'd never get him to go back to camp again. She hugs him. "I'd like that, Mikey, but just think of what you'd miss — soccer, swimming, snack. . . ." Her voice has taken on a coaxing quality.

He folds his arms across his bare chest. "I'm *not* wearing that shirt."

"Where did you put my sneakers, Mom?" Kate calls from the other room.

"I didn't put them anywhere. Where did *you* leave them?"

"I don't remember. Will you come find them for me?"

"Just a sec," Maggie hollers back, looking at her watch and realizing that despite their early start, the camp bus is only fifty minutes away. *Late, later, latest*, chants a small inner voice. How is she going to get this shirt on him? And where *are* Kate's sneakers? There are times when she feels it is too much for her to cope with all by herself. Sometimes the problems the children present enclose her, weblike, until it is hard to breathe. She thinks of how her own mother would have resolved this argument: one stroke of her hard, flat palm and the child submits. (She represses the memory and a wave of anxiety passes through her stomach.)

Eight years ago when she had pictured being a mother, and longed to be pregnant, she could never have imagined a scene like this. Instead, she would have painted herself as perfectly calm and patient. Yet here she is, fighting for control. It is all a cruel reminder of her own childhood: all those shortcomings in mothering (for which Maggie refused to forgive Vanessa) now park themselves right here on her doorstep as undeniable parts of her own personality — despite all her determined resolutions to be so different. (The unconscious is an excellent scorekeeper.)

"Mikey, put this on," she says, taking a deep breath and stuffing the shirt into his fist. "I'll be back to help you with your pants."

She locates the elusive sneakers under the bed, helps Kate with her buttons, and brushes out a mean snarl in her hair; her daughter selects a barrette to coordinate with her soccer jersey.

Kate allows her mother to brush her hair back and insert the clip — a rare exchange that fills Maggie with nostalgia for the days of Kate's toddlerhood, when this same bounty of curly brown was soft and nearly blond. She smiles as Kate pauses before the mirror, admiring the way the barrette and the jersey match. (Kate's concern for the finer details of fashion is typical of Scarsdale, a town where mothers and tiny daughters are often seen dressed in matching handpainted warm-up suits.) Nevertheless, it is foreign to Maggie, who pulls on her jeans and sweater in the morning and is glad if she gets the chance to put on her mascara and blush.

When Maggie finally gets back to Mikey, he has taken all the shirts out of his dresser and pitched them backward over his shoulder, where they are scattered, brightly colored flags, over furniture and toys. "See," he says, holding out last year's battered camp rag. "Here's the one I wanted."

"That's too small for you."

"No, it's not." He smooths it down over his round, balloon-taut stomach, where it ends an unfortunate inch shy of his belly button. Looking at the shirt, Maggie realizes with a start just how much he has grown. She catches him up in a hug and holds tight, wishing they could just stay this way. But he nestles his face against hers for only a second before squirming free. "Ghostbusters don't kiss," he informs her.

"There's no more toothpaste," Kate yells from the bathroom.

"Try the linen closet," Maggie yells back.

"No, you!"

"I'm getting your brother dressed! I can't be in two places at once!"

Maggie hears Kate grumbling as she goes out into the hall and opens the linen-closet door. *Squeak.* She looks back to Mikey, who is still waiting with that expectant expression in his brown eyes, hoping that she will not make him take off this favorite. She wonders what the counselors will say — his tummy sticking out through the gap between the outgrown shirt and his brightly colored Transformers underpants — and then stifles this thought as unworthy. *Who cares?* she thinks. She turns to the dresser to hand him a pair of shorts and grins despite herself. Without argument now — he's won his point — he sits down to tackle his socks and sneakers.

"I can *do* it!" he says, pushing her hand away when she tries to help. His fingers work hard to manipulate the laces as she watches, but coordination has never been his strength. Every morning they go through this routine: he tries, the tip of his tongue licking his lower lip in concentration, while she holds her breath, hoping that when he cannot manage it and has to ask for help he will not erupt in frustration. She respects his need to do things on his own, even those he cannot yet manage, but it is difficult for her to stay out of these small motions toward independence. Today he carefully makes the first loop by himself and then starts to make the second (bunny ears, they called it when she was little), but she's sure he will never be able to push them around and through. Kate comes in and plops herself down on the floor to watch.

"The baby's having trouble again," she observes, paying him back, Maggie thinks, for the wake-up call half an hour ago.

"I'm not a baby!"

Swiftly Maggie moves to squat between them. She loves them both: it hurts her when they fight. "Kate, help him," she urges, thinking that advice from his sister may be easier to accept than advice from his mother. "Undo your shoe and show him how."

Surprisingly, Kate obliges, undoing her lace with a swift pull and then demonstrating how it is done, her curly head bent in concentration. With pride, Maggie watches her daughter teach; with pride, she watches her son try. She balances with her fingertips, chin against her knees, elation filling her: she has managed some harmony this morning after all. Of such small moments is her day made.

✌

Sy stops short outside the bedroom door: he can see his wife, bent between his two children, trying to maintain her equilibrium in what he immediately knows has been a trying morning — the linen closet agape, an empty toothpaste box halfway down the hall, the shirts helter-skelter across Mikey's room. Mothering does not come easily to his wife, who finds elusive the patience required; but from her tenderness with the children now, he sees once again how good a mother she can be: her stubborn insistence on self-improvement is one of the things he admires most about her. Sy is grateful that she quit her job in Manhattan when Kate was born, although, even then, such an action was considered by their city friends to be decidedly bourgeois.

Sy stands in the doorway undetected, his crumpled suit jacket slung over his shoulder and the smell of his own tired body surrounding him, and takes significant pleasure in watching the family he has not seen for four days. He has looked at them every night before falling asleep in his hotel room, but he feels hungry for the touch of them now. Even when he only stays one night in a city, he unpacks the leather photo set from his suitcase before he so much as takes out a shirt; this ritual, religious in its exercise, is accompanied by an equally automatic snap of the on-off button on the television set. Though he mutes the volume, the presence of the silent, moving pictures from the television and the photos on the dresser make his hotel rooms seem less empty.

In the beginning, there was an air of romance about traveling, working hard all week long and then coming back to the quiet, his home, a wife who looked up with weary delight at his entrance and a baby who thought Dad was a new toy. Just before Kate came along, he had left his predictable (and boring) job at Morgan Guaranty (a commercial bank) for the promise of more (money, prestige, work, glamour) in M&A at First Boston. He'd felt triumphant then: they had thrived despite the challenges and the sacrifices. Partners. It had seemed a game: to win, all they needed was a little team effort. Eight years later, he is tired. Maggie is tired. His children miss him, and (hard as he tries not to know it) he suspects he is missing a great deal.

Maggie's crouched posture now reminds Sy of a memory that he reels back in as he stands there silently observing; setting his briefcase down, he is overwhelmed for a moment by the vivid force of time unspooling in his head: Harvard Yard in January, the trees bent under snow, Maggie bent over her bicycle. He was on his way to Lamont Library to get a book from reserve that he'd neglected earlier in the semester. Intent on his purpose, he nevertheless stopped (without quite knowing why) beside Maggie, who was struggling to pry the inner tube off the wheel rim. Another girl might have pushed the bike down into the Square to be repaired. Another girl might have accepted his offer of help. But Maggie just squinted up at him as he stood backlit by the sun, and shook her head, throwing her chin up, a gesture that made her seem, if anything, even more vulnerable.

He continued to watch her while he stood inside at the circulation desk waiting for the book, as she kept wrestling with the frozen rubber. Even muffled up in a parka and scarf, she was unusual-looking — tall, slender, with fiery hair that belied her air of fragility. When he came out a few minutes later, now allotted a mere three hours with his precious book, he found himself offering to help again. There was dirt on her chin, and when she looked up at the sound of his voice, he could see an odd mixture of emotion in her eyes: exasperation, anger, and maybe even a bit of desperation.

With one flip of his wrist, he remounted the tight rubber tube on the rim for her. She gave him a grateful smile of relief, and he saw in her eyes, quickly downcast, that she was a woman who believed she should be able to do everything herself — but who (secretly) loved to be rescued.

Now Sy steps through the doorway into his son's bedroom and is immediately assaulted. Mikey shinnies up Sy as if he is a tree trunk, wrapping his short legs around Sy's middle; Kate runs to her father's side, but contents herself with hugging his arm against her face, happiness percolating out through her grin. Maggie rocks back on her heels and smiles. "Welcome home, stranger."

He smiles back. "Sorry I'm late," he says, each muscle in his body releasing its hold on tension as if he is in a warm bath: the love of these three makes him feel rich, adored, secure. "Cab got stuck on the Van Wyck."

"Get any sleep?" Maggie stands and comes to kiss him across the tangle of the children's bodies. She puts her arms around him and feels his solidity: for an instant, they stand that way, all four interlocked. To have him home is positively luxurious. When he is there to put his arms around her, she feels protected from her own nameless anxieties.

He shrugs and answers her. "Enough to get by." For the first two years in the new job with First Boston, Sy was unable to sleep at all on a plane. Finally he asked a friend who was also a physician for a prescription; now Halcion knocks him out — fast and neat — for a few hours on each cross-country trip. Procuring a window seat at any cost, he props his head on a pillow against the glass, pulls his cheaters over his eyes, inserts a pair of earplugs, and wraps a blanket around his head.

Maggie doesn't respond: it makes no sense to her that Sy comes home from such an arduous trip and does not go to bed before going into the office. At first she blamed the firm for its impossible demands, but with time she has come to recognize that Sy is the one who pushes himself so hard: he does not like to waste time sleeping any more than Mikey does. As a result, there is a permanent gray-brown smudge under his eyes.

"Let's get some breakfast," she says, heading out the door toward the stairs. Sy follows, still carrying Mikey, and leading Kate by the hand. Maggie checks her watch as she hurries down the wide staircase: it is nearly seven-thirty and she hasn't gotten breakfast on, or the kids' lunch boxes made up yet.

She pours two coffees and begins to work on lunch and breakfast simultaneously: frozen waffles into the toaster (she likes them to start off with something hot), two glasses of juice for the kids, syrup from the cupboard, bread from the frig, a knife for peanut butter and jelly, wax paper packages of grapes and cookies. As she deftly fills the two lunch boxes and thermoses, her own mother skims through her mind — Vanessa, who could never seem to wake up in the morning and who made sure everyone else suffered right along with her. When Maggie turned six, she began packing her own lunch and helping her father to fix breakfast so that Vanessa could sleep: he made terrible sunny-side up eggs, the whites quivering like something unspeakably embryonic. She slid them into her napkin, unwilling to hurt his feelings.

Vanessa saved her best for nighttime, Maggie reflects now as she pops the waffles out of the toaster; a concert violinist who gave up a promising beginning in New York City to come to Boston (her husband, Turner, had begun his analytic training at the Psychiatric Institute, and their only child, Margaret Thompson Adams, had just been born), Vanessa rehearsed with her chamber group three nights a week.

Because of her mother's schedule they ate dinner as a family only twice a week; Maggie most often ate alone, fed by the housekeeper at five o'clock, at the kitchen table. By the time she was old enough for such perceptions, Maggie took umbrage at the restrictions her mother's career placed on their time together; as the years went on she also became increasingly aware of her mother's resentment over the now-distant yet omnipresent career sacrifice, which resentment moved like a cold and inexorable wedge between her parents as Maggie moved into adolescence.

Maggie learned early in life to question nothing. (As the daughter of an analyst, she knew that when you ask questions you sometimes find answers you don't want to hear.) For all that childhood and adolescence is reputed to be a time for just such questioning, her own had depended on a fragile equilibrium she was afraid to upset: her parents' marriage tenuous even in a child's eyes; her mother's career thwarted in the name of motherhood; her father's silence. And a year-long period when she was three (buried but never forgotten) when Maggie was separated from her family and sent to live with her grandparents because her mother could not cope and was hospitalized. All these circumstances were the boundaries of both her world and her imagination. To question anything at all (certainly not her parents' authority, or the view of life they presented) was too risky: she accepted instead whatever they offered (no matter how little) and believed herself to be grateful. Her very presence kept a certain sort of peace. To her great surprise, when she left for college they did not divorce or even separate, casting confusion over all her assumptions.

Now, outside her kitchen window, a streak of yellow flashes. *Oriole*, she thinks, and stops midstride, staring through the glass for a minute: *are they nesting somewhere nearby?*

At the kitchen table, Sy is trying to keep the kids' wreckage to a minimum. Mikey in particular likes to flood his plate with syrup, turning each waffle into a well-soaked sponge. His orange juice goes over onto the floor, and Maggie tosses Sy a roll of paper towel as she begins to shove things back into the refrigerator. Sy mops up the mess and wonders how his wife manages all this by herself on the mornings he is not here.

While drinking his coffee and talking with the kids, he begins to shuffle through the week's mail: Mastercard, Amex,

Con Edison, mortgage, lawn service, dry cleaner. As he opens the envelopes, his chest and throat constrict in the sort of discomfort that makes him want to snap at the children's bickering over whose turn it is to get the stickers off the back of the cereal box. But he doesn't; he knows he ought to be grateful that there aren't envelopes from Bloomingdale's, Bergdorf's, and Saks. He ought to be grateful that Maggie is a different sort of woman from their next-door neighbor, Irene Karp, who confided to Sy last week that the only thing that helps *her* anxiety is using her charge card at Needless Markup (Neiman Marcus).

"Daddy?"

He looks up into Kate's earnest gaze.

"Uh-huh." He smiles at her face with pleasure.

"Could we hit a few balls when you get home tonight?"

Sy frowns, trying to remember his schedule. "If I make it before dark," he promises, thinking nevertheless of how tired he will be by then.

"That's what you said last time and then you were too late!" Her voice is indignant, warning him she will not be fooled with another empty promise.

He sighs. "If I don't make it tonight, then first thing tomorrow morning. O.K.?"

"O.K.," she agrees grudgingly, stirring her last few Cocoa Puffs through the sea of remaining milk. "I've been working on my serve — you'll see."

Sy smiles at her and goes back to flipping through the bills and sorting them into piles, but when he comes to "Paccabella & Sons, Plumbers," he tears it open and quickly scans it: "Removed son's toilet from floor, removed dinosaur toy from same, reinstalled toilet . . . $73.01."

"What's this?" he asks Maggie, waving the bill in the air, a little irritation showing now, but it is irritation mixed with amusement. " 'Removed toilet from floor'?"

"Ask Mikey," she answers, nodding in the direction of their son. "Ask him why the plumber had to take the toilet totally apart, right off the floor, so he could get down into the drain."

Sy looks at Mikey and waits.

"I don't know." The boy hangs his head and pokes at his waffle with his finger, leaving a soggy indentation. Then he looks up at his father with a nervous smile. It is not clear if he is scared or sorry or delighted with the stir he is creating. "I flushed my dragon down."

"We went through all this two months ago," Sy answers, angry now. "Why on *earth* would you do it again?"

"But Daddy," Mikey says miserably, sliding down off his chair and going around to stand next to him. "That dragon — he's really fierce! He bited me!"

"You flushed him down because he bit you?" Sy knows he mustn't let Mikey see the laughter building inside, so he rubs his hand across his mouth to get control, remembering, for a minute, the sheer joy he'd felt at ten, when he and Nicolas, best friends, snuck out of Hebrew school to go play handball on the roof of the temple. Although Sy is well settled into his thirties now, a man weighted by responsibility, inside of him still lives a spunky child.

Mikey nods solemnly. "He did! He bited me *hard!*"

"Where is he now?"

"Mommy made me put him in the garbage — she said we can't have dangerous reptiles in this house!"

"Mommy was right," Sy says, the grin leaking out at last to spread across his face. He turns once again to his wife, who is also repressing a smile as she snaps the lids of the lunch boxes closed. "Did you punish him?"

"She said I can't watch Ghostbusters for a whole week!" Mikey interrupts. "And no dessert for three days!" He pouts.

Sy fights hard to keep a straight face. "Never mind about that — you just know that if you ever do it again, you're going to get spanked. By me." He sighs, sobering then, and runs his hand through his curly hair. He rubs his scratchy face as he looks at the bill again. "Jesus, Maggie, we've got to find a cheaper plumber."

"Look — this guy comes right away when I call."

"For seventy bucks he ought to sprout wings."

"When was the last time you got stuck mopping up the crap from a plugged toilet?" This sort of nagging about money angers her.

"O.K., O.K." Sy puts up his hands in surrender and changes the subject. "Did you find out when your parents are coming down?"

"I don't know," Maggie sighs. "They're as elusive as ever.

You'd think they'd want to see the kids. Six months was a long time ago."

Sy gets up and wraps his arms around his wife. Maggie has never been able to accept her parents' distance or their lack of curiosity about her life. With sadness he rests his head against her cheek as he thinks of the kind of grandparents his own parents would have made had they been alive: his mother's broad bosom, a comfort for a child's head, her arms warm and soft as the dough from her kitchen; the faint smell of a pot roast (they had called it brisket then), with its onion, tomato, carrot, and brown gravy all simmering in a deep round pot; her apron, the curtains, even the rugs in their small apartment at Stuyvesant Town, an apartment complex on the Lower East Side of Manhattan, held these smells (smells associated with love) while the windows steamed over from the endless parade of strudel from the oven; his father, a tall man who stooped, quiet, with deep-set eyes that never stopped probing.

Sy's parents had wanted to know everything about him, the only difference being that his mother asked with a question, his father with a look. He was their only child and nothing was too personal or private. Even now, he keeps himself from knowing certain things, his own emotions, as a way of keeping his parents from knowing. Their deaths came suddenly, when Sy was a sophomore at Harvard in 1970, on a drizzly spring night, as a taxi jumped the light while they were in the crosswalk at Twenty-third and Second, right in front of the deli they owned and operated.

From the street comes a series of staccato honks. "Bus!" Maggie calls. "Let's go, kids!"

There is a general scramble in the direction of the front door and a few seconds later the house is quiet. Magic. Maggie comes back to sit down for a minute at the kitchen table. She sips her coffee. "Eight thirty-three express?"

Sy nods and they head upstairs together, Maggie to dress and Sy to change his shirt and to shave. In the bathroom they crowd around the sink together.

"Maxine reminded me that the firm outing is coming up in July. Have you marked it on the calendar?"

"You two on the plane home together?" Maggie asks, nodding. Maxine McClellin is Sy's mentor, a managing director in

Corporate Finance who recruited him years ago, and one of the people who will (or will not) push to get him promoted to partner sometime in the next two years. Whenever Maggie encounters Maxine at a firm function, she is intimidated by the other woman's cool professionalism and by the power she holds over their lives, even though she is the same age as they. (The three years Sy spent at Morgan Guaranty do not count toward partnership now.)

"We sat together," Sy answers. "But mostly we slept."

Maggie leans across Sy to grab her hairbrush and gets shaving cream in her hair.

"Here, wait," he says, catching her to rub it out with a towel. She reaches up to kiss him absentmindedly.

"We've got to get a double sink."

"No room."

She surveys the cramped space and nods; whoever built this house didn't believe in spacious bathing. Shaving, Sy watches her in the mirror as she pulls the nightgown over her head, hangs it on the hook on the back of the bathroom door, and walks into the bedroom. He stands for a moment, his face scraped clean, but the razor still aloft; he loves her body: the line of her hips curving into a small circle of waist, the slope of stomach attesting to the birth of his children, long thighs, tapering ankles. Physically, she is everything his mother had not been, he reflects as he bends to rinse the shaving cream from his face (and there is safety in that).

Maggie is taller than he. When they first met, he had loved that defiance of custom. His compact body elongated next to her lovely elegant stretch. He thinks now of their first time in bed together — how shy she was about her breasts. He found them lovely and told her so, but she stayed shy nevertheless. She hadn't known anything about sex, really, seeming to comply simply to please him, as if the whole thing bewildered her. She turned away when asked about what pleased her or did not.

Drying off with a towel now, he follows her back to the bedroom and nuzzles the nape of her neck as she stands in her closet, looking for a clean shirt.

She leans against him and he lets his hands drift from her waist up around to her breasts. The nipples harden under his palms. He puts his nose deep into the shampoo smell of her

long hair. Around them motes of dust drift through the sunlight that comes into the closet by way of a small end window.
For a moment he closes his eyes and sees her spread out there
on the floor, arms cradling her head so that her breasts lift to
the sky, her knees up, her hipbones thrusting forward to meet
him, her chin snapping back to the slanted ceiling when she
comes, all her angles reflected in the angles of the dormered
closet — a gritty sort of sex, tangled up in the smell of shoes
and bathrobes and dust.

"Don't you want the eight thirty-three?" she says in a low
voice, as his hands continue to caress.

He opens his eyes, grabs her arm, and rotates her wrist so
that he can see her watch. "Eight-fifteen. Damn!"

"Of course, you could go later," she says, turning to face
him and lacing her arms up around his neck. She wasn't much
in the mood before, but the idea of keeping him from his train
gives her a kick: in college she used to be able to keep him in
bed even when he had economics.

She puts her mouth against his and lets her tongue slide
between his lips just a little. *Tease*. She sucks his lower lip
between her teeth: he tastes of coffee and maple syrup. His
penis thickens, grows hard, as he pushes it against her thigh;
she answers his motion, bringing her pelvis forward against
him. He groans.

"I've got to go," he says, breaking himself away from her.
"I can't."

"Come on," she says, getting bolder, licking from the hollow of his collarbone right up to his ear. "You'll get the next
one."

"We'll make time tonight," he says, turning to go to his
closet, where he pulls out a fresh shirt. "I promise."

She stands still for a minute, one fire dying down inside her
as another starts to glow. Then she shrugs and pulls her jeans
off the hanger: what difference does it make? She can wait
twelve hours — she's already waited four days. And maybe
when he is ready, he'll discover she isn't. (Fair play.)

At the station they sit for a minute, waiting for the train.
Maggie rolls her window down and dangles her arm out into
the sun. "I got a sitter for tonight."

"You want to go out?"

She nods. "Just us, though. I thought we needed some time alone."

"What do you feel like?" he asks, wondering if she has made a reservation yet.

Maggie puts her head back against the seat, her mind suddenly filled with the smell and taste of moo shu pork — the rich hoisin sauce, the slightly sour, thin pancakes, the crunch of cabbage, ginger, and scallion. "I don't care," she answers. "Whatever you think."

Tonight he would love just to stay in; tonight nothing sounds better than a bologna sandwich and a scotch. Curling up in front of the TV together. He is sick of restaurants and hotel beds. But he doesn't say that: he knows how she feels shut up in the house while he is away. "Steak then," he says, choosing the next best alternative. "And maybe tomorrow we can get Jon and Christa out for tennis again."

"If it's nice," she agrees. As much as she likes Christa and Jon, she wants Sy to herself for a little while. If the others are around the only thing discussed will probably be business. "If it's nice," she repeats. "And it's not meant to be. Besides, I thought you and Jerry were going to get started fixing that fence."

The 8:33 crashes down the tracks into the station, flooding the space with a rush of air, blowing stray papers and trash up like a confetti cloud. Without answering, Sy gets out of the car, blows her a kiss, and sprints. Maggie waves as he runs with his briefcase banging against his knees. He is headed for the very first car (where he may have to stand for the thirty-seven-minute ride, even though farther back there are plenty of seats). He will do anything to avoid the crush at the stairs in Grand Central. He hates waiting in line.

〜

As Maggie sits in the station waiting for Sy's train to pull out, she watches women in business suits, briefcases and newspapers under their arms, boarding the train in tandem with the men. She wonders what she is doing here — sitting in a station wagon, dressed in jeans and a T-shirt — instead of up there on that platform, about to steam away to the city? Suddenly she longs for the years when she dressed in pumps instead of sneakers, read the paper over breakfast instead of packing

lunches and arbitrating arguments, when she headed downtown to the scurry and bustle of *Esquire*, instead of heading
upstairs to make beds and start laundry.

There was a certain self-absorbed quality to that old life that
she craves now. What had she given up when she quit her job
as the fiction editor? All that work, and just as she grew comfortable, sure of what she was doing . . . a baby, a baby she had
wanted desperately to carry to term after having already mis-
carried that year. When Kate had arrived with her pure and
simple needs, pink and soft, summoning up that exquisite rush
of newborn love, it had been so easy (delicious, in fact) simply
to continue to stay home, to push her maternity leave into
something permanent. Her mother had been aghast.

But Maggie had so wanted to be different from Vanessa that
she could only hear the prejudice in her mother's tone, not the
concern or the love or even the wisdom. And so she had, like
women in other generations (and despite the warnings of her
own), allowed the children's world to become hers, however
trying and exasperating and boring that world might be on any
given day. And there were compensations, oh, yes, many compensations: for as confined as she felt on one day, she might
well feel joyful the next. What pleasure she had taken in making her own baby food out of fresh vegetables, starting a garden, taking Kate to Gymboree, coloring and painting the
afternoons away.

Until Kate and Mikey started preschool and kindergarten.
And camp. And the house grew more and more silent. And the
fear grew louder and louder. And *the* question (what are you
going to do now?) more and more undodgeable. And all the
while, Sy continued to travel and advance, growing increasingly
distant from their everyday life, even as his direction seemed
clearer and clearer — and hers more and more uncertain.

In her stomach she now feels a familiar lurch. Other wives
wave good-bye, start up their Volvos, and begin a morning
round of errands and self-improvement: with marketing and
laundry handled by housekeepers, there is plenty of time for
the hair and nail salon, an aerobics class, a quick stop at Bloomingdale's before a set of tennis at Century or Sunningdale or
Metropolis or Old Oaks or any of the others. But Maggie does
not want to fill her day like this.

It has taken her several years to get used to the way things are done here (New York being very different from her own, provincial, Boston), and she being the sort of person who finds it difficult to make new friends. It took time to adjust to the sense of entitlement displayed by women who openly upbraid her if they feel she has usurped their place in line at the checkout counter while they run back and forth for "the one last thing" (number three) they've only "just this minute" realized is missing from their cart. And she'll never get used to women with rhinestones on their sweatshirts and designer running shoes under their full-length ranch minks. Or with their sunglasses matched to their bathing suits.

Ellie Weiss pulls up in her wagon and honks. Maggie rolls down the window and smiles, concealing her melancholy. Ellie is the last person she would complain to. Having submitted six months ago to a modified radical mastectomy, Ellie is now drawn and bewigged, both by-products of the merciless chemotherapy.

"Can I give you a ride to your treatment this afternoon?" Maggie asks.

Ellie nods. "I didn't want to ask you again, but I can't find anyone else."

Maggie shakes her head vigorously. "Count on me to take you every time, Ellie. I *mean* it."

"Thanks." The smile is grateful but tight. "I've got to scoot to the market now. I'll see you at noon."

Maggie nods and waves as Ellie drives off.

That the events of her life might unfold so uneventfully — that she might spend her day doing errands, taking care of a house, and helping out a neighbor — had never occurred to Maggie, and it is hard to admit, even now, even to herself, how disappointed and restless she is. Back in college, she and Alexis planned their futures as obsessively as they watched the boys and studied for exams. They left no margin for error because it never occurred to them that they would need such a margin.

She, Alexis, Nicolas, and Sy were a tight foursome during the early years of their friendship at college (Nicolas at N.Y.U., the other three at Harvard). As the years went by, they remained sentinels at the crossroads of their collective lives, guarding each other's crises and successes, ensuring that they remained as intertwined as possible: when Sy was promoted at First Boston, it was Alexis and Nicolas who threw him a bash; when Nicolas expanded his family's business and needed financing, it was Sy who structured the deal and found the outside investors; when Maggie and Sy had their children, it was Nicolas and Alexis who stood up as godparents. Nevertheless, as the years passed, reality intruded: they could no longer stay up all night for a game of Diplomacy or for a party; there was work to be faced in the morning, children with whom Sy and Maggie had to deal, and they could no longer concentrate so exclusively on one another — or on themselves.

A train slams into the air of the station and passes in a blur of glass and metal, without stopping, onward to some other destination. Watching it, Maggie knows she should start her engine and leave the deserted platform; there are so many things she is meant to be doing: hair ribbons to be bought for Kate's party dress, a repair job on Mikey's bike, Friday is a big laundry day, and the beds have to be stripped. But — just for a minute — she leans her forehead against the rim of the steering wheel, and allows herself to acknowledge what she is actually feeling: a swamping, homesick wave of desire for years past — when things seemed simple.

⌒

They met during their sophomore year, in 1970. Maggie and Alexis were roommates in Lowell House, and Sy dropped by Maggie's room unannounced one night in January before exams, with Nicolas in tow. Having just finished his midterms, Nicolas was ready to carouse; while Maggie and Sy began to talk, Nicolas and Alexis began to flirt. Maggie discovered she liked this short boy (shorter than she) with his New York accent and curly hair: his intelligence drew her and his warmth made her comfortable.

Nicolas was the opposite of Sy: tough, sharp, a bit suspicious. Over the years, he continued to arrive on Alexis's doorstep with a new story of some scrape he'd just avoided, and Maggie had recognized from the moment they were all introduced that he was not the sort of man upon whom you could depend.

Here was chemistry of a different sort: Alexis felt a hot, compulsive attraction to the dangers he represented, and to his elusive, unpredictable qualities. Her parents were concerned that their only daughter marry the right sort of man (they had sent her to Chapin — a launching pad for bright girls from well-to-do, social families); after she had known her roommate awhile, Maggie decided that on some subterranean level Alexis needed to fly in the face of all she had been raised to be and powerhouse her way through life.

Maggie sits now in the train station in Scarsdale, her head pressed against the wagon's steering wheel. A horn from a nearby car startles her and she raises her head, roused from her lethargy. The sight of a sparrow, balanced high on the electrical wires that run from telephone pole to telephone pole through the station, brings a glimmer of memory. His tiny feet are curled tight, his wings held close. This feat of balance summons the mental picture of Alexis one night during the giddy week just before graduation — on a walk the four of them had made from the Business School back to Harvard Square, across the Lars Anderson Bridge, which was the site for the fatal leap of Quentin Compson in Faulkner's novel *The Sound and the Fury*. Alexis had swung herself up onto the top of the stone wall that served as the guardrail for the bridge. The cool June wind streaming down the Charles had billowed through her pale shirt and long black hair. Maggie, afraid that Alexis (on the Harvard diving team) would do a double gainer right down into the slick black water, was paralyzed. But Alexis was invincible, high on her own power as the river passed beneath her dancing feet, and she fell, to everyone's relief, into their upstretched arms at the other end.

Alexis's drive (daring) has served her well, Maggie thinks, quite enviously. After graduation Maggie had settled for a traditional woman's job as an assistant to an editor in a Boston publishing house, and lived in the spare room at her parent's house until she and Sy married the following year. But Alexis had taken on something infinitely more ambitious: as she had planned for years, she'd gone to Wall Street as an analyst for two years and then entered the Harvard Business School; the reward for these years of diligence and direction was a position with a top investment bank after graduating from HBS in 1977 as a Baker Scholar. In the last nine years Alexis has become a significant force in the toughest and most male-dominated department on the Street. She wouldn't be caught dead sitting in this little suburban train station, mourning her life. She is out there in the thick of it, getting what she wants. Angry at last with herself, Maggie reaches down and turns the ignition key; the engine roars, startling the sparrows from their high wire into a random pattern of flight far above her head.

~~~ FOUR

Flight Patterns

Entering her office on Monday morning, Alexis sets her briefcase down and takes her jacket off to hang it in the closet. Then, sitting back in her chair, she surveys her desk and picks up the sheaf of papers from her in-box. As a principal in the firm, her office is medium-sized, with one window, not two; in the fall, if she makes partner (a fantasy, prospect, and worry that occupies her more intensely than anything in life right now) Alexis will receive the prestige of an office with two windows, a secretary whom she has to share with no one, and a piece of the firm's annual profits.

Because she is in her office more often than she is at home, Alexis has taken care in furnishing it; the green glass lamp on the desk throws a warm light into the room on those nights — several each week when she is not traveling — that she must stay late. A leather armchair and couch, good for all-nighters, stand next to several big bookcases that dwarf the room and hold a variety of tax regulation binders and bound closing volumes — and even some more ordinary books she likes to peruse when she has lunch in her office, which is more often than most people would suppose: Mergers and Acquisitions leaves little time for dining out. Lately she has not even had time to get up to the pool to practice her diving.

The desk with which the firm provides her is an old piece, generously-sized, of well-worn and scratched mahogany; she often traces the grain of the wood with her fingertips, and this tactile incantation soothes her in even the most tense of moments. Such moments occur regularly in this side of the business, and have to be handled with precision, finality, and self-assurance.

Or chutzpah, as her father would say: daring, guts, balls. Not surprisingly, Martin Somers had not supported his daughter's decision to plunge into M&A after she had done a stint in the municipal bond area during her first two years at Hewett Lowell. He didn't care that she craved the challenge or the risk. *M&A isn't a place for a woman — you'll never be anything but a background player*, he announced to her the day she announced her move into the department, his dark eyes scowling out from beneath the winged eyebrows she had also inherited from him; now, as she glances at the photo of her father that stands on the corner of the desk, she remembers well the disappointment and depression she felt when she realized he was, inexplicably, neither pleased nor proud. His reaction to her news had made her want to cry (although she hadn't) and angry (she buried it deep).

Since 1975, her second year as an analyst at Goldman, Sachs between college and business school (when she watched her father scramble, as head of the then third-tier firm Bear Stearns, to find a lucrative new angle of the business to pursue after commission rates were deregulated), Alexis had dreamed of being in on the ground floor of what her father foresaw as the great bull market of the eighties. She believed then that nothing would impress him more than her success in such a competitive field. It had been a coup for her to land the position at Hewett right out of business school, as it was considered one of the premier firms. But the following year her father retired, quite suddenly, turning his attention to fund-raising for the Mount Sinai Medical School — where her brother David was head of a cancer research project — eventually being elected chairman. The irony struck Alexis then: though time moves on quite inexorably, people and their relationships often do not.

Two years later, when she switched into M&A, Alexis had discarded all his objections (old-fashioned ideas): he'd been on the Street for over thirty years and she reassured herself that he couldn't imagine what was possible for a woman in any field right now, let alone M&A. But once she started working in the department, she had seen his point: unless she made a strong and unique start, it would be difficult (perhaps impossible) to acquire a name for herself here. The prejudice was rampant, and every woman suspect. Chase Porter was a typical problem: he worked Alexis hard and then took all the credit without so much as a backward glance.

M&A was a megacompetitive clique previously unbreached by a woman. The hours were grueling, the travel infinite, and the work difficult, contentious, and sometimes outright hostile. Ordinarily, even the most high-powered young woman eventually wanted to make a family life, to slow down and take fewer hours in the office and more at home. But these conditions distressed Alexis not in the least. In fact, they provided her with a dare — and a dare was just the incentive she needed.

Now, as she concentrates on the papers in front of her, she fiddles absentmindedly with a piece of hair that has escaped from its clip; her long hair is a matter of pride to Alexis. Her clothing is subdued only in deference to taste — not gender; her hair is drawn back — not cut off; her makeup is simple — not nonexistent. A beautiful woman at thirty-six, she sees no reason for her beauty, or her sex, to put her at a disadvantage in her work. She is too smart and too sharp to be mistaken for a secretary, and it never even occurs to her to hide behind a blouse with a bow at the neck.

She picks up her pencil and begins to initial the memos that had been typed for her last night. The silver of the pencil is tarnished, she notices; she ought to take it home and get it polished. Nicolas gave it to her for her birthday the first year they were married, when she was still in school and her parents had been so angry. She turns the pencil in the sunlight coming from the window. There is an inscription running down one side: *"me to you, 1975."*

She and Nicolas were good at enjoying themselves back then; it took little to please either of them, possibly because they were very poor, extremely daring, and a little crazy. They savored acting like adolescents once in a while, sneaking into movies through the back door without paying, parking in illegal spaces and then tearing up the tickets. The silver pencil was an extravagance Nicolas charged at Tiffany's, knowing full well it would be months before he could afford to pay the bill.

He was commuting back and forth from Manhattan to Boston that year. While Alexis worked on getting her M.B.A., he worked on turning his family's business around. Linden's, the current sportswear chain, had once been a single store called Lindnerhoffman's, owned and operated by Nicolas's father, Sam; originally a small garment store aimed at Bronx housewives, it had become old and dumpy as the character of the neighborhood changed over time. The plate-glass windows had clouded, the mannequins were dated and fly-specked, the name of the store was run out in large scrolled letters that had faded from magenta to puce. When Sam died of a stroke after Nicolas's graduation, neither Aaron nor David — Nicolas's older brothers — were interested in the store, except insofar as how quickly they could get rid of it. For them, plastic surgeons both, the store brought back less-than-savory associations: growing up in Stuyvesant Town; the public school system; the way their father smelled of cigarettes every night over supper. They exported their mother to Miami Beach, where they kept her in reasonable style at a residence hotel.

Nicolas alone had sensed the opportunity and discovered that while he, too, might hate the color and smell of the past, that did not mean he could not use it. He bought out his brothers, changed the store's name — and his own — to Linden, used the shop as a base to open several branches in Westchester, and learned that he did not need to escape that which he could transform. With his brothers watching angrily from the sidelines, he made money and so passed them on their genteel climb up. And this was the part of Nicolas (his gritty determination, his ability to take big risks with aplomb) that Alexis had fallen in love with.

Despite the difficulties of that first married year, their weekends together were filled with love and lovemaking and a sense of purpose — to make it work against all odds, against the time apart and the studying, against the disapproval and abrupt financial withdrawal of Alexis's parents, against their own idiosyncratic natures. And it had worked, maybe precisely because the odds were so stacked against them.

In the eleven years since, he has built a discount sportswear chain that boasts twenty-three stores in the New York area. It was a success, a solid one, until last year — *when he got greedy,*

Alexis thinks now, twisting the pencil in her hands. Buying *Le Sport* — an existing chain of sixteen sportswear stores spread across the Northeast — and merging it with Linden's had given him higher visibility and many more outlets, but it also put a big financial drain on the company. He'd borrowed to finance the acquisition. From the beginning Alexis had worried that the merger would overextend them, but he was so eager for the deal Sy had put together (he would never have backed down in front of Sy anyway) that he had not been willing to listen to her admonishments. Discontent with his success, merely rich, he craved a new challenge — and this was something she well understood. She'd let her empathy with that sway her judgment.

There is no pleasure in being proved right. But she would be able to deal with her anger if only Nicolas would be willing to deal with reality. Now even a quick look at the books shows the enormous cash drain — all the carefully tended resources hemorrhaging out just to meet the overhead and carry the debt — and Alexis is disgusted with the way Nicolas is wavering; he cannot decide what to do next when the solution is obvious: sell off some of the branch stores and consolidate. But he gets emotional every time she brings it up. She can't bear the lack of resolve in him: *where has his instinct gone?* she wonders. *Where is the old Nico — who repositioned his father's store ten years ago with such a sure hand?* She was glad her work kept her at the office all weekend long. They would only have argued more about it all. She strokes the barrel of the pencil and her irritation with him and her fear for the company give way to sadness, a sadness that now swells inside her: something (precious, young, hopeful) is gone, something that can never be replaced or re-created with anyone else. Life seems infinitely more complicated than it used to; it occurs to her now that she and Nicolas have only been children playing at being adults.

She keeps staring at the pencil and as she turns it between her fingers, she sees (as if she were watching a movie of a woman sitting at a desk) that it is getting wet. In fact, the desk beneath it, under her hands, is getting wet. She is crying, she realizes with a start, she is actually letting tears fall. The sorrow taps its message out loud and clear at last: she doesn't want to go home and face his blindness and immaturity for even one more night; she wants out; she wants to meet Jon Stratton for a drink. *What are you doing?* she asks herself now. *Why are you sitting in your office full of crazy thoughts?*

She tries to straighten up — but cannot. Overwhelmed, she feels a premonition of waste, of unfulfillment, of — she can barely name it — age. It is perhaps the first despair she has ever known in her life, and she has never felt so alone. And scared. Swiveling her chair so her back is to the glass door, she gives in, puts her head down on the edge of the desk, and sobs.

After a while, she shakes herself, straightens her back until the sense of anguish (pitiful, childish) leaves her body. She wipes her face and blows her nose: the noise helps, makes her sound busy and industrious — if she can make such a loud honk how bad off can she be? She shuffles the stack of papers in front of her and clears her throat, instructing herself to concentrate and get back to work, which is when (thank God) the phone rings.

ᔗ

"I just sat there and cried," Alexis says to Maggie six hours later, relieved to be talking with her at last. "I don't know what's the matter with me."

"A blue day," Maggie answers, resting her feet on the foot rail at the bar in Palio. "I have them all the time."

The two women sit in companionable silence for a moment, sipping their drinks. (This is what Maggie offers: the space to talk or be silent, and so feel your way through your own problem.)

"Actually, I was feeling blue myself this morning, which is why I called you," Maggie goes on.

Alexis arches her eyebrows, surprised.

"I was sitting in the kitchen thinking about all the things I ought to be doing — getting depressed. Which made me feel like rebelling. So I called you." She grins and sips a tart gin and tonic. She very quickly abandoned her plans when, on phoning Alexis's office this morning, Alexis suggested they get together for a drink at five. Maggie (who always makes a point of being at the door when the children get off the camp bus) had called the baby-sitter; her depression, having begun last Friday at the train station, had still been upon her (not banished even by

Sy's presence at home all weekend long). She thinks she cannot stand another minute.

"You? Rebel?" Alexis tilts her head to one side and laughs.

"Well, maybe that's not the right word," Maggie admits, embarrassed. "But not being there when they get home — breaking the routine that way." She shrugs. "So I asked the sitter to feed them supper and cornered Sy into taking me out."

"You should get into the city more anyway," Alexis agrees. "You're too shut up out there." She sips her white wine spritzer — light, because she has to go back to the office tonight — and looks around, scanning the crowd. It is rare that Alexis does not know at least one person most every place she goes, although Palio is far from her office on Broad Street. Maggie suggested it because it is close to Sy's office, and the restaurant upstairs is wonderful. She made a seven-thirty reservation and asked Alexis to come uptown.

"Don't you miss this?" Alexis asks, waving her hand at the crowd. "Don't you miss getting up and going *somewhere* every morning?"

Maggie hesitates. She is torn between the urge (defensive) to justify herself, and the need (newly felt but equally strong) to talk out all her ambivalence about still being at home. It occurs to her in this moment that she never really made a decision to stay out of work for such a long time; somehow, it just happened — the same way it just happened that Sy started working longer and longer hours and traveling more and more. (Or so it seems.) But before Maggie can open her mouth, Alexis's beeper goes off, an adrenaline-inducing intrusion, muffled but persistent, from the depths of her purse. She draws it out, clicks it off. "Be right back," she says, excusing herself and rising to go to the phone.

Maggie sighs and watches her go. She hates the way all the M&A people carry beepers with them in and out of the office: those times she and Sy manage to get free for dinner they are so often interrupted that it seems worse than being married to a doctor.

But this difficult, stressful sort of life must surely agree with Alexis: never has her old roommate looked more beautiful. Maggie tugs at the waistband of her silk dress, which is of a feminine sort of small print (frumpy). Alexis's dark suit is slim, tailored, padded across the shoulders. Maggie hooks her feet back up under the bar stool, hiding her low-heeled pumps.

To distract herself from herself as she waits for Alexis to return, Maggie scans the room: a vivid mural by Chia Sandro circles the vaulted ceiling, bright orange and blue, a Renaissance festival complete with horses, pennants, men in ballooned tunics — a playful poke at Uccello; the bar itself is horseshoe-shaped and of polished granite; and there is an elegant elevator that transports patrons to the elaborate restaurant upstairs. As she surveys the beautifully dressed men and women around her, she realizes that Alexis is right: what a relief to feel anxiety and claustrophobia (suburban isolation) flag and then fade back under the pulse and throb of Manhattan — the color and pungent smell, the clatter of barware, the growing crush of bodies, the loud even-beated hum of genuine adult conversation.

"Sorry," Alexis says, sliding back onto her seat. "The deal I'm working on is about to close and I've got to stay in touch." She pulls her sleeve back, glances at her watch. "I've got a conference over at Morgan at six, which gave me a lucky excuse to leave early and meet you."

"So what's going on?" Maggie asks curiously, not at all interested in the daily business of M&A, sipping her gin and tonic again. "You sounded so unhappy this morning."

Alexis sighs again. "I don't know, Maggie. It's just . . ." She pauses, unsure of how to talk about the way she feels. "The mess Nico has gotten into with the company, for instance. He won't listen to any realistic advice — just keeps pretending everything is fine. He wants to stay in bed all day with the covers over his head." Her voice is angry now. "Like a little kid!"

"I didn't know things were so bad." Maggie's voice holds a tingle of alarm.

"They're bad — but at this point probably rescueable. Except that Nico won't *do* anything." She picks up her drink. "And I don't know —" again she hesitates, almost afraid to go on (to voice what she feels and so make it real). "We're just not getting along very well."

Maggie sits silent, waiting, trying to understand what Alexis is leading up to.

"I'm just not sure we're going to make it, that's all."

"You mean Linden's?"

"I mean Nicolas and me."

The air sails out of Maggie's lungs with an audible *whoosh*. "Sometimes marriages go through bad times," she says, after a moment.

"It's more than that." Alexis shakes her head. "I don't feel any respect for him anymore. You know, he's like an old friend, in a bad place, but *I* don't want to be there with him." She pauses again. "And then, there might be — could be — I might want — someone else." She looks up at Maggie's face. "Don't look so shocked — it's not like I've got cancer or something."

Her friend's voice is tinged with annoyance now, and Maggie realizes that it does indeed seem as though Alexis has just announced something drastic and terrible (threatening), some important sort of news with which Maggie does not want to deal.

"You're just moving a little fast for me, that's all," she manages, stalling for time by taking a large gulp of her drink.

"You've known for the last year that we haven't been getting along." Alexis seems puzzled by her reaction.

"Maybe I just didn't want to take it seriously. I mean, not getting along — sure." Maggie nods, slowly. "But an affair . . ." she trails off, feeling dubious and disapproving even though it is not her place. Her heart pounds, anxiety again, but anxiety from an unnameable source: after all, this is Alexis's life they are discussing, not her own.

"Who said 'an affair'?" Alexis picks up the matchbook from the ashtray in front of them and snaps the cover back and forth. "I just said there was someone else I was *interested* in."

"Is he someone I know?"

Alexis cocks her head again, sizing Maggie up speculatively.

Under this scrutiny and the silence, Maggie realizes instinctively that she has failed some sort of test; she has been unable, in that quick second of visceral reaction, to provide the sort of unlimited, nonjudgmental support by which close friendships are characterized.

"Is it?" she repeats, more insistently this time, determined to override her own feelings and so rectify the lapse.

Alexis traces the lines of beaded sweat on the surface of her wineglass with one long sculptured fingernail, and, at last, nods. "Jonathan Stratton."

Maggie's face pinches with distress and she looks away from Alexis. "Christa's in love with him," she says, almost to herself (as in many stressful situations, such a diversionary detail is the first thing of which she thinks).

Alexis sighs. "Look, *he* called *me*. It isn't like I was the one went looking."

Maggie moves her glass on the cocktail napkin, making a pattern of rings, concentric, overlapping, with its wet bottom.

"He asked me for a *drink* — but it could probably be more." Alexis pulls her purse up onto her lap and begins looking through it.

Maggie stares at her. She can't quite believe the confidence Alexis has, nor the fact that they are sitting here discussing the prospect of adultery the way they once discussed the prospect of getting a date. She struggles to maintain a neutral expression.

"He could have called you for a drink — pure and simple. You're reading so much into it." Maggie's voice rises a little. "After all, you do work in the same field."

"He didn't call me because he wants to be friends." Alexis's voice stresses the last word. "A drink is just the overture."

"What about Nicolas?"

Alexis, rooting around in her purse, at last finds her cigarettes, buried at the bottom. "That's the problem."

"You're worried he'll find out?"

Alexis shakes her head, extracting a cigarette from the battered leather case she's had since college. "If I want to keep something secret, I can. But we spend so little time together right now, there's hardly anything . . . hardly anything *real* anymore."

Maggie hesitates. "You mean sex?"

Alexis shakes her head again. "Nico and I don't get to bed much anymore, but when we do, it's good —" She shrugs and smiles. "But after all — sex is, well . . . it's just *sex*. Even when it's terrific. If the feelings aren't right —" She flicks her lighter up against the end of the cigarette and drags in deeply. Smoking is a habit Maggie quit during college because Sy hated it so, but Alexis had been under no such restrictions. Even if Nicolas had disliked it she would not have given it up. Into Maggie's mind flashes a picture of Sy, making love to her six weeks ago (that had been the last time), missionary, each of them working hard toward his own orgasm; she thinks of being able to say terrific sex is "just sex." Over Maggie settles the depressed realization that she has never felt anything like that. Not once. Her sex with Sy is . . . nourishing is the word that comes to her mind: like hot cereal, the comfort of it fills you up, but it is bland, bland, bland.

She watches Alexis's mouth closing over the cigarette, leaving behind the rosy bloom of her lipstick on the filter, and realizes that she is jealous.

"No," Alexis goes on now, but haltingly, "the problem is that I don't know if I meet Jon for a drink, if I start something — well, I'm just not sure I'll ever be able to go back." Her voice drops, very low, dispirited. "Which says a lot about staying in any case." Maggie has to strain to hear her now. "And that scares the shit out of me."

"There's so little left that you'd jeopardize everything —" Maggie breaks off, incredulous. Alexis and Nicolas have always seemed so perfect together (as perfect a match as she and Sy have been). On top of the bar her hands knit themselves together, clasping and unclasping.

Alexis's face is luminous with sadness. "The part of him I loved best — that nutsy part, the crazy guy — I don't know, it's just gone. Thank God we don't have any kids."

Maggie flinches. "Kids might force you to work it out."

Once again Alexis looks at her as if she is crazy. "Kids only get trapped in between."

Maggie inhales sharply; the idea spreads out through her body like a stone thrown into a pond, dropping down through the lukewarm and murky layers of memory: a summer night, late, the stars bright pricks outside her bedroom window, honeysuckle vines' sweet musk over her bed, the acrid exhaust of traffic; a night when she looked down from her window to see her mother returning from evening rehearsal with a colleague; Maggie, nose pressed against the wire mesh of the screen, watched her mother press against a stranger's body in tight embrace; only thirteen, she had felt both fury and arousal; she had worried that her parents would get divorced, that she would be left in some limbo, separated and alone, sent off again to live with relatives.

Like the time she stayed with her mother's parents on Cape Cod. Months that were terrible and strange for a three-year-old, alone in the big house by the sea with no one her own age, no one to talk to, no one to explain this painful quarantine, the exile of months. Nothing but overheard whispers and voices that stopped short when she came into the room. She waited in slow motion that summer, suspicious, sure she would be sent elsewhere, to strangers this time, certain her mother was really dead, certain she had caused it all, and full of dread, unnamed (for how should a three-year-old speak of anxiety?), which would never entirely leave her.

Finally, after three months spent drifting, flotsam on the waves of the adults' reserve, she was returned to Vanessa's side, where, safe at last, she became a cool, smooth pebble in her mother's palm, forever afraid and praying to be never again cast out.

"You and Sy are so close — I guess you can't understand what I'm talking about." Alexis sighs with impatience, her eyes scrutinizing Maggie's face, probing. Maggie drops her gaze, wishing she had not come here today at all.

"Haven't you ever, even once, been tempted?" Alexis's voice sounds plaintive, almost vulnerable, now.

"Sex just never seemed that important to me," Maggie says wanly, feeling embarrassed — as if she needs a justification for having never once looked at another man besides her husband.

"I'm not talking about sex! I'm talking about something else, entirely different, some excitement — a connection — that's gone, just gone. Broken."

Her face is angry, despairing, and Maggie realizes that she is failing to comfort her best friend. She reaches across now, filled with chagrin, to take Alexis's hand, and, at her friend's touch feels the strong urge to cry, so full of her own conflicting emotions that she believes she can no longer contain them all. She clears her throat, but her voice still comes out as a whisper. "I don't mean to sound like some nun."

She takes a deep swallow of her by-now watery drink, looking for the strength of the gin. "But this is scary. You make me wonder about myself, about Sy and me, and about the four of us. We're like family. You know that. Besides, it reminds me of my mother and all those men she always had hanging around." She shakes her head against the tears and reaches across the table to steal one of Alexis's cigarettes.

"What's this?" Alexis smiles, ruefully now, and scratches the wheel of her lighter to light Maggie up. "A *little* rebellion, you said?"

Maggie smiles shakily as she inhales (more controlled). "This isn't a good time for me, Alexis. So much being alone . . . I don't know."

Alexis looks remorseful. "And here I am burning up the wires with my problems, not even thinking about yours. I guess I never realized how much all that stuff with your mother upset you. You always seemed so distant about it."

"Did I?" This strikes Maggie as odd. "I guess I don't like talking about it. I always took my father's side. I never understood why she did it."

"Maybe your father didn't keep her happy."

"Maybe. She *was* unhappy. A lot. But I hated her for the uncertainty she dragged into our lives — wondering whether they were going to stay together. I didn't understand why she couldn't *control* herself better."

"Maybe it didn't have anything to do with control."

Maggie shrugs. "Maybe not." She inhales again, quickly, and as the smoke fills her lungs, stinging, she realizes that she'd forgotten how good it felt; she wonders if Sy will be able to smell it on her later.

"And, if he cared, why didn't he do something about it?" Alexis asks pragmatically.

"I don't know." Maggie shakes her head slowly, feeling somehow dazed. "I never understood it. But it's just how he is — you know, so calm. He ignored it. It always was hard to get his attention."

Alexis laughs dryly. "I know how that feels, for sure."

Maggie sighs and smiles wryly. "Do you know anyone who's satisfied with the relationship they have with their parents?"

Alexis laughs. "No."

"When you get married," Maggie says, "it seems like you'll finally be able to get back to the warmth, the safety you had once, as a child, and then time goes on and you start to understand it's not at all the way you remembered it. You begin to want something altogether different."

"Insatiable for love and approval. A search doomed from the start." Alexis laughs. "Maybe we never grow up, we just get older."

Maggie smiles and doesn't answer, sipping her drink.

"So," Alexis says after a minute, "tell me how you really are."

"I'm depressed." Maggie takes a deep breath. "I sat for an hour in the train station on Friday morning after I left Sy off, just thinking. What the hell am I doing with myself?"

"Are you and Sy O.K.?"

Maggie shrugs. "I'm just beginning to realize how much he's away and how much I hate it." Her voice is bitter. "I never thought I'd be so alone."

"When he isn't traveling — how are things then?"

Maggie looks into her glass and stirs the ice with the stirrer. The lime bobs up and down. "Fine," she says.

"And the kids?"

"The kids are everything to me. More, maybe — it's just —" She drags on the cigarette again, but now it is beginning to make her feel a little queasy. She stubs it out.

"Nobody said that kids should be enough, Mag."

Maggie is silent; Alexis's words make her angry even as it is a relief to hear them: she doesn't want to admit it, not yet.

"You could go back to work."

"And what about the kids?"

"It's not an either-or proposition, Maggie." Alexis studies her friend's face.

"I guess," Maggie says, in a dispirited voice. Right now she feels more trapped than ever before.

"It's all a question of proportion," Alexis answers. "What about Sy?"

"Sy doesn't like the idea," Maggie answers gloomily.

Alexis raises her eyebrows, and her beeper goes off again. "Damn! Hang on one sec, O.K.?"

Maggie watches her go: how much there is for Alexis to do, how many important things hinge on her; it is a measure of her accomplishment that they can't do without her for even a half an hour. Maggie tries to imagine a reason she would be called away from a drink or a dinner. There is only one: domestic crisis — an overflowing toilet, or if one of the children threw up.

Alexis hurries back. "I've got to go," she says, apologetically. "My client moved the time up on us." She pauses. "But I feel terrible, running out on you like this."

"That's O.K.," Maggie says, lifting her chin. "I'll be fine." She smiles and steals another cigarette from Alexis's case, using the lighter again before Alexis puts it back in her purse. "What are you going to do about Jon?"

"If I stay with Nicolas it has to be because I *want* to, not because I hid under the bed." She grimaces and reaches for her purse, taking out her pill case and hurriedly swallowing a tablet. "If you'll excuse the pun."

"What's the pill?"

She shrugs. "My last two periods have been murder."

"Have you gotten it checked out?"

Alexis shakes her head. "No." She begins to gather her things from the bar, slipping back into her jacket, and picking up her briefcase. "So, maybe I'll call Jon." Her voice is almost gay now, but her face seems white. "What the hell." She stops and looks at Maggie again, speculatively.

"I'm all right!" Maggie says, leaning across to give her a hug. "Go on," she says, "scoot. You don't want your deal to fall apart. But let me know how things go, O.K.?"

Alexis nods, hugs her again, then goes. Maggie looks at her watch. It is nearly six-thirty. She'll just wait for Sy right here, have another drink. She smokes for a while, watching the gray ash climb, and wonders if Jon could make Alexis happy, if Nicolas will be hurt. She grinds the cigarette out in the ashtray.

The waiter comes over and slides a slip of paper across the surface of the bar toward her. She unfolds it: "Your husband can't make it. Please call him at work."

"Damn!" She crumples the paper into a tiny ball and tosses it beside her glass. She fishes her first half-finished cigarette from the ashtray and then realizes she has nothing with which to light it.

"May I?"

She turns to see that a man has taken Alexis's seat at the

bar, to her left. She nods and he lights the end of the butt. She inhales, smiling her thanks.

"I couldn't help noticing." He smiles back at her, gesturing toward the message in the ashtray. "Get stood up?"

"My husband," she explains lamely. She's never struck up a conversation so casually with a stranger before; she's never been alone in a bar before.

"He's stuck at work?"

She nods.

"What's he do?"

"Mergers at First Boston."

He nods understandingly. "Those guys work like schvartzes."

She draws back a little. "I shouldn't be mad," she goes on, covering her reaction. "I was just so disappointed." She looks at him again: *nice-looking, late-thirties, respectable suit, elegant tie. Tall. Good teeth.* She smiles and drops her eyes. *And no wedding band.*

"You come to Palio often?"

She laughs. "I don't even get to the *city* often. I've got" — she breaks off abruptly, changing her mind about what she was going to say, about children and their demands — "a full load." She doesn't want to talk about who she is and what she does all day because she is embarrassed by it.

"And home is? Where?"

"Westchester," she answers, evasively.

"You work?"

"Publishing. Editorial." She shrugs. "What do you do?"

"I'm a partner at Davis Polk."

She nods, allowing the fact that she is impressed to register on her face. He is telling her something by including the fact that he is a partner. It puts him in the right league, on the right level, but it also betrays a certain insecurity.

"Hey — I'm on my own tonight myself," he says, smiling at her. "I mean — I'd be happy to stand in. Dinner upstairs is too special to miss."

She stares at him and flushes. *A stranger, Maggie.* Her heart begins to pound, a double triple thump. "I couldn't." Quickly, she puts the cigarette out.

"Why not?"

She can't think of why not. *Haven't you ever, even once, been tempted?* Fumbling with her purse, she scrambles for her wallet and leaves a twenty-dollar bill on the bar.

He shrugs. "Don't let me chase you out."

"It's not you. It's —" She breaks off, at a loss to explain why she needs to leave in such a hurry. "I have to get back to take care of some work, that's all." *I am such a bad liar,* she thinks.

"Good-bye," he says, smiling at her again.

"Good-bye," she mumbles, looking away as she slides down from the stool and walks quickly to the revolving door. *A near escape,* she thinks. Her heart keeps pounding, even as she spins herself out to the sidewalk, clutches her bag firmly under her arm, and begins to walk rapidly toward Grand Central, pounding and pounding as a question begins to revolve, spinning, spiraling through her mind: *a near escape from what?*

~~~ FIVE

Gamesmanship

"I told her I couldn't make it — that's all." Jonathan shrugs and unfolds his napkin, as the waiter carries their drinks over from the bar. "I don't explain myself to Christa. Why?"

"Maggie tells me you two have a standing squash date on Monday nights," Alexis answers (betraying her interest), as she sips her gin and tonic. "I knew you'd have to break it."

"Is that why you called this afternoon?" He seems amused: his eyes flash black in the pools of yellow light cast by the table lamps of Le Bernardin. He settles back in the armchair and scans the large room. The oil paintings with their museum lights, the fat upholstered chairs, the wooden beams crisscrossing the ceiling — all of this gives the restaurant on Fifty-first Street an air of understated elegance and intimacy, as if the patrons are at home in their own living rooms. An interesting concept this, to cosset the diner with such comfort, as if what you want most in the world is to be the sort of person who can live every day in the middle of easy opulence, to pretend the chef and tuxedoed waiters are your personal staff — as if you own it all.

Even as Alexis shakes her head, she knows there is truth to the idea that she has purposely picked a night that will break a regular date between Jon and Christa (although she would never admit it). "The deal I'm doing let up for a millisecond, so I decided to take advantage," she says, sipping again and looking into his intense stare. She wonders if his assumption that she's been just sitting around plotting to call him is self-confidence or egotism. She is still in her work clothes — a navy suit and silk shirt — and has come straight from the office, toting her briefcase; the only concession she has made to the social aspect of the situation is to unpin her hair and brush it loose over her shoulders.

"Deal?" He breaks a hot roll in two and butters one side of it, raising an eyebrow with his question.

"Finishing up the NavCon merger."

"A nice little scalp to hang on your belt," he observes. "It was some piece of work to keep that one from crumping."

She turns her wrist so that she can read the face of her watch. "I probably should check in with the office around ten. I left my beeper on my desk by mistake." She smiles at him.

She has been thinking about him for several days now, ever since her drink with Maggie a week ago, debating the question back and forth in her mind. In defense of her marriage, she even took time out of a working weekend so that she and Nicolas could spend a little extra time together. But the effort had been wasted: they only ended up arguing.

Nicolas's obstinance helped her lift the phone this morning to call Jonathan. She felt justified, somehow.

"I'm glad you did."

"Glad I did what?"

"Left your beeper."

She nods, resolutely putting thoughts of Nicolas aside. "Ordinarily I don't mind bringing it, but . . ." Deliberately she lets the sentence drift off, unfinished, not saying what she is really thinking — that leaving the beeper behind is an unconscionable oversight on her part, one that could land her in a lot of trouble.

"M&A is tough on your personal life."

"Funny." She pauses and fiddles with her glass. "I'm sure it must be for some people — and my husband certainly complains enough — but I've never felt so. Never minded."

"That's because it *is* your life."

She looks up, startled to be so instantly understood, and waits for him to continue, her hand dragging the stirrer around and around the glass.

If she were to count the events important to her over the

last few years, the way Maggie counts her children's developmental milestones, she would be naming her deals: Rubbecki-Sloan, Brigham-Highbee, Sandscripts, GCX, Limorix, Slearner Brothers, now NavCon. Like the concentric growth rings inside a tree, each is larger than the last in the sense that with each she has earned for herself an increasing amount of responsibility and power. The work has not deprived her: it has stretched her and taught her her own potential.

"And you?" she asks, when after a minute he does not continue, but allows their silence to deepen instead. "Do you mind the sacrifices?"

"What I mind is that there aren't thirty-six hours in a day. More time is what I'd like — for work, more reading, more sleeping, more exercise, more sex —" He breaks off, laughing. "And what did you tell your husband about tonight?" He smiles, once again enigmatic. "If that's not an indiscreet question."

"I said I was having dinner with a colleague. The truth, of a sort."

"Of a sort," he agrees. "*Is* that why you're having dinner with me — because I'm a colleague?" His gaze holds her across the table, the dark stare unreadable.

"Is that why *you* asked *me?*"

He tilts his chin back and laughs.

It has been a long while since she's played this kind of game, direct, eye to eye (apart from the hondeling she does for work — and this is very different from that). Alexis feels as if her body temperature has risen a degree; this is a match she wants to win. She notices everything about him: how he slouches back in his chair and then moves forward toward the table when he speaks, his motion revealing a restless energy; how he rests the line of his forearm against the edge of the linen cloth, but never his elbow; how his fingers stroke the tines of the fork, one by one, over and over again, very slowly. His nails are closely clipped, without any rime of white showing.

"Shall I order for us?" he asks, flipping open the menu.

She suppresses a grin. "I always have the sea urchin."

He raises his hand for the waiter, who comes forward immediately, pencil poised, and Jon lifts one eyebrow in Alexis's direction, whereupon she does order the sea urchin. He chooses the lobster à la nage, and they agree to share a platter of malpeques on the half shell to start. After mutual consultation over the extensive wine list (during which their hands brush twice) they select, at Alexis's suggestion, a bottle of vintage champagne.

"So you're just friends with Christa," she says, without preface or explanation. "That's not how it looks to me. Or Maggie."

"Look." He puts his head to one side, sizing her up speculatively, obviously surprised that she's brought the subject up again. "Christa isn't pleased that I broke our date tonight, and she probably isn't pleased that I broke it for you. But that doesn't mean —"

"You told her you were meeting *me?*" Alexis interrupts.

"Is there some reason I shouldn't have?"

"Discretion?"

"Are we doing something indiscreet?"

Those black eyes of his tease her with the question, and she starts to laugh. The waiter sets the plate of oysters down in the middle of the table. Alexis picks up the lemon and squeezes it over, waving off his offer of a mignonette sauce. "I thought you said you didn't explain yourself to her." She arches an eyebrow.

He acquiesces the point with a shrug.

"Here," she says, delicately separating the first oyster from its barnacled shell with a quick twist of her wrist and extending it across to him. As he takes the fork, their fingers brush again and she feels her face warm as she bends to take one for herself. Under the table their knees bump. She looks up and finds him staring at her once more. This time the look is even longer. She meets his stare and does not break away until the champagne cork breaks the silence. The waiter pours a puddle into Jon's glass, waits a beat for the requisite nod, then fills Alexis's to the brim.

"I don't mean to pry. It's just been a long time since I poached onto someone else's territory. Except at work," she amends, lifting her glass. They both laugh. The fruit of the Cristal '82 washes over the brine of the oysters. "This is my favorite champagne."

"Do you see yourself as Nicolas's *territory?*" His voice has a curious edge.

She takes another oyster. "Once we were each other's territory . . ." Her voice drifts off.

"And now?" He reaches for another oyster, his long, narrow fingers bracing the shell as he pulls out the raw meat. He lifts the fork to his mouth quickly; the opalescent flesh is speared precariously, shiny and dripping salt water, and his tongue shoots out, pink, wet, to tuck it back into his mouth, where he cradles it for an instant against his teeth, and then, with a gulp, swallows it whole.

Alexis watches as he puts down the fork impatiently and picks up the next oyster with his hands. Tilting it, he purses his lips around the rough stony edge of the shell, rakes his teeth across the meat, and sucks hard. The oyster disappears neatly, without a drip. *He didn't learn that move at finishing school*, Alexis thinks, picking up her fork again.

"Now?" She chews a moment, thoughtfully, wondering how to characterize the present between Nicolas and herself. "Now is eleven years later."

"You've been together eleven years?"

"We've been married eleven years," she elucidates. "Together seriously, one on one, something like thirteen. Or maybe it's more now." She sighs. "We met as undergrads."

"Thirteen." He raises an eyebrow and picks up another oyster. "Are you superstitious?"

She laughs and shakes her head. "I don't believe in unlucky numbers or black cats. Not even in destiny."

"You mean if you were Anna Karenina you wouldn't throw yourself in front of the train?"

"I mean if I were Emma Bovary I'd leave the arsenic for my dolt of a husband."

"But you'd deprive literature of its most tragic heroines," he protests, wiping his hands on the linen napkin and leaning back again.

She shrugs. "I'd rather be someone more modern. Who wants to die of love anyway?" Careless, face warm with the effort of eating, drinking, and flirting, Alexis finishes her glass and wonders what they are really talking about. The wine has gone to her head very fast, she realizes a bit blurrily, remembering too late that she hadn't had time for lunch today. "Where did you go to school?" she asks, taking refuge in a straightforward question. "You're certainly well versed."

"Cal Tech after prep school, then I designed electronic subsystems for Hughes Aircraft for a while. Stanford B-school. When Keufel Ross offered me a job I came to Manhattan."

She translates this catalog of events into three ideas: solid family, private schools, moderate money. Why should it sound so rehearsed? she wonders. "How did you get interested in defense stocks?"

"You have to play to your strengths."

"It must put you in a unique position," she agrees. "In fact, you could be a very useful person to know," she teases, playing with her spoon. "Just think of all you could tell me about some of my own clients."

"Just think of what you could tell *me* — most definitely not dinner-table conversation," he says with a laugh. "On the other hand" — he looks now at his watch — "I wonder how it would go down over breakfast?" He grins.

Her face gets hot: his bluntness disconcerts. She is not used to being with someone who refuses the silky webs of illusion (or is that an illusion in and of itself?). She avoids responding directly to his suggestion by watching the waiter clear the platter of empty oyster shells. He refills their champagne glasses. Jon's hands move over the tablecloth, tracing an invisible design on the linen. They are small hands, with slender fingers and a large pad of muscle at the web of thumb and first finger: they look like hands that *do* something, strong hands that do not fit with the rest of the polished image, Paul Stuart suit and Hermes tie — any more than eating oysters with your fingers fits with his background. She remembers how he looked on the tennis court, the hair on his chest curling up silky and dark — and then thinks inadvertently of her husband's skin, hairless and smooth.

And as she sits staring, mesmerized by the motion of his fingers painting their unconscious patterns, she has a quick fantasy of his hands on her breasts. Then he lifts his arm, the white cuff of sleeve tugs back, and a tangle of black hairs over his wrist is exposed; the warm weight of his hand comes down over hers where it rests motionless next to her spoon. His skin is soft, surprising against the impression, already created, of strength. Without even thinking, she turns her palm up against his and feels the ridge of calluses that comes from gripping a racquet. Now his fingers thread up and down over the lines of her palm. The waiter puts new plates down in front of them.

They remain so still that she can feel the pulse in his wrist running against the tip of her index finger. It has been a very long time since anyone has touched her in this way: although it is only his hand on hers, it is intensely sexual, and she feels this single caress over her entire body. She is surprised to realize, in a blur of perception, that she has no guilt, but only sorrow, at being so excited. To feel this way again brings a marvelous rush. She looks up into his eyes for the first time since their hands met.

"Are you hungry?"

She doesn't answer.

"Would you like to leave?"

She hesitates a fraction of a second, knowing what it means to say yes, as his fingers stroke her wrist. "Do you think they'd give us a doggie bag?"

He laughs; to her horror, with total aplomb he asks for, and is given, a beautifully wrapped package containing their warm supper.

Leaving the restaurant is a blur. A quick credit card, an apology; the noise of conversation and the clatter of china passes over them in a Doppler effect of lopsided sound. Outside the night is warm and wet. The soft rain allows them to huddle together under Jon's golf-sized umbrella for practical reasons. She puts her arm through his, and because there are no taxis, and because his apartment is on Sixty-first, off Lexington, they walk.

Jonathan's building is a new high-rise; he has a one-bedroom (known euphemistically as a three and a half room apartment because in Manhattan practically even the bathroom counts) on the twentieth floor, with the sort of small balcony that always makes Alexis feel as if she is standing in a teacup suspended above the street. The lights of other buildings twinkle across the dark apartment as they come through the door, and she stands there in the dark, motionless, and waits for him to touch her.

He gropes instead for the light switch. Alexis squints against the sudden wash of cold bright; a minute elapses before she can open her eyes and focus again.

While he rummages in the kitchen, fixing them drinks, she goes to sit in the living room but changes her mind about the couch. To her surprise she is now feeling nervous and uncertain of why she has come; she stands in front of the bookcase instead. The shelves are crammed, some in double rows, with every sort of book. In fact, there are books all over the room, Alexis realizes, as she turns after a minute to head for the leather couch, books overflowing from the shelves and piled beneath the windows and up against the stereo in free-standing stacks. Magazines too — *Forbes, Fortune, Newsweek, Time, Esquire, New York, The New Yorker, The Atlantic, Aviation Week & Space Technology* — with coffee stains ringing their bright covers, curved over the sofa's arm and down behind its cushions, scattered in disarray over the round glass coffee table. Crowded to one edge of the table is a carved chess set of ivory. Alexis sits down, pushes the clutter aside, and picks up the king, running her fingers over its face. She shivers, though the room actually seems stuffy: tobacco smoke and sweat mingle faintly in the air.

As Jon comes and sits down beside her, Alexis pulls a running shoe from beneath her seat cushion; he sets their drinks down on the coffee table, balancing them on a stack of magazines.

"Sorry the place is such a mess," he says, kicking the shoe back under the sofa. "Maid's day tomorrow."

She nods, and, made even more nervous by the closeness of his body, stands to set the chess piece back on the board. "Point me at the bathroom?" Her mouth is dry.

Jon extends one arm as he takes a sip of his drink with the other, and she finds her way into a short hall crowded by three sets of skis, several tennis and squash racquets, and a loose basketball. Threading her way around these objects, she manages to find the toilet. She closes the door, pushes the button lock, pulls skirt up and panty hose down, and sits on the padded seat, which startles her by hissing air. Pressing on Alexis now is an important consideration: does she really want to ruin the possibility of further anticipation by rushing this? (Is she really ready?)

It has been a very long time since she's taken her clothes off and been naked under someone else's eyes. How will he know what she likes and does not, how will she be able to describe needs she has been communicating wordlessly, effortlessly, for the last thirteen years? She sits there for a minute, feeling vulnerable.

Finally she stands, washes her hands, and splashes her face with cold water. Succumbing to a habit left over from childhood, she slides open the mirrored medicine cabinet. Its top shelves are crowded with several contact lens solutions, a pair of horn-rimmed glasses smeary with disuse, aspirin, mouthwash, a tube of imported shaving cream, razor, toothpaste, and floss. On the bottom is a cache of hotel pilferables: miniature bottles of shampoo, conditioner, body lotion. Tampax. Toothbrushes wrapped in cellophane. *Everything a woman could need for a single overnight stay*, she thinks wryly.

As she combs her hair in the mirror, she hears the phone ring and Jon answer. While he talks, she turns right in the hall rather than left and peeks into his bedroom. On the floor is a rowing machine. The sheets on the unmade bed are white (of this she approves subliminally) and the comforter is trailing onto the floor, kicked off — the sign of a restless sleeper.

His voice travels down the length of the short hall: he is still talking on the phone, but his tone has become brusque and he is now speaking so loudly Alexis cannot help but hear.

"I don't want to talk about it anymore."

She walks toward the living room slowly, not wanting to intrude. Who is he so angry with? she wonders, feeling curious and a little nervous.

"No, don't apologize. You said it, you meant it. Call me tomorrow when you've calmed down." He hangs up the receiver, with a bang, and looks up to see Alexis standing, poised in the doorway.

Unsettled, she hesitates before coming back into the room: he has revealed a great deal of himself without intending to.

"Sorry about that," he says, gesturing toward the phone.

"No problem." She sits down in the chair across from him, picks up her drink, and waits, not knowing what to say.

He begins to pace back and forth around the room. "She gets me so mad sometimes!" His hands slice through the air, and Alexis is reminded, again, of his strength.

"Who?" she asks, pursuing the obvious.

"Christa."

"That was Christa?" Despite what she knows about the other woman's feelings for Jon, Alexis is still surprised that Christa has stooped to calling: it's a weak move.

Jon shrugs. "She's really ticked about tonight." He comes over and sits down again. "She shouldn't be — after all, I date a lot of women, and she's always known."

"Why did you call *me?*" Alexis asks, curious now.

"Why not? You know that hitting on the women in the business is a Wall Street tradition." He smiles and looks away. There is a silence between them. He looks back at her, directly, with a serious expression. "I called you because I wanted to be with someone like *me* for a change. I've had my fill of airheads."

"What about Christa?"

"Christa will never be more than a friend." He sighs. "Right now there's doubt in my mind that she'll even be that."

"Seems like a lot of people don't want us to get together," Alexis observes, leaning back and lighting up a cigarette.

"Who else?"

"Maggie gave me a big guilt trip last week."

"Why?"

"It threatens people who are married when someone they know strays from the flock."

"Are you planning to stray?"

"I don't know what I'm planning." She squints at him through a curling haze of blue smoke. "Except maybe to finish this cigarette and then get a cab back to the office."

He stretches to take a cigarette from the pack on the table, and she cannot read his reaction. If she expected him to protest she is obviously going to be disappointed, and this frees her: she gets up and goes to sit beside him on the couch.

He puts the cigarette down in the ashtray and takes her hand, running his fingers over her fingernails, then the lines of her palms, just touching her. She knows he is staring at her face, and so she waits a minute, then looks up, right back into his eyes. The silence extends, unfolding around them. Her face flushes, grows warmer.

He leans across the small distance between them and kisses her, at last, his lips circling hers, his tongue sliding in just over the edge of her teeth. Every doubt dissolves. Forget music and romance, forget beds and sheets and foreplay.

She pushes away and stands. "I have to go."

"You do?"

"If I stay any longer I won't leave at all."

He rises to stand directly in front of her. "You're worried I won't respect you in the morning?" he asks. He puts his hands on her waist, pulls her close.

"More like I might not respect you." Their faces are so close now that his breath (whiskey, tobacco) is palpable against her lips. She aches for him to touch her again. Slowly then — as if there is some resistance in the air between them — he moves his mouth down over hers. His tongue outlines the shape of her lips, licks inward, the edges of her teeth, then deeper. Their noses bump. She laughs, puts her arms up to him. He smiles, buries his face in her hair. Contours of their bodies align: adjusting for high heels, they are nearly the same height; the muscles of his chest meet her breasts, his hipbones are sharp against hers. For the first time in years she does not have to break her neck upward to kiss.

She pulls back an inch.

"I'll come down and put you in the cab," he says, his voice still muffled by her hair.

"The doorman can do that," she says, breaking away to pick up her purse. She heads toward the door, sounding determined but feeling unsteady.

"I'll call you." He throws the bolts to let her out.

"Good," she says, ringing for the elevator.

The doors slide open. She waves good-bye quickly, and only then, doors closed, does she allow herself to sink back against the wall and catch her breath. She smiles slowly to herself as the elevator drops toward the lobby: it has been too many years since she last felt this way.

Out on the pavement, she considers going uptown to the

apartment. To Nicolas. She thinks of the questions and the charade, the lies she will have to create about where she has been. The doorman helps her into a taxi with his umbrella. Leaning forward on the seat, she speaks to the driver. "105 Broad Street," she says, and so speeds downtown through the rain-slicked night.

✎

Christa, who had been wandering through her apartment for the last several hours trying not to call Jon, is now wandering again, berating herself for having given in to the urge. Finally, she gives in to yet another impulse and heads toward the kitchen.

Cash trails Christa as she pads barefoot down the hall in her nightshirt and snaps on the kitchen light. She opens the refrigerator door and pulls out a half gallon of Rocky Road, then changes her mind, takes instead a carton of chocolate milk and a box of Fig Newtons. She settles herself on the stool at the counter, which serves as a pass-through between the small kitchen and slightly larger living area in her one-bedroom apartment. Unwrapping the long cellophane stack, she watches Cash as, legs extended fully, he makes a curving, languorous bend, bringing his stomach all the way to the floor. With a yawn, he pads over to twine himself around and through her bare legs as if she is a Maypole, purring and rubbing his sleek red coat against her.

"Feel good?" she asks, reaching down to rub him with the flat of her fingertips, on his back, in that special place just in front of his tail.

"Mighty good," he answers in his Southern growl.

"These Fig Newtons are going to cost me five fat ones," she groans, licking crumbs from the corners of her lips. "Possibly more," she says reflectively, extracting another. Christa is the sort of person who is always dieting but never losing weight. She could be attractive, with her pale silky hair, blue eyes, and dimples, but her pretty features are diminished by the impression of roundness she creates. Bearing witness to that roundness is her telephone (calls from friends, not eligible men).

Alexis Somers, Christa is sure, never needs to diet: she skims across the surface of life untouched, getting everything she wants exactly the way she wants it. (Plainly put, Christa hates her.) She goes into the living room now, taking three more cookies and swigging from the carton of milk, and flips on the light switch. A cozy room, its sofa and chairs are covered in sun-faded velour; throw pillows are scattered around, and a mess of magazines litter the coffee table, crowded out by a framed photo collection of Cash in varying poses. This is the thirty-eighth floor of a glass-and-steel, doorman building at Fifty-seventh and First: what it lacks in architectural charm it makes up for with a spectacular view of the East River. The living room is Christa's cocoon, and she retreats into it with relief at the end of each long working day. Ordinarily she and Jonathan spend Monday nights here, cooking up a storm and working on her latest jigsaw puzzle as they watch cabin cruisers, yachts, tankers, and garbage barges roll by. But not this Monday. Not tonight.

She goes to the puzzle table and sits down, carrying Cash and stroking him absentmindedly as he drops his weight into her lap. Once she hoped that after a time she and Jon might settle down into a house somewhere, have children. Though Jon always dated freely she was sure one day he would look up across the puzzle table, put his hand over hers, and then they'd go — as in the movies — to the bedroom, without a word of dialogue. She felt certain that he never really shared himself (ideas, thoughts, feelings) with his dates, so many different faces and bodies he could barely keep them straight himself. And then he'd met Alexis.

Next Monday is her birthday. Number thirty-nine, in fact. She hasn't told anyone. Certainly not Jon (she doesn't want him to know how close to forty she is). She has been fantasizing that next week they would come back from squash and on the spur of the moment, he'd dial up Lafayette, whisk them over in a taxi for champagne and sweetbreads and chocolate truffles. And then, hazy with alcohol and desire, they would stroll arm in arm through the warm summer night to his apartment.

Christa studies the puzzle and reorients herself around the spot she left off with last night. She tries an oblong piece with three wavy curves to its left side in the upper right corner of the puzzle. In this scene, mountains drop away sharply into a lake, and there is enough blue in the background and a field of yellow poppies in the foreground to make it an extremely difficult puzzle. She only likes the hard ones; "stumpers," as her father calls them, make her concentrate, and while she is concentrating, some other part of her mind is free to wander over other problems, working them out in a silent, indirect fashion. (She often has her best ideas about a problem when she is deliberately not thinking about it.)

Christa began with jigsaws as a young girl, spending hours on the porch of their home in North Carolina with her father, fitting one piece to the next. He taught her to sort the wooden pieces by color and shape, by location, by the number of juts and holes, straight and wavy edges.

It is never just a question of trial and error, but rather, a mental exercise to try and hold in the mind the shapes and configurations already seen, possibly incorrectly tried, and to remember where the necessary piece has been laid (not unlike the art of psychoanalysis). The porch light cast a dull glow over the table, changing the browns and blues and reds before them, and the wind moved across their arms, which were bare in short-sleeved shirts. The scent of magnolias and newly mown grass wafted back and forth over them in that wind, overlapped occasionally with the charred smell of someone else's barbecue. It is a game of the mind, utterly obsessive and absorbing, a feat of balance between conscious and unconscious rhythms.

Now her attention snags on a space at her elbow, bounded by three jagged edges. She reaches reflexively for a blue piece to her left and for a blue piece with shading into yellow to her right. Turning them around, she lays them side by side into place with a sigh of satisfaction. And suddenly this is enough. She is tired. She will be able to sleep now.

She turns off the lights and moves down the hall to her bedroom, Cash close on her heels. As she enters her room, her glance falls on the photo her father sent with his last letter, a snapshot of him standing outside his church, the spire an abrupt thrust into the sky behind him, the graveyard where her mother is buried a symmetrical blur of squared shapes to the right. He is smiling in this picture, the flesh of his chin drooping down over his black and white clerical collar. He called a few hours ago to say hello and she was falsely cheerful. He wasn't fooled; he'd been waiting for her to admit how lonely she was, how empty New York has become for her. He wants her to come back home. But she knows if she goes back now she'll end up moving in with him, giving her life away to take care of his.

She reaches out and touches his face in the photograph, gently, with her fingertip. He always seems so sure, just when she is the most unsure. His faith is the long, slender pole he holds for balance as he crosses the high wire of everyday life; it is a faith she once tried to emulate. In the end (especially after her mother's cancer and surgery and slow painful death, when Christa was only thirteen) she couldn't believe — much as she might have wanted to. She stopped going to church. They stopped doing puzzles together. Now she would like nothing more than the comfort of a hug from him. But she is not ready to ask. She climbs into bed and pulls Cash tight against the curve of her hip. She turns out the light.

Darkness for them all now: darkness for Christa and Cash, whose eyelids shutter down toward sleep; then for Sy, propping his head against the window in the darkened plane on its way to the coast; for Alexis, restless on the leather couch in her office; for Nicolas, who slips under with columns of figures still scrolling through his mind; then for Jon, who kicks his sheets off in the humid New York night; and at last for Maggie, on her side of the king-sized bed, who sleeps and dreams, adrift.

SIX

Comfortable Deceptions

Maggie drives (quite fast, as is her habit) around the curves of the Hutchinson River Parkway (the Hutch) while Sy glowers at her out the corner of his eye. She feels him gauge the distance between their station wagon and the car directly in front, so she pulls out to pass on the left, pushing the speedometer up to seventy.

"Sing the ants go marching," Mikey begs his mother now. Maggie smiles. Family singing is a pastime she loves, and she knows his next request will be "Ninety-nine Bottles of Beer on the Wall." Just these two songs will keep them occupied until they are nearly there. The latter reminds Maggie of her own adolescence, of long bus rides on class trips where each verse was sung with gusto. Sy reaches over to pat her hand and, lustily, they both begin to belt it out.

The Whittens are on their way to the First Boston annual firm outing, held every year in the first week of July at the Wellport Bathing Club on the Connecticut shore. Every year the entire family's attendance is required at the outing, and every year Maggie tries to think up some excuse that will enable them to wriggle out of the commitment. But Sy is obligated to bring them all — Maggie with her smile at the ready and their handsome children freshly pressed and scrubbed — to make a good impression on all those partners who, as the countdown for promotions and bonuses begins, will vote for or against his person and/or his performance. He will be considered for partnership in the firm — managing director, they call it now — sometime in the next two years, so that each year, as Maggie grows more and more bored with (stifled by) their requisite appearance at all these functions and outings, their attendance itself assumes an exponentially greater significance.

Year by year, there is something else that has begun to make her resentful (though she has never articulated it either to herself or her husband): she is in a peculiar limbo at these events, having little in common with either the women members of the firm, the younger secretaries and analysts, or the other wives. No one seems to realize that at one time she was a working woman and that this is something to which she someday intends to return: her sense of dignity smarts as she is labeled, quite simply, *wife of Sy Whitten, mother of two*. Buffeted by sensations of envy, she has to sit and smile as the First Boston women like Christa and Maxine McClellin — not just the men — get to talk shop with her husband; nonworking wives are limited to warbling a supportive chorus. Certainly she never (consciously) intended this role for herself. And yet, here she is.

"Don't forget Maxine asked me to be her doubles partner," Sy inserts quickly a half hour later, as they hit the thirty-third bottle of beer on the wall and Maggie clicks her blinker to turn off the highway.

She looks over at him, startled: she *has* forgotten, though she now recalls he mentioned it only last night. She had blocked out both the pleasure on his face and her own concomitant surge of frustration. She knows it is a compliment that Maxine asked Sy; he certainly cannot say no.

"Don't forget you promised to take Mikey swimming." She is being argumentative (there will be plenty of time for both) but she finds herself unable (unwilling) to keep an accusatory note from her voice.

He sends her a look. "There'll be time."

From the backseat comes Mikey's voice. "I want to go swimming, Daddy."

In the rearview mirror, Maggie sees her son's face, vulnerable. His body is braced, stiff, against the back of the seat (against disappointment). She smiles into the mirror at him. "There'll be plenty of time for both," she says reassuringly. "Mommy was just being silly."

Sy leans over the front seat. "Right after lunch," he promises.

"But Mommy said —"

"Don't worry about what Mommy said," Sy cuts his son off. "*I* promised and *I* never break a promise."

"What about me?" Katie pouts. "You always take him — and I brought my float!"

"You, too, sweeting."

As they pull into the stone-arched, tree-lined entrance to Wellport, Maggie realizes how, in a second of selfishness and anger, she has used the children to get at him. She puts her hand on Sy's arm. "Sorry." She keeps her voice low.

He shrugs.

"It's just all this politicking — I hate it. I wish we didn't have to do it anymore."

"If I make M.D. we can cut back some," he promises. She sees from the set of his jaw that even mentioning the word makes him tense. "You know I really spend a lot of time with the kids." He turns his head away to look out the window.

A suffocated feeling fills her chest. "When you're here."

"More than most fathers who are around all the time," he answers shortly.

She presses her lips together, tired of assuaging his guilt over how much time he does, in fact, spend away from all of them. It's nice that he's around full-time most Saturdays and Sundays, but that still leaves her close to being a single parent, making the decisions and meting out the discipline for more than half the week. And when Sy does come home, the limited hours he has with the kids are too precious to waste being anything except a best friend.

"I forgot to tell you that I did manage to get Katie's appointment with the ophthalmologist moved to Friday," she says, striving for a positive note over the swift protest of her emotions.

Dr. Lewison is concerned about Kate's mildly crossed eyes, and so her vision has been regularly monitored for over a year now; this week's appointment will decide whether corrective surgery to tighten the eye muscles will be necessary in the autumn, or whether the glasses she's been wearing for the last year will suffice. Last week, Sy asked Maggie to switch the checkup to Friday so that he could go with them.

He frowns and a vague expression crosses his face.

"You'll be able to come?"

"I said I would, didn't I?"

"Yes, but —"

"But what?"

"It just looked like you'd forgotten."

"I said I'll be there." He releases his seat belt as she maneuvers the big wagon into a grassy parking space. "Though I still think you're up to handling it by yourself."

By yourself. A prickle of anger climbs Maggie's back as she turns the key and kills the engine. She rubs her hand over the cool plastic of the steering wheel. Sometimes the distances between them astound her. How can he not understand why he ought to be at this appointment?

"I'm just saying that we'll do whatever he recommends anyway," Sy points out (as always the pragmatist). "But I changed my meeting in Philly so I can be with you if you want."

"If it's inconvenient . . ." She lets the words hang in the air, not meaning them in the slightest.

"If you want me, I'll be there," he repeats.

They load up with two distended beach bags, Kate's inflatable raft in the shape of a dinosaur, their sweaters — barbecue supper on the beach will be chilly — and a volleyball, as well as Sy's tennis racquet and his whites, carefully pressed, on a hanger. Thus burdened, they begin to walk toward the low main building.

The Wellport Bathing Club was built on a stretch of white beach along the Long Island Sound in the early 1900s, in an era when croquet, swimming, and racquet sports were the major summertime occupations of a certain class of Americans. The main clubhouse is a single story of cement and red brick, the roof of Spanish tile. (Through its simple architecture and its somewhat ramshackle condition it proclaims that old money is never afraid to be, or to look, exactly as it is: old.)

And that is precisely the reason, Maggie muses, as they walk up onto the wide front veranda, with its dilapidated fleet of green-painted rocking chairs and wicker swings facing out onto the ocean, that the women here take off their jewelry when they put on their bathing suits. Unlike in Scarsdale, where ladies at "the club" accessorize their bikinis with gold earrings and necklaces. The sea air permeates everything here: even the individual dressing cabanas, handed down generation to generation like a precious heirloom, have brass door plaques so green with verdigris that it is difficult to read the name of the original owner, and walls and chair cushions alike are stained with mildew.

Several top officers of First Boston are members here, sponsoring the outing, and, to Maggie, Wellport is a reflection of the place Sy works. In addition to being O.M.O. (Old Money Only), the club is still N.J.A. (No Jews Allowed), and Maggie hates coming here because she is embarrassed for Sy. Some rebellious streak in her would like to sign the register Mr. and Mrs. Seymour Whittenberg, which used to be Sy's name, before his father removed the last four letters at some point prior to Sy's birth. Sometimes she wishes that Sy had joined a firm like Bear Stearns, where his Jewishness would not be so out of place, but that would only be trading one sort of homogeneity for another. Besides, breaking into the ranks of a not-so-long-ago solely WASP investment house tickled Sy in exactly the same way it tickled Alexis to join Hewett Lowell.

There are unspoken rules here everywhere you turn, and these rules serve to set apart those who belong from those who do not. You never go into the main part of the clubhouse in your bathing suit, even with a cover-up and shoes. On the tennis court, whites are not only required but strictly observed. You do not sign a chit or give an account number when ordering your lunch on the deck, but merely the family name. Children conduct themselves with decorum, everywhere but on the beach, or are quietly removed. It is a languorous place, swept by the sea air, baked under the sun, and leisure is the art to be perfected.

"Maggie! Sy!"

They both turn at the shout and see Christa, down the long expanse of porch fronting the ocean, looking happy and relaxed in Bermuda shorts and a straw hat. The day at Wellport has begun.

"Hi!" she says, arriving breathlessly next to them. "I thought maybe you weren't coming." Her smile is wide, genuine, and Maggie finds herself warming to her obvious good humor.

"It always takes us a while to get ourselves together," she says apologetically, gesturing over the heads of the children.

"Can we build a castle?" Mikey tugs impatiently on her arm.

"In a sec, sweetie."

"Now, now, now." He pulls again on her hand.

"You go along and get started." She disentangles his sand-pail from the five other objects she has dangling off her arms. "I'll be right down."

As the children run off toward the water, a tall black man comes up and puts his arm around Christa's shoulders while simultaneously greeting Sy.

"Weldon, this is my wife, Maggie," Sy says, making the introductions. "Maggie, this is Weldon Robb — a fellow drone in the M&A department."

Weldon laughs, low-timbred and husky, and offers his hand; he holds her fingers a second longer than is customary. His skin, obsidian, shines with a film of perspiration in the hot July sun; his cheekbones are high, his nose aquiline. His hair is cut to reveal the oval of his skull and the length of his neck. His eyes are amber, the color of glass washed smooth by the sea. Flustered, she frees her hand and turns to look for her children at the water's edge.

"I better make sure the kids don't drown." She starts down the steps onto the sand. "Nice to meet you," she calls back to Weldon.

"A pleasure."

"I'll come with you," Christa offers.

"Be there in a sec," Sy shouts as they walk away, but when she looks back he is already deep in an animated discussion with Weldon. Whatever he says, it will be some time before he joins them.

"I've never met him before," Maggie says, as they struggle across the sand toward the spot the kids have picked to drop their pails and shorts.

"Weldon keeps the rest of them sane — never gets hepped up." Christa's smile is broad. "Unless you cross him. He can be mean as a yard dog."

"Seems as if he has a soft spot for you," Maggie observes,

throwing the beach bags down and rummaging for the blanket and towels.

A blush creeps over Christa's skin. "Weldon's a lady-killer, that's all."

Christa unbuttons her shirt and takes it off. Her bright pink suit looks new, undoubtedly bought especially for today's outing. The pool is the singles hangout, just as the beach is where all the kids and mothers end up. Maggie always avoids the pool, where every lounge showcases a woman in her twenties without cellulite or stretch marks; they pose for each other provocatively while drinking iced fruit punches from the bar and flirting with co-workers.

"Kids!" Maggie's voice dissolves into the wind, so she has to call two or three times before she snags their attention. They come, reluctantly, to the insistent semaphore of her arms. "Lotion," she says, uncapping the bottle of number fifteen.

"That stuff is gross," Kate protests. "Besides," she pouts, "I want to get tan."

Maggie rolls her eyes at Christa and both women laugh.

"Have to," Maggie answers, squirting a liberal layer across her daughter's back. Slowly she rubs it in, savoring the feel of the young bones beneath her fingers. Despite her initial protest, Kate cooperates by holding still, arching her back against the pleasure of her mother's hand. Maggie kisses the top of her head and tweaks her ear to let her know she is finished.

"Yuk-ko," Mikey cries, planting his feet and refusing to come any closer, and then doing everything possible to escape once he is kneeling before her — writhing and wriggling, making the job even worse than it already is. By the time she gets the back of him covered and turns him around to start the front they are both miserable.

"Hello, Maggie. Christa."

They look up to see Maxine McClellin standing above them. She puts her hand out toward Maggie, but Maggie's hands are so greasy by now that she can only gesture with the bottle of lotion. "If I gave you my hand you'd ruin your racquet," she says with a laugh. It's inevitable: no matter how she tries, she always seems to be at sixes and sevens whenever Maxine is around.

Maxine laughs, too. "A messy job," she agrees. As usual, she looks perfectly put together: in a white tennis dress of expensive cut, she wears a visor and Vuarnet sunglasses. Her cropped hair doesn't even ruffle in the stiff wind off the ocean. Maggie feels conspicuously inadequate, her hair tousled and snarled, her own sunglasses left back on the dashboard of the station wagon.

"How have you been getting along this year?" she asks Maggie. Christa has scrambled up to stand, which is exactly what Maggie wishes she could do (to gain some sort of a hold on the conversation), but Mikey has chosen this lull in the greasing of his body to begin a new construction project: starting at his mother's ankles, he is now dumping pailfuls of sand over her calves and thighs. Maggie doesn't even bother to protest, but instead shades her eyes against the sun and cranes her neck.

"Fine," she answers politely. "How about you, Maxine?" She caps the tube of lotion.

"Mommy!" Mikey has finished entombing her legs in the ton of itchy sand and is now tugging on her arm. "Mom-my."

"Great, thanks. Things look about the same with you." Her expression is one of amusement.

"Yes," Maggie agrees. "They're a year older but I'm just the same — when you already feel ancient you've got nothing to lose one year to the next."

All the women laugh. "Good to see your sense of humor is intact," Maxine says affably.

"Mommy!" Mikey tugs again, shoving his plastic sailboat in her face for emphasis.

"Last time I saw you you were thinking about going back to work," Maxine goes on.

"I want to go swimming now!" insists Mikey.

"Back to work? No, I —" She redirects the sailboat away from her face so she can see Maxine, but Mikey dances back, directly in her line of vision.

"Let's go swimming, Mommy!" Mikey's voice is louder as he realizes he has not yet caught her attention.

Maggie laughs self-consciously, trying to cover her annoyance. "Isn't the beach fun!" she says brightly.

Christa laughs. "Sometimes I wonder how women talk themselves into being mothers. This seems much harder than what we do day to day."

Maggie sends her a grateful look, while Maxine looks back to Maggie, clearly waiting for an answer to her question about returning to work.

"I still can't bring myself to leave them with some stranger," Maggie explains, her tone apologetic. "Though don't ask me why, because today I'm ready to auction them off to anyone at all!" Again she laughs and again Christa and Maxine laugh with her. Maggie flushes with pleasure at this moment of camaraderie. Sometimes (too caught up with being envious), she forgets how friendly Maxine can be.

"Mommy, you're not listening!" Mikey interrupts again, voice stubborn and loud, face earnest and angry. "I *said* I want to go swimming!"

"So go ahead, dear." She gestures toward the water. "I'll watch you from here."

"It's hard not to worry about it," Maxine goes on, above his head, continuing as if they have not been interrupted five times by now (a tactic all mothers learn as soon as their toddlers begin to talk). "But I've been leaving Maxie since she was four months old with this Guyanese woman I've got and she seems to be just fine. She's with her today."

"What luck to have the same person looking after her."

"Well, actually this is the third one, but she's nearly as good as the first." Maxine smiles uncomfortably. "As long as I'm not in the house too much — the woman would drive me crazy if I had to be with her all the time!"

"I hear really good help is hard to find and impossible to keep," Maggie says. It seems remarkable to her that Maxine has no trouble leaving her child with a woman she herself can't bear to be around. "In the end neither one of us felt comfortable with the idea of leaving a three-month-old — or for that matter a three-*year*-old — with someone else from eight to six, five days a week. But *now*," she adds, "they're both ready for school full-time and it's a more realistic possibility."

"I didn't really have a choice," Maxine says. "The firm gives you three months. Period. And even if they gave you more, you wouldn't take it because you'd be too scared that they'd forget who you were and replace you on all your accounts. Can you go back to *Esquire* after all this time?"

"Swimming!" Mikey says again, tugging again on his mother's arm.

Maggie points toward the water. "I'm watching, Mikey. Go ahead."

"I want to go with *you!*"

"In a minute," Maggie promises. "When I'm finished talking to Maxine."

"No — now."

Why is it that whenever she tries to have a conversation with an adult he is always interrupting? Especially now, when she is so hungry to talk to other women with something more on their mind than diapers and nursery schools. This is one of the first times she can remember ever being asked about herself at one of these functions. This moment is important to her. "Kate?"

Her daughter looks up from smoothing, with great delicacy, the front wall of her sand castle.

"Could you take him in the water?"

Kate frowns. "I'm busy now."

Maxine laughs. "Go ahead, Maggie. I'll catch up with you later."

Maggie smiles and takes her son's hand. "Sure." She does not let the disappointment overwhelm her, but pushes it to the back of her mind.

"I'm ready," Sy announces, arriving on the edge of the blanket, changed into his whites, with racquet in hand.

"Just in time," Maxine says, looking at her watch.

"Have a good game," Maggie says, picking up the sailboat, a forlorn tinge creeping into her voice despite her resolve.

"Maybe we could play some singles afterward," Sy offers.

"I'd like that," she says slowly. "But how?" She gestures at the children, running now across the sand.

"I'd watch the kids for you," Christa volunteers.

"You would?" Maggie brightens at the generous offer. Christa must need to circulate with her colleagues today, after all, just like Sy. In fact, why isn't she lounging by the pool right now, showing off the new bathing suit?

"Sure. You two never get a chance to do much alone."

Maxine nods in agreement. "These things are supposed to be family events, but it always seems like the mothers wind up getting stuck."

"Is Jack here?" Maggie asks.

Maxine shakes her head and grins. "Another Wall Street truth: husbands of female officers are not expected to attend these events — only wives."

"That's true," Sy says, dragging his toe through the sand. "And it ought to be different."

"I was thinking next year we should set up some sort of 'moms' tennis tournament," Maxine goes on.

"Being a beach potato does get boring year after year," Maggie agrees, as Mikey begins once more to cover her legs, ankle to thigh, under a thick layer of sand. Again Christa and Maxine laugh. Maggie reaches out to ruffle Mikey's hair.

"Oh, come on, don't make it sound so bleak," Sy says gruffly, embarrassed.

"Quit while you're ahead, Sy." Maxine gives him a light shove with her hand and drags him off across the sand.

Maggie frees herself from the burial mound Mikey has built around her. She stands up and walks with Christa down to the water's edge as he bounds ahead of them, frisking in the ocean's froth. She thinks of all the hours she has spent during the last six years, fingerpainting, tying shoes, doing laundry, wiping asses, spooning chicken and prunes, spreading peanut butter, cleaning up thousands of tiny Lego pieces, waiting in line at the supermarket and at school for the afternoon car pool, smoothing over the disruptions and the disappointments in their young lives. All those activities that carry little or no currency in life outside the home. The endless tedium set so tightly against the love. She wonders if Sy understands her situation at all.

As she pushes Mikey's sailboat back and forth in the shallow water, she reprimands herself: it is shameful to be upset when there are people in the world with real trouble. She and Sy are financially secure, they have two healthy children and a beautiful home. How can she complain? And she is certain (almost) that when she decides to return to work he will be supportive.

After a while, Mikey wants his raft. Christa and Maggie take turns blowing it up. When it is nearly done, Maggie takes a quick dip in the water and then breaststrokes back in. Her feet graze the sand and hit bottom. Kate waits at the edge of the surf, waist-deep, her back to the sea and her mother, the dinosaur raft bobbing around her.

Maggie dives underwater and swims through the beat of the waves to grab Kate around the ankles, provoking screams of glee. Cavorting with her daughter, Maggie wonders if any of these issues will be more clear when it is Kate's turn to be a woman and a mother.

Christa wades in, up to her chest, pushing Mikey in front of her on the float. "Is everything O.K.?" she asks after a minute, when Maggie stops horsing around long enough to catch her breath. "You got awfully quiet."

"It took all my breath to blow up that raft!"

They both laugh.

Maggie sobers and then sighs. "Seriously . . . sometimes these functions are tough. That's all."

"Just remember even surefooted women like Maxine are ambivalent, too."

"Maxine always looks like she knows what she's doing."

Christa shakes her head. "Just like the rest of us — stumbling around in the dark."

"Why do I have to take everything so seriously?" Maggie asks, laughing at herself. "I get upset in a flash over nothing."

Christa smiles sympathetically.

"You're a sport to help me with the kids like this."

Christa's face is still shaded beneath her hat, but Maggie can see the smile regardless. "I love kids." She shrugs. "I always wanted to have my own. . . ."

"How's Jon?" Maggie asks, without thinking; a few weeks have passed since she had drinks with Alexis at Palio and she has heard nothing further. Maggie has not tracked Alexis down to find out what transpired when — or if — she met Jon for that infamous drink. Perhaps, she thinks now, she does not really want to know.

Christa looks out at the ocean. "We had a fight. I haven't seen him in a couple of weeks."

Maggie waits a minute, but the other woman's silence invites more questions. "A fight about what?"

An expression of disgust crosses Christa's face. "Your friend Alexis, I'm sorry to say."

"Why did you fight about Alexis?" Maggie keeps her face impassive; protocol clearly calls for her to feign ignorance.

"He's started to see her." Christa smacks the top of the water with the flat of her palm a few times. "It doesn't matter one iota that she's married." Her voice is sarcastic and bitter. "Not one iota. When Jon makes up his mind, you can never talk him out of it."

Maggie's stomach drops, her breathing is tight in her chest. Not only has Alexis decided to see Jon, but already it is public news, a piece of gossip bait — and she, the best friend, did not even know. It hurts to think that Alexis did not call to confide in her; on the other hand, perhaps she deserved it for her reaction that evening at Palio. Christa pauses, looking at her speculatively. "I'm sorry," she says, "I know you all were close. I assumed you already knew."

Maggie shrugs and trails her hand in the water. "Alexis can be unpredictable." She smiles. "Just because you love someone doesn't mean you always like what they do. Besides," she goes on, "I feel bad for Nicolas. And you."

"I *am* jealous," Christa admits slowly. "I always thought that when he got tired of all that running around he'd look to me." She laughs with bitterness. "I just don't understand it. Her husband is smart, successful, handsome." She shakes her head. "It's downright greedy."

"She hasn't been getting along with her husband for a while now."

"Still. You think they'd separate or something first."

"Or something," Maggie agrees, wondering what Nicolas will do if he finds out. She can't imagine them separating or divorcing.

"The worst part is I just can't seem to take anyone else seriously." Christa stares up into the sun. The waves sway her body. "I'm not getting any younger, either," she says, ruminatively. "I turn thirty-nine next week. I keep thinking about kids. When I see people like you and Sy —"

Maggie stares at her. "Don't be fooled, Christa. We've got problems just like everyone else."

"But he loves you so much. Do you have any idea how hard that is to find?"

"Do you have any idea how hard it is to keep?" Maggie asks, an edge coming into her voice. "After twelve years, and him away so much?"

"But you're so happy together."

That idea brings Maggie up with a start. *A good front*, she thinks. "We're no paragons." She feels her confusion rise again, sap in a spring thaw. "Everyone talks about the sacrifice he makes for his work — but how about me? What about all I've given up just to keep the four of us together. Suppose I *did* go back to work now — how would it be for the kids to have a father who is away four days a week and a mother who limps home, tired out, to face them alone at six or seven every night? What kind of a life is that?"

Christa nods.

"The last few years have been impossible."

"Is his traveling worse?"

"Probably not," she reflects, squinting against the sun, which now seems extremely intense. "It's just that in the beginning I fooled myself that it was temporary. I thought a time would come when we'd have real family dinners and he'd be there for me every night —" She breaks off. "The other day, I was sitting talking to Alexis, and I realized — well, now I know this is how it's going to be. For a long time."

"You're right," Christa agrees. "Unless he changes jobs."

Maggie laughs sarcastically. "Are you kidding — he loves this stuff! And we're addicted to the money. No," she says darkly. "I've just got to get used to it."

"How?"

"Some wives seem to."

"Maybe those wives don't really want their husbands around so much. Maybe they like that separate life-style."

This has never occurred to Maggie before, but before she can pursue the thought, Mikey tumbles off the edge of his raft into the water, sputtering in the waves. Maggie and Christa both jump to rescue him against the undertow, but he stumbles out onto the beach, and without a pause runs to pick up his sand pail and shovel.

"Well," Christa says then, continuing as they stand monitoring Kate's progress through the water on her raft, "what about the Tokyo job? If you move then he'll travel less."

"Tokyo job?" Maggie repeats, puzzled.

"If he gets it."

"What job?"

"The Tokyo office." Christa's tone is overly patient, as if she can't understand what Maggie's problem is. "I'm sure he'll get it if he puts his name in. I'm sure. It was Maxine's idea to sponsor him."

Maggie, stunned, says nothing; she just stands there with her hands hanging by her sides, mouth agape.

"He *did* tell you about it?" Christa asks, slowly.

Maggie shakes her head.

"Nothing?"

"Not a word," she whispers. The rush of the water around them is all she can hear, overlaid with the sound of excited children running up and down the beach (gull-like whoops diminished by the vast space and the pounding of the surf).

"Christ." Christa wades through the water to come nearer, as if she wants to put her arm around Maggie. "I never meant to —"

"You couldn't have known." Maggie shakes her head. "It's natural to assume that he'd tell me he was considering accepting a job in *another country*." Her voice rises now shrilly. "You'd *assume* he'd discuss it with his wife. What man wouldn't?" Tears tip over the edges of her eyelids.

"But why wouldn't he tell you? I don't understand this at all. And why wouldn't you want to go, for that matter?"

"He's afraid — that's why," Maggie answers, wiping her face with a vicious swipe of her hand. "He knows I've been thinking about going back to work. I'd never be able to get a job in Tokyo. I'd have to put my life on hold all over again."

"Well, he'll have to broach it with you at some point. He can't very well just keep on avoiding it."

"When?" Maggie demands. "When he cancels the newspaper subscription? When he buys the airline tickets and rents the apartment?" She is furious, humiliated to learn of this job offer from someone else. "It's outrageous."

"If it's any consolation — it's a fantastic opportunity."

"Are you joking? That will just make it harder to turn down."

"There's no possibility that you'd go?"

"I can't imagine it. How can I think about transplanting myself now? I'm not ready for another six-year sabbatical from life." She wades out of the water and paces back and forth through the green and foamy lap of the waves where they meet the shore. "So what is it, anyway?"

"Director of the new M&A effort we're setting up in Tokyo. It's a real compliment that they're considering him. It'll push him into partnership faster."

"Or out of it."

"Out?" Christa cocks her head to one side.

"Marriage is a partnership, too."

"I wish I had never brought it up," Christa groans. "Lord, why didn't I keep my mouth shut?"

"It's not your fault. You just put your foot in a hole dug by somebody else."

"What are you going to do now?"

"I'm going to wait," Maggie answers, planning it all in her mind as if she is staging a battle. "I'm going to wait and see when he gets around to telling me."

By the time Sy returns to the beach from his doubles match, she has regained her composure. She seals the rage beneath a mask of goodwill. All afternoon she sits on her beach towel and plays at being the perfect wife and mother, and the fury within provides a backbone of patience, the mien of love. She wonders how long she can keep up such a facade. Sy is oblivious, enjoying his romp with the children on the beach: he runs to the snack bar for sodas, takes them swimming, builds a sand castle big enough for Mikey to climb in, and plays tag.

By the time the day is over, the Whittens climb wearily into the car to head for home, their bodies itchy with sand and sunburn. The children fall asleep as soon as the car begins to move. In the front seat, Sy takes Maggie's hand and tells her he loves her. Maggie smiles back and repeats his words. But from behind the glass wall of her face, she sees only a man who has betrayed her by keeping a secret.

∽

At ten-thirty in the evening, on Independence Day, Alexis and Jon saunter into Greene Street, a jazz joint cum restaurant in the Village; she moves comfortably within the circle of his arm, having blocked out, quite deliberately, that she has a husband.

This morning it was not as difficult as she'd anticipated to lie to Nicolas — telling him that she would be at the office all day, when in fact she intended to spend only a few hours there. And she used work again as an excuse to join Jon that evening for the fireworks on the tip of Manhattan at Battery Park. Everyone in the thick crowd was infused with camaraderie as fireworks from four barges moored just at the base of the Statue of Liberty shot out over the water and illuminated the skyline of Wall Street. How glad she was that they did not go to some chic rooftop, but instead, incognito in their jeans among thousands of others, held hands through the two-hour spectacle.

She hadn't seen Jon since that night at his apartment because both of them had been traveling, he in L.A., she in Chicago, Miami, and Denver. But when she returned to the office yesterday she picked up the phone without a moment's hesitation.

The maître d' greets Jon warmly and escorts them to a table. Jon frowns, requests another a little farther back and to the left. Once seated, Alexis raises an eyebrow.

"The sound is much better this side of the room," he explains.

"You come here a lot?"

He shrugs noncommittally.

She unfolds the napkin across her lap and settles back in her chair, smiling to herself. While Jon will rarely answer such a direct question (he fancies himself inscrutable), she nevertheless is discovering it possible (if not easy) to interpret his silences. What would strike some women as impossibly annoying only seems titillating to Alexis, who knows that more can be understood from what he does not say than from what he does. His enigmatic posture is a compliment to her (the more intensely a high-powered man wants something, the more secretive he becomes).

She scans the room, which looks to be an old garage with several levels, converted to a cabaret. Small lamplit tables are scattered around the central platform where the musicians now prepare for their next set.

"Hungry?" Jon asks, extending the menu toward her.

She nods. "Recommendations?" She flicks through the menu, not really wanting to make a choice, feeling that almost anything would do.

"Pasta's terrific. Especially anything with shrimp. Or clams. Or mussels. And desserts."

As the jazz starts, they choose a good bottle of red, and pasta, then settle back. Alexis puts her head against the back of her chair and closes her eyes. They sit and just listen. His hand creeps across the table to take hers, and she intertwines her fingers with his.

"Jonathan?" The voice that interrupts them is female, twangy, self-assured.

Startled out of the reverie created by the soft blues and her fatigue, Alexis looks up to see a young blond woman, her hair blunt cut to emphasize her jawbone and wide mouth, standing beside their table with her hands on her hips. Jonathan immediately withdraws his hand to his own side of the table.

"Mick." His voice falls, betraying dismay, although his face, eyes, and smile all remain neutral.

"Coincidence. Again." She looks toward Alexis, whose mouth lifts at the corners in a smile she does not mean.

"Mick Harrington, Alexis Somers," Jon says.

Mick puts her hand out, and as she takes it (the other has a hard, quick shake) Alexis realizes why her name sounds familiar. She read several short stories by Mick Harrington in *Esquire*, back when Maggie was still an editor there. Maggie was so excited about publishing her — one of the first major magazines to give her an audience — though Alexis couldn't (and still can't) understand it. Her prose style is flat and reveals nothing more about her than does her name: she adopts male and female viewpoints with equal ease. (Some critics consider this a strength.) Her characters live in trailer parks strewn with empties and shadowed by mongrels; people who eat cat food for breakfast, smack their kids around over lunch, and scream at each other during dinner. Over the last five years, Mick Harrington (now a wealthy Manhattanite) has spun the litter of human life into gold. Alexis wonders how Jon knows her.

"Mind if I sit a minute?" Mick says, sliding into the chair next to Jon, without waiting for an answer. "You ran out on me the other night," she chides him, turning to face him so that her shoulder is at right angles to Alexis (and so closes her out). "Before we talked at all. Where'd you get to anyway?"she asks in a petulant voice.

Jon looks over at Alexis. "Mick and I ran into each other last week at an anniversary party for *Tattletales* — you know, the magazine."

The spaghetti arrives, steaming, redolent of tomato, garlic, sea brine. The clams and mussels are still in their shells.

Alexis and Jon both pick up their forks.

Mick reaches over and takes a sip of Jon's wine. Contrary to what Alexis expected to see in a woman connected with Jon, there is little to recommend Mick physically: the width of her mouth emphasizes the narrow point of her chin, and even the wealth of hair could not make up for the peculiar lashless look of her eyelids. Finished with her scrutiny and bored now, Alexis begins to cut her pasta with neat strokes of her knife.

As she does so, Mick breaks off mid-sentence to stare. "I haven't seen anyone cut their pasta since grammar school."

"*His* pasta? Or *her* pasta?" Alexis asks dryly.

"How about eating Chinese food with a metal fork." She taps her finger against Jon's knife. "Do *you*?"

Alexis, her silverware suspended and her eyebrows aloft, just looks at her.

"It ruins Chinese if you don't use chopsticks," Mick explains. "You destroy pasta unless you twirl it."

Alexis shrugs, lifts a bite, and begins to chew hungrily. "Delicious," she says — to Jon.

"Aesthetics," Mick murmurs.

"Nothing aesthetic about tomato sauce down my front."

Mick lifts both of her large square hands toward Jon. "Jane's new book is up for the NBA," she goes on.

"I heard," he says. "But I thought the two of you weren't

speaking." He picks up his fork and knife and cuts his pasta.

Mick watches him do it, quizzically. "Oh, we resolved all that. *Ages* ago." She hooks her hair behind her ears, one of which has three ebony studs in it.

"You're still working on *The Yellow Omnibus*?"

She shakes her head. "Finished. I'll send you a comp next fall. I got a jacket by Fred Marcellino this time." Her hands are flying through the air now, sculpting in tandem. "He does Anne Tyler, all the really good people."

Something about the name-dropping reminds Alexis of her mother's friends, sitting poolside in the Hamptons and gossiping about which jeweler, which designer, which architect has done what for whom.

"Who's your publisher again?" Alexis asks curiously.

"Knopf."

"A friend of mine was the fiction editor over at *Esquire* when you first published there."

Mick answers with a shrug. She looks irritated — either at being interrupted or at being reminded of her beginnings, Alexis can't tell which. Reaching for Jon's cigarettes, imported, Mick takes one, lighting it with a match from the ashtray. "I've missed these," she says, inhaling appreciatively. "Especially — well —" She breaks off, with a sideways glance at Alexis.

Especially after sex, Alexis fills in silently. *What a pretentious bitch.*

Jon lifts his wineglass and drinks from it very slowly, considering how he is going to get Mick out of here and away from Alexis. Still, he can't help but appreciate the way Alexis just sits back and watches, eyes open to every bit of information and each nuance.

"Are you here with someone?" he asks now, hoping to remind her that she isn't spending the evening at their table.

"Upstairs," she says reluctantly. "I guess I should get back."

"You should," he agrees, taking his napkin off his lap and rising politely, so that she has no choice about it.

"Could we get together?" she asks, bending across to give him a kiss on the cheek. "Soon."

"Right."

"It's been long enough, don't you think?"

"Have a good night."

After she leaves, Alexis eats a few more bites. Finished, she aligns fork and knife on the edge of the plate, wipes her mouth on her napkin, and settles back with her wineglass. She can tell Jon is relieved that she has not started up a barrage of questions about Mick. *Later*, she thinks.

"How did you manage to finesse your way into a party for *Tattletales*?"

"My friend Lawry Stenowitz works there now." He loads his fork with more pasta. "I don't see him much anymore — I thought it would be fun."

"Sounds like it would be."

He looks over at her as she draws a cigarette from her case. He takes up her lighter and holds it under the tip as she inhales. "It wasn't."

She drags and waits, just looking at him.

"It was depressing."

"How come?"

He moves restlessly in the chair. "Too much money, too much glitter, too many pretentious people strutting their stuff. I don't know . . ." His voice trails off, awkward.

"I read about that party somewhere. Sounded like a lot of deal-making went down."

"Probably," he says, sipping his wine. "You know the kind of scene — paparazzi like a cloud of mosquitos, so many limos you'd have thought it was a funeral for Elvis. And the guest list!" He laughs, short, punctuation. "Handpicked for major marquee value." He shakes his head.

Alexis is puzzled. "But you must have to deal with that sort of bullshit function all the time at work."

"This was different." He looks at her directly, remembering the way the scotch lay heavy and sour in his mouth; the sense of isolation, as if he'd rocketed off into outer space and were watching a new ritual on a foreign planet. "Like I said to you the other night — I'm getting sick of a lot of the things that used to turn me on. I had a better time tonight, doing this with you." His face grows moodier. "Till Mick turned up."

"Case in point," Alexis agrees.

He pours himself another glass of wine. "I was surprised you knew who she was."

"Hey — I'm literate. But I can't say I like her writing much."

"Why?"

"All those detached people." She shrugs. "Nothing to make me care. Laugh or cry."

"I didn't expect her to be here. We came a couple times, but mostly she prefers Brett's."

"I hear that place is like some replay from *The Sun Also Rises*."

Jon shrugs. "A lot of types hang around together there. Talking about writing ad nauseam."

"Which makes you wonder how they ever get any writing done."

"It's like a business lunch. Probably something gets done — not much of it on paper."

"She's pretty possessive of you — or is that her way in general?"

"Let's just say I broke it off. And she didn't like that."

"I had a few of those in my time." Alexis smiles at him. "The music is terrific here," she says then. "I'm glad we came. In spite of the unexpected guest."

They sit for a while, listening again, but Alexis can tell his mood has changed. He refills his glass once more and his face gets a little sadder, unfocused, as if he is caught somewhere else. Alexis is surprised at the change, but not annoyed. She reaches over to take his hand.

"What about Nicolas?" he asks, looking at her directly.

She looks away. "I'm not sure." Hesitating then, she opens up a little. "Even though there's not much left — we've still been together a long time."

"Does he know where you are?"

She shakes her head. "I lied." She drinks some more wine. "The lies are worse than no more love. They make you feel so sad." She sighs. "Sometimes I just want to be alone for a while. Soak my brain in work and nothing else."

"Sounds like that's what you've been doing anyway," he observes, swirling the wine around the edges of his glass without spilling a drop.

A jolt of recognition as he says it: her life now — work and nothing more and suddenly that idea seems bleak. She looks at her watch. "It's getting late," she says, thinking for the first time of what she will say to her husband and loathing the idea of another invention.

"Nearly twelve. Let's catch a cab."

They pay their bill, go out onto the street, and hail a taxi. "Seventy-seventh and Fifth," Jon says to the driver, "and then back to Sixty-first and Lexington." In the dark of the backseat, his mood seems to lift and they begin to kiss as the car bounces over potholes and flashes through traffic lights.

Alexis pulls away from his embrace just long enough to speak to the driver. "We've changed our minds," she says. "Just Sixty-first and Lexington, please."

⟿

Jon turns on the overhead light and they stand there blinking at each other in the glare. He snaps it off and reaches instead for the reading lamp beside the bed, then turns back to face her, shrugging off his unbuttoned shirt. He sits on the edge of the bed and pulls her around to stand in front of him. (A moment's awkwardness.)

He begins to undo the buttons on her blouse. She watches his fingers pull at the sides of the material and then go up to cup her breasts. Her nipples come erect and she reaches around, unfastens her bra. He sucks his breath in at the sight of her standing there topless in her tight jeans, and puts his face forward into her.

Looking down at the top of his head she can see the wavy black hair threaded with silver, the pulse at his temples, his cheeks hollow in and out, his tongue flickers over her. She reaches down and with a small tap of her fingers, pushes him over onto his back.

Quickly she unzips her pants and then, just in her panties, she unbuckles, unzips, pulls his pants over his hips, strips off his socks and briefs. Lying side by side, for a minute they pause, trying not to rush, to savor a little. She puts her face into the silky mat of hair on his chest and rubs her cheek against it hard, then with her tongue she draws a line down, down until she slides his penis in over her tongue. He's smaller than Nicolas, a pleasure in her mouth, no jawbreaker.

After a while he doesn't say a word, just reverses their positions and pulls her panties off. Lying between her legs, he strokes, kisses, licks.

"Inside now." She feels breathless. "Please."

They reposition. Side by side, legs tangled. He slides in and she opens up down deep as he uses his hand on her at the same time. The advantages of being face to face. Kissing, the rhythms heat up, the ferny odor of their bodies fills the room where they've forgotten to turn on the air conditioner and she sees him grit his teeth trying to wait for her, and she laughs, tightens down around him, whispers and squeezes, *go ahead*, and he pumps very hard, face red, sweat gathering, then with a groan, three beats, he lets go.

They lie still. He opens his eyes. "Sorry."

"Don't be."

"But you didn't —"

"Ever hear of round two?"

He laughs, kisses her again, and she rolls over onto her back.

Later, she slips from the bed where he has fallen asleep, one leg over the edge, sheets trailing onto the floor. In the bathroom, she studies her face in the mirror. She brushes her teeth and washes her face, armpits, and crotch. She wonders what it would be like to stay and make him scrambled eggs for breakfast.

∽ SEVEN

The Mien of Love

A hot Monday in July. On her way to an appointment with the managing editor of *Esquire*, Maggie is wedged between a messenger reeking of sweat, whose roller skates and pouch are slung over his shoulder and into her face, and a fat woman who smells as if she has washed her underwear in dime-store perfume. The elevator doors slide closed and Maggie packs herself farther to the back irritably. It is lunchtime and they are stopping at every floor, taking on more people than can possibly fit. Her dress is shellacked to the small of her back, and the crotch of her panty hose has migrated downward — all of which makes her feel as if she is coming unstitched at the seams like a dilapidated stuffed animal.

Her decision to call Sarah Mills had been precipitant, provoked by the escalating anger toward her husband. All week long she had waited for Sy to bring up the Tokyo job. Worse, although Sy had promised to accompany her and Kate to the ophthalmologist's appointment last Friday, when Maggie suggested that she take Kate by herself, he quickly rescheduled his appointment in Philadelphia and booked a flight.

And so Maggie had found herself alone at a time when both she and Kate wanted Sy there. Her daughter never said a word after her initial *where's Daddy?* and Maggie did not bring it up with her again. He had let them both down by not insisting. The loyalty that prevailed in Maggie and Sy's marriage (the naïveté that the two of them cultivated with such determination) began to dissolve as she sat there in that waiting room. With steadfast blindness, she and Sy had always looked away from each other's (and their own) shortcomings in the sort of comfortable deception that sometimes keeps a marriage stitched together.

Her anger now compels her to ask questions for the very first time: Why is he gone so much? Why doesn't he want to be with them on some sort of regular basis? She hates his devotion to his work more than she would hate another woman sharing his bed: in fact, a passionate deception would be more comprehensible to her than this numbed betrayal of the spirit. Her innocence (he travels because it is required) of the nature of people has begun to erode under a new clarity of vision (he travels because it satisfies something inside him). She is no longer willing to grit her teeth and smile.

As she sat there with Kate in the doctor's office, reading aloud until they were called, she let none of her own inner turmoil show. Determined to calm her daughter, she kept herself cool throughout the examination despite her anxiety: she held Kate's hand and stopped her own from the slightest shake; she joked with the doctor despite her dry mouth. And when surgery was recommended, either immediately or in the fall, Maggie made the decision. By herself. Sy had been right, she realized as she paid the receptionist for the appointment and helped Kate out the door: she had not needed him at all. The discovery was a bitter one.

The culmination of this event led Maggie (in a moment of uncharacteristic spontaneity) to allow Kate to take their check to the register after their lunch in Lindy's that day — Lindy's was a special treat designed to balance the tension of the doctor's office — while she made a phone call to Sarah Mills. Sarah, who began as Maggie's assistant at *Esquire* and then replaced her when she left for maternity leave; Sarah, who was now the managing editor. Maggie had arranged to stop in at the office around lunchtime the following Monday. And now, as the elevator doors slide open and shut one last interminable time, Maggie experiences another quick plummet of nerves: she has kept in touch with Sarah since leaving the magazine but has not actually been back to the offices for nearly four years now. The doors open and she pushes her way out.

Intersection: past butts against present. She closes her eyes for an instant and sees a dirt road (was she there once, perhaps as a child), smells the dust, sees a white hedge, in May, and through her mind drifts a line of poetry: *What! are you here?*

Maggie turns, looking for direction, and spots the reception desk. The girl smiles up at her and jiggles her earrings, neon, in the shape of IUDs. "Can I help you?"

"Sarah Mills, please," she says, but in her mind that other voice is still speaking, providing a voice-over commentary on all her actions. *Suspended in time, between pole and tropic.*

"Name?"

Maggie moves closer, shaking off the distraction of the words, but still trying to remember from which poem they come. She focuses on the girl, her question, the way her bleached hair is sprayed straight up into a spiky crown on top of her head: what feat of aerodynamics permits it to remain fixed that way in such heat? She looks like the Statue of Liberty. The waiting area is humid and stuffy with filtered air.

"Maggie Whitten," she returns at last, speaking over her own interior monologue with an effort.

The girl lifts her receiver. Maggie leans against the desk, unused to walking in high heels on scorched pavement. *Between melting and freezing, the soul's sap . . .* It fades out and she can't catch the last word.

"Ms. Mills'll be out as soon as she can," the girl says.

Maggie nods and goes to sit on the bench under the window, which is upholstered with the same industrial carpet as the floor. *Quivers. Soul's sap quivers.* That was it. A good description of her state of mind right now.

She looks at her watch twice. Despite the delay in the elevator, she is nevertheless early. *If you came this way, taking the route you would be likely to take.* What the hell is it from? Once she had known it well. Now, half-recalled, the bits and pieces swarm through her mind, unsettling her.

She pages through last month's issue of the magazine, stares again at the receptionist's hair, wishes she had a cigarette, keeps searching with her mind for the poem. At last the inner door swings open and out walks Sarah, older now and still plump, but nevertheless looking chicly New York. Maggie smooths the front of her dress before being enveloped by a warm hug. "Wonderful," Sarah says. "You look wonderful."

They walk back through the large open space where a lab-yrinth of desks provide the only partitions: people buzz over layouts and artwork with feet up on desks, phones ring, there is a general cacophony of laughter, argument, and work. Nothing looks as it did when she left, but it still smells and sounds the same. With an excited smile, Maggie searches for a familiar face.

Inside her office, Sarah pelts her with questions: how is the family? The suburbs? Has she seen the magazine's last issue? What does she think of the piece on Jerzy Kosinski? Maggie sits up straight in the wooden chair, feeling she has returned to a place that is as far away as childhood. Suddenly, insecurity clouds her excitement at being back.

"So show me a picture of the kids," Sarah demands, making neat stacks of paper on her desk.

Maggie opens her purse and takes out a snapshot: last winter, the asymmetrical snowman in the front yard listing to one side, propped up by Kate and Mikey.

"They're so big!"

"Yes." Maggie smiles with pride. "Big enough for me to come back to work."

Sarah looks up, startled. "You're thinking of going back to work?"

"That surprises you?"

Sarah taps the photo's edge against her desk. "I just remember how happy you were to leave."

"Well, I was pregnant then and that was about all I could think of," she says, fiddling with the catch on her purse. *What you thought you came for is only a shell, a husk of meaning.* "But I always knew I'd come back."

Sarah nods, pokes at the piles on her desk with her hand. There is still no band on her left ring finger. "How has it been to be away from all this insanity?" she asks curiously.

"Good. Hard." Maggie smiles, a little tightly now, wondering why they are still discussing her decision to remain at home (the past) rather than her decision to return to work (present and future).

Sarah fiddles with her pen. "What does Sy say?"

"He thinks it's great." Which is a lie of course; she has not even mentioned this appointment to him. "The kids are in school nearly all day now."

"So, have you started looking yet?" Sarah asks, leaning forward on her elbows with a smile.

Maggie stops short, a bit disconcerted. "Well, this is the first place I've been."

"Why, yes, it's natural you'd start here." She slowly nods, thinking.

"You and I worked together for so long . . ." she trails off.

"The problem is, we haven't *got* any editorial openings right now — not even for associates." Sarah's smile is kind. "But I think you should set up an appointment with Lee anyway. You never know what might turn up. And I'll start making some calls for you with the people I know at other places."

"Some of those young writers I brought in are now New York's big guns." Maggie's anxiety reasserts itself, surpassing the rapid-pulse stage to attain a level that makes all the objects in the room overly bright and too sharply defined. Her eyes ache with the strain of trying to keep all those throbbing edges steady. The poem in her head has stopped as suddenly as it began.

Sarah looks up at her, quietly, steadily. "That's true," she agrees, swiveling her chair and looking out the window. She turns back to face Maggie. "But I know you want me to be honest with you. You were here a *long* time ago, Maggie. If you want to get back into the business, you've got to be realistic," she continues. "I wouldn't be doing you any favors to butter you up with a lot of nonsense. Eight years back is an aeon in this industry. Most of the people who were here then are gone now. It's going to be hard to do."

Maggie sits silent, stunned by this idea. She thinks of all the strange faces they passed on her way into Sarah's office. "What about Melanie Barker?"

Sarah shook her head. "M.E. over at *Glamour*."

Maggie is swamped by a sudden sense of standing on a platform, watching a train pull away.

"Look," amends Sarah, "I just meant — you've really got to want it, then you've got to get out there and hustle. And don't be too proud. You may have to go back a few steps to get yourself up to where you were." She flips through her Rolodex.

"I'll call Phyllis Geiringer over at *Vanity Fair*, and Lucy Reinhart at *Redbook* for a start." She checks her watch as she scribbles the names on a piece of her letterhead. "I've got a one o'clock lunch midtown, want to share a cab?"

"I feel like a walk," Maggie says, forcing herself to smile. "And thanks for giving me a hand." Not knowing what else she could say, she picks up her purse.

"Call me when you've seen them. I'll try to get through to them today." Sarah stands up and hands the photo back, lingering over it a minute. "Your kids are so cute," she says. Her voice is wistful. "You'd be surprised how many women here would trade places with you." She laughs abruptly. "How many of them would say two kids are definitely worth having given this up for."

Given up? It never even occurred to me that I was giving it up. Maggie makes her way back out, and in the reception area walks blindly past the smile of the girl at the desk, blinks to cover the tears. *This was supposed to be a short-term leave — not a retirement plan.*

She pushes the elevator button, understanding, for the first time, that she has always been counting on having the opportunity to come back here, even if she hasn't admitted it to herself. How naive of her to assume (even unconsciously) that all she has to do is walk back through the door.

Slowly she trudges to Grand Central, oblivious to the heat and the stretch of pavement that burns the bottom of her feet. She looks up at the sky and sees towers of stone that shut out sun and air and direction. She asks herself whether she has the courage or tenacity to work her way back. Does she want it enough? She is out of practice for both the politicking and the hard sell; it has never been her forte and she feels too old to start all over again now. And does she have the energy? she wonders. She pictures her time at home, bounded morning and evening by the commute: the scramble to get the children dressed, fed, and out the door single-handedly, in time for the eight o'clock train; the rush to return home in the evening before the baby-sitter leaves and then help with homework, cook dinner, do the dishes, make up the lunch boxes — all before sitting down to her own work. Or the alternative she has (in the past) always avoided — live-in help, with its attendant price tags.

All at once, the idea of returning home and telling no one (surely one more reason why she did not mention this appointment) suddenly seems safe and comfortable. Desirable even.

But how can she? (She pursues these questions as she walks.) What will she do about the discontent and restlessness she feels nearly every day now? How will she escape the anxiety that descends each afternoon when she finishes the household chores? When she sits with nothing to do except read a book or play in the garden? She craves something quite simple: purpose.

Through the heat, traffic, and human noise, Maggie walks as if encapsulated in silence. As she steps off the sidewalk at the corner of Forty-eighth Street, she finally remembers the poem lost so long ago in memory: "Little Gidding," in a brown hardcover collection of T. S. Eliot's poetry, bought at the Coop her junior year, the pages growing more and more annotated and dog-eared throughout her years at school. It depresses her further that it took her so long to place the poem: at one time she could have recited nearly everything he'd written. (At one time she'd thought all the answers were to be found in poetry.) Her own poetry, private, secret, stored in binders in the attic; recent attempts now kept in the black-and-white ruled notebook, her journal, at the bottom of the dish-towel drawer in the kitchen. Writing is another way of thinking things through, of getting to the bottom of how she feels.

"Got any spare change, lady?" asks the man, who has, like a snail dragging his own house, parked his shopping cart topped with newspapers, balls of twine, a blanket, and a pair of crusty boots over a subway grate in the shelter of the station's shadow. "Help me out?"

There is something in this man's upturned grimy face, the slope of his shoulders, the stained undershirt, the stench, the despair. She digs in her purse for a five-dollar bill and extends it to him; their fingers do not touch.

He neither looks at nor thanks her. She walks into the cool dark cave of the station and buys a ticket for the next train, which leaves in half an hour. As she slides her wallet back into her purse, her fingers brush the sharp edge of the stationery on which Sarah has written the contacts at other magazines. Inside of her, a butterfly spreading its wings, anxiety looks for a way out. Maggie exhales around it while simultaneously noting its power. Then she turns back into the roar that is Grand Central and makes her way to the public phones.

❧

"I'm sorry, I can't hear you." She taps the receiver impatiently with her fingertip. "Are you still there?"

". . . here." Sy's voice floats through an irritating cloud of static. "We just went through an underpass, that's all."

He is calling her from a phone in a taxi, on his way to a business dinner in Manhattan. Maggie hates talking to him in transit: they are always getting cut off or shorted out, and this seems to her an ironic metaphor.

"What did you do today?" he asks. "How are the kids?"

She pauses a minute, realizing that he always links the two questions. "O.K., I guess," she answers finally, uncertain whether she should tell him now about Mikey's latest prank. She returned home from the city to find he had used a sharp stone to sketch a Tyrannosaurus rex — his favorite dinosaur — onto the hood of her car while the baby-sitter was watching *Guiding Light*. The scratches are too deep to be compounded away and Jan, who stopped in to tell Maggie about a last-minute P.T.A. development, agreed with her that the hood will have to be repainted. But Maggie (experiencing anger, bewilderment, and frustration) doesn't really feel like telling Sy all this now while at the mercy of an unpredictable phone that might at any moment sever their connection. Besides, then she would have to explain where she was while their son (however talented) was executing his art project. She wipes her hands on a dish towel and puts down the paring knife and the carrot. "I'm sort of in the middle of making supper."

"I shouldn't be home too late," he answers. "How long can this dinner take?"

"Will you be here for breakfast?" she asks, somewhat impatiently, pushing the carrot peelings down into the disposal. "Mikey says I don't pitch the baseball the way you do."

"Yeah, I'll be there, but —" Static intrudes again, drowning out the rest of his sentence.

"What? Are you there?"

"— else is happening?"

She sighs. She doesn't feel like telling him about the meeting with Sarah Mills — or about the appointments at *Redbook* and *Vanity Fair* she set up from the pay phone in Grand Central for later this week — because she wants to see his face when she tells him. "Let's get off," she entreats. "The car phone makes me feel like you're on Mars." She is anxious to get a half hour in the garden, a little time to think quietly before dinner begins.

"Well, see you around eleven then." He sounds annoyed.

And with that they hang up, Maggie feeling both guilty and defiant at having cut the conversation short. As she heads out the back door to the garden, the doorbell grates against the silence of the house. The kids are upstairs watching television and she hears no clatter of feet to answer it. It peals a second time, and, with a sigh, she turns from the door and goes to the front of the house.

As she reaches the front hall, the phone begins to ring. Maggie swings the door open, with the intention of asking whomever is there — probably Jan again — to wait while she runs to answer the phone. But it is Nicolas who slouches against her doorjamb, greeting her with his lazy smile, and Maggie is so startled to see him that she simply stands there.

"Aren't you going to get that?" he asks as he saunters past her into the front hall.

"What? Oh, the phone." She runs past him to the study and snatches up the receiver.

"You sound out of breath," says Alexis.

"I was at the front door. What a coincidence." Maggie laughs. "Both of you at exactly the same time — he just walked in. Where are you anyway?"

A beat. "Who walked in?" Alexis asks.

"Your husband."

"What the hell is he doing at your place?" She sounds indignant.

"You're asking me?" Maggie laughs again and peers over her shoulder, but Nicolas is nowhere in sight. "I just answered the door as the phone started up — and there he was."

"Damn."

Maggie pauses, alert now to the tone in Alexis's voice. "What's wrong?"

Alexis sighs. "I told him I wanted to separate. He stormed off last night and I haven't seen him since."

Maggie sits down abruptly in the desk chair. "Are you all right?"

"I guess so." Alexis's voice grows husky and she clears her throat.

"Are you sure about this? Maybe —"

"Maggie, I'm sure," she interrupts. "I've never been *more* sure."

"I'm sorry, Lex. It's just . . ." What can she say? It all sounds crazy to her — how is it possible for two people who love each other so much suddenly just to stop?

"Listen, I've got to go," Alexis says. "There's someone at *my* door. Can I call you later?"

"Well, sure." Maggie traces a circle with her fingers through the dust on Sy's desk. "Sy's not home till late, so I'll be up." Her palms are clammy and she wipes them on her skirt. "What d'you suppose Nico wants?"

"I don't know. Comfort, maybe."

"This is damned awkward, Alexis."

"Maggie, I'm worried about him." Her voice softens. "He's *so* alone — and you're *his* friend, too."

"But —"

"Just talk with him. And I'll call you back later."

She hangs up and Maggie sits for a minute in silence, trying to collect herself. A phone rings and intrudes without her consent; a few words, and the threatened landslide occurs, burying a relationship upon which she has leaned, until recently, for its constancy.

She thinks about getting up, but doesn't. The idea of trying to comfort Nicolas makes her nervous: they have been friends for years, but in all those years Alexis has been the focus between them. Maggie has rarely been alone with him for any length of time, and certainly never in such an extreme circumstance. She sighs and gets up to wander through the house, looking for Nicolas, whom she eventually discovers sitting in the backyard, a beer in hand, next to the bed of Japanese iris Maggie put in last year. In spite of her distress, she feels a distracted flush of pleasure at seeing these flowers, so vivid, nod in the low sunlight; she loves their wild profusion, the way they grow in a haphazard riot of green leaves and saturated blue. Iris seem to her the most sensual of all flowers, their large plum-purple petals parting in a flash of yellow to reveal the velvet, cradled interior.

She kneels at the edge of the bed and pulls her pruning shears from her pocket. She begins to deadhead, cutting away spent flowers, keeping her hands busy as a way of concealing her awkwardness with the situation. "That was Lex on the phone."

"She told you?" His tone is curiously flat.

Maggie nods. Feeling self-conscious, she stops for a minute and reaches over to take his hand, which is cold from the beer bottle. "Are you all right?"

He shrugs. "I'm not surprised." He looks away.

"Well, *I'm* surprised."

He shook his head. "We've been at each other for a while."

"You hid it pretty well."

"It was private."

"Didn't you ever talk to Sy about it?"

He shakes his head. "Both Lex and I wanted to keep our trouble a secret. Especially from ourselves."

She leans back on her heels, and speaks with exasperation. "What could be so bad between you that you can't work it out?"

He just shakes his head. "Hard to explain, Maggie."

She stretches to get a blown bloom at the center of the bed and sighs. "I guess I always imagined that marriages break up over something catastrophic — you know, like an affair. But not quietly like this." She is thinking of Jonathan, but of course does not say so. "I thought there were always fireworks."

He smiles at her and his face creases with sadness. For the first time she notices the fine lines that groove his forehead and the silver cast of the hair over his ears. They've all put on age, she realizes then; it has slipped up unremarked, like the cusp of late afternoon light crossing into dusk. Forty (that unthinkable number) is not so far away.

"More marriages die from silence than noise," he observes. He leans back in his chair and lifts the bottle to his mouth. "A few years back I met a woman — for a while I really thought I loved her. I even daydreamed about marrying her, having the life — the kids, being together at home every night — that I wanted, Alexis didn't. But after a while —" He breaks off and shrugs.

Maggie swallows, stunned by his disclosure, and thinks of Alexis, confiding in her at Palio, unaware of Nicolas's infidelity and considering her own. With a rush of anger, Maggie hates them both for being so duplicitous. "I never knew you wanted children." (She picks up on the least difficult part of what he's said as a way of covering her reaction.) She gets up and goes to sit in the chair by his side.

He shrugs again. "Ten years ago I didn't. But your feelings about things like that change."

"Lex never said anything about it at all."

"That's because she couldn't even discuss it, let alone consider it." He lifts the bottle again, tipping his head back. "She's totally obsessed with her work. That's all she can think about. At first it was like a game, where the goal was to have absolutely everything. For a while that was fun. But when she started working just to work — there was no goal anymore. . . ." He falls silent. "It's as if the chemistry changed. The worst thing you used to be able to say about the investment-banking types was that they were boring. But now" — he shakes his head — "now they take themselves so seriously they're dangerous."

Maggie laughs. "Come on, Nico, you're being melodramatic."

"No," he protests. "I'm not. They're shut into their own world, with their own rules and codes of honor. It's just like the Mafia."

Maggie doesn't like what he's saying, or how it reflects on Sy. "Back to the point," she says, changing the subject. "You can't weasel out of telling me about this other woman."

"Nothing happened."

"Well, why didn't you leave Lex and marry her?" She picks up her shears and fiddles with them.

"One night I looked over at her and the danger of it all had worn off. She was a nice girl, beautiful, great in bed —" He smiles. "But she wasn't Alexis. We didn't have a long history together. I decided I was being an ass. So I went home."

"And?"

"For a while it *was* better with Lex — maybe just because I'd been away from her. It reenergized things. But . . ."

Maggie looks over and waits, silent.

"Well, it was an illusion," he goes on. "Everything that had made me go looking someplace else was still right there waiting to be fixed. And Lex wasn't really all that interested in fixing it."

"Did she ever find out?"

"I never told her — no midnight confessions. And I was very careful."

"You make it sound so easy — just go off and be with someone else for a while, then trot back home when you feel like it?" She sounds angry, she realizes: she is.

"Not at all." His voice sharpens under her criticism. "It was a bad time, and one that cost both of us a lot. Even though we didn't want to admit it at that point. You've got to understand how alone I felt!" His mouth twists in an ironic smile. "A man isn't supposed to admit to feeling lonely. You're supposed to be independent and self-reliant." He sighs. "Another myth. So you see, having the affair wasn't a casual thing at all. It was desperate." He pulls on his beer again. "The point is — the affair didn't end our marriage. We did."

She shakes her head, still unconvinced.

"You want everything clear-cut," he continues with exasperation. "Black and white, good or bad, sad or happy. Neither you nor Sy can deal with ambivalence. But that's how things are, all the time. Everything pours over your head at once."

"Probably true," Maggie admits with a half smile, letting go a little. "I never did like the color gray."

They sit for a minute then, each thinking. "Still," Maggie goes on. "I don't see how it was that Alexis wasn't interested in working things out. She isn't the kind to back off from a tough situation."

"Look, I'm not saying it was all her fault. Maybe she *couldn't* face it. Or at least, maybe not right then." He sighs again. "I remember one night, she came in late, around one A.M., and I was watching her get ready for bed. She was all stoked up over some deal in the office and I was feeling low because business has been rough recently. I just wanted her to get into bed and put her arms around me and be with *me* for a while. Forget all that stuff. I listened to her go on and on about her big success —" Here he breaks off with a small forced laugh. "She got into bed and we just lay there. There was no holding, no talking, nothing. I guess maybe if you've got kids you at least keep talking about them."

"Or fighting over them," Maggie interjects.

"Yeah, well," he agrees. He pauses a minute. "Maybe there was some sour grapes on my part," he admits. "After a while, next to what she was doing, I felt smaller and smaller. The vanishing man." He smiles moodily. "But during the last fifteen years we changed a lot. And when you can't remember how you used to feel about each other, when there's just this dead zone between you. . . ." He shakes his head. "Silence and distance are the enemies — not some other person." He studies the beer bottle for a minute; then slowly he sets it down on the grass and pulls his wedding band off his ring finger. He puts it in his back pocket.

Maggie bites her lip. Alexis and Nicolas are part of her family. She wants to shake him by the shoulders to stop him, but she tells herself to shut up; she was unfairly judgmental with Alexis a few weeks ago, and today she is equally judgmental with Nicolas. It is not up to her. What he needs now is room in which to talk, and he has probably come here for just that. "I'm glad you came, Nico." She reaches out to touch his hand. "I wish this weren't happening, but if it has to — well, just know we're here when you need us." She smiles at him. "I wish Sy were home," she frets. "He won't be back till late."

"I don't mind." He smiles at her, and that smile, so incongruous against his tired face, illuminates his sadness; he is more stripped than she's ever seen him, all bravado doused, and it arouses in her a sensation quite maternal.

"I like talking to you," he goes on. Again that smile; the sadness makes her throat ache. "With him I'd feel like a failure. He'd probably lecture me on how I hadn't tried hard enough."

"Not unlikely," she concedes, thinking of Sy's unremitting

search for perfection. She checks her watch and pushes herself out of the chair. "I was in the middle of getting supper when you rang the bell. It's only meat loaf and baked potatoes, but will you stay?"

"Thanks."

As they walk back to the house he puts his arm around her and she puts hers around him. "You never talked with Sy about this other woman?"

He shakes his head. "Imagine his reaction?" He laughs and so does she.

"He's a very loyal sort of person," Maggie says thoughtfully. "I don't think he would understand it."

"The kids are where?" Nicolas asks as they go inside.

"Television." She gestures up the back stairs. "Supper's just about finished, I've only got salad to fix."

"Make you a drink?" he asks, going to the liquor cabinet.

She hesitates. Ordinarily she doesn't drink on a weeknight when Sy is not home (a safeguard against a tendency to become sloppy over her own loneliness). "I'd love one," she says, relishing the idea of both a drink and some company. She sets the iris she has cut on the counter and begins to scrape carrots, chop celery, shred lettuce. She pulls a can of artichoke hearts from the cupboard. After pouring them both a scotch, he stands and watches her, which makes her nervous.

"I haven't had a great day myself," she says, checking the meat loaf in the oven.

He lifts an eyebrow, waits for her to go on, and hands her her glass.

"I was in the city for a job interview and when I got home I discovered Mikey had wrecked the paint job on the station wagon."

"Back up a minute!" He laughs and shakes his head. "What job interview?"

She smiles. "Boy, I didn't get that by you, did I?"

"You're going back to work?"

"Well, I'm thinking about it," she amends.

"Where was the interview?" He picks up a carrot and begins slicing it for her.

"Oh, I went back over to *Esquire,* but they haven't got anything right now. So I made appointments at *Redbook* and *Vanity Fair* for Friday." She takes a large glass from the cupboard and fills it with warm water.

He laughs again. "Not wasting any time."

"I haven't got much time," she answers grimly, sticking the iris in the impromptu vase and setting it on the table.

He looks up from the cutting board inquiringly.

"Though he hasn't seen fit to mention it, I happen to know Sy's considering a job offer in Tokyo." (Sarcasm in her voice belies the casual tone.)

Quietly, Nicolas scrapes the carrots into the salad bowl, digesting this new information. "Doesn't sound like you two are doing very well either."

"I'm mad at him for not telling me." She turns the oven off and sips her drink. "*And* he's never here. I don't need to tell you Mikey behaves a lot better when he's around."

"What's this about the car?"

She sighs and shakes her head. "He did a little engraving on the hood with a stone."

Nicolas starts to laugh.

"You're not supposed to laugh!" she protests, although his reaction is contagious. "You wouldn't believe the stuff this kid comes up with!" She shakes her head again in distress. "Why is it always my job to discipline him? Whenever Sy travels for long stretches I have trouble with him. Nightmares. Bed-wetting. You name it."

"Whenever Sy travels?" He laughs. "You must have problems all the time."

"You said it."

"Hey, I was a kid just like Mikey — my parents spent most of my childhood trying to keep me in control and out of trouble. See how great I turned out?"

"*You're* supposed to be some sort of consolation?" she jokes, poking him in the ribs.

Mikey and Kate appear, in a clamor for supper; when they see Nicolas, they beg for a game of Chinese checkers. He looks to Maggie. "Is there time before we eat?"

"You don't mind?"

He shakes his head.

"A quick one, then," she relents, taking the silverware

from the drawer and beginning to set the table around them. Rapidly the game takes a predictable turn: Kate winning and Mikey whining. As Maggie glances over, she sees Nicolas deliberately make a mistake so that he won't move ahead of her son. She remembers what Alexis had once said about Nicolas being unable to allow anyone else to win — with children it appears he isn't so set on being number one. She takes the meat loaf from the oven and begins slicing it. "Finish up," she warns.

"We're not ready," Mikey insists stubbornly.

"No arguing with your mom," Nicolas interjects, putting his arm around the small boy's shoulders. "We'll play some more after supper." He rises and lifts the board from the table, carefully setting it down on the countertop.

Amazed at her son's obedience, Maggie fills their plates at the stove and they sit down to eat.

"How come you're here by yourself?" asks Kate with curiosity.

Maggie busies herself scooping salad onto their plates and glances at him sideways.

"Alexis is working late." He begins to eat.

"Like our dad," Mikey says. "He's always working." Slowly he chews a bite of meat loaf. "Does she sleep on the eye plane, too?"

"On the what?" Nicolas is puzzled.

"The red-eye, he means," explains Maggie, smoothing Mikey's cowlick down. He twitches away from her touch.

Nicolas smothers a laugh. "All the time," he says to Mikey. He gestures with his fork to Maggie. "This is great."

"Remember the days when I used to make those ten-course Chinese banquets?" She laughs self-consciously. "Meat loaf is for the kids."

"I love this kind of stuff. It reminds me of being little."

"Nursery food," Maggie agrees.

"Like brisket."

"Tapioca pudding," she says.

"Bagels with peanut butter," he continues, shoveling in another huge bite.

"Minced lamb on toast."

He makes a face. "Sounds awful."

"How about roast-beef hash?"

"*Corned*-beef hash."

"Uh, oh, I think we're getting into fine ethnic distinctions here." She laughs. "Well, I guess they all comfort you somehow."

He sighs. "Haven't had anything near to my mother's potato pancakes in years. With warm applesauce." He grins and drains his scotch. "Maybe I'll stop by for dinner more often."

"Let's have shepherd's pie next time," Kate suggests. "That's *our* favorite."

Maggie smiles and groans. "What a pleasure to have another adult at the table."

There is watermelon for dessert and Nicolas shows the kids how to have a contest on the stoop: who can spit the seeds the farthest. Kate wins because the gap between her two front teeth makes a nice slingshot effect. Then the children go upstairs to put on their pajamas. Nicolas convinces Maggie to sit and talk instead of doing the dishes, promising to help her clean up later. Around eight Maggie tucks the kids in, but only after "Uncle Nico" reads them three chapters of *Stuart Little*. Maggie is grateful to him: how wonderful it is to share the scramble of bedtime rituals.

As they come downstairs, Nicolas shows no signs of leaving. The fatigue Maggie felt earlier has dropped away and she feels almost gay. The kitchen is such a mess that they desert it for the front porch, taking the bottle of scotch with them; outside it is cool, and the dark has just started layering itself in around the rhododendrons. The wicker furniture creaks as they lean back, get comfortable, and start to rock. From two stories up, the murmur of Mikey's radio filters down to settle in the air about them in a net of distant sound. Maggie does not turn on the porch light. They sit in the dark for a long time, just listening to the tree frogs and the cicadas and the low music, until the darkness is complete.

"When's Sy coming home?"

"Who knows? It's a business dinner."

He nods. "Do you realize that Sy's been my best friend for" — he pauses now, counting silently — "for over thirty years. Christ."

"A long time." Maggie is awed by the thought of it: she has long since lost track of any of the girls she grew up with.

"You don't find many friends like that," Nicolas continues. "He's bailed me out of a lot of scrapes."

Maggie laughs. "I bet he always was the good boy. Never in trouble."

"You know, I remember this time, we must've been about ten. He was the kind of kid who never gave up on *anyone*, no matter how rotten or nerdy they were. There was this schmuck named Dickie Weinstein, and he stole a pair of skates that Sy had saved for months to buy — lugging dishes down at the deli his old man ran. I came up with at least three real clever plans to get revenge. Sy wouldn't even hear about them. He just walked up to Dickie's front door and told him that when he was through borrowing the skates to please return them."

Maggie smiles and sighs. "He always likes to see the best in everyone."

"Actually Weinstein did give the skates back," he muses. "And d'you know what Sy did then?"

She shakes her head.

"Asked him to join our secret club! I was ready to kill him." He shakes his head and laughs out into the dark. "Maybe I was jealous."

Maggie laughs too.

"This guy was the president of every club we ever formed, he got straight A's in school, he even made Mrs. Whitten a wooden trivet in I.A. for Mother's Day when we were eleven. When we were eleven most guys wouldn't even admit they *had* a mother!"

"Hard to imagine now," Maggie says slowly. For no reason, she thinks again of Sy not coming to Kate's ophthalmology appointment. She cannot see much more than the movement of Nicolas's profile as he rocks back and forth in the darkness. "You used to be just as much of a fanatic about work as Lex — what happened?"

He sighs. "When your work doesn't go well it changes your perspective. Makes you think about what it's worth to you." He gets up and refills both their glasses from the bottle, which he had placed on the floor at their feet. "Both of us were working so hard on our own things that we didn't make time to be together." He shrugs helplessly. "I know you understand, because Sy's doing the same thing." He gets up and stands at the edge of the railing, looking out into the darkened yard. How he envies Sy this life: a rambling house filled with warm smells from the oven and flowers from the garden, overflowing with the rambunctious antics of a spunky son who is dirty behind the ears and unstoppable in his questions, the adoration of Kate — as well as the loyalty of Maggie, who waits night after night.

Slowly (unwillingly) Maggie picks up on what he has said. "Sy and I aren't in nearly the same place you and Lex are."

"The writing on the wall isn't exactly done in invisible ink." He wants to make her see it. "What about Tokyo?" Maggie has always gone along with whatever Sy says or wants. Initially, both Nicolas and Alexis had looked down — affectionately — on the Whittens for their more traditionally structured relationship, but now he sees only that if Alexis had been more like Maggie he might have a family with whom to eat supper every night.

"I don't know." Her voice is dejected. "He's got to tell me, sooner or later."

"He might not — what if he's afraid of getting you pissed until he's got the job nailed down?"

"There was a time when he'd have told me right off so we could discuss it. Like a team."

"Past tense," Nicolas observes, his hurt easing a little as he realizes he is not alone in being lonely. "And how much longer can you keep on? After a while the light between you goes out." He comes to sit down again; she hears the splash of him refilling her glass in the dark. "There's always a consequence, Maggie, that's what people like Lex and Sy ignore. If you're so committed to your work that you take yourself away from your family four nights a week, that means you are *not home* for over sixty percent of the week." He hands her her glass. "And don't believe Ma Bell — no phone call covers that kind of distance." Leaning forward, he taps his foot against the planking of the porch with frustration. "They want marriage to be some sort of magical garden — one that grows without water." His anger drills into her silence. "The hardest thing is watching it

happen — I begged her to listen — but she's so stubborn, she
just kept saying we had to hang on a few more years. Till she
made partner. What kills me is that we don't need that kind of
money — the money is incidental now. Alexis works that hard
for something else. And it's not worth it."

Maggie bows her head, a little dizzy from the scotch and the
motion of the swing. The words strike her: *Till I make partner.*
How many times has Sy said exactly that? She loathes hearing
it from Nicolas now. In her mind stands an invisible but stout
wall behind which she stores certain unacceptable emotions
(those she does not wish to acknowledge — much less endure).
Wedged behind that wall, her anger is bottled up, but, like lava
through fissures, it now begins to leak out along with fear,
sadness, and loss. Everything she feels about the distance between them moves forward on a wave of expanding emotion
and, with the alcohol lowering the line of her defense, she lets
it all run through her. Tears streak down her cheeks, over her
chin.

"People are stupid. Think they don't have to choose." Nicolas tilts his glass again, unaware she is crying. He is starting to
feel a little drunk and the idea of going home rouses itself at the
back of his mind but he bats it away. "They think they can just
work harder. Or run faster. Make everything they want happen. But you can run till you're blind tired — and when the
feelings die they're gone for good."

He looks up and sees the way she sits, head hung forward.
Stumbling in the dark, he sits down beside her in the wicker
swing and puts his arm around her shoulders. "I didn't mean
to make you cry." He loves Maggie: she is sensitive, caring,
fragile. He berates himself for pounding on the subject, and
feels a sudden wash of shame. "Hell, I'm just striking out —"

"No," she says, leaning against him and putting her head
down on his shoulder. "What you said is true."

"It's true. And I hate it." His voice cracks now and he, too,
starts to cry, but with anger. "Why couldn't she just have listened! I loved her so much!"

They cry against each other, old friends who feel they are
the last two on earth. After a time, they sit in silence, tucked
into the swing together. Maggie finds cuddling with someone
taller than she reassuring. It seems to Nicolas that he has not

been held by a woman in a very long time. Every once in a while they pass the glass back and forth between them; neither of them care that they are thoroughly loaded.

Nicolas puts his head back and lets the swing rock him. Maggie's hair tickles the side of his face and he rubs his cheek against it, like a cat. After a while he gets up and pulls her to her feet. "C'mon." She comes up and into the arc of his arms and their bodies move slowly toward each other, bump, settle in. "I haven't danced like this in years."

"No one does anymore."

They shuffle across the porch, their feet tracing a loose circle over the wooden floor as they slow dance to the distant sound of Mikey's radio. They hold each other in a dazed, somewhat sleepy trance for a long time, until the headlights of a taxi sweep down the driveway and startle them awake. Shielding her eyes against the glare, Maggie realizes her husband has come home, and, as she hears his footsteps come up the walk, irritation flashes through her.

Sy stops short on the porch steps, startled to see them there in the dark. "What's this?"

"Out of the worst of times come the best of times," quips Nicolas, a bit blurrily, his arm still tight around Maggie. He pulls her over to the swing and they sit down together, like Siamese twins, and begin to rock back and forth.

"Hasn't been a good day," annotates Maggie, downing the rest of her scotch.

"How long have you guys been out here? I couldn't raise anybody on the car phone and I got worried!"

"Been enjoying ourselves — running through old times." Nicolas's tone is sharper now that Sy is here. "Right, Mag?" He gives her another hug around the shoulders.

"Right," she says, lightly punching his arm. "Comrades in misery."

"You two are blotto!" Sy is indignant.

"Could say that," agrees Nicolas. "Blotto and divorced."

"Who's divorced?" Sy looks confused.

"About to be," Nicolas says, peering into his empty glass owlishly. "Divorced from reality."

"He means it, Sy," Maggie interjects, trying to look serious but starting to giggle.

"Means what?"

"Lex kicked him out."

"You guys are too shitfaced to make sense," he says, swooping down on the table and capping the scotch. "I'm putting you both to bed."

"In the same place, I hope," says Nicolas, with a wink.

Maggie whoops.

"You're going to be hung in the A.M.," warns Sy disapprovingly, putting his arm around Maggie and supporting her over the doorjamb into the front hall. "I'll be back for you in a minute, you old shikker."

Slowly they begin to make their way up the curving staircase. "Is he serious? Is Lex divorcing him?"

She nods solemnly, turning her attention to negotiating the risers quietly, so as not to wake the children.

"But why?"

"Still not sure."

"Well, it's ridiculous. They probably had a fight. They'll make it up in the morning."

"Don't think so," she says.

"What could possibly be so bad? I mean, you can work anything out."

"Some things — yes. Some things — no." His casual, dismissive attitude sets her off and suddenly her anger seems both righteous and no longer containable. The walls and the framed oil portraits of Maggie's family and ancestors waver as she stands there on the staircase; the emotions she wants to voice are dangerous and powerful (and the words to express them seem absolutely within reach).

"Well, I can't picture anything so dreadful."

"I can."

They have reached the landing, where her mother presides with her painted smile, violin laid carefully across her lap; Sy is guiding Maggie toward the bedroom. He drops her arm and stops when she says this, but she keeps walking, so that suddenly they stand separately, she just over the threshold and he still in the hall. She turns back to face him, the knob of the bedroom door cool and round against her palm.

"Like what, for instance?" He sounds taken aback.

"Like a husband who won't talk to his wife."

"I talk to you," he protests.

"Really?" She squints at him in the harsh overhead light, leaning on the doorknob. "Is that why I had to find out about Tokyo from Christa Brooke?" The impact of her words smacks across his face. Satisfaction.

"I was going to tell you," he says defensively. "I was waiting for the right moment."

"Well, I guess you waited too long." The sarcasm clears the blurry feeling from her head and suddenly she feels sharp. "That ought to teach you something about *right moments.*" She reaches out and shuts the door on his nonplussed expression.

As the heavy wooden door swings closed so unexpectedly, Sy stands there without moving. The news that she's found out about the Tokyo job telegraphs itself through his weary body in a staccato of despair. He can't believe she's known and has said nothing — that she has, in effect, set a trap for him. Now, he realizes with mounting frustration, it will be much harder to convince her to agree to relocate. He has not brought up the possibility in part because he wants it so much and he is not ready to hear her put the kibosh on his dream.

He has nearly killed himself to get home and spend a few hours with her — ducking out of his dinner meeting with a client at an unseemly nine-thirty — and now he walks in to find her pissed with him, and drunk with his best friend. Who is, in the meantime, about to be divorced. It all seems like a histrionic episode from a soap opera and he would laugh if he weren't so tired. (Too many red-eyes.) He leans his forehead against the door and sighs. "Is there a full moon tonight or what?" He tries the knob but the door is locked.

He decides to go back downstairs and check on Nicolas. Maybe by the time he comes back, Maggie will have cooled off and they can talk. Nicolas is still sitting on the porch.

"Let's move to the kitchen," Sy suggests, swooping down to retrieve the bottle. "I feel like a coffee."

To his surprise, Nicolas pushes himself up without protest — though unsteadily — and docilely follows Sy down the hall into the darkened kitchen.

"What a mess!" Sy exclaims when he flicks on the light. The table is still covered with plates and glasses, the sink barely visible beneath its heap of dirty pots.

Nicolas looks around, dazed. "We forgot. We got talking."

Sy begins to set up the coffee, then rolls up his sleeves and turns on the water.

Sitting down at the table, Nicolas shoves the plates aside and leans his chin on his hands. He stares off into space, blinking slowly, as Sy clatters back and forth from sink to table.

"What's going on with Alexis?" Sy asks, taking the plates from the table and stacking them along his arm.

"She's divorcing me." As Nicolas utters the words, his face bunches up as if someone has twisted his arm. Without warning, he starts to cry.

Disbelieving, Sy just stands there. He's never seen Nicolas cry — not when Pop Lindnerhoffman died, not when he broke his leg fooling around on the high wall over at school when they were nine. He slides the dishes into the sink, turns off the water, and goes slowly back to his friend. He stands at his side for a minute, and then, awkwardly, pats his shoulder. "Maybe she'll change her mind," he says, hopefully.

"Only hurricanes and women change their minds."

"You *are* pissed," Sy observes, going back to the sink and turning on the water.

"Well." Nicolas shrugs and wipes his face with the back of his hand surreptitiously. "I think she's got someone else."

Sy stops in the middle of soaping a pot, thunderstruck. "You're joking!" In the sink the water runs on, splashing high and unattended.

"She didn't admit it," Nicolas continues. "But I know her pretty well."

"I don't believe it," Sy declares flatly.

"That's because you don't want to hear anything negative about the people you like," Nicolas says, irritated now. "Like the little kid who insists Santa Claus is real."

"Well — if you're so sure, then who is it?" Sy asks, deciding to plow ahead and ignore the criticism.

"Don't know or care." He clears his throat. "Look, I don't want to talk about it." His voice is flat and depressed. "Why does everything have to go wrong at once."

"What's 'everything'?" Sy asks (relieved to change the subject).

"Money, for one."

"Now that's a trouble I know how to handle," Sy answers, glad that Nicolas has moved on to another subject. He goes over to the stove and pours the coffee into two mugs. Maybe coffee will wake him up enough to help him give Nicolas some decent advice.

"Six months ago I was short my payment on the loans," Nicolas says. "So I mortgaged a few other things to raise a little cash."

"Like what?"

"What's it matter?" Nicolas evades, shaking his head impatiently. "All that's important now is the interest — it's like quicksand."

"Why didn't you come and tell me?"

Nicolas looks at him for a moment, then speaks slowly. "I didn't want anyone to know how bad it was."

"What did you put up?" Sy repeats (his way of asking how deep the trouble is). Setting the mugs on the table, he rubs his eyes with his forefingers, pinching the skin over the bridge of his nose. He sits down across from Nicolas with a thump.

Nicolas shrugs and looks away uneasily. "Some of the out-buildings up in the Bronx."

"You are a crazy man!" Sy lets his forehead drop forward into the cup of his palms.

Nicolas sips his coffee and again shakes his head, as if to clear it. "Alexis was right. Too much quick expansion."

Sy looks up, irritated somehow by the entire discussion. He is just too tired for all of this. "Moving in little increments has never been your style, Nico."

"I was so sure the new stores would just skyrocket."

Sy shrugs. "The question is, what to do now? Maybe cut bait," he says meditatively, taking refuge in solving the problem pragmatically. "Maybe close a few branches down."

Nicolas shakes his head, stubborn as always. "I won't do that."

"You may have to," Sy says, pulling a notepad off the counter, starting to work up some figures. "Let's look at it together so you can make a clear decision."

"Forget about it!" Nicolas stands up, swaying. Leaning on the table, he glares with anger at Sy. "You may have gotten me into this mess, but I'll get myself out."

"*I* got you into it?" Sy repeats slowly, looking up at his friend, bewildered by Nicolas's resentment. The whole world is topsy-turvy tonight, all its inhabitants doing strange dances he can't interpret. "It was your company, your decision."

"*You* set up the deal!" Nicolas leans in closer.

"I *executed* exactly what you asked for," Sy corrects carefully.

"And now you get to sit here in your safe house with your fat salary — no risk here — and with a terrific wife who'd follow you anywhere. Too bad you won't give her the time of day."

"What's this got to do with Maggie?" His voice is sharp now. "Has she said something to you?"

"Like to know, wouldn't you?" Nicolas laughs shortly, rocking the table with his body. "Maybe you should try listening to her sometime."

Sy sits up very straight. "What's between Maggie and me is none of your business," he flares, angry at last.

"Well, you sure haven't made it *your* business, have you, old buddy?" answers Nicolas. He comes over and gives him a clumsy punch on the shoulder. "Ambition's got you blind." With that, he turns and stumbles out into the dark hall.

After a minute, the front door slams, footsteps move unevenly over the front porch, and then the engine of a car grinds, catches, roars. Sy (thinking to stop him from driving) makes a halfhearted motion to get up out of his seat, but then sinks back: he doesn't want to deal with Nicolas's problems anymore tonight. There are enough of his own waiting upstairs.

Hurricanes and Women

The doorknob to the master bedroom does not yield to Sy's hand, when, after midnight, having washed all the dishes, he trudges upstairs again. Turning from the door of the bedroom, he goes down the hall to Mikey's room, where he sits on the foot of his son's bed and watches him sleep; the child's eyes slide from side to side in some sort of dream, his hands open and close, he breathes through his mouth in little puffs and snorts like a windup toy fallen on its back but still running. Maybe he is dreaming about playing baseball. Since spring, Sy has spent every Saturday morning teaching him how to catch, and a few weeks ago they went together to buy the right-size glove.

As a boy, Sy saved for months to be able to buy his own first glove, waiting table and helping out at the deli; his father and he stopped by Paragon every Saturday morning to daydream about the one he wanted. He'd been eight before he knew what that glove felt like on his hand. What joy to leave the store at last, leather stiff over his fingers, and begin breaking it in, oiling it before bed and then sleeping with it under his pillow to soften it. Little League, with his father cheering him on; Yankees games on summer nights, hunched around the black-and-white set, he and his dad, eating pretzels and having a contest to see who could remember the batting averages better. Many nights during those years he would dream he was playing center field for his Little League team: he heard the crack of the bat and tilted his head back to see a high, deep drive spinning toward him in slow-motion; as it arched across the sky he knew he would never catch it, and the fear of not catching it was like a cloud across his vision. He panicked, losing the ball against the bright blue sky. Then, as suddenly as he lost it, he found it again, descending in a long curving arc, backlit by the sun, falling more and more slowly in a blur of canvas and red stitching. Eventually it thudded into the pocket of his well-oiled, magical glove. But when he opened the glove to hurl it back to the shortstop — a boy named Robbie Marcus who lived down the hall from him — he saw that what he had just caught was in fact his father's pocket watch.

This watch, handed down through the various Whittenberg generations for many years, transferred from father to son at bar mitzvah, was a plain-faced, gold-rimmed timepiece. When it was Bernie's turn to give it to Sy, he had done so proudly; looking into his son's eyes after his Torah reading at shul, he said that though he had never had the proper suit with which to wear the watch, he was certain that Sy would. And although Sy does now indeed wear the suit to which his father alluded, he chooses to leave the watch in his top drawer. It occurs to Sy that maybe he's been concentrating too hard on the right kind of suit, and not enough on the watch itself.

He lays his finger across the middle of Mikey's palm, but the boy does not curl his hand shut as he used to when he was a baby. Sy straightens the sheet up under Mikey's chin and bends to kiss him. "Daddy's home," he whispers in the boy's ear, wishing he might wake, but tonight his sleep is impenetrable.

He goes down to Kate's room, stopping on the threshold before tiptoeing across to the large white bed where she sleeps curled on her side, looking inexplicably younger than her brother. Maybe the way her hair curls down over her forehead, damp with sweat, makes her seem vulnerable. Or maybe it is the way she snuggles next to Silver, the gray felt horse Sy had as a child, which he passed on to her when she was born.

The fine tissue of time dissolves as Sy sits there, remembering the year when he gave Kate her two A.M. feeding in the rocking chair on the other side of the room; he remembers diapering her on the changing table that now serves as a doll chest; he remembers the first time she walked the balance beam without falling off, the first tennis ball she hit with her small racquet, how just this year she learned to tell time and he took her to Bloomingdale's to buy a Swatch. It is hard to believe (to understand with his heart) that his parents will never see or hold this child, that she will never spend a winter afternoon steaming up the windows of the apartment in Sty Town baking strudel with her grandmother. He wishes he could pick up Kate now and hold her, rock her, take comfort from her warmth. His mother always said there was no cure for grown-up loneliness like the sweet weight of a child in your lap. He puts his face down, cheek to her cheek, and inhales the soapy scent of his sleeping girl entwined with the scruffy, woolly smell of his past.

But he does not to disturb her. Slowly he eases himself off the edge of the bed, contenting himself with one more kiss on her cheek. He walks down the hall to the guest room where, in the narrow single bed, he sleeps in fits and starts until the first streaks of sun finger their way into the summer sky. His travel alarm clock reads nearly six, but he turns it off before it can ring and just lies there, listening to the birds wake in the tree outside the window and the thud of the newspaper as it lands on his porch. Shortly, he gets up and goes downstairs in his underwear to put on a pot of coffee. The morning air is cool against his legs as he reaches out the front door and scoops up the paper quickly — so that Irene Karp won't catch sight of him in his boxer shorts. From next door, Jerry Kirchenbaum waves from his own front porch and Sy smiles and waves back, thinking he'd like to get Jerry over onto the court this weekend.

He is standing at the kitchen sink draining a glass of orange juice when Maggie comes downstairs. Seeing him, she hesitates on the threshold. Then, averting her gaze, she crosses to the refrigerator and gets out the milk. Like a cloud, it billows up through her mug of coffee; she sips slowly and rubs her eyes with the back of her hand in a childlike motion. Her mouth is sour and her head aches.

"How could you not have told me?" Her words come as a surprise to her. (She did not know she was ready to ask the question.)

He turns from the window to look at her, hair a red nimbus around her face, bathrobe belt trailing to the ground. "Because it was important to me," he says slowly, "and I didn't want you to say no."

"How could it be so important that you wouldn't tell me about it? Is it the money?"

He shakes his head. "The opportunity." The fatigue on his face gives way to excitement. "I'd be the one heading up a brand new branch of the firm — my own show, with everyone reporting to me. A chance to let everyone see what *I* can do. And think of what it could mean for you."

"For me?" she echoes, startled.

He nods. "A chance to live abroad. The firm'll set us up in a terrific place, we could do all the sights. I'm sorry I didn't tell you right off." He smiles at her.

It's a bribe, she sees — he is holding out temptations in an effort to distract her from what she needs (and wants) to do now. He thinks a quick apology brings them back to the start and that all will be forgiven. *Do not pass Go,* she thinks. *Do not collect $200.00.*

"And what about me?"

"What about you?" His face is genuinely puzzled. He takes his coffee to the kitchen table and sits down.

Maggie remains standing by the counter, her coffee cooling untouched; she feels more and more nauseated. "I want to go back to work," she says.

"You've said that before. But I never thought you really meant it. You like being home."

"I liked being home when the kids were little, when they really needed me — the whole of me. But they're gone nearly all day now." Her voice rasps a little and she fights to keep her emotions in check. "What we need now is a cleaning lady."

"Oh, come on," he remonstrates. "When they get home at three o'clock is some cleaning lady going to read to them, do art projects? Don't denigrate what you do."

"I just need to feel like I'm doing more with my day than making beds and folding laundry."

"Well, you can. Without going back full-time and making your life hard. Why not volunteer for something?"

"I don't want to be a *volunteer*. I am an editor." She paces back and forth between the sink and the table.

"And a mother, and a wife," he corrects, turning to follow her movement. "Don't forget the things that are important to you."

"Why do they have to be mutually exclusive? You're a husband and a father — does that keep you from going to work every morning?" She shakes her head.

"The fact that I'm away from home so much is a damned good reason for you to be here most of the time. What happens when one of the kids is sick? Is a cleaning lady going to be here for them then? Are you going to call into the office and tell them you won't be in because Mikey's got a fever?"

"All those things can be worked out," she insists, even though her own questions about the effort required to return to work in the city surface again. "Other people manage." The more he argues with her, the more adamant she becomes.

"Since when have we wanted to be anything like 'other people'? I see women all the time who work their asses off, and I admire them for it. But we've always been different — we always wanted to be different."

"You just don't want anything to change," she accuses. "If I stay at home you can keep up your insane schedule with impunity."

"My first priority is the children."

"Your first priority is your work! *Masquerading* as concern for the family."

"It's not an optimal time," he replies stubbornly.

"And when would be 'optimal'? When they're off at college? When they're married?"

He stares her down. "Don't go getting sarcastic."

"Well, then listen to yourself," she answers angrily. "You don't want me to go back to work because it'll cramp *your* style. If I go back to work then I'm not as transportable as a sack of mail, and you'll be pressured to put in more time at home. Isn't that really it?"

"You're being ridiculous," he says calmly.

"If I go back to work how can we go to Tokyo?"

"If it really matters to you, then when we go to Tokyo you'll find a job there." His voice remains practical, low-key.

"*If* we go to Tokyo I wouldn't be able to get work and you know it," she says acidly.

"I may never see an opportunity like this again. And you could always wait a few more years to go back."

She hears the logical turn his tone has taken now and knows he is convincing himself of the value of this idea. "I put myself on hold for the last eight years," she says, furiously. "I gave up work with the understanding that when I was ready to go back, you'd be supportive!"

"It's not my fault that this offer came along right now," he flares at last. "I don't control these things."

They just stand and glare at each other, each feeling betrayed.

"Look," he says then, breaking the tension by changing his face and voice from angry to placating. "Let's put all of this on hold. Wait and see whether I even *get* the job. I'll know in a few weeks and this entire argument may be moot."

She takes a step closer to the table, staring at him. "You mean, you've already told Maxine you definitely want it? For sure?" The words come out of her mouth very slowly.

Sy looks uncomfortable. "You know how these things work — your name comes up and you either lean into the suggestion or against it. Maxine knows I'd be pleased to get the job."

"How's it going to look if they ask you and you turn it down?"

"Terrible," he acknowledges. A look of distress (panic) crosses his face before he manages to stifle it.

Watching that expression, Maggie realizes that he has never considered the possibility that she might refuse to move; he'd been that confident he could make an effective sales pitch.

He runs his hand through his hair. "Let's put it on hold," he repeats.

"You should know," she says, stunned to realize that he could have taken this definitive a step without discussing it with her, "that I had an interview at *Esquire* yesterday. And I've got two more with other magazines next week."

"How could you do something like that without telling me?" he flares.

She just looks at him.

He turns away, suddenly vulnerable. He had thought they'd make up this morning; that in the face of his opportunity she would acquiesce, out of love, and the recognition that the move was designed to help them all. Now they are at even more of an impasse than they were last night.

The children stumble downstairs, sleepy and growling for their breakfasts. Maggie sets out cold cereal and milk, then begins the lunch boxes. Her head pulses with the hangover and handling greasy pink slices of bologna makes her stomach leap again. As she spreads the mustard and mayonnaise, she sends Sy a look that means the rest of their discussion will have to keep until they are alone. Into the midst of the triumph she feels at having stood up to him intrudes despair: the realization that he has yet to inquire about the results of her interview at *Esquire*. It is not real to him; she is not real to him. All that he knows is the angry burn of his ambition. She sees how much he will sacrifice to feed that interior fire.

He looks so miserable, hunched over his coffee mug, that she feels almost sorry for him — but not quite. All through that long breakfast, Maggie keeps silent and restrains herself from reaching out to pat his hand or reassure him. She wants the tension to continue, for it seems to her that they have passed some threshold. It is the first time in their twelve years of marriage that she has not given in, immediately and automatically, but instead has held her ground on a major issue. To her surprise, there is little he can do or say, and this empowers her in a new way. She realizes that they have come, nearly without recognizing it, to the end of an era: of feeling a particular way about each other, of making assumptions about how they will live and who will set the tone. This feeling of power frightens her. She does not know what it means, for their future as a family or as a couple or even as individuals who have vowed (with one ingenuous, hopeful promise) to love each other for the rest of their lives.

Nevertheless, entwined with the anxiety is a concomitant surge of new and itchy curiosity: she wonders if she has the courage to continue the game, press the point and call his bluff. For the first time ever, she wants to find out just how good her hand really is.

ᕗ

The tug of war between the Whittens lasts all summer long. Though July is hot and August hotter, the impasse about the move to Tokyo is handled in cool acts of sublimation: Maggie makes persistent, fruitless phone calls in search of a job; Sy, with a hearty enthusiasm, brings home brochures of everything they will be able to see and do during their years abroad, spreading glossy possibilities across their dinner table like so much tempting smorgasbord. The children (resistant at first) begin to succumb to the lure and become excited. By mid-August, with the tide of family sentiment running more and more against her, Maggie is silently, absolutely, desperate. Sy's determination frightens her. The box around her seems to grow smaller and smaller. Grim and depressed, she packs the family up for their two-week vacation to Maine, rationalizing that nearly everyone, including the publishing industry, leaves Manhattan in August anyway.

She hopes that amid the high bush blueberries and the porcupines, in a house borrowed from someone Sy knows at the office, on a tiny year-round island off the coast at Bath, she and her husband will sit down and talk, rediscover the warmth and rapport that always used to sustain them. But this is not to be — though Maine itself lives up to all expectation — for on their second day a crisis calls Sy back to the office. The client sends a private jet to collect him, and as Sy packs, Maggie is too tongue-tied with anger to say a single word, too frozen in the inertia of their life. Alone, the children bathed and in bed, she spends three straight evenings on the screened-in porch, with the yellow bug lamp to read by and a large, refillable glass of wine. By midnight, having climbed the stairs to bed, she is unable to sleep. Despair pushes her against the walls of the room, where she flattens out with barely a whisper. Sy's lack of respect for their family's privacy makes her respect him less, and she cannot understand why he is so unable to draw a line with these people. It is as if every priority they had ever set as a couple is being trampled on. Is this how they will spend the rest of their lives? she wonders. She has never felt more separate and lonely. What a cheat it all is, she thinks: a man who promises you love but gives you absence.

When Sy returns four days later, he brings with him an unexpected guest: Nicolas, who is glad to escape the heat of the city. At the end of July, he took a sublet in Chelsea, throwing a few suits and some underwear into his suitcase, but leaving most of his belongings behind in the apartment. (He refuses to be too accommodating. It isn't his style.) He resents being relegated to such quarters while Alexis continues to relax in luxury, accompanied by God knows who, on Fifth Avenue. He has nothing in Chelsea except his clothes. Still, he was lucky to get the sublet, and his finances give him little alternative. This is hardly the time to rent an apartment at the Carlyle (though he did consider it briefly). When Sy offers him a week-long retreat on the island, he hesitates not one minute, eager to escape not only the heat but the loneliness as well.

Nicolas's presence prevents any discussion (fighting). No one brings up Tokyo, Maggie's job hunt, or Alexis. Instead, they divert themselves: the children, the Scrabble board, lobsters and steamers three nights in a row, paddling the canoe around the tidal river, picnics, swimming, and swatting greenheads on the beach, arguing amicably over whose turn it is with that summer's Tom Clancy thriller, *Red Storm Rising*. When, during the second week on the island, Sy is once again called back to the city (the same crumping deal), neither the children nor Maggie seem to mind, because they have Nicolas to keep them company.

The morning after Sy leaves, Maggie wakes Nicolas early, appearing in his room before daybreak to snap up the shades and flap his covers back in the chilly air, ignoring his groans of protest; she pulls him out onto the mud flats at ebb tide. Shivering, they roll their pants to the knee and set out barefoot. She teaches him how to clam, using a small rake and then his fingers to dig down into the mud. They feel the sunrise when welcome heat travels up across their cold feet and bent backs. The rank smell of ocean's bottom and salt rises around them. Under the new light, the detritus of shells across the flats glitters like a field of mica. Across the booming expanse of mud and sea, their voices are diminished.

Her pail filled at last, Maggie stops and looks around the flats. A sharp wind whips the morning clean, and the world is laid bare by the sun: the backside of life right here, in the hard-packed, still expanse of mud, the tidepools teeming with life; the snowy egrets hunting above their heads, criss-crossing on steep currents of air; gulls swooping in raucous chorus — dip and fish, dip and fish. All of this activity leads the eye down toward endless motion at the curling lip of the ocean. Soon the vast plane of water will reverse itself and begin to pull, once again, toward the shore. It seems to Maggie that this moment of tides and moons, of suck and sigh, ebb and flow, waiting for the invisible pivot from low to high, can only be called holy.

Nicolas comes over and sets his bucket down, filled to the top with muddy clams, and puts his arm around her. She twines hers into his, glad to share this with him. They watch the rest of the sunrise, cresting orange above the thick line of evergreens, without speaking. As they pick their buckets up and begin the hike back toward shore, he catches her hand and squeezes it. "Thanks," he says.

Maggie makes a kettle of chowder, thick with the cherrystones, potato, salt pork, and cream. That night, they feed the children first and then wait for dark. With Mikey and Kate bedded down, the two of them douse themselves with Woodman's, fill the thermos with the hot soup, cut a slab of corn bread, and go to sit on the end of the dock. Anchoring a bottle of Chardonnay with the halyard from the motorboat, they drop it into the water to chill. The waves suck in and out against the pilings — *a comforting noise*, Maggie thinks, as they down the bread and the chowder, which steams up into the chilly Maine dark. More jokes about nursery food. Wine straight from the salty neck of the bottle. Nicolas does not speak of Alexis, but Maggie knows he is thinking about her, learning to live, bit by bit, with his loss and his anger. The mosquitos (supersonic) drive them indoors.

In bed that night, wind tumbling through the pines outside the window, ocean a distant sough against the rocks, Maggie contemplates the curious position in which she now finds herself: painful as it was to accept initially, she had assumed that after her friends' separation an inevitable schism would occur within their foursome. Nicolas and Sy have been friends too long for them to be pulled apart now, and Maggie was certain that she and Alexis, too, would continue as before, with the friendship between the two couples absorbing the brunt of the divorce. But instead, she now sees, Alexis has withdrawn to devote whatever free time she has to Jon, and Maggie and Sy are simply not ready to accept someone new so fast.

Even then, if Maggie were not so close to Nicolas, she would undoubtedly be the natural recipient for the outpouring, detail by detail over the phone, of Alexis's newest obsession. As it is, however, a silence has developed between them, fueled by the conflicted feelings Maggie has (her anger with Alexis for deserting Nicolas, her anger with Jon for having separated her two best friends, the increasing isolation within her own marriage) and Alexis's obvious distraction with love. It hurts Maggie to hear Alexis rhapsodize — even briefly — about Jon, when Nicolas is so profoundly alone; it hurts her to see him avert his eyes every time Sy puts his arm around her waist or kisses her cheek: Sy's insensitivity to Nicolas's feelings makes her short with him and invariably she slips away from the embrace. (Which rationale serves, of course, as a neat excuse.) And there is also her newly deepened friendship with Nicolas itself, a bounty in her lonely life.

Alexis's unabashed happiness brings to Maggie's mind words like callous, unfeeling, selfish — words she tries to push away because she feels guilty over even thinking them. (The truth is that she is envious.) The lilt of Alexis's voice, the rapturous manner in which she describes the most simple events, clearly comes from this vitalizing wave of enchantment. Alexis sounds remarkably young and Maggie resents it. Also, Maggie senses that Alexis does not sympathize with the stand she has taken about Tokyo; whenever Maggie brings up her feelings, Alexis changes the subject as a way of not appearing to side with Sy. The two women have never been so distant.

⌒

Such is the battered condition of the friendship when, in early September, Alexis scans the ballroom of the Sheraton Centre from her elevated position on the dais, and runs smack into the face of Sy. He is sitting fifty feet away at the table First Boston has subscribed for the Man of the Year Award Dinner syndicated by the Harvard Business School Club. This year the benefit is in honor of Paul Volcker, head of the Fed (Federal Reserve), at a thousand dollars a table.

Alexis and Sy stare at each other for a minute, and then both look away quickly, embarrassed. Bad as things are with Maggie, she has not seen Sy, or even spoken with him, since Nicolas moved out. Having heard from Maggie, upon the Whittens' return from Maine, that Nicolas accompanied them on vacation, makes Alexis feel even more awkward; all summer long she was not invited out to Maggie and Sy's for so much as a drink. Perhaps Sy will avoid her tonight, she thinks. Perhaps he no longer wants to be friends. This idea makes her eyes sting: years ago when they were undergraduates, Sy was the only one willing to brave with her the arctic Boston freeze on midnight runs to Tommy's for cheesesteak subs, and though in recent years they've talked more about their mergers than about cheesesteaks or the Allman Brothers, she always, intuitively, believed in his loyalty. That same sense of loyalty, she now realizes with despair, may require him to side solely with Nicolas — his best friend. She blinks rapidly and wipes her mouth with a napkin. (The last thing she can afford to do right now is look as if she is ready to cry.)

Alexis does not know what to say to either of them, especially Maggie. She wants (needs) to share both her joy about Jon and her sadness over Nicolas, but there is a hard and stubborn edge in her best friend's voice: Maggie doesn't want to hear anything about any of it. During the last few years, the pressure of work has pushed most of Alexis's other friendships into the background, but Maggie has always been a constant, no matter what they are talking about or how much time has elapsed since they last spoke. Their estrangement is, for Alexis, a sharp, additional loss.

She is certain that had Nicolas left *her*, cheated on *her*, Maggie would have been by her side instantly. And so Alexis now feels betrayed: Maggie is making not the least attempt to understand the pain and difficulty of divorce — even when you are the one doing the divorcing — nor does she begin to comprehend the way Alexis's happiness keeps bumping up against the botched commitment to Nicolas. When Alexis looks at Jon she wonders if he, too, will someday bore and irritate her to the point where she will once again want to leave. This sense of disillusionment with the human capacity for love and fidelity backlights even the most minor of details: a little dandruff cannot be simply a little dandruff. She quickly grows defensive with Maggie — as if she needs to justify every move she makes — and retreats to her most cool and distant.

To distract herself from these painful thoughts, Alexis looks around the noisy room: nearly all of the 150 tables are syndicated by Wall Street investment banks or the major consulting firms. At each candle-lit circle, there are one or two senior partners and their spouses: the rest of the chairs are filled by junior associates who have been strong-armed into attendance (the firms pay, but the tables must be filled). Alexis is program chairman for the benefit and it was her idea to honor Volcker, sitting to her left, tonight. He is an old friend of her father's, and though there was general excitement at the proposal of his name, the committee doubted they would be able to entice him to appear and be so honored. Craftily, Alexis did not volunteer her connection to Volcker, or offer to help in approaching him through standard channels, until Tom Berels, the head of the committee and an important partner at Goldman, Sachs — who, at this very moment, is introducing Volcker to the crowd — tried and was given the polite turn-down. Then, and only then, did she step in behind the scenes.

Berels finishes his speech as the waiters go on changing plates, taking the salad off, putting the salmon on, and Volcker strolls up to the podium to speak. His tall frame dwarfs the microphone, and he is having difficulty straightening the gooseneck. Alexis (lit up inside) bustles over to help him make the adjustment. She loves performing, assuming whatever role a situation provides. Tonight, her speech — the first of the evening — was well received, and she knows that in the eyes of Berels, at least, she has scored big by snaring Volcker, who is a hero to most of the people in this room. Despite typical American-media second-guessing, Volcker screwed the money door tight over at the Fed; when inflation dipped and interest rates dropped back down, the financial community took off. Berels, a friend of Sam Waterston — the managing partner at Hewett — can now be counted on to drop in a good word for her.

She sighs as she returns to her seat. The cat-and-mouse routine is stale these days. To play such games, with so much riding on subjective perceptions from the right source, seems altogether too haphazard. At a time when nothing else about her life seems certain, she craves the sure knowledge (nothing on the Street is ever sure) that she will be rewarded this year with a huge bonus and a promotion next year to managing director (a guarantee that she will rise above the frantic struggle of ordinary Wall Street drones). The familiar pressure about bonuses and promotions is just beginning now, in September, with the results of this particular footrace to be announced sometime between Thanksgiving and Christmas. The competition is relentless and merciless — with everyone comparing figures and achievements. *Lucratocracy*, she thinks.

Unable to concentrate on Volcker's speech, she instead glances to Jon, on the far side of the ballroom, at the table his firm has taken. He, too, is watching her instead of Volcker. She smiles, so slightly that no one else will notice, and feels suddenly less depressed. In a little while they will leave separately and a few minutes apart, then meet on the corner of Sixth and Fifty-first. Alexis has no intention of being the subject of the trading floor's newest dirty joke.

Jon has been in Chicago for the last three nights, and Alexis missed him enough to scare herself. Organizing this function on top of her impossible schedule has meant next to no sleep, and now a wave of nauseated exhaustion hits her as she pushes her plate back to get away from the odor of the fish. It has been a rough week, complicated by the arrival of her period and more pain (still unexplained). The codeine she is relying on has washed her gray with fatigue.

Following Alexis's smile to the other side of the room, Christa sees Jon and pushes her plate away from her, scraped clean, with disgust. She is not listening to a word Volcker says. Alexis sits on the top of their world like king of the castle. On the sidelines, her lover pays court.

Her sense of spite loosened by two glasses of wine (she's never been much of a drinker), Christa leans over to whisper to Weldon, who has developed a rep around the firm as a major leaky pipe. "They're about as subtle as Ivan," she says, nodding in Jon's direction. "Or not even."

"Stratton?" Weldon follows her gaze with interest. "You kidding?"

Christa shakes her head. "Like a catcher and pitcher sending signals in the ninth."

He laughs and studies Alexis on the dais. "Lot of scuttlebutt about her these days. They say she was the one who bagged Volcker for tonight. And there's a rumor she might be up early."

A wave of disgust. "Sure," Christa comments bitterly. "She's got everything else — why not promote her ahead of the peons, just settle every little detail in her picture-perfect life." She snorts. "Some people are blessed."

"Got green eyes?" He grins at her.

"Who me?" She strives for a light tone but inside she feels dark and troubled, a hurricane sea.

"Why do you care so much?"

He misses nothing, Christa realizes. "Jon is a good friend." She looks over at him again across the room, where he remains fixed upon Alexis. "That woman is a disposal. She couldn't understand a man like him if she took a Ph.D."

"And *you* do?"

His tone mocks her and she flushes. "We came from the same place, that's all. I understand the way he thinks, down to the ground." Christa pauses and clears her throat. "Hey, Sy —" She drops her voice and turns to Sy, seated on her right. "What's the word on Tokyo?"

"Still haven't heard." He shrugs. "Soon, I hope." Though he strives for nonchalance, the question brings on a crunch of nerves. Hasn't heard. Not a good sign. More nervous with each day that goes by, Sy wants to ask Maxine if she knows anything — but he is afraid to sound too eager. Maxine, sitting opposite him tonight, appears not to have picked up on Christa's question: at least, she keeps right on talking to the wife of one of their associates to her left. He decides now that if she still hasn't said anything by the end of the week he will bring it up. Around him conversation buzzes past: who is up for promotion this year, who will be in the first-tier of bonuses, who is sleeping with whom around the office.

Back on the dais, Alexis is making a pretty speech that will bring the formal program to a close. Sy watches the way she escorts Volcker down the steps, as comfortably as if he is an old friend. Volcker laughs at something she says. Suddenly Sy knows — the way he often senses such things, the smell of a good deal — how successful Alexis is going to be. She will be at the very top, a major partner in a very short time. He both envies and pities her: what will be the cost of maintaining her balance at such a lofty elevation? he wonders, thinking of himself, of Maggie and the kids, of Tokyo. He aches for his own opportunity, to pitch in the major leagues, just this once.

"If they offer it to you, will you go?" Christa's voice interrupts his train of thought and he breaks his gaze away from Alexis and Volcker who now stand at the head Hewett Lowell table with Tom Berels.

"I want to." He sighs. "But I'm not the only vote."

"Maggie's still opposed?"

He nods.

"She find a job yet?"

He shakes his head. "It's not fair of me, I guess, but I keep hoping she won't —"

"Sy!" Christa is horrified to hear this remark from Sy, from whom she expects something more noble. "You can't be so low as that, so mean spirited. You know you want her to be happy."

"Right now she doesn't know what she needs to be happy," he says, irritably.

Christa just looks at him, allowing his own words to sit in front of him.

"O.K. You're right." He sighs. Twirls his wineglass on the tablecloth. "It's just —"

"It's just you want it so bad," Christa amends.

"I want what's good for her, but I also want what's good for us!" His voice picks up. He looks around, and then continues more quietly. "I'm only asking her to wait. Not to give it up."

"She's been waiting a long time already," Christa admonishes. As much as she likes Sy, as long as they have been friends, in this instant she feels (woman to woman) quite fiercely loyal to Maggie.

"Damn it, I know that." He runs his hand through his hair, rumpling himself thoroughly. "But she's so mixed up about what she wants right now, and I've been *working* for a long time, for just this kind of thing."

She looks at him quizzically. "Which is more important to you?"

He groans. "Don't. Just don't."

"Sorry." She smiles, but it is not truly a smile of sympathy.

Sy looks away, knowing she finds him to be unfair. This bothers him. He sets great store by Christa's opinions, professional and personal. He admires her guts (for being one of the best in such a competitive field); he admires her courage (for living alone without complaining).

Once again he is distracted by Alexis, standing at the Hewett table, introducing Volcker to a variety of people. Excusing himself, he stands and starts to work his way across the room between the tables.

Alexis is getting extraordinary pleasure out of introducing Volcker and Hewett's head merger partner, Sam Waterston. After Volcker moves on to speak with others he knows, Berels stops to talk shop with Waterston, an old HBS classmate, and to thank him for subscribing the table for the dinner. He puts his hand on Alexis's shoulder. "If you ever want to trade this player here, be sure to give me a call," he says to Waterston, smiling at Alexis and giving her a squeeze. Then he lowers his voice. "When *I* call Volcker's office, they practically give me the dial tone." He makes an abrupt hang-up gesture with his hand. "But when Alexis calls," he smiles at her again; there is a chunk of orange fish wedged in between his teeth, "it's a done deal." He laughs. "Though she's still zipped shut on how she managed it."

"Inside information, Fred," Alexis replies in a tone of reproof.

Waterston gives her a speculative look. "She pulls rabbits out of hats all the time, Tom." Although he is speaking directly to Berels now and not looking at Alexis at all, the words are portentous. "And, as you know, she's not for sale."

"Would you two excuse me for a minute?" Alexis asks demurely, knowing it is not politic to stand here lapping up their praise. (Although the suggestion of a job offer from Goldman ought to be worth at least $100K at bonus time.) She flashes a look at Jon, and then walks calmly through the tables toward the exit.

Once outside, she goes around the corner toward the ladies' room, but does not go inside. She waits there until she sees Jon approach, so excited she thinks she is going to float up through the roof of the place like a helium balloon. Her depression is gone.

Waylaid by a colleague from Morgan Stanley, and then by Jerry Kirchenbaum, Sy stops for a moment to talk. When he starts back toward Alexis, he sees her moving quickly through the room, *probably to the ladies,* he decides. He changes direction and threads his way through people and conversations after her. But he is stopped several more times and so, hurrying now toward the washrooms some five minutes later, he fears he may have missed his opportunity to speak with her. Approaching the corner, he hears her voice, carrying in excitement above the whisper she obviously intends. He stops short.

He wants to catch her alone, in a situation where he can get right to the point. *And what is the point?* he wonders. *What is it you want to say?* He almost turns back to the ballroom, but the urgency of her tone intrigues him.

"No, I'm telling you, he said it right in front of Berels! 'Not for sale'!"

Sy begins, without even thinking about it, to eavesdrop.

"You're phenomenal." A man's voice, familiar. "I bet they promote you this year."

Sy hears the hiss as she draws her breath in, sharp. "A year early?" She laughs. "They'll never go for it."

"Why not?"

Sy leans forward against the wall, straining to hear.

"They'll never do it for a woman. Never."

"Maybe you should give them some incentive."

She laughs again. "Got any ideas?"

Silence for a minute. Sy wonders if they have moved farther down the hall. Curiosity pushes at him and he takes a fast peek around the corner.

Not five feet away Jon Stratton has his arm around Sy's best friend's wife. Quickly, Sy draws back, feeling as if someone has knocked the wind out of him. A waitress comes down the hall, eyeing Sy as he stands leaning back against the wall, trying to calm himself. Startled by the intrusion, he moves forward, toward Jon and Alexis, pretending to head toward the bathroom.

"Hey, Alexis!" he says, adopting a tone of surprise, one that sounds transparently false to his ear. Then with reserve and a nod, "Jon."

"Sy." She smiles at him, tentatively it seems.

The two men shake hands reflexively, and then they stand there for a moment, surrounded in awkward silence.

Alexis turns back to Jon. "See you later?"

He nods, takes the hint, leaves.

Alone, they stand in more silence. "How are you?" he says then, smiling at her a little despite himself. Maybe he ought to ignore her, but he can't bring himself to do it, after all these years.

"O.K.," she says slowly. "I miss you guys."

How he admires her style. Always direct. No games. Just: *I miss you*. Just: *can we still be friends?*

"Come out for supper some night soon."

"I'd like to." She hesitates. "How's Nico doing?"

"Fine," Sy replies, knowing his friend would want this answer. He looks at the floor and shuffles his feet. What is he supposed to say, anyway: Nicolas is still chasing every brain-free blonde from one end of the city to the other.

"I'm worried about him." Alexis swallows, and he can see her throat tighten as she speaks. Her concern is real, and that puzzles him: it seems strange that she can still care enough to worry about Nicolas, but not enough to want to work things out.

"It sounds as if you still care a lot."

"Don't get started!" She cuts him off with a vehement shake of her head. "There's no way we can get back together."

"O.K." He puts his hands up. A surrender. He cannot bring himself to mention Jon. "Well, call Maggie for a date — she's got our calendar."

"Good." Alexis smiles and reaches to give him a kiss on the cheek. He puts his hand on her shoulder, and, surprising them both, catches her up in a hug. Holds tight. Warmed by the press of her small body, he feels his eyes sting. He does not see how they can all still be friends, but they will have to manage somehow.

"You tell her if she doesn't call me, I'm going to call her. You tell her that's a definite threat!"

He laughs and she turns to go, stopping once to look back at him and smile.

He goes into the men's room, blows his nose, pees, washes face and hands. He studies his reflection in the mirror. The sorrow clings. He sighs, pushes the swinging door open.

"Sy?"

His turn to be surprised.

He waits till Maxine catches up with him. She motions him into an alcove off the corridor.

"I was hoping to snag you. I got the word on Tokyo this afternoon."

He stares at her, feeling his heart thud in three distinct beats. *At last.* Blood pushes up into his brain. Air seems elusive.

"I couldn't get you," she goes on. "I stopped by your office but you weren't in."

"No, I was out," he manages at last, anxiety making every nerve in his body stand on end like an electrified field of grass. Why doesn't she get to the point? The noise coming from the ballroom increases in pitch, up from a drone, approaching a roar. As if there is a ball game going on a few feet away. The escalating babble crowds his head.

"I'm so sorry," she says then, her eyes full of sympathy. "But they gave it to Marty Frost."

"Marty Frost?" he repeats dumbly, his face flushing red and hot and then draining in a sensation that makes him nauseated. Her voice sounds tiny and out of sync, as if it is stretching across a long distance, hard to hear over the noise inside his head. "They gave it to a woman?" His voice sounds faint and incredulous. "This place is changing."

"Pretty amazing, isn't it?" She shakes her head.

He just stands there. He doesn't know what to say. "Why did they pass over me?"

She shrugs and looks away. He is sure her evasive motion means something bad.

"These things are arbitrary," she says. "And they're a bunch of jerks." She grins at him.

"It'll affect me next year, won't it?"

"I doubt it," she answers. "Relax."

But he knows that to try for a position like this and fail to land it is worse than not having tried at all. Worse than just waiting for his ordinary promotion to managing director, due next year, or the next, if he is lucky and the merger market holds.

Maxine puts her hand on his arm to reassure him. "There'll be other chances, Sy. It's got more to do with politics than merit — I promise you that." Again, she pats his shoulder and then makes an excuse about getting back to the table.

As soon as she moves away instinct leads him to the men's room. Leaning on the door, he fights the urge to kick something. He has jeopardized so much with Maggie — all these months wasted in anger and recrimination, all the energy spent over absolutely nothing.

He wants to punch out whomever made the damned decision and remembers Nicolas, in a Harvard Square bar ten years ago: "When you can't get revenge, get release." Sy pushes his way out of the men's room and takes the elevator to the street. He walks until he finds the right sort of neon sign. *Line them up,* he says to the bartender, and watches them double in reflection on the shiny surface. One bullet after another, he goes down into oblivion.

NINE

Fantasies

Maggie and Nicolas sit on the dark porch again, this time side by side, companionably, in the swing. The cool September night stretches out around them and Maggie feels remarkably relaxed. Just for this one minute, when she and Nicolas are talking about the kids and how quickly they are growing up, she forgets all the other problems hanging over her. This was the children's first day back at school, and their excited stories had dominated dinner. Sy has a business dinner at the Sheraton Centre and Nicolas dropped in, unannounced again, just as she was taking the casserole out of the oven. Maggie likes the habit, and (without realizing it) now makes slightly larger suppers just in case. Every night between five and six, she lingers at the front of the house, listening unconsciously to the traffic on the street. Since their trip to Maine, he has become a regular, and important, face at their table.

She cradles the coffee mug on her lap and leans her head back. The luxury of silence. Of not being required to answer any more questions. Nicolas's arm stretches along the top of the wicker swing. Its warmth just touches her hair.

His hand moves down to stroke the back of her neck, tickling, sending goose bumps up and down her body. He twines his fingers into her hair.

"You have the most beautiful hair," he says, tracing a finger down her cheek, then across the outline of her lips.

The pleasure of his touch floods her. Her face is getting hot.

She squelches temptation by reaching up and removing his hand, gently. "Don't," she says.

"Why not?"

"I don't want anything to change between us. I need you just the way it is."

"Mommy?"

Maggie jumps, startled, at the sight of Kate hovering in the doorway, watching the adults. She is a little uncomfortable that her daughter has walked in at this particular moment. "Kate," she sighs. "What are you doing out of bed?"

"Mommy —" She comes up to them, smiling out the corners of her mouth, eyes downcast.

Maggie keeps her face stern. "Kate, you know the rules." Bedtime arguments are always the most infuriating to deal with: it is now nine o'clock and she needs some time to herself, while they must get to sleep or be tired tomorrow for school.

Her daughter does not answer, but just sends her another imploring look, and Maggie is moved despite her good intentions. She catches her hand and pulls her to sit between them. Kate snuggles her head against Maggie's shoulder. To discipline in such a situation is the most difficult; how she would like to rock Kate to sleep right here, sheltered in her arms as if she were a baby. But that sort of coddling isn't the best idea for her daughter, who at seven, needs to be more self-reliant. Still, how good it feels for them all.

"What's the trouble, sweet Kate?" Nicolas asks, taking Kate's other hand. "You want Uncle Nico to put you back in?"

"I came to tell you Mikey was drinking this," Kate says, looking up at him and handing over a plastic bottle without a cap.

"Where did you get that?" Maggie asks.

"I went to the bathroom and he was in there with this."

Nicolas hands the bottle over to Maggie, who holds it up to the light coming from the streetlamp. "Dimetapp."

"How much was there?" he asks, peering at it in the dark.

"It's empty, and I just bought it yesterday," she says slowly. "He's got a snuffy nose. He loves this stuff, like grape candy."

"Well," Nicolas says, putting his arm around them both. "It's only over-the-counter — it can't do too much damage."

She wants to believe him. In that instant, how she longs to

let it go, sit back and enjoy her coffee. But the question catches
inside her throat like a hiccough. "How did he get the cap off?"
she wonders irrelevantly.

"Is Mikey O.K.?" Kate asks now, worried.

"Sure he is," Maggie answers, forcing calm and a playful
note back into her voice. "I'll go put him to sleep and Uncle
Nico will tuck you in."

Quickly she climbs the stairs; the two of them trail behind
her. In the light from the hallway she reads the bottle's label: *In
case of accidental overdose, call poison center immediately*. Her knees
chatter out of alignment; she concentrates on walking.

In his room, Mikey looks up as she comes in. "Mom! I'm
making a G.I. Joe jungle with my pillows!" He is surrounded by
every action figure he owns as well as all the pillows from
Maggie and Sy's bed.

"Did you drink this?" she demands, holding out the bottle,
hoping he will tell her he poured it down the toilet.

He looks sheepish. "Candy medicine." He laughs, delighted to be caught in such naughtiness. She restrains the urge
to slap him.

"How did you get the cap off?"

He rummages around in his pillows and comes up with the
defeated childproof mechanism: a cap within a cap. His stubby
fingers demonstrate how he simply dismantled the interior
locking mechanism. *Trust your mother, but you cut the cards*, she
thinks, and wonders how she could have been so stupid as to
leave it in his medicine cabinet. All medicines are ordinarily
kept high up, in the shoe box on the top shelf of the (locked)
linen closet.

She paces back and forth for a minute. A new idea strikes
her. She comes quickly to check his sheets. "Mikey, did any of
it spill?"

He just looks at her, mischievous as a chipmunk with a
winter kill of acorns.

She races into the bathroom, hoping for a large purple
splash on the floor. There is none. Reflexively, she reaches
down to flush the toilet, because Kate always forgets. Then she
pushes shut the medicine-chest door and stands for a minute,
looking at herself in the mirror. "I'm going to have to call," she
says to her reflection. She picks up the bottle again, remem-

bering it is important to take it with her to the phone, though she can't recall why.

She hurries back into the hall and dials from the extension in the master bedroom. Sy has taped the number for the poison center (along with police, fire, and pediatrician) to the underside of the handset. Two rings.

"Poison center." A man's voice. Clear and calm.

"My little boy drank a bottle of Dimetapp cold syrup and I need advice," she says. To her surprise, her voice is as composed as if she's giving an order to Gristedes for eggs and milk.

"Name and phone number?"

She recites both slowly.

"Let's confirm what he took. Get the bottle and bring it to the phone so you can read me the label."

"I have the bottle with me here," she says, feeling a beat of competence over her fear. She reads the ingredients off slowly, and hears him type them into the computer. In the other room she hears Nicolas asking Mikey questions about his jungle. A wash of gratitude for his presence spreads through the fear.

"He's forty-four pounds, five years old," she volunteers. Behind her she feels Nicolas come into the room. He does not try to touch her or take her hand. He just sits on the edge of the bed. He seems to know that she cannot deal with more than the phone.

The computer keys clack. A minute more. An eternity. "That's a hefty overdose. You must make the child vomit."

"Oh, God." As prepared as she is, she is not prepared enough.

"Do you have any ipecac in the house?" He leaves her no time for feeling — just one step after another, all quickly set out.

"Yes," Maggie confirms. Sy insisted, back when the children were still babies, that they must always have ipecac on hand.

"How long ago did he ingest the Dimetapp?"

She forces herself to calculate. She put Mikey to bed at eight. "What time is it, Nico?" she asks.

He looks at his watch. "It's nine-fifteen. He probably took it sometime in the last hour."

"An hour — five minutes ago — we're not sure."

"It might be better to take him to the E.R. and have him lavaged. If he falls asleep before you get him to vomit, you'll be in trouble. Let your husband go check how he looks now."

"Looks?"

"Sleepy, awake. Are his eyes O.K.? I'll hold," he says. "Hurry."

She hands the phone to Nicolas, who answers more questions while she runs back to Mikey's bedroom. He looks up, quick as a tick. She switches on the light and he blinks in the sudden brightness. How can she know for sure? She begins to sweat. From the top bunk, he watches her curiously. His eyes are clear and he can say her name without yawning. She charges back into the other room and grabs the phone.

"He looks awake."

"Give three tablespoons of the ipecac right now, followed by at least six ounces of water. When he vomits call me back."

"How long will it take?"

"Twenty to twenty-five minutes. Keep him awake, whatever you have to do. If he doesn't vomit in that time, call me back."

Maggie hangs up and runs to the linen closet, where she scrambles through the contents of the box on the top shelf to find the small, brown bottle.

"Are you all right?" Nicolas catches at her arm.

She looks up at him. Nods. He hugs her, hard. "I'm right here with you."

They go back into Mikey's room. Maggie lifts him down from the top bunk, searching for words of explanation. "The medicine you drank will make you sick. We have to get it out of you."

"Get it out how?"

"I have another kind of medicine," she says, showing him the bottle. "This medicine will get it out."

"Will it taste good?"

"Probably not too good," she says, pouring it into the measuring cup.

He lifts the cup to his open mouth tentatively. After one sip he makes a face and breaks off. "Horrible."

She urges him to continue, threatens a spanking when he refuses, and at last it is down. "Water," he begs, gagging.

She gives him a large glass. He drinks it all.

"Can I go to bed now? I'm tired."

"Not yet." Keep him away from that warm soft bed. She pulls him onto her lap and takes a deep breath. "In a little while the new medicine will make you throw up the bad medicine."

"Throw up!" His chin quivers and his eyes fill, instantly, with tears. "I don't want to throw up!"

"I'll be right here," she says, putting her arm around him and hugging him tight. His body trembles. "I won't leave you till it's all over."

"I won't throw up!" he says defiantly. "You'll see." He slides down and heads back toward the safety of his bunk.

"Hey sport," Nicolas says, intercepting him. "How about you show me that baseball glove again."

Mikey starts to giggle. "Mommy's silly," he says, whispering confidentially to Nicolas. "I don't feel like I'm going to throw up."

Maggie checks her watch as the two of them talk, get down the mitt, toss a ball back and forth (a strictly forbidden activity inside the house). Five minutes pass. She goes into the bathroom, turns on the light, gets out a stack of towels, and lifts the lid on the toilet seat. When she comes back into the room, Mikey is swaying in front of Nicolas. He giggles. "Mommy's *so* silly. I feel fine."

Maggie and Nicolas exchange glances. His speech is slurred and his balance off. As if to confirm their worries he sits, suddenly and with a thud, on the carpet. "He's just drunk," Nicolas whispers to Maggie. "That stuff's got a shitload of booze in it."

"I feel funny," Mikey says, peering up at the two of them owlishly. "I wanna go to bed."

"Let's read," Maggie suggests.

"Sleepy," Mikey says. "Go to bed."

He starts to crawl toward the ladder at the foot of the bed.

Nicolas catches his foot, and, quickly stripping the slipper off, tickles him. Mikey starts to laugh, ascending and descending crescendos of pleasure. "How long's it been?" Nicolas asks after a minute, giving Mikey a chance to recover from the tickling.

"Fifteen."

"Pretty soon. Do you want to call Sy?"

It had never occurred to her. "I can't leave him now."

"Do you want me to try and track him down?"

"*You* can't leave *me* now!" she says, trying to make the truth sound like a joke. She scrambles to her feet. No longer being actively stimulated, Mikey is already nodding off. "Come on," she says, hauling him to his feet like an old drunk. "Let's go for a walk."

For the next ten minutes, with Nicolas on one side and Maggie on the other, they walk him from bedroom to hall and back again. They drag him. Pinch him. Tickle him. Maggie feels desperate. Twenty minutes have passed and he is now fighting to stay awake. They drag him in bigger and bigger circles, exchanging worried glances over his head, until he is nearly drowsing in their arms, swaying heavy-headed like a tulip in the wind.

Suddenly, with no warning, he clutches his stomach. "Sick," he mumbles.

Maggie holds him over the toilet. The room fills with the purple stench of grape and sugar. She flushes and flushes and wipes his head with a cool towel. Nicolas drags the extension phone to where she sits on the cold tiles of the bathroom floor, Mikey limp on her lap, and dials the poison center for her. She reports that he has vomited three times.

"He won't be finished for a while yet. After he vomits the last time, keep him awake another hour."

"Another hour?" she cries with distress, "he's practically asleep in between rounds right now."

"Well, a half hour," he amends. "We've got to be sure."

She dials the pediatrician. Service asks her to hold. "It's an emergency," she protests.

"I've got another doctor on the line," the woman informs her. Click.

Dr. Nelson, who calls back in five minutes, confirms that the poison center has given her appropriate instructions. "In half an hour, let him sleep it off," he advises. "Call again if you need me."

With the tension lessening, Maggie begins to shake. Mikey keeps retching, though there is nothing in his stomach left to vomit, horrible dry heaves, his stomach wringing itself inside out: a terrible thing to watch. Made more so by the knowledge that she could have prevented it all.

"It hurts," he cries, with tears running down his face, over the edge of his chin.

She shakes him to keep him awake.

"I *hate* you." His eyes are pinched into little slits. "You're so mean," he says. "You made me throw up." She wants to cry for him. She wants to make it better and put him to bed. She pinches him awake.

Time bounces off the white glazed tiles of the bathroom, moving neither backward nor forward. At midnight Nicolas carries him to the bottom bunk. The crisis past, Maggie is still too frightened to leave her son. She sits on the floor and leans her head against Mikey's bed, finally allowing herself the luxury of tears.

Nicolas puts his arm around her and rocks her slowly, back and forth. "You were fantastic," he says. He kisses her cheek, strokes her hair.

"It was my fault. I left it where he could get it."

"Don't be so hard on yourself."

"I can't just forget it."

"No," he agrees. "But now you'll know. And *he'll* know — how many times have you told him that stuff is off limits?"

"A lot," she admits. "Still . . ."

"There's no better lesson than the one he just got. And you *did* handle it. That's the point."

"What would I have done if you hadn't been here?" Her gratitude, her love for him, has never been more intense. "I felt so alone."

"Just what you did do," he says, with a smile. "Just what you always do."

There is a new bond between them. For an instant she has the fantasy that Mikey is *their* child. She looks at her watch. Nearly one. For the first time, she wonders about her husband.

"Where the hell is Sy?" Nicolas asks, echoing the thought. "That dinner must've been over hours ago."

"He's an adult," she answers (meaning she is too tired to worry about someone else). "He must have gone for drinks after."

"If he'd come home at a reasonable hour, he'd have been here," Nicolas says.

Maggie does not reply. Just reaches up to put her hand on Mikey's back, to feel that feather-light up and down, angel breath.

She and Nicolas fall asleep that way, camped on the floor at the edge of Mikey's bed with their hands linked.

Sometime later, Maggie wakes to the slam of the front door. She gropes for her watch to see the time.

"Two," she murmurs, and rubs her eyes. Nicolas is still asleep, sitting up with his back against the bed. She pulls the quilt from the top bunk and covers him. From downstairs she hears a thud and a curse.

"So damn dark!" Sy's frustration travels upward.

In the hall, Maggie finds her husband sitting on the landing with his back to her, leaning against the banisters and rubbing his shin.

Exhausted, she stares at his back and wonders why he is still sitting there. As she watches, he lists sideways, curls up on the floor, and begins to snore. She can smell the whiskey. Disbelieving, she moves not one step toward him: in all the years they've been together, she's never once seen Sy drunk. (For all she knows, he's never in his life been drunk.)

Staring at him, she nudges him with her foot. He doesn't stir. His tie is missing, there's a stain down the front of his shirt. This hardly looks like the remains of a business dinner. *What the hell has he been doing?* she wonders. Suddenly she doesn't care. It sweeps over her then: while she's been here dealing with yet another crisis he's been out carousing.

I'd like to give him a quick shove down, she thinks, pivoting away and leaving him there. Going back to check on Mikey, she discovers Nicolas, in the bottom bunk with her son, the two of them jammed up tight together. She watches them sleep for a moment and then pulls the covers up.

In her own room, she strips the bedspread off and lets it fall to the floor. She slides in between the sheets and then, despite her exhaustion, finds her mind will not allow sleep. Instead, the image of her husband (crumpled) on the landing of the staircase floats past her closed eyes, followed quickly by that of

Nicolas, curled in tenderness around her son. Her stomach begins to churn with the feeling of having overeaten, of being bloated with something disagreeable. She tosses back and forth on the mattress, but there is no relief from the nausea. Bile rises into her mouth and she runs to the toilet.

She grips the bowl and her stomach lifts and twists violently once, twice, three times. Around her the darkness shifts. She vomits up her anger and it stains the porcelain as it has stained the muscle of her heart. It cannot be flushed away.

✑

"I didn't get the Tokyo job," Sy says the next morning, his head low over his coffee mug.

Maggie stands in the kitchen and stares at him. "You didn't get the job," she repeats with disbelief.

He says nothing.

Nicolas gets up and refills his coffee.

Kate and Mikey thunder down the stairs and out into the front yard to wait for their mother to take them to school. The kitchen reverberates, first with their passage and then with silence.

"But you were positive you'd get it," she says, dumbfounded by the thought that Sy has been rejected. "What happened?" (Several feelings fight for dominance now: joy that a move is no longer to be required, fear over what such a setback will mean to his future with the firm, and finally, distress for her husband's injured pride.)

"I don't know." He runs his hand through his already-rumpled hair. "I only know what Maxine told me, which is that the decision was political." He looks over at Nicolas, whose face is devoid of expression. "I guess I got a little upset," he admits, tapping his spoon against the china mug. "I was pissed off."

"So you hit a bar," Nicolas continues for him.

"Or it hit me," Sy says, trying for a grin. "I'm not sure which."

Nicolas puts his coffee mug down on the table with a click and stands, unamused. "I don't understand you at all anymore," he says, anger infiltrating his tone at last.

"What are you talking about?" Sy asks, his smile dropping away.

"You're so wrapped up in yourself." He crosses to the sink

and puts his mug under the faucet. "But we've had this deaf-ears discussion before. Maggie —" He walks over to where she stands by the stove, arms wrapped around herself, and kisses her on the cheek. They hug.

"Thanks," she whispers. "I couldn't have —"

"Shhh." He stops her by putting his finger against her mouth. "Just shh."

She smiles at him and nods. From the other side of the table, Sy watches this interchange with bewilderment. (Something is going on here and he doesn't like the fact that he's not in on it.)

The minute Nicolas is out the door, Sy turns to her. "What was all that about?"

She just looks at him over the rim of her mug.

"Did I miss something? Did he get drunk again and have to spend the night?"

She turns to put the breakfast dishes into the dishwasher. Silverware clatters under her hand. "Don't project," she says, sticking a plate in: china grates against china. "He stayed because I needed him to."

"What are you talking about?" He is exasperated now.

"I'm talking about *your* son." Her voice underlines the word sarcastically. "Who drank an overdose of cough medicine last night and could have died."

"Cough medicine?" His voice glitters with fear.

"A whole bottle of Dimetapp. I had to call the poison center and give him ipecac." Her voice is vengeful. (The anger inside her lifts off.) "Nicolas helped me."

"How did Mikey get at the Dimetapp?"

"It was in the medicine cabinet." She turns now and begins to scrub the bacon pan. Water slops up and over, onto the front of her shirt and jeans.

"You left it where he could reach it?"

"It had a childproof cap on it." The skillet bangs against the tap as she turns it in the rinse water.

"You know how smart he is — you can't be careless about leaving stuff like that around."

With the water still splashing up and over the lip of the sink, she freezes; the word "careless," spoken so quietly by her husband, screams inside her head.

"At least we know the kid's got first-class parents," she says with bitterness, "one careless — the other nonexistent."

"Knock it off," he answers angrily. "That kind of talk isn't productive."

"Productive!" She turns on him. "Don't make this sound like one of your deals, some piece of strategy. Don't try to get around the facts!"

"And just what are the facts, Maggie?" he asks, patiently, wearily, refusing to get angry, leaving all the heat to her.

"The facts are that while you were off being self-indulgent and getting drunk, I was here fighting another fire!"

"The fact is that *you* left the cough medicine out. And I wasn't being *self-indulgent*. I was upset. Not that my feelings matter here!"

"You want it like that? O.K., fine." Dropping the pan in the sink, she turns the tap off with a sharp twist. She picks up a juice glass to put it in the dishwasher and almost pitches it at him. Barely in control, she sets it back in the sink and stalks from the room.

Sy follows her, close behind.

"Leave me alone!" she cries, running up the stairs.

"What's the matter with you? What's going on?"

"Go away!" She slams the door behind her.

He looks at his watch. Leaning his head against the wooden panels of the door, he knocks. "Maggie," he entreats, "come on out. It's time to take me to the train and the kids to school."

The door opens so suddenly under him that he falls inward. Maggie sprints past him, keys in hand.

"Where are you going now?" he shouts.

"Out," she shouts back.

"Out where?" he yells after her now, confused.

"Somewhere. Anywhere."

"But what about the kids?"

"You've got a Harvard degree — you figure it out!" A wave of laughter breaks through her as she slams the front door and runs across the lawn.

∼

She doesn't trust herself to drive. She just walks. At first with an open stride that steams out some of the anger, then slower, until her pace subsides into a tired stroll. How she wishes Jan were home. How she needs to talk with someone. Two hours later, thirst drives her home. It is a very warm September day, and overhead, the sun shines through leaves beginning to color. Sweat circles the armpits of her shirt by the time she walks back up her driveway.

In the house, she drinks two large glasses of water before she notices the note Sy has left on the table for her: "Took kids to school, taxi to station."

She sits down, suddenly ashamed of herself. Were the children upset this morning to discover her gone without warning? she wonders. The way in which she handled the argument with Sy now seems childish — nearly a tantrum. She wishes she could rewind the incident like tape on the VCR, and do it over differently.

She begins to fix herself some lunch. The phone interrupts. It is Dr. Lewison's office, calling to book the hospital reservation and the operating-room time slot for Kate's operation in two weeks. After Maggie hangs up, she puts her salad back into the refrigerator and sits down for a minute, overwhelmed.

Without bothering to discuss it with Sy, she has already decided to postpone her search for work until Kate has recuperated from the surgery and is back at school. The delay in her job hunt is not ideal, but Maggie refuses to be distracted by herself while her daughter needs attention. At least this is the rationalization she uses to push away the suspicion that she is actually using Kate's operation as a good excuse to procrastinate. Though she knows the risks of this particular operation are rather small, she is nevertheless afraid for her daughter. Some doctors do not even require an overnight hospitalization, but Maggie and Sy have chosen an extremely conservative surgeon — and they take comfort in this choice, even if it means Kate must be admitted to the pediatric ward overnight, and Maggie as well. As Maggie sits at the table on this fine September day, a new image enters her mind: the memory of her own general anesthesia, when she was eight years old, for a tonsillectomy. Alone in the operating room. The stink of the ether as it dripped down onto the wire-mesh mask; the frightening spin — faster and faster, as she was sucked down into the vortex of the world's biggest drainpipe: unconsciousness. (Separation. Death.)

She pushes herself away from both the memory and the

table to go outdoors to the toolshed, where she slides her feet into her mud-covered clogs. With basket, trowel, and pruning shears as weapons, she heads toward the annual garden she started this spring in the backyard.

Down on her knees in the dirt, she is glad that weeds have run wild while they were in Maine, that grass has encroached up and over the neat stone border, that flowers have bloomed and then dried on the stalks. She will rake and deadhead and prune until her heart is still again, until the only hunger she can feel is one soothed by food.

The sun beats on her back and she takes a barrette from her pocket, twists her hair up in a messy knot (anything to get it off her neck). Jamming on an old canvas hat to protect her skin, she sets to, pulling out everything that does not belong, using her hands as a rake through the moist loam. Dirt builds in a crust beneath her fingernails. The smell of earth baking and green stems snapped fills her nose; beat by beat, the anxiety does recede; this work is a tide that bathes the dangerous shoals of her heart.

The sun moves overhead. Her hands reach with care through the green leaves, creating order and symmetry. Her knees ache. The back of her thighs ache. Her shoulders. The glow of labor fills her.

Nicolas stands on the far side of the yard, watching her work. She does not know he is there. There is something erotic about her position, down on her hands and knees, her ass round beneath blue jeans worn threadbare and soft, her feet naked where they have come free of the clogs that lie tipped on the grass. He moves across the yard stealthily, wanting (for a reason he does not understand) to surprise her.

He reaches her before she turns around. Unnoticed, he stands silently above her: the shirt clings to her back, and through it he sees the bones of her scapula rise and fall as she digs; he smells the damp, black loam, freshly turned, and the salt of her sweat. Aroused, he drops to his knees in the grass behind her, puts his hands over her eyes.

Frightened, Maggie struggles back against him, against his arms and chest, then with a sharp twist manages to see who holds her. With a laugh of relief, she relaxes against him. "You scared me!" she scolds.

He grins. "I know." He does not let her go.

Her ear is pressed to his chest and she can hear the lopsided thuds his heart makes. Smell him. His chest is hard beneath her cheek.

He lets go of her and she rocks forward. Away. "What are you doing here in the middle of the day?" she asks, turning to sit down crosslegged on the edge of the lawn.

He shrugs. "Had to take lunch sometime. I was over at the White Plains outlet and I wanted to make sure you were O.K."

She is silent.

"You didn't look too happy when I left this morning."

She pulls her hat off and undoes her hair, which floats out around her face in a damp cloud. "We had a big fight after you left. He started blaming me for last night and I —"

"*He* blamed *you!*" Incredulous, furious, he sinks back on his heels.

She nods and shrugs. "If I hadn't left the Dimetapp out . . ."

"Right." His mouth is a tight line. "And if he'd been here — if he'd been home at a normal time, what then?"

"Ah, Nico, I don't know." She brushes, ineffectually, at the dirt on her knees, ground deep into the fabric of the denim. "I'm not sure I even care anymore. I'm so damned tired of fighting it all." She stares at the black crescent of dirt beneath her thumbnail.

"I know," he says, comfortingly. He reaches over and brushes the hair away from her face, back off her brow. (It is the same motion she has used many times with her own children. Comfort.) He takes her hand, and turns it upward. She watches him study her palm, then looks down at it herself. Dirt colors her skin in the creases; the calluses across the top are faintly yellow. Embarrassed, she closes her fist reflexively.

He looks up at her, and smiles. "Silly." One by one, he unfolds her fingers. Her palm is exposed again, stained and rough. Slowly he brings it up to his mouth. He kisses the center, with tenderness, as if it were hurt.

Maggie gasps as his tongue, warm and wet, licks her palm, licks the crevices between her fingers. He sucks at the pad of her fingertips, a soft pulse of lips and teeth and tongue. Her nipples harden against the soft cloth of her shirt. She watches him; she watches her body pull toward him. In response, her mouth opens slightly, the tip of her tongue slides out over the edge of her lip.

He looks up at her. Stops. Sets her hand back down into her lap.

She turns her hand over, tucks it away under her arm. Clears her throat. "Why did you do that?" she asks after a minute.

"Which? Stop or start?"

His eyes are deep gold, she feels as if she is falling. She does not wipe the moisture from her palm. She curls her fist around it, slips her fingers across the wet. She cannot answer him. He is teasing her and the tease burns — to think it was all some sort of joke.

"I wanted to taste you," he says then.

She blushes. This is not a joke. The air between them is static. She wants to look away from him, but instead is paralyzed, as if watching the arabesque of a snake: danger, symmetry, beauty.

She stands up, brushing her knees off. Her heart pounds, but not from anxiety this time, from something she cannot (will not) name. She moves before he can touch her again; gathering up her pruning shears and trowel, she walks, barefooted, back toward the toolshed, confusion swarming through her mind.

"Are you going to have lunch?" he asks, following her.

"I already did," she lies. "I've got some errands to do before I pick up the kids."

He nods. "I should get back, I guess."

He expects her to offer him something to eat, but right now she needs to be alone. To sit in some quiet place and calm herself. She smiles, but does not look at him. She can't.

"Is Sy coming home tonight?" he asks.

She nods. "At least he says so. Family dinner," she goes on brightly. "I've got to get down to the supermarket."

"Right." He smiles. He moves to kiss her good-bye and she turns her face so that his lips brush her cheek, not her mouth.

"See you," he says then. Watching him walk away, around the side of the house into the front yard, she sinks into a lawn chair and drops her face forward in her hands. The wet from his mouth is still there; it comes up against her lips and before she can stop herself she licks his spit off her skin. After a minute (horrified), she straightens up and banishes the memory of the instant. *You're being silly*, she tells herself.

The feeling that something is missing comes over her, as if she has left an object behind. She checks for her rings, her watch, pats her pockets. All is intact. The hair clip is back in her pocket, though she cannot remember putting it there. Still, the sensation of loss nags at her. She looks up to the other side of the yard: her clogs are tipped on their side by the edge of the garden. She gets up to retrieve them, walking slowly over the cool, damp green in her bare feet. *Dirty feet*, she thinks. *I'll have to wash.*

✑

But she does not. Instead, she spends the afternoon making blueberry pie, Sy's favorite dessert (expiation). When he comes home, at an unusual seven o'clock, they all sit down to eat together. After the children are in bed — he having given them their baths and read the nighttime stories while Maggie sat on the porch — she tells him about the call from Dr. Lewison's office. And then, without meaning to (or understanding why), she begins to cry.

He puts his arm around her and strokes her hair. After a while, she stops crying. They do not speak. They do not discuss how he feels about Tokyo. They do not discuss their fight this morning. They just sit, in a state of emotional ruin. After a time, they go up to bed.

As they undress, she turns to him. "You will write the date of the operation down on your calendar?" she asks, naked now.

"First thing in the morning," he promises.

She goes into the bathroom for a shower. Under the scour of hot water, she washes off all the dirt from the garden, which is ground like powder into the pores of her skin. She soaps three times. A final cold rinse. Then she towels off. The night is sticky and humid and in spite of the rinse, it is hard to get dry. Still damp behind the knees and between her thighs, she comes back into the bedroom.

He looks up as she stands in the doorway naked, toweling herself.

Feeling his eyes on her, she crosses to her dresser and reaches into the drawer for a nightgown.

"Don't," he says, getting up to come over. He puts his hand on her arm. The front of his pajamas tents around his erection. "Don't?"

"Wear that. Come to bed like you are." He smiles at her. Fatigue has worn a crease between his eyes. She feels exhausted, but knows he wants them to make up by making love; she cannot say no to him tonight.

She lays herself down on top of the covers. The sheet is cool and slick against her back. Her toes point toward the ceiling. Her thighs seem impossibly heavy and thick. Her body feels like a layer of sludge at the bottom of a lake.

He lies beside her. Tentatively, he touches her: she is a white wall he is afraid to mark. His hand strokes her belly, makes a quick circle up to her breast. Over his shoulder, she looks at the mullions of the window, which are backlit by the halo of the street lamp and outlined against the shade in eight rectangles. She can feel his thumb and forefinger circle her nipple. She concentrates: now she should feel something. Anything. Against her leg she feels his penis, hard and impatient. Already ready.

He bends to kiss her. She closes her eyes. His tongue in her mouth, her tongue in his mouth: it reminds her of the games they played as children. Taking turns. By the rules. With her hands she urges him on top of her. "You're not ready," he whispers. "Wait." He slides down the length of her, uses his mouth and tongue to get her excited. This is hard to resist. After a few minutes he surfaces, leaving her just as she is getting close. Now she is wet but still tight. Not quite ready. When he enters her he hurts. "I want to make you come," he says, his face a white moon above, glistening. She smiles. Moves with him. Two minutes later, she pretends.

He hears what he wants to hear. Free at last from worry about her, he concentrates on his own sensation. A minute later, he bends his locked elbows and his weight drops down. He groans. Whimpers. She puts her arms around him and hugs him hard.

They lie in the dark without speaking. She can feel him going to sleep on top of her. Though he is not a large man, she will suffocate if she has to lie under him much longer. She shakes him, makes him roll off. Shifting to her side of the bed she lies awake, staring into the dark. Sadness engulfs her. She touches herself, down where she is still wet from his mouth. Her finger brings back the heat he began and then left. She closes her eyes; over the slippery bud, her finger slides up and down. Her breasts swell. The picture paints itself against the dark: he kisses her hand in the garden, he licks her fingers, they lie in the dirt, he opens her, petal by petal. Silently, without even a shudder, she comes. Sy sleeps on beside her. She opens her eyes. All that remains of her fantasy is the sharp angle of her own hand between her legs.

⟡ TEN

Rumors

She rings the bell again.

Jon opens the door. "A little impatient tonight?" He grins at Alexis. In his hands is a white carton of Chinese takeout with the fork still in it.

"No jokes, please," she answers, pushing past him to throw her jacket over the back of the couch and drop her briefcase onto the floor.

"I just got in a half hour ago," he says, coming over to give her a hug. He yawns. "Want some?" He jiggles the paper carton.

She shakes her head. "Not hungry."

"Almost midnight and you're not hungry?" he asks, surprised. "Did you already eat?"

"I'm just not hungry."

"You're upset," he says, looking at her more carefully now.

"Upset would be putting it mildly," she says with bitterness.

He disappears into the kitchen for a minute, then reappears with a tray bearing a bottle of scotch, two glasses, and three more Chinese-food containers. Nudging her with the tray, he shoos her down the hall into the bedroom, where he sets it amid unmade sheets. She unbuttons her blouse, while he hangs up her skirt and his pants. Naked, they slide beneath the comforter.

He pours them both a drink, leans on the pillow, and waits for her to talk.

"How was your day?" she asks at last.

He just looks at her, still waiting.

"O.K.," she sighs, his persistence winning out after a minute. "I heard a rumor."

He sips his scotch.

"Except I don't think it's just a rumor." She takes a long swallow from her glass. "I think it's a leak. From Zuckerwise's office." Another long swallow. She swishes the ice cubes around the glass with a finger. "Supposedly, Hewett will go public after the first of the year. Off year-end numbers."

Jon rests his glass on his chest. The cold makes him wince and he moves it. "I heard it too."

She looks up quickly. "From who?"

"Herm Thomas over at the *Journal*." He sighs. "And the guy's always reliable."

"I don't think it's just scuttlebutt," she says angrily. "I think it's going to happen."

He nods. "Agreed. At the least — it's likely."

"Where the hell does that leave me?" she asks rhetorically. "And all the rest of us who haven't made M.D. yet?"

"On the outside."

"Shit!" Hearing him say it makes her even angrier.

"On the other hand," he says, casually, "for those who make partner *this December*, it'll be incredible. Each share they give you in the partnership package will be worth a fortune a few months later."

"This December," she scoffs. "What are the odds of that?"

"Maybe the odds are what you make them."

She leans back against the headboard and drinks again. The alcohol has relaxed her some. "I'm doing well," she concedes after a while. "I know they'll promote me next year, if I don't fuck up. But if we are going public, everyone who's up for M.D. next year will be mad as a hornet. There'll be a lot of pressure. They're not about to open themselves up by promoting one person early. *Especially* not a woman."

"Also agreed." He turns on his side to face her. "But if that woman's so valuable they're afraid to lose her — that's something altogether different. Remember that people will *leave* if the rumor's confirmed. Everyone knows that making partner after Hewett goes public is worth jackshit." He thinks. "Suppose you make yourself too valuable — and then give them an ultimatum."

She sits up, shoves the comforter back and pulls the tray of food toward her. "What've you got?" she asks, poking through the containers. Just talking to Jon makes her feel better: his intuitive grasp of the politics makes her feel less stymied.

"All spicy — chicken, pork, shrimp. And cold noodle."

"Yum." She picks up a container and, settling in crosslegged, starts to eat from it.

He takes the container of sesame noodle and balances it on his chest.

"You might be right," she says around a mouthful. "And they know I can get a job anywhere — even Morgan or Goldman. Still, you'd have to be mega-valuable for them to do early promotion in this kind of climate."

"Are you?" he asks, around a trailing bite of noodle.

"Maybe." She takes another bite and chews a minute more, licking brown sauce off her fingers. "But great deals don't grow on trees. Switch," she says, extending her container. They do, and eat for a while longer in silence.

"But, if I *was* able to bring in one more big one, *before* they vote," she muses, "I might swing it. There's still a month or two before the decisions get made."

"I'm working on a great one myself," he says casually, spearing a shrimp. It slips from his fork midway to his mouth; she picks it up off his chest with her fingers and eats it herself. Playfully she bends down to lick the spot clean. It warms her that he waits with his news until her depression has lifted a little.

"What kind of great?" She sits back and looks up at him with interest. This is one of the best things about the relationship between them: they both *want* to hear about the other's work. Naturally, there is a certain amount that must go unsaid (firm privacy and ethics); nevertheless, they get around this by speaking in the abstract, talking of situations (disguised). Intuiting the delicacy of the position, they never even mention it when they see the results of the other's work in the news. It is an unspoken pact that frees them to share.

"I'll be writing the report next week." He chews for a minute. "Great takeover opportunity."

She just keeps eating. The cold noodles twirl out of the box and down her chin as she takes too big a bite.

"What if you don't make M.D. this year," he says then, shoving the box of shrimp back onto the tray with a groan and rubbing his stomach. "Will you leave?"

"I don't know," she says, depressed again at the thought. She can't imagine herself somewhere else. (For nine years now she has envisioned herself at the top of Hewett Lowell M&A — not just any firm, but Hewett, the top.) "If only Hewett promoted in eight years, like Morgan."

Jon shrugs. "You knew it was a ten- or eleven-year track from the start."

"Sure, but having them go public just before I make M.D. wasn't exactly part of my game plan."

"Well, ask yourself this —" He takes another bite. "Could you be happy someplace else?"

"Maybe." She shrugs. "I suppose I've got some skewed sense of loyalty."

He nods.

"I guess I'd have to leave, though," she says, her voice following the thought through to its logical conclusion. "I mean, who wants to be partner in name but not in stock?"

"There are never any guarantees — no matter where you are." He puts his arms up behind his head and stares at the ceiling.

"Most of these guys have been waiting for me to take off and have a baby." She snorts. "When I got separated from Nicolas, they were crushed."

"Don't you ever think about that?"

"Babies?" She looks at him, surprised, and puts her carton down on the tray. "It doesn't seem to have much to do with who I am right now, that's all. Maybe it will later."

"How old are you, anyway?"

"You mean you still haven't guessed?" Her age is one of the secrets she's been keeping from him (not out of pride, but simply to tantalize). He is so secretive about himself that she refuses to be totally open. "Want to count my growth rings?" she jokes, with a suggestive smile.

"Seriously, Alexis."

"Seriously?" She looks at him, considers the question. Then for no reason she can fathom, she answers. "Thirty-six."

"Have to make up your mind pretty soon."

"You can have babies past forty, you know." She shrugs. "What about you?"

"I wasn't planning on being a mother in the near future," he says, starting to laugh.

"Very funny. I meant" — she reaches over to pick at the noodles again — "do you want kids someday?"

"You look cute with sesame paste on your face," he says, bending over to lick it off her cheek.

"Cut it out!" She shoves his shoulder. "I'm serious. *Do* you?"

He shrugs. "Not really. Family doesn't have good associations for me."

"Why not?"

"It just doesn't."

"Why not?"

He shrugs again.

It's clear to her now that she is pushing him. Still, she doesn't want to stop. She wants to know everything about him. "Why not?"

He sighs. "It just feels too close for me, that's all."

"You never talk about your parents. I still don't know anything about how you grew up."

He pushes the blanket back and goes over to his dresser. "That's because it's not very interesting," he says, opening his wallet and pulling out a stack of receipts.

"It is to me."

"I don't like talking about it." He shuffles the stack of Amex carbons.

"What's to hide?" she asks, teasing him now. "A nice California family, a prep school, then Cal Tech?"

"When there's nothing worth remembering it's better to forget." He puts the receipts down on the bureau. His back is straight and stiff. In the mirror she can see his face, as he studies his hands. "I grew up in a two-family house where we rented the top floor. My prep school gave me free tuition because my father was the custodian. I got teased year after year about being the janitor's kid." His voice is low: he releases the words quickly, as if it hurts to hold them in his mouth. "Scholarships to both college and B-school. I'd like to forget it all."

She sits cross-legged and wordless on the bed. She hadn't even suspected. He'd done an incredible job of buffing himself up, of watching everything he wanted to be and then absorbing it all. To rise past his past. No wonder he didn't want to introduce her to his parents, as she had suggested one week in August when they both wound up in L.A. on business.

"It doesn't matter to me, you know," she says at last.

"How can it not matter?" He is still standing with his back to her, leaning on the dresser.

"It just doesn't. It will matter to my mother — but not to me." She laughs and he turns back to her. "I like gutsy people. Nicolas was gutsy in the beginning. Making his own way. Maybe I really liked your rough edges all along and just didn't recognize them for what they were."

"What rough edges?" He looks up.

She shakes her head, laughing, and holds out her arms. "Come here."

Slowly he walks back to the bed. He lies down beside her and, leaning on her elbow, she feeds him another shrimp with her fingers. He licks off the brown sauce. "You're going to smell like fish," he sulks.

"I thought women did anyway."

They start to laugh. "I love you," she says, looking down at him.

He stares at her. Several seconds float by. She realizes it's the first time either of them has used the word "love." With all they have talked about, all the intimacy they have shared, they haven't dared to wield this one emotion-laden word. Now that it is out and floating in the air (*Pandora's box*, she thinks), it seems dangerous. The moment extends and her throat grows tight. She waits for him to say something. (She wishes she could take it back.)

But then he reaches up to her. "It's mutual," he says, and she sinks off her elbow down into his arms.

She loves that they fit together in this way, too: the way his chest meets her breasts, the way his ear fits into the hollow of her collarbone when he rests his head on her. How can it be that she never even knew that place was a part of her body?

After they cuddle for a while (this is how they always begin now, very slowly, with a lot of touching, almost as if the sex that inevitably follows is not at all the point) they begin to stroke each other. She sits beside him and runs her hands up and down his body. He lies very still and she uses her finger-nails like tiny combs, through the hair on his chest, over his nipples lightly, then teasing down over his belly, around his penis (but not touching, not yet) and deep between his legs. He sighs and stretches out under her. He relaxes into the idea that she can do whatever she likes. Then she stops. He opens his eyes.

She moves astride him, and bending forward, flips her hair forward across his face. She uses it like a fan of feathers, swing-ing the silk of it back and forth across his body. As the strands brush against his penis, he groans and arches up against her. She is sitting on his knees. Her hands again, a tickle of fire up and around his cock and when she knows he can't wait any-more, she puts her face down next to him, rubs her cheek against him, takes him into her mouth.

Alexis refuses to surface, when, a minute later, he starts to tug on her hair, signaling her to move up to his lips. He is trying not to come, and if she persists much longer it will be too late. But she ignores the pressure of his hand: there is too much pleasure in the sweet motion of her mouth. She wants to drink him. The muscles in his thighs are growing rigid beneath her palms, his body vibrates now in little spasms. He is losing control. She caresses him with her fingernails just under his balls and the loose sack tightens, crinkles upward and hugs his body. With a cry, he shoves himself against the back of her mouth; three quick jerks and the brine spurts over her tongue like mother's milk. *Oysters*, she thinks, and remembers their first meal together.

She is wet. She is leaving smudges on the sheets. Luckily, he is still hard. Before he softens, she slides her mouth off and her cunt on, groaning with pleasure as he spreads her open. Balancing over him, she moves up and down, her breasts dangling above him. His eyes are still closed. She keeps hers open. Her heat builds up around him, and she moves faster, rubbing herself against the ledge of his pubic bone; his penis pushes into a buried spot high inside; the expansion and contraction begins, as if this pink muted mouth inside of her is nothing more than a bellows designed to kindle fire. Sitting up straight, she can see herself in the mirror as in a painting: wailing woman at the horizon. The cusp of earth and heaven. She reaches for the sky but instead grabs her breasts. Their round shape in her hands brings her back to herself.

For a minute more she moves against him in some instinctive, animal motion programmed by the neurons of her body, then slows, then at last folds herself down to blanket him with her body. She molds herself to his form. She trembles. He shrinks out of her as they lie together.

After a while, she slides off and he cradles her against him. They lie in the dark for a while. As usual, they don't speak. The hair on his chest bristles against the soft shell of her ear. She can hear the regular whoosh of the blood moving through his chest.

"MicroFlight," he says.

She says nothing. She lies there like a sponge. In time, they both sleep.

✧

MicroFlight, Christa repeats, sipping her second cup of coffee. She is reading Jon's latest analyst's report at her desk on the trading floor of First Boston. Despite their differences, Jon has not taken her off his mailing list, but they haven't gotten together — not even for a squash game — in two months now.

It is eight forty-five and the large room of traders and salespeople is still comparatively quiet. Around her hundreds of computer screens hum silently, already warmed up (are they ever turned off?), but there is no screaming back and forth yet, no shouting over the hoot. No neon numbers or letters running over the electronic ticker tapes on the far wall. Her phone console — directly in front of her with three hundred–plus direct-dial buttons to her contacts and clients across the country — is still relatively dark. Behind this are her Quotron and Telerate machines as well as four other video screens of data. Hanging directly above her head are several monitors mounted on swinging arms, which provide other sorts of facts and figures. Against the far wall, the New York Stock Exchange tape will shortly begin to spew out activity from the floor of the exchange — current trades in round lots of one hundred — while the Broad tape will carry the breaking news stories related to the market.

Once the tapes begin to run and the phones light up, everyone gets crazy. (Smile and dial.) But in these early quiet moments, when many are still in morning meeting, Christa grabs the chance to look through her mail, read the paper, trade scuttlebutt. Even though this room is "off the Street" in midtown Manhattan, it is umbilically linked through a vast cable system: the floor here is ramped up fourteen inches above the level of the other offices on the fifteenth floor to accommodate a spider's nest of wiring.

Tilting her chair, she puts her head back and contemplates the ceiling as she thinks about Jon's report. She's not in the least surprised to see he's put his finger on an extraordinary deal. It is Jon's forte to find little-known divisions of large companies whose products can be used for defense purposes, and his opinions are respected enough to guarantee a visible reaction in stock price as a result of his recommendations. Micro-Flight is a partially owned division of Geneco, a petroleum company that's invented a new composite material destined (in Jon's opinion) to become the skin of the Stealth bomber; Jon demonstrates that the division itself is worth far more than the parent company — a great investment, but an excellent takeover opportunity as well. Christa is sure Geneco will be heavily traded in the next few days.

She tosses the report back onto her desk and quickly glances through the rest of her mail. Around her, the beat of the room intensifies. The buzz of voices increases. The bond market seems dead today, but equities will be hot.

A knock on the top of her computer makes her look up: Weldon, with his coffee mug in his hand. "How about dinner?" he asks.

"You're asking about dinner when we aren't even near to lunch?" She moans.

"Tapas, Christa," he wheedles. "I made a reservation at the

Ballroom for seven-thirty. Now — what do you say?" He grins, knowingly.

As his smile predicts, she can resist neither the grin nor the tapas. She nods.

"I wanted to ask you about those Telephone Bo Dereks," he goes on. (Bo Dereks: bonds that mature in 2010.)

"I refuse, absolutely refuse, to talk business at dinner," she warns, waggling her finger at him and realizing (a beat too late) that she has just escalated the evening onto a personal level.

Weldon throws back his head and laughs, a boom that travels across the honeycomb of people. She can't help herself and starts to smile. Perhaps she enjoys Weldon so much because his humor is a near match for her own.

Across the room behind her back, she can see the first quotes come over the NYSE tape.

"You've got yourself a deal," he says with a nod.

Her phone begins to ring. "Gotta hop," she says, swiveling her chair away from him.

"Later."

She reaches for the console, but, before she can answer, the Broad tape activates on the far wall. She glances over: *Trading in MicroFlight suspended. Announcement at 10:00.*

What a coup! Christa thinks, as the room buzzes with speculation. Anytime trading is suspended it generally means a takeover is either in progress or imminent. Those of Jon's clients (all of whom would have been informed of his opinions several days prior to the publication of his report) who bought into Geneco last week will be sky-high.

Her phone lights up again and this time she takes a call from her guy at CREF (College Retirement Equities Fund), who owns some Geneco eleven and a halfs, due 1997, and wants Christa's advice on what to do (trading in the stock may be suspended, but the bond market remains very, very open).

She fields close to thirty-five calls in the next half hour, on a variety of subjects, but her eye is always on the tape. When the announcement unfurls across the screen, it is just what she expected: a hostile tender by General Dynamics for Geneco. She calls CREF back and tells them to hold: if the merger goes through, the bonds will almost certainly be upgraded.

She sits back, and goes over it in her mind one step at a time. While pleased for Jon's success, she also feels an increasing consternation. Gradually the phone begins to annoy her and it becomes more and more difficult to focus on anything. When she snaps at her trading assistant, who comes by with an innocent question, she decides to take a break. She goes to the ladies' room for a while; sitting on the toilet lid, she pulls the *Times* crossword puzzle from her purse and concentrates on filling in the blanks.

Something about the Geneco deal bothers her; as she puts *suspicious* in the ten spaces allotted to the definition "distrustful," she berates herself for being such a poor sport. Is she so bitter about the loss of Jon that she would begrudge him success in his work? Even as she chastises herself, the unsettled feeling tugs. (Instinct.) When she finishes five words — the maximum allowable for a bathroom break — she goes back to her desk, still troubled.

Sitting in front of her console, she punches up Sy.

"Long time no talk," he says, pleased to hear her voice. The friendship between them has gotten stronger since Nicolas and Alexis split up and since Alexis took up with Jon.

"A pleasant surprise to find you in," she drawls, though she knows from Maggie, who called her last night, that Sy is home this week.

"I'm trying to reform."

"Sure you are. *This* week."

They both laugh, but that laughter is colored with resignation.

"How's every little thing?"

"O.K., I guess."

"That sounds less than promising," Christa answers dryly. "More fallout over Tokyo?"

He sighs. "Actually right now Maggie and I are both pretty wound up over Kate's operation tomorrow. We're all a little strung out."

"Maggie mentioned it, but she sounded strong." Christa shifts in her chair, checking the NYSE tape as she speaks. "It's just one overnight in the hospital, nu?"

"Yes." He sounds a little annoyed, as if she is minimizing it.

"Anything I can do?" she offers quickly.

"Come out for supper and cheer us up with some cat jokes."

"You tell Kate she's got herself a deal. Can you hang on there for one minute, Sy?" She takes two fast calls, then returns. "I apologize," she says quickly, "and before we get interrupted again — do you know who's doing Geneco?"

"Geneco is a Goldman client, of course, and Dynamics is ordinarily us, but this time they went to Hewett. I'll bet it's Alexis's deal. Why?"

"I've got a customer, a nosy one, who wants to know," she says, which isn't an outright lie. (She does, in fact, manage her own bond portfolio, and she really is nosy.)

"Thanks," she says, as her console lights up on three different lines simultaneously. "Back to you on supper." She begins to handle the calls. For the next several hours she works nonstop. She has no time to think about the connection between Jon and Alexis, or the Geneco merger, or Jon's report, or Hewett's involvement.

But at lunchtime (two-thirty), she takes a walk and does not stop to eat. The October day is cool and blue — Manhattan at its best — but Christa paces the blocks, oblivious. An embryo of suspicion has seeded itself inside her. She hypothesizes as she walks: if Alexis hinted (leaked) to Jon that Geneco would be in play shortly and if Jon took that information and advised his clients it was a lay-up, that would be trading on inside information, with prestige — not profit — as the motive and the gain. (Assuming he himself didn't then trade on his own information.)

In early 1986, trading on inside information is done, albeit covertly, somewhat more than most Wall Street people would like to acknowledge and quite a bit more than most outsiders realize. It is a fact of life on the Street that a handful of people ignore SEC regs; such activity is frowned upon but largely glossed over.

In the abstract, Christa has always thought of insider trading as basically stupid. Why would Jon do anything so transparent that he risks being caught? Surely he does not need this to improve his reputation.

You ah' one remarkably judgmental person, Cash reminds her. Christa smiles. *M.Y.O.B.*, Cash reiterates now, and with that advice tucked away under her heart, she stops at a Sabrett's cart for a hot dog covered with sauerkraut and onion, even though she knows the onions will repeat on her all afternoon long.

Back in the office, the phone swamps her. At six o'clock, when the room quiets, Christa punches Jon's button on her console. "Squash," she says, when he answers. "In one hour, and this time I will not accept any mealymouthed excuses."

~~

He meets her on the court at the DAC; they give each other a polite kiss on the cheek. Feeling almost shy, she realizes what a long time it has been since they've seen each other. She makes a joke. He smiles. They warm up.

His timing is off today and he's slow to get to the ball; she squints at him through her safety glasses. What has Alexis been feeding him? she wonders. (An image crowds her: the two of them in bed, naked, spooning caviar into each other's mouths.) She whacks the ball ferociously.

"Easy," he cautions, giving her a look.

Restraining herself, she serves. "Nice call on Geneco," she shouts over the smack of the rubber against the front wall. "Nice."

He returns the ball.

She polishes it off with a boast into the far corner.

"Lucky shot," he says.

"Geneco?" she asks again.

"Right." He laughs. "A real lay-up."

"How long you been chewing on it," she says, casually, as she stoops to retrieve the ball.

"I wasn't sure about their contract with the Feds coming through when I went out to see them last January — so I waited to recommend. I like to make sure none of my clients get blown up." He grins.

She serves again. They play for a while, just rallying. The old rhythms return.

"From the timing of the deal, I wasn't the only one who noticed what a great asset play it was," he goes on, after a while, as they take a quick break between points to towel off. "Daniel Hertzberg's doing a column on it in tomorrow's *Journal*." Jon tosses the ball up and down, catching it in his palm. "He called me this morning."

She settles in to play with something like relief. It sounds clean. Like coincidence. If the *Journal* is doing a story on it and Jon is this relaxed, there can be nothing to hide. Now she begins to concentrate in earnest on the game. She is winning. The anger about Alexis strokes out through her arms and hands and legs.

She takes him five games to three.

By nine, they are sitting in a local bar, their hair still wet from the showers. Their muscles hum from the exercise, stomachs riot. They order Bass ale on tap and chiliburgers. Jon hasn't mentioned Alexis once. Christa thinks of ice cream afterward and then, back at her apartment, doing a puzzle together. Like old times. She hasn't been this happy in months. As she takes her first bite and spicy red beans drip down her chin, Christa looks up in the mirror and laughs at her messy reflection. Which is when she remembers her supper date with Weldon. She has stood him up.

ELEVEN

Ascension, Declension

"Stand up, sweetheart," Maggie says, as she pulls the faded cotton johnny around Kate and ties it. So exposed, her daughter's back looks vulnerable above white cotton underpants.

"This is for *babies*." Kate pouts and plucks at the fabric dotted with bunnies and chicks.

Maggie sighs and sends Sy a look.

"It's just for the operating room, honey. We'll put on your own nightgown as soon as you're back upstairs."

It is now two o'clock on Friday afternoon. Kate's surgery, originally scheduled for eleven-thirty this morning, has been pushed back twice. Sy, enraged, has confronted everyone from the operating-room supervisor to the director of the hospital — only to realize (after three hours of irate ill will) that operating-room slots are dictated by politics. Kate's eye surgery has been bumped by an emergency appendectomy and (unbelievable) a liposuction. Maggie and Sy resign themselves to the wait. But Kate (having gone without food or water since the night before) cannot. By noon she approaches the irrational. By one o'clock the frantic. Hunger, thirst, and tension make her shrill and whiny. Her parents are helpless. There is nothing anyone can do.

At two-thirty, an orderly with a stretcher appears in the door of her private room on the pediatrics floor. "O.R.," he grunts.

Maggie smiles brightly, falsely. "Hop on, Kate," she says. "Let's take a ride."

Kate shrinks against the bed and begins to cry. "I don't want to go."

Sy scoops her up and piggybacks her across the room. He tries to tickle her but she won't be cajoled. Tears bead at the corners of her eyes. Bored, the orderly pulls the sheet up over the nervous child. Maggie and Sy surround the gurney, each holding one of Kate's hands; they roll down the pediatric floor and into the elevator.

In the holding room, patients come and go, either unconscious or silent on their stretchers. Kate continues to cry without sound. The anesthesiologist tries to jolly her into a smile, but she won't look at him and chews on a corner of the sheet. Inside Maggie fear twines. She wraps her arms around herself tightly. The time now speeds by as they endure one more wait, answer a few last questions. Kate's face is a bleached bone beneath the mask of her freckles.

At last the orderly wheels her away. She lies very still. She does not look back at them or call out. Clutching her daughter's glasses, Maggie stands and watches the stretcher move away into the maw of the O.R. She begins to cry.

Sy puts his arms around her, leads her into the waiting room down the hall where she sits without moving on the couch. Time passes. Sy reads work from his briefcase. She just sits, iced by anxiety. He tries to get her to eat or drink but the fear has stretched her body into a strange shape. There is no space for anything more. She knows nothing will go wrong, but she doesn't believe it with her heart. Outside the windows, day slides into autumn's early dusk. Through the branches of a tree, light shifts unreliably.

Later, in the recovery room, Maggie's hands flutter over her daughter where she lies on a stretcher; she counts fingers and toes the way she did once, seven years ago, in the delivery room. Kate's eyelashes are crusted into clumps and there is a thin wash of blood on her cheek. Maggie reaches in between the bars of the stretcher to hold Kate's small hand as the orderly wheels them to the elevator.

Back in the room, they transfer the child to the bed. She rouses briefly, hugs both her parents, and then falls asleep again. The nurse reassures them that she may sleep a long time now. Sy goes to the cafeteria, brings them sandwiches and coffee. Still, Maggie cannot eat.

The room is filled with flowers and balloons: from Sy's firm, from Maxine, from Maggie's parents, from Christa, from Alexis, from Nicolas, from Jan and Jerry. Everyone has sent something for Kate. Maggie takes Kate's watch from her purse and fastens it back on the fragile wrist. They watch the news; they watch Kate sleep.

At eight o'clock the phone on the bedside stand rings. Sy gets up to answer it. From the tone of his voice, Maggie knows instantly that it is the office.

The talk continues for ten minutes. Into Sy's tone has crept a slight, polite resistance. Maggie fights a rising sensation of worry. A premonition.

Sy hangs up, and stares moodily at the phone for a moment before turning around to face her, very slowly. "There's an emergency," he says.

She says nothing, just looks at him. Kate does not stir.

"The damned deal is falling apart in Baltimore."

"So?" She wants him to say this out loud, flat and straight. No mistake. She is not going to help him with a single word.

He sighs. "So I have to go down there. On the earliest plane."

She just stares at him.

He strives for a light tone. "I'll go down first thing and be back in time for dinner."

"Don't they know what's going on here?" The words fly from her mouth. "How can they be so insensitive?"

"They held off calling me earlier. The client wanted me to come today."

"That's supposed to make me feel better?"

"Look," he says, his tone both tired and conciliatory. "I have to go, but it'll only be for the day. You've got to realize that since the news came down about Tokyo, I feel like I'm walking the line. Do you understand?"

She understands one thing: once again he is making a choice that will take him away. "Someone else can't handle it?"

He shakes his head. "Not really. And I don't want to ask."

"And what does 'not really' mean," she asks, incredulous,

wondering if he sees how he creates his own theater of the absurd.

"It means it's not open for discussion or negotiation," he answers, defiant now. "If it were, I would have gotten out of it. You *know* that."

Maggie doesn't answer.

"I've been here *all day*," he says angrily. "She's fine now — Lewison said so."

He's angry because he's defensive, she thinks as she stares at him, as she tries to calm herself so that her voice won't wake Kate. He's defensive because he knows he's wrong. She looks at him and doesn't answer. How can she explain that, to Kate, to spend this weekend with her father may well be the most important part of this traumatic time? How can she explain that if they were really a team her partner would not ask her to trade away one moment for another.

"So go," she says, frozen in defeat but knowing, somehow, that something is different this time.

"I can't go if you're angry."

"You'll go no matter what I feel. So just go." She leans her head back against the chair and closes her eyes. On the bed, Kate shifts in her sleep and moans. They both stop and look. When she doesn't move again, they relax.

"I'm not sure you'll be all right," he says then, shifting from one foot to the other.

She meets his eyes steadily. How tired she is of being viewed as incapable and neurotic: she, who holds the entire equation together. "Why don't you stop deluding yourself?" Her voice is very calm now. "You know perfectly well I'll be all right." She wants to continue: *we will make it without you. Can't you see we already have?* (And that, of course, is what has changed.) But she says only: "You probably should get home to Mikey now. This has been hard on him too and I'm sure Nicolas is ready for a little relief."

"I'll ask Nico if he can spend the night and come over to pick you up tomorrow. Seems like he's not doing much these days except hanging around with us anyway." He shifts his weight from foot to foot. "I'll definitely call a couple times tomorrow from Baltimore. Put the phone in beside Kate's bed."

She nods and leans her head back again. He stoops to kiss

his daughter, softly, on the cheek, and settles Silver in closer under her arm. Then he turns, puts his lips to Maggie's cheek, and squeezes her hand. She closes her eyes. The sound of his footsteps clicks and gradually recedes, as he walks out of the room and down the hall.

The night stretches out in front of her like an empty highway. If he were dead, she thinks, if we were divorced, it would be like this anyway. She gets up out of the chair and begins to make a few calls — Jan, her parents, Alexis. Kate continues to sleep through it all. At ten, Sy calls: Mikey was upset with Kate and Maggie away, but Nicolas had cajoled him into fifteen games of checkers, and Sy has just gotten him into bed.

Later, Maggie folds the reclining chair back and gets a sheet from the nurse. She scrunches her body up on the vinyl seat and tries to sleep. But every time Kate turns over, Maggie gets up to check. At three, Kate wakes, crying.

Maggie scrambles to her side and turns on the light. The whites of her eyes are filled with blood, the pupils barely visible. While Lewison had warned her of this, no amount of preparation could make it a less revolting sight. Maggie averts her eyes as her stomach rebounds. She busies herself with ringing for the nurse, who comes in and gives Kate medication for the pain.

She continues to cry. Maggie sits on the edge of the bed and strokes her hair. "It's all over now," she says to her daughter.

"I can't see. Why can't I see?"

"In the morning I'll give your eyes a bath with a cloth and they'll feel better. Keep them shut now and it won't bother you so much." Maggie turns off the light.

"Am I O.K.?"

"You're fine. Dr. Lewison said you were very brave when they put you to sleep."

"I was scared."

Maggie squeezes her hand. "I was too," she whispers. She keeps stroking Kate's hair back from her forehead.

"Can you sleep in my bed, Mom?"

Maggie climbs over the railing and stretches out beside her daughter, cradling her just the way she used to when she was a baby; they wait together for the pain to stop.

Kate sighs. "I'm glad you're here. Can you tell me a story till the hurt stops hurting?"

Maggie smiles, picks Kate's favorite. "The day you were born Daddy and I were so excited," she begins.

"Where is Daddy?" Kate interrupts.

"It's the middle of the night, sweetheart. He gave you a kiss before he left."

"He was supposed to be here when I woke up." Her voice quavers.

"He was." She goes on with the story; after half an hour, she begins to feel desperate with fatigue, and finally Kate's breathing deepens into sleep. Maggie stops speaking and waits. As she waits, she too drowses off.

At six o'clock the nurse returns to check Kate's temperature and pulse. Maggie sits up and shakes out her stiff limbs. Kate's eyes are sealed shut with exudate, frightening her; Maggie quickly sponges them open, and then clean.

As promised, Nicolas is at the hospital by eight, Mikey in tow. To show his sister how much he has missed her, Mikey clambers up on the electric bed and begins to push all the buttons. "Hey, cool," he says, as he pauses to study her sanguine eyes, "you can go as Dracula for Halloween."

The children ride up and down on the bed for the better part of an hour, while they wait for Dr. Lewison to sign the release papers. Nicolas drives them home but doesn't come in, giving Maggie a quick hug at the door. He has to go back to the Bronx to catch up on yesterday's business. With regret, Maggie watches him drive off.

The doctor requires that Kate stay in bed, so Maggie devises endless games that can be done in between the sheets. Jan drops by with a kettle full of chicken soup on her way to work the afternoon shift, and brings Kate a get-well card Rachel made. This visit momentarily buoys Maggie's spirits. Sy calls in at noon and speaks with Kate, which brightens her despite her discomfort.

For once, Mikey's noise and exuberance is welcome. He runs up and downstairs for sodas, cookies, and books to read; he makes his big sister a lot of pictures to hang around her room. "I'm taking care of her," he boasts to his mother as they make a tray of P.B.&J. for lunch.

Bleary with lack of sleep, at three Maggie nods off on the end of Kate's bed as the children build a Lego castle on the lunch tray. At four o'clock the telephone wakes her.

"How's it going?"

Sy's voice, she realizes fuzzily, shaking her head to clear it. "O.K.," she answers, still groggy.

"Are you all right?"

Even through the fog of interrupted sleep she hears that damned question again. Maybe he would like it if she said she wasn't all right — if she threw a tantrum and demanded he come home. "I'm fine," she answers irritably. "I just fell asleep on Kate's bed, that's all."

"The night was rough?" he asks, hesitantly.

"I didn't get much sleep."

"Sorry," he says. She has the feeling that he is sorry for more than her lack of sleep, but again she refuses to draw him out or say it for him. This time she just waits.

"How's Kate doing now?" he asks, after a minute.

"Fine. Considering."

"Any pain?"

"I gave her some codeine."

"Is Mikey behaving?"

"He's been a big help," she says, warming to the subject with a little laugh. "I think he likes being the boss for a change."

Sy laughs, too. "Listen," he blurts out then. "I'm not going to make it home tonight."

She sits abruptly on the edge of the bed. "You're not at the airport." This is not a question — it is a statement of fact. She is so tired.

"No. This is taking longer than I thought. We were up all night and will probably be again tonight. But I promise I'll be home for supper tomorrow night. O.K.?"

"Sunday night," she repeats dully. He sounds like a little boy asking his mother (quite anxiously) if he can stay out an extra hour. How is she supposed to respect a man who is always running away and, worse yet, asking permission to do so?

"Is that O.K.?"

"Sure." Though he cannot see her, she shrugs. Right now, she doesn't care what he does.

"I sent Kate something. It should be there soon."

"I'll listen for the bell."

Another hour passes in front of the television (reruns of *Leave It to Beaver*) that Maggie has wheeled in to the foot of Kate's bed. She starts thinking about dinner. She should get up and do something. But she is so comfortable just sitting, snuggled amid pillows and comforters, with a child nestled under each arm. The sun slants, low and lemon-colored, into the room to warm them. The love here soothes the wound the phone call left.

At five-thirty the doorbell rings. Mikey plays postman and returns, staggering under two large boxes. Inside the one marked for Kate is a doll. Maggie's is a florist's box filled with long-stemmed reds.

"From Daddy," Maggie says. She looks at the roses. The color seems obscene right now, dark red. She slides the lid back on.

Kate cuddles the doll against her chest, stroking its long, beautiful hair. "I knew he'd send me a present," she answers disdainfully. "But you're not sick."

"She's beautiful," Maggie says, ignoring the resentment in her daughter's voice.

Kate hugs the doll closer. "Daddy really loves me." Her tone creeps toward the shrill. "When will he be home?"

Maggie looks at her daughter and sees tears crowd her red eyes, glittering.

"Tomorrow," she says in a whisper.

"But you said *today!*"

"I know I did." She sags under the weight of disappointing them again. Of being the one to tell them.

"You lied to me!"

"I did not."

"You're such a mean mom!" Kate's face contorts and she bursts into tears. "It's your fault that Daddy went back to work!"

Stunned, Maggie stares at her. Then fury boils up inside. *She* is the one who spent the whole night sleepless beside Kate; *she* is the one upon whom everyone depends. And now she must take the blame for Sy's absence? She opens her mouth and then closes it with a snap.

Kate sobs. Mikey stares, then turns away. Suddenly pity breaks through Maggie's anger. Her daughter is only seven. She reaches over to put her hand on the thin pajama-clad arm. "You know that's not true," she says. (Time-out for reality.) The anger colors her voice with sternness. "I want Daddy at home as much as you do." (Even as she says this she wonders if she does. If she really wanted him home wouldn't she have insisted that he come tonight?)

Kate continues to sob.

"Kate, *I've* been here with you the whole time. I *love* you." Her voice holds an entreaty: in this instant she wishes Kate would put out her arms and cuddle her, reassure her that she understands; in this instant — and just for an instant — she wishes Kate were the mother and she the daughter. She wants something the child cannot give. She stares at her, huddled in bed with her red eyes, sobbing unabated. Maggie straightens up with a sigh. Kate defiantly wipes her nose on her sleeve, thrusts her chin up and turns on her side, toward the wall.

Maggie just stands there, angry and defeated. She knows it's not Kate's fault — the frustration has to be turned somewhere and a mother is often the nearest available dumping site. Nevertheless, it hurts. She waits until Kate starts to play with the doll again, until the tears subside. Then she scoops the florist's box under her arm and runs downstairs. As for generations of women, the kitchen offers her sanctuary amid its pots and pans: a good place for privacy. But when she pushes open the swinging door, she stops short. Ginger and garlic and coriander.

Slowly she peers around the corner. Industriously, Nicolas sets white paper cartons out on trays. She starts to laugh, but that laughter borders on tears. It surprises her to hear this sound coming from her mouth. She strides past him to the sink, flips on the garbage disposal and the water. One by one, she feeds the roses to the blades.

"Hey!" he shouts over the noise. "What's up?" He has followed her to the sink and now puts his arm around her shoulder. "Why are you doing that?"

"Because they're not enough, that's why!" she shouts back, taking another from the box and putting it down head first.

He shuts the disposal off and then makes her turn to face him. "Are you going to tell me what's going on?"

"Nothing's going on," she starts to say before her voice quivers. "Everything's the same as usual." Tears cut hot streaks over her cheeks. "I'm so tired, and Kate is mad at Sy and she's yelling at me!" She starts to sob.

Nicolas puts his arms around her and pulls her tight.

"I'm the only one here and I'm not the one they want! Damn him anyway!"

"He'll be here soon, won't he?"

"He sent flowers instead."

"Well, when *is* he coming?"

"Not until tomorrow. Suppertime maybe." She puts her head down on his shoulder and he pulls her in tight against him. "Why does he even bother — he'll just have to leave again on Monday!" His shirt is ringed with her tears and the black of mascara.

She continues to cry, for a long time. It feels as if she's been holding her body upright for so long. The crying washes her white and clean. Nicolas rocks her with his body.

"Hey," he says, after a while, as the sobs begin to subside. He lifts her chin so that she looks him in the face. "I brought Chinese so you wouldn't have to cook."

"I smelled it," she says, lifting her head to wipe her nose on the back of her sleeve. "What'd you get?"

"Well," he says in a teasing tone, "I seem to remember that someone here loves moo shu pork."

"Moo shu!" A smile, at last. She gives him a kiss on his cheek, then draws back diffidently.

When Kate sees they have company, she recovers her humor. Nicolas fixes Maggie and himself drinks and they build a fire in the family room. They have a picnic of spareribs and spicy chicken off trays. Mikey gets out the checker board.

At bedtime, Nicolas helps Maggie tuck the kids in. There is something, Maggie decides, about having someone beside you as you do this sort of everyday task that makes you feel less fatigued. Tonight she gets simple pleasure from watching her son crawl up into his bunk bed and under his comforter, face eager for her good-night kiss. While Nicolas gives Mikey one last glass of water and one last story (the third of each), Maggie goes into her bedroom, kicks off her shoes, and drops onto the bed. There is no point in getting too comfortable, she thinks drowsily, as Kate will surely need one more thing before she falls asleep. But the bed is soft; the scotch she had with supper edges her toward the bliss of rest; she closes her eyes, for just a minute.

∼

When Nicolas wanders into Maggie's bedroom, he finds her asleep on top of the comforter. The room, even with its windows closed, is cool with the October evening, and he can tell from the way she's lying, hunched on her side, arms hugging her knees, that she's cold. He goes to her side of the bed and flips the comforter up from the bottom, covering her as best he can. He sits beside her and watches her sleep.

Her shirt has rucked itself up in the back, exposing the knobs of her spine and the skin of her waist. Asleep, she looks unusually fragile — vulnerable. When she cried in his arms tonight, he found he wanted to cry with her. For an instant, he closes his eyes and imagines that this (not the cold apartment in Chelsea) is his house, that Mikey and Kate are his children (not just his godchildren), that he does not face empty space in his bed night after night, that Maggie is his wife.

Her breathing is deep and even. Slowly, he reaches out, with just one fingertip, to touch her, lightly, at the hollow where her shoulder and neck meet. His heart quickens, as if he is sneaking something, as if he is a small boy doing the forbidden. Her skin is warm and soft against his finger, faintly damp; perhaps she is not cold after all, he thinks. He slides the comforter down. He wants to see all of her. He traces his finger up the line of her neck, all the way to her ear and she stirs slightly under his touch. Falling into the rhythm of it, he begins to rub her back, a light touch that makes her skin prickle up into goosebumps.

Something tickles. Something light and feathery. Itchy. She twitches her shoulder to get it off. When it doesn't go away, she begins (reluctantly) to surface from the warm lake of sleep. The tickle changes to a stroke. She wants to stretch out under it and be caressed like that for hours.

The hand follows her. It traces a gentle line behind her ear, down the back of her neck. It twines itself in her hair, pulling gently at the roots until the nape of her neck prickles with pleasure. It rubs her scalp. After a while, she turns over.

"Hi," Nicolas says.

"Hi." She smiles, again shyly — a little surprised to see him, but not so surprised after all. "What a nice way to be woken. Sorry I konked out."

"You were tired." He smiles back. "I was having fun watching you sleep."

"What time is it?"

"Ten." He reaches over and draws the edge of his thumb down along the line of her jawbone, up and over her lips.

Slowly, he bends down and fits his mouth over hers.

She closes her eyes automatically. Then she opens them, rocked with amazement that there can be so much in a kiss. He kisses big. His mouth covers hers, dominates, wet and deep, probing, thrusting, sucking. Tentatively then, as if she is embracing a stranger (and not quite believing she is doing this), she puts her arms up around him. She keeps thinking they'll stop in a minute. Still kissing her, he sinks down to lie beside her. She feels the hardness of his chest, the round muscles of his arms, the press of his long body. She breaks away. "What are we doing?"

"Are you afraid?"

Awkwardly, she wipes her wet mouth with the back of her hand, and answers in a whisper. "Yes." His touch makes her feel anxious. Heightened. It feels good, but it's wrong.

He keeps touching her, stroking her cheeks, her lips, her throat. Her hand is weighted to the bed. She doesn't raise it.

"This isn't what we want."

"It's exactly what we want." He reaches over and starts to unbutton her blouse, somehow pleased by her diffidence.

"But that's not the point." She tries to sort out what the hell she is doing, lying here kissing her husband's best friend.

"And what is?" he murmurs, covering her cheeks, her chin, her eyelids with tiny soft kisses.

"What I mean —" She is trying to talk over the clamor inside her body and to ignore what he is doing. As he is ignoring her protest. "What I'm trying to say —"

"Go on." He pulls her shirt open, cups her breasts with his

hands and starts to kiss them. Reverently. His persistence in the face of her protest is an aphrodisiac. Mesmerized, she watches as her nipples go instantly erect.

"We can't." An agonized whisper now. She wants to turn her face away and not see what they are about to do. But she is spellbound.

"We are." He looks up at her as he starts to lick her. His tongue is very wide and pink. And wet. A gasp from her throat as he sucks on her, pulling hard. He murmurs with pleasure, kneading her as he sucks. She is tangled in the comforter, pinned under his weight on the fabric. She should say no. Her body disagrees.

She closes her eyes. Tongues twine. Bodies twine. Clothes are in the way. Without breaking the embrace, they struggle to get past buttons and zippers. His shoulders are broad and freckled, his body is tall and smooth — everything so different from Sy. His skin is soft, a surprise under her fingers. Her hand burrows in his pants to touch him, hesitantly at first; she is afraid she will do something wrong. His penis seems enormous and for a brief suffocating instant she wonders if it will fit.

Her tentativeness excites him. There is in her a banked fire and he will break down whatever wall he has to to get at it. He pulls her jeans off, and kisses (nibbles) her through her panties, getting the fabric wet with his mouth. The heat of his breath is more exciting in that moment than his tongue could ever have been. He can tell from the way she moves against him, the way her mouth opens and her tongue slides back and forth over her lips, that he's doing something to her she's never felt before. He keeps nipping and nuzzling until she is begging him with her body, and at last he pulls the panty aside and rubs his face in her, lapping up and down with his tongue. He reaches up for her breasts and rolls her nipples between his fingers.

She is getting close, he sees, and he doesn't want her first time to be like this, with him below and out of sight. He wants to be deep inside her, her eyes open, the two of them face to face — so that she knows who she is with. He waits until she is just on the edge of coming and then slides up her body, rubbing their sweat slippery skin together, until he rests, top and bottom, at the entrances to both her mouths. With his knees he spreads her legs apart.

She is trembling. She cannot wait another minute. He puts his lips against hers and pushes his tongue in; his prick nudges and separates and opens more soft folds below. Slowly he moves his hips, side to side, sinking down into her inch by slow inch, reaming her open. Her eyes widen beneath him, she no longer sees him, she feels only his entrance. His presence fills her body.

Deep inside now, he begins to build a rhythm. Their bodies are some miraculous match, just the right height for each other. She is not touching herself anywhere. For the first time in her life, she is not touching herself to make herself feel. Instead, she is touching him: the map of his chest, the bones in his back, the round muscle of his ass. She feels every part of his body as it moves over and around and inside of her. His penis stretches her out and it is as if there is a nerve-soaked sponge inside her, a new organ distended with heat and pleasure, and it is getting tighter around him until at last he picks up the rhythm, hammering himself into her, and she meets him with her hips, her legs curl up somewhere above her head, she is spiraling right up off the bed; she levitates, she is lost, she is flown out of her head. Looking down she sees the two of them a long way away, different people, a voice is raised in a scream that does not end. She does not know where she is. She has evaporated: no mind, only body. There is the pounding between her legs, there is her cunt, there is the electric tingle through her breasts, there is a pleasure that goes on and on because Nicolas goes on and on. *This is me*, she thinks, *Oh, God, this is me.*

She opens her eyes. He is watching her. His face is covered with sweat. It drips down on her breasts, which are now freckled pink and splotchy, and then melts into her own slick skin. Eagerly she licks the wet from his forehead. She would be his forever. If only he would do this to her again. And again.

He puts his hand down in between the junction of their bodies and strokes her. Embarrassed now, she wants to push his hand away.

"It's your turn now," she whispers.

"Who said anything about turns?" He kisses her neck, her earlobe. "We've got all night." He keeps rubbing her. In just the right place. She closes her eyes. Moans. He is still hard inside her. Slowly he moves in and out. As he rubs her, he fucks her. She lies spread beneath him, his experiment. The sweat flies off him, a salt spray, when their bodies smack together. And then, quite suddenly and easily, her body rolls in on itself. She is coming again, small circles of pleasure that lap up inside her body like a rising tide. She cries out. He moves even faster, he is flying over her and her body begins to sing again; it is a musical scale where one note easily follows the last. Higher and higher. Over and over. He flies. She ascends. After a long time, as he senses the ebb in her, he slows.

He flips them, so that now she is on top. She is quivering. She has lost control of her body. She closes her eyes, she does not want to see his face. He guides her up and down on him. She is quivering so hard she can only think of collapsing against him, but his hands insist. Her cunt insists. He reaches down and strokes her some more. Excites her again. *Not possible*, some distant voice says, but now she is flying over him, pumping herself up and down, lost once again in herself. As she climaxes she opens her eyes.

His eyes are closed. His face is wet, red, his chest mottled. He groans and they thrust against each other, he sighs, a paroxysm. Then she drops on him and they rest.

They doze in that position, their bodies pasted together with wet and salt and semen. After a while Maggie cracks an eye open to look at the clock. It is midnight.

She rolls off him and goes to the bathroom. She is too tired to think. She takes a towel and washes herself, then stumbles back to bed.

As she gets under the covers, Nicolas wakens. He comes over and stipples her face with small soft kisses. She puts her arms up to him and they hold each other. She does not mind the sticky press of his body. She feels she belongs to him.

"Are you O.K.?" he asks.

"You are incredible." She is deeply, immensely grateful, and swept away by the sense of debt: what she owes him for having brought her to such pleasure. He owns the sensual part of her now.

He smiles, holds her tightly in the circle of his arms, kisses the end of her nose.

"It was never like that. Nothing like that." And she laughs, giddy with her discovery. She was an amputee: now she can run.

They fall asleep that way, tangled into each other's bodies, reeds in the wind.

Sometime in the middle of the night, Maggie feels the bed rock. Nicolas getting up. From the other side of the room, she hears him moving around.

"Shit!"

In the half-light from the hall she can see him bend to rub his foot. "What is it?" she asks, sitting up on her elbow.

"I just tripped," he answers, holding aloft one of Mikey's sneakers. Sighs. "The guilt of little shoes."

In the dark she laughs, quietly. "What are you doing fumbling around in the dark anyway?"

"The kids might wake up early. I think I should go." He comes to sit beside her on the edge of the bed.

She is silent in the dark, grateful again that he would consider children not his own. The thought of her children suddenly makes her anxious. She is ashamed to admit that she wishes he would go: she is afraid to have him here in the morning, to see his face next to hers on the pillow.

"I'll call you tomorrow," he says, and kisses her one last time. Then he is out the door, moving with stealth over the staircase. His car starts in the driveway and then backs out. She closes her eyes and waits for sleep to return.

But it eludes her. Restless, she gets up, goes down to the kitchen, sits in the dark drinking a glass of milk. She sets the glass in the sink, climbs back upstairs. On the way to her bed, she stops to check Kate.

She is curled with her arms around the doll Sy sent. Maggie sinks down on the side of the bed and strokes her hair. Kate shifts under the pressure of her hand. Maggie stops, afraid to waken her. Her daughter's innocent sleep is a reproach: Maggie has corrupted the tight circle of family. She wishes she could talk to Alexis, but realizes how impossible that would be. There is no way she can talk to *anyone* about this. She puts her face forward into her hands. She has never felt so confused. For the second night in a row, she lies down beside her daughter. After a while she makes herself get up.

She wakes with the sun in her eyes, her mood changed. She has been dreaming about him, she realizes: she is aroused. Her body feels substantial. Buoyant. Thinking of Nicolas, she stands in front of her mirror and examines her face. He has given her to herself, she thinks. (The prize.) She knows she ought to be ashamed of what they did, but as she gets back into bed and stretches luxuriously among their sheets, she doesn't. Instead, pride fills her. After all these years of failure in bed, last night seems a triumph. She rises to float dreamily through the house like a young girl in love. She hugs her children awake and then makes them pancakes. Nicolas phones. They talk for an hour. They plan for him to come during the week when Sy is away. For the first time in months, she is full and happy.

Until Sy comes home, and the guilt (the price) descends like a guillotine. She can barely kiss him hello, barely meet his gaze. Anxiety rules with a vengeance. Her mouth goes dry as she begins the lie.

"It wasn't so bad," she says when he inquires about last night. "Nicolas brought over Chinese and gave me a hand with the kids."

"That was nice of him," Sy says absentmindedly as he sits on the edge of Kate's bed, holding her hand. He is clearly upset by his daughter's appearance. He strokes her arm and studies the sheets.

"After he left, I watched some rerun from *Masterpiece Theater* and then went to sleep early," she goes on, detailing her empty hours though he has asked for no further clarification on any specifics. She wonders what kind of a woman she has become (like her mother?) that she can stand there so cold-bloodedly and invent a different life for herself — as if she is telling a story about another person. And as relieved as she is when he seems to accept everything she says (freedom), her respect for him nevertheless dims: why is he so trusting?

As they head downstairs to make supper, he catches her hand. "I'm real sorry about how this all worked out," he says, as she tries not to flinch away from his touch. "You were an incredible trouper." He stops her on the landing and, turning her toward him, puts his arms around her. "I know how hard it must have been."

The words clamor in her ears. "It wasn't, really," she says.

"Come on, Maggie. I *know*."

The touch of his hand on hers is abhorrent. When he bends to kiss her she can think only of last night. She closes her eyes so that she will not see her husband, but that increases the spin of pictures in her head: Nicolas above her, the beauty of his face, herself floating off the bed. She has shared pleasure with another man when she could share no pleasure with Sy — and this betrayal seems the most dreadful of all.

"I'm surprised you got back even now," she says, breaking the embrace, afraid she will suffocate under his mouth. She takes a step backward.

"I told you I would."

"But you'll be leaving again tomorrow morning, so I thought —"

"I rescheduled my trip to the coast," he interrupts, grinning at her.

"Oh," she says, and her heart drops with disappointment. She forces herself to smile.

"Don't look so pleased," Sy says, puzzled. He moves closer and puts his arm around her again.

"Whatever you do is fine."

"I thought you'd be happy."

"You were expecting a medal?" she asks. "Or maybe a marching band on the front steps — a yellow ribbon around our old oak tree?"

He stares at her. "I said I was sorry."

"Yeah, well." She shrugs. "Look, I'm just tired," she says, stepping out from under his arm. "Could you watch the kids so I can take a bath?"

"Sure." He just stands there, alone, his arms dangling empty, as if he does not know where she has gone to.

She turns and goes back up the stairs, then runs the water for her tub with the door closed, so that he cannot hear her sob. She has destroyed it, she now sees, an innocence between them, and it cannot be replaced. Once their most intimate life was shared only with each other; now there has been an invasion. Yet, accompanying the sorrow, there is also a confusing wave of pleasure: to know, at last, for whatever reason, that she is capable of ecstasy.

Later that night, when he crosses (somewhat uncertainly) the gulf of their king-sized bed, guilt opens her arms. She pretends passion, but it is not at all the same. He is so tentative, so unsure. The rhythms are wrong. He annoys her in every way. As they struggle there on the bed, her mind floats above them and judges critically every move he makes, the way he touches or does not. She hates him. Right now, tonight, her body is yet again a failure. She forces herself to endure the awkward grapple. Or perhaps he is the failure, she thinks with anger, as her husband pumps and strains above her in the dark. Beneath him on the cool sheets, she keeps herself gravity-bound.

TWELVE

In Name Only

The weather moves forward. Trees give up their leaves with a sigh, the way long-haired women relinquish their bounty to the beauty shop's floor. While the earth in her front yard becomes riddled with apples, while the children are in school and Sy on the coast, Maggie invites Nicolas in. Day after day, she invites him to unfold her. He knocks on the front door, mid-morning, two quiet raps; she answers, feeling concomitantly shy and yet filled with a desire so great it makes her want to drop on her knees and pay homage. They move up the staircase to the attic room (they never again use Sy and Maggie's bed) where there are storage boxes piled high, old porch furniture, garbage bags leaking outgrown children's clothes — and a yellowed mattress left over from college dormitory days. Here they lock themselves together and dusty space becomes a fortress.

She cannot get enough of the smooth gold of his skin, the pale circles of his nipples, the five blond hairs on his chest that thicken into down across his belly. She loves the elongated ovals of his long calves and thighs, the flat hollow of his abdomen where his semen pools if she does not catch it all with her tongue. She loves the feel of him in her mouth.

She has never before loved a man's body nor released herself to follow the magic of her own. For years she believed (or wanted to believe) that there was something wrong with her. She envied women who spoke of lust — and she protected herself from knowing her failure by scoffing and refusing to believe such sensations were possible. She had slept with only a few other men before she'd met Sy and retired with relief to monogamy; after the first few times she and Sy made love, she began to lift her hips, moan decorously, and behave as she guessed a sexually aroused woman would. And there was a glimmer deep down, some movement beneath the surface (an inner space waiting to be found, touched, and unfolded), but the sensation remained elusive. Unexplored. She took her satisfaction in the cuddle that came afterward, the warmth of another body tucked safely against hers in the dark of night — and in the babies.

Sy still does not expect anything more than this, it seems: she chose him because he did not, because he was safe, because she believed that he would never summon forth her passion and that she would never want him to. He is not sure enough to do so. It takes Nicolas, imperious (imperial) in bed, to teach her how to *want*. She wants him when she wakes in the morning, curled in a damp nest of sheets; she wants him while she is peeling potatoes or mulching the garden or choosing fruit at the market. Desire shimmers off her skin. Other people sense it: for the first time men stare at her when she walks through the middle of town on an errand or gets out of her car to pump her gas at the self-serve; women ask if she's lost weight. Everyone notices — except Sy, who just rushes from coast to coast, blurry with airline fever, accumulating more and more frequent-flyer miles for vacations they will never have the time to take.

While Maggie discovers the power that goes with desire itself. Their bodies are talking: mouths mute, brains mute — their bodies know (and hers for the very first, most miraculous time) just what they are doing. They are swinging higher and higher, as if climbing some sort of splendid tropical fruit tree, a tree whose crown stretches so high into the sky that only someone insane would willingly go there.

She learns that she is not a stone, but that she has made herself a stone. She loves everything she and Nicolas do, each act their love requires. Never once does she have to work toward a climax, either with her mind, or with her hand. With

Nicolas she reaches some inner plateau wherein the pleasure just keeps rolling over her in one long sinuous wave.

Sex becomes an addiction. It makes anxiety stop. It makes depression go away. (It makes thinking freeze.) All that exists is the fucking.

Until he puts his clothes back on and leaves. And her children come home. And Sy calls from the road to ask what she's been up to today. Then the guilt heats up, singeing her with a fire that is, ironically (or perhaps intentionally), similarly intense.

She stops looking for a job. She no longer wants to return to work. She can only think of getting through the hours until it is time for Nicolas to knock on her door again. Nicolas himself spends little time at work, turning up on Maggie's doorstep most mornings around ten-thirty, often staying through lunch and leaving just before the children's car pool pulls into the driveway from school.

In her mind, Maggie splits her life and imagines herself as two different people. One: the sensual human (animal) who seeks every opportunity for pleasure. Two: the mother who continues to provide the basics — folding laundry, making meals, driving the car pool, dispensing kisses. (Her role as wife now seems a vague concept, as distant as the cities to which her husband travels; intellect and reason appear temporarily paralyzed by sensation.) She does not like to have Nicolas come over on the few days when Sy will be in town for the evening: then these divisions grind against one another like the lips of a wound, provoking anxiety and guilt. In bed at night, no matter how many times she has bathed, she worries about being clean. She despairs of feeling whole again, all selves merged. But the question now surfaces: was she ever whole before? And, if so, does she want to return to that particular sort of unity?

ᐢ

Nicolas draws her shape on the sheets, his hands trace the outline of her body the way children trace their shadows in the snow with sticks. "Arms up," he says, and she complies, laughing; breasts rise and draw taut, the blue-tinged skin of her armpit is revealed. He draws her first that way, then continues, pushing her legs apart, to do the deep V up to where a cloud-shaped stain wets the mattress. "I love her," he says, and bends for a taste.

Maggie laughs again, stimulated once more by his lips and fingers and being found beautiful. She shivers under his touch. "I always thought it was ugly."

"Most women do." He raises his head a minute. His fingers trail through her bright bush as he resumes nuzzling her.

It is Wednesday, early afternoon. The attic fills with late-October sunlight; low and slanted, this light catches the dust drifting under the rafters; Maggie watches the shifting screen of air and thinks that time here is in visible slow motion; it reflects the inertia of their now-stilled bodies. She waves her hand and the dust, accelerating, disappears.

She looks down at him between her legs, and strokes the nape of his neck. "Hungry?"

"Famished," he answers, exploring for a minute more with his tongue.

"I meant," she says, "for food."

"This *is* food," he says, lifting his face away from her with a grin. They laugh.

As is their habit, they have already been here for several hours. In this lull, they rest before returning to feast on one another. He rubs his face, slowly, back and forth in her, then moves up, spreading her wetness across them both, over their bellies and thighs. Their pubic hair is matted, glistening. He enters her quickly. She comes again as he presses in to fill her, bucking her hips up in a shudder that travels throughout her body. In the last few weeks she has discovered that during a long interlude like this, it is possible for her to climax many times, over and over, and from nothing more than a single touch or a single entry. No longer does she require a lot of time or hard work or manipulation in just the right spot. His mouth alone on her nipple or on the back of her neck or his finger or his voice — any of it can bring her off. She looks up into his eyes and sees that the golden iris is now just a rim against the white, a sun setting into the oblivion of pleasure. He moves faster and faster until he is just a blur inside and above her, part of her. His motion casts her sideways on the mattress; her head falls over the edge, the blood rushes up behind her eyes. His chest is flushing red, his hands grasp and clutch the mattress on either side of her neck. The window behind him throws light over his body and sets him on fire.

He pushes himself into the main artery of her body and she dances outward; blackness clouds her eyes until all she can see is his face silhouetted against the sun, rushing away from her; all she can feel is the pounding of his body into hers. In the fever of blackness, she starts to climax, again: merged with him she has ceased to be herself alone. The waves break in her head and in her body and she can't (she won't) stop him. She would die now, all of her sex, and nothing else. She wants to go out on high, seized, swept through the glass and up into the sky.

A cry, from far away, hoarse, from a raw throat. He shudders and slumps against her. His hands release the mattress. She picks her head up, her lungs expand, fill with cool air, her vision clears. Her head still spins.

They catch their breath. They turn on their sides to face and hold one another. To speak would reduce their magic with words. After a while she rolls over and away, easily; she pulls the paper sack he brought with him from the deli up onto the bed.

Fragrant in slick white paper is greasy, garlicky salami sliced thick, a wedge of melting Camembert; a plastic container of sweet pickles; a loaf of sourdough. He props his shoulders against the old bureau that serves them as a headboard. She gets up and fetches the red wine they shoved behind an old carton of books for safekeeping; they pass the bottle back and forth as they eat. There is something about eating on the mattress with their fingers, mixing up the smell of love with the succulence of food, taking each other in one more way, satisfying themselves on yet another sensual plane.

"I've been thinking something radical," he says, after a while, swallowing some wine to wash down the rough crust of the bread.

She raises her eyebrows and licks her fingers. "A new exotic position?" She reaches over and tugs gently on his penis. Then, embarrassed, she looks away.

"Seriously," he goes on, tapping his finger on her knee to refocus her attention. He passes her the wine bottle. How he loves the cold kiss of her wedding band on his skin. (It is the irony he loves: this ring, which once was entrusted to him as Sy's best man.) "Picture a house in Maine on the edge of the ocean." His eyes gleam. He licks his fingers. "And us. Clamming every day. Making love every night. No interruptions."

She stops chewing for a minute, then tilts her head to one side. "You're going to buy a summer place all the way up there?"

"Not exactly." He smiles. "Better than that. I want us to be together every day."

"I couldn't go with you to Maine," she says, irritably. "Not for a weekend, not for a night." It angers her that he tempts her with such an idea; he knows the preservation of the affair depends upon secrecy. She cannot (will not) take a risk like that.

To be Nicolas's lover now requires no complicated plans or lies. Sy is away so much that they have only to take advantage of the opportunities that arise three or four days every week. It's easy to pretend that the affair doesn't interfere with her family life in the least. "I just couldn't take the chance, Nicolas," she says now. "You know that."

He smiles at her, the happiness radiates out from him like heat. "I'm not talking about sneaking off, or inventing some excuse to get away. I'm talking about being there, together, all the time."

"What do you mean?" Her eyes get wide and round; gooseflesh nets the skin across her breasts and she crosses her arms over her body.

"I'm going to start looking for a buyer for Linden's. I'm not going to sell off a few branches like Sy wants — I'm going to unload the whole damned thing and start something new."

She stares at him. "You're joking."

"No." He shakes his head and reaches across to cup her breast. "Hey, relax, little one. It's a good thing, I think."

"Why on earth would you do something like that?"

He smiles. "Because of you."

"Me?" Her voice rises in pitch and she draws her sweater toward her, pulling it on over her head. She doesn't like anything unpredictable, and Nicolas's mysterious expression frightens her. "I don't get it."

"Being with you." He looks down, fingers the button on the striped mattress. After a minute, he looks up, shyly. (As he reveals himself she is moved to empathy for his vulnerability.)

"You pushed me to think about what I want." He smiles at her. "I want to start over, do something different. I've always needed challenge and this is the right time, I just know it."

"What would you do instead?" Maggie asks, wrapping the remains of her meal in the waxed paper.

He leans forward. "When we were up there on vacation I realized how much undeveloped land there was — that entire island for example — and farther down the coast, too. I made a few calls yesterday. It's a great area to invest in." He lifts the wine bottle again.

"Real estate? You mean, sell houses?"

He puts his head back and laughs. "No — I'm talking development. Taking land and making something on it."

"It sounds awfully risky," Maggie says doubtfully (disapprovingly), thinking of the silence of the island.

"Risk is what makes me go."

"Well, couldn't you do it all from here?" Her voice quavers, just for an instant. She doesn't say anything more but runs her fingers up and down the stripes of the blue ticking. He touches her, his hand warm on her cool flesh.

"You don't get it, do you?" He lifts her chin in his hand, tenderly. "I'm talking about us being together. All the time. Never sneaking." She looks up to see that his face is alight. "Go out to dinner, the movies. Whatever we wanted. No more hiding. I'm talking about the *two* of us moving there."

She stares at him, speechless. He is suggesting they run away together. Such an idea never occurred to her, not even in her most vivid daydreams. The fantasy heats her with its audacity. As they sit there, she imagines a scene far beyond this room: a gray shingle house on the edge of the ocean; a porch where they take their morning coffee, the steam lifting off the surface to float over the salted air; she fries eggs in an iron skillet and they wait for the sun to edge up crimson over the jagged line of the pines; at night, she stirs a pot while waiting for him to come home; on the table, the typewriter where she has worked all day long, sheets of paper mounting on the left side, the writing for which she'd never before had the time; below, the sea stamps on the rocks, music, the rhythm of their blood. "You and me?" she repeats slowly. "Together?"

"Think about it." He squeezes her hand.

"You're not even divorced yet."

"I will be," he says, "soon."

"Soon?" He and Alexis have filed, just last month, in the no-fault system, which makes everything quite pro forma and supposedly painless. Nevertheless, Maggie hasn't allowed herself to think of what this will mean in terms of his freedom. She looks around her at this attic room where they sit and suddenly it seems as if all the objects here are a mere facade: this is a world of cutouts, like the cardboard towns she constructed as a child, complete with houses, streets, gardens, and railroad tracks (that was all a town needed then) vulnerable to being knocked flat by one clumsy move. "But what about me?"

"That does seem to be more the question," he responds dryly. "What about you?"

"And Sy? And the kids?"

"I love the kids," he says. "We could be a *family*."

He stresses the last word, and with that inflection offers Maggie the one thing she has always craved: a nest where all related birds fly in for the night to browse together, feed, and warm themselves — all she thought she was creating with Sy but that seems to be in name only.

"I'm the one who's here night after night playing checkers and doing the bedtime thing." His voice is righteous with indignation. "You know they deserve more than he's giving."

She bows her head, acknowledging the truth of his observation. "But is that what you really want?" she asks, her voice doubtful (thinking to herself that men must have a love of fairy tales as well as big lies).

"I love you, Maggie," he answers, stroking her cheek softly. "You know that. And I love them. In time, maybe we could start a family of our own."

His words drop on her, a shock. An image flashes through her mind: her body, ungainly with another pregnancy; shared space. Her body, which for the first time seems to belong only to her. Abruptly, and without warning, she begins to cry.

"What's wrong?" asks Nicolas, startled into distress; he had thought his plans would be greeted with pleasure, not tears. This changeable, fickle side of Maggie is not one with which he

has much experience. To him, Maggie has always been an un-
complicated song. He feels a flicker of irritation now that he
must comfort her rather than rejoice. But he reaches across to
stroke her hair nevertheless.

"This is all just so much —" She breaks off, and tries to
wipe her face on the back of her hand. He offers her the tail of
his shirt. "So much *bigger* than I thought it would be. It's a tiger
out of its cage." In her mind she sees their love now rampaging
dangerously through the room, tearing holes in her life. "And
there's Alexis, too. We're *friends*, you know." (This last is a sad
defense, as she has avoided even talking to Alexis on the phone
since she started sleeping with Nicolas.)

He stares at her. "Maybe you should have worried about
that before. What did you think we were doing here anyway?"
he asks, anger edging his voice. "This isn't a game of charades,
you know. I'm in love with you!"

She stares up at him, her mouth open. His anger makes her
meek.

"Don't you love *us?*" he demands. "You can't possibly love
him!"

"Nico, Nico." Her voice and her hand stroke him down.
"It's just so much, all at once. And you sprung it on me, besides," she adds. "Don't you think —"

From downstairs comes the distant noise of the back door
banging shut. Maggie freezes. "What time is it?" She fumbles
in a panic for her watch.

"Who cares!" Nicolas stands to scramble for his pants.
"Hurry."

Hearts thudding, sweat breaking out all over again, they
thrust their bodies into clothes, buttons askew, zippers rasping
with haste, shoes without socks. (The film runs backward now,
with fear replacing passion.) Nicolas grabs their lunch and
shoves it under the bed. From downstairs they can hear
Mikey's voice calling, room to room, in search of Maggie.
"Mooooooooom! Where are you!"

Maggie struggles to tuck her shirt into her jeans. He mustn't
catch them here, beside the mattress; she rushes to the head of
the attic stairs just as he tramps up to the second floor. "Coming," she shouts.

Rushing down the flight of stairs, she nearly collides with

him in the hallway. "Oh!" she says, her hand flying up to her face, "you scared me."

"Where were you?" He squares his shoulders angrily. "I called and called."

"I was up in the attic." Behind her she feels Nicolas come down the stairs and close the door. She doesn't turn.

"Why is Uncle Nico here?" Mikey asks with curiosity.

"He was helping me move that big old couch."

"Can I see?"

"Oh, there's nothing to see now," Maggie says casually, steering him by the shoulder toward the staircase to the kitchen. "Let's go get you a snack."

Distracted by the thought of food, Mikey bounces ahead, while Maggie surreptitiously checks her watch. She is mystified: it's only one-thirty and school isn't ordinarily dismissed until three. Thank God Mikey has never listened to her admonitions about looking for her quietly instead of yelling for her from five rooms away. From the window on the staircase landing, she waves at Jan and thus frees her to back down the driveway and reverse into her own.

"Why are you home now, Mikey?" she asks as she goes to the refrigerator for milk. Nicolas gets the cookie jar. "You're not sick, are you?" Hurriedly she lays her hand against his forehead to check.

"Cut it out, Mom," he says, wriggling under her touch. "I brought you a note yesterday. Remember?" This is said with the scorn of a five-year-old who insists *he* knows and remembers everything.

"I forgot," she groans. "Teacher conference day. Lucky it wasn't my turn to drive car pool."

"Lucky it was Josh's mom," Mikey affirms. He takes a cookie from Nicolas. "Can we play some checkers?" he asks with his mouth full.

Nicolas hesitates.

"Please," Mikey pleads. "Just one game? It won't take long."

Nicolas checks his watch. "I've got to get back into the city pretty soon."

"I'll be your best friend," Mikey says, with a winning grin.

"Who could refuse that?" Nicolas says, looking over to Maggie with a smile. She busies herself at the sink as they open the checker board. Ordinarily the sight of Nico and Mikey playing checkers gives her pleasure. But not today.

What fidelity does she owe her children? she wonders as she roots through the refrigerator in search of the makings for supper. Would they like to go and live in Maine, leave behind their real but absent father in favor of someone new and present? Would it be the best thing for them? Does she love Nicolas enough? Does she still love Sy? The questions swarm in and she cannot answer any of them, neither the children's nor her own, much less those Nicolas has put before her like so many hors d'oeuvres on a plate. But she now sees that if she does not decide which to choose, she may well be hungry the rest of her life.

✑

"You can't be serious," Alexis says, dumbfounded. The buzz in her head grows louder. "Don't talk to me about getting pregnant — I'm in the middle of a divorce!" To hear there is something wrong with her body comes as a shock.

Lia Bates smiles at her with kindness and leans her white-jacketed elbows on the desk. She is a birdlike, small-boned woman. "I'm not telling you what to do, Alexis. I'm just pointing out the options. That's my job." The phone buzzes and Lia answers, smiling apologetically.

Waiting, Alexis scans, for a moment, all the medical degrees that hang behind the desk. She and Lia have been friends since junior year, when they sat next to each other in Chem 20. Now Alexis sighs and, as Lia hangs up, tries to focus again. She was depressed before she came in for the appointment; now she doesn't know if she can deal with the pressure of another problem. Especially one that is health-related, and therefore beyond her immediate control. She hadn't taken any of it seriously enough to even make a special appointment: today she simply came in for her yearly Pap smear.

"Look, all of this is guesswork," Lia continues. Her voice is direct but her brown eyes soften the words. "Unless you let me do a laparoscopy to determine whether the cause of the pain is due to endometriosis, I *can't* be sure," she continues. "I can surmise certain things from a physical exam, but we need to know."

"And if that's what it is, getting pregnant is the only way to fix it?" For an instant she feels her voice quiver, then she regains control.

"No." Lia shakes her head and explains again, patiently, gently. "If it is endometriosis — and I palpated several sizable cysts on your left ovary — then getting pregnant or using a drug regime will send it into remission. Pregnancy or the drug course gives your body a rest from the monthly cycling that feeds the endometriosis. That's why we're seeing more and more of the disease as women postpone childbearing. On the other hand, if you leave it untreated, at some point it will become impossible to conceive."

"What is this drug?" Alexis asks, dispiritedly.

"For some the birth control pill is enough. For others — there's a more effective drug now called Danocrine."

Alexis sits in silence.

"It doesn't sound like you're in the right place for a pregnancy."

Alexis shrugs. "This is a bad time for me."

"Your work still keeps you on roller skates?"

"Yes," she admits, and her face darkens. "But maybe not for long."

Lia raises her eyebrows in a question.

"My firm announced it was going public today," Alexis explains, dejected. "Making partner there *next year* is like being named chief of staff in a hospital that was just decertified."

Lia wrinkles her nose. "In that case, maybe this is *just* the time for a baby. Are you and Jon permanent?"

Alexis makes a face. "Who knows? And anyway, he says he doesn't want kids."

"What about you?"

"What about me —" Alexis shrugs moodily. "I've never thought about it much. It doesn't seem like a part of my life *now*. I just want to make partner this year and spend all my free time with Jon. But I have to admit, once in a while, sometimes there are moments where I wonder." She hesitates. "I worry that when I'm fifty, I'll look back and regret it in a way I can't foresee right now." She is distraught, she realizes; it has been a long time since she has opened herself up, and it strikes her now how much she misses talking to Maggie. When she separated from Nicolas she had not known that one of the worst prices would be the simultaneous separation from Maggie. "I don't feel like less of a woman now," she continues, "but I wonder if I'll feel like less of a woman then?"

"How can you know something that's so far away?" Lia shakes her head.

"This isn't like any other choice I've ever had to make. Even with your career you figure that you can finesse some things and change your mind. But at a certain point this is irrevocable." She sighs.

The buzzer goes off on the desk again. "My waiting room's stacked up," Lia says, with regret. "Let's get together for dinner soon? I still haven't met Jon."

Alexis sighs, pushes herself up out of her chair and nods.

"In the meantime, you've got to come in for a lap. Women do have babies into their forties these days, you know. You've just got to protect those family jewels." She grins.

"I'll think about it," Alexis promises unhappily, as Lia opens the door.

"Don't put it off. Call me," she urges, "by next week at the latest."

Alexis nods and makes her way out, emerging from the building in a blur. She dreads telling Jon anything about this appointment. The idea that he might feel pressured frightens her and even worse (more repellent) is the thought that he might regard her with pity. All her life she has been in perfect health, except for the occasional broken bone. The idea of surgery terrifies her. Staying fit has always been another way of delineating the differences between her and her mother. She flags down a cab and gives him the address of the Columbia athletics building.

After spending an hour diving angrily into the pool, she finds another cab despite the rush-hour crush and talks the driver into stopping at Gristedes so she can run in to pick up the order she phoned from work. She arrives at Jon's apartment close to seven o'clock. Having been out of town all of the week before, she is profoundly grateful to be at home tonight, and early at that. She and Jon made plans to have supper here together, alone. She struggles to balance the sack of groceries as she unlocks the door.

The apartment is dark. She goes to the kitchen, puts the bag down, but does not turn on the lights. With a glass of ice and a bottle of scotch in hand, she goes to hibernate in the living room. There is plenty of time for making steak and salad; Jon won't be home for another hour, at the inside. She kicks off her shoes, pours a generous slug, puts her head back, and closes her eyes, relieved to be here; how she misses him when they have to be separated now.

The idea of a shower occurs to her and, unwillingly, she considers it. It will require energy, but she can still smell the chlorine in her hair.

Taking the scotch with her, she turns the taps on full, drops her clothes in a heap on the floor, steps into the water. Lets it beat down, soaking skin and scalp. The rhythm of the water soothes, it washes her backward into childhood, when a young maid named Claudia — charged with temporary care of the two Somers children in a gap between nannies — calmed any kind of a temper tantrum in the bathtub. The water soothed then as the water soothes now. Claudia squeezed the wash-cloth, water trickled in a thin, delicious stream down over the ears, neck, and back. The tantrum floated away like magic.

Thinking of this makes her sad and Alexis begins to cry. She leans against the wall, the tiles cold against her overheated skin. The water continues to stream across her body, this body of which she has always been so proud, a body now flawed and troubled. Betraying her in a low moment. She does not know what to do.

The sobs echo and she feels ashamed. She tries to stop, putting her forehead against the soap dish and resting there. Totally wrung out, she shuts off the tap after a minute and steps out. Blowing her nose, she wipes the fog off the mirror to peer at her red and swollen eyes. Even her fingertips are pruney. She shakes her head and sighs. In the bedroom, she takes out Jon's flannel pajamas, wraps her hair in a clean towel, secures it up on her head like a turban. In the kitchen, she pours another drink. The liquor is depressing her even more, making her more weepy, but she doesn't care. She is in the mood to feel sorry for herself, for just this minute. She is tired of being invincible.

She goes back to the still, dark living room and sits down at Jon's desk, where today's *New York Times* lies in sheaves across the desktop and floor. She flips through disinterestedly. There is nothing new to read. She sits back, sips, eyes the deep drawer on the side of the desk. This is where Jon stores the files he is currently working on in the office. Like Alexis, he works late every night at home when he isn't on the road.

She watches as her hand reaches out and tugs that drawer open. Her stomach knots. Casually, as if she's looking at dresses on a rack, she flips through the files. Many of them are companies for whom the reports were written some time ago, secrets now public knowledge. But not all.

At the front of the drawer there are two files under the heading "Current" and it is these her fingers nudge at with determination. *What the hell*, she thinks, and pulls them out. On top of the desk, the first is of no interest to her, and both disappointment and relief well up. She hesitates. Almost puts the files back where they belong. Then she folds back the second cover slowly: Aviation General. She starts to read, and hears Jon's key in the lock.

"Christ!" She stuffs both files back into the drawer, shuts it, puts her feet up on the desk, and pulls the newspaper onto her lap.

Jon opens the door and waves at her, holding an orange and black paper sack in his teeth. He crosses to give her a kiss and drop the bag in her lap. It feels heavy: glass. She raises her eyebrows. "Happy Halloween to you, too."

"Consolation champagne," he answers, as she pulls out a bottle of Cristal.

He is obviously referring to Hewett's announcement earlier in the day. She shrugs. "Well, it's not like we didn't expect it."

"Hang on for that promotion." He hugs her. "You never know."

She smiles at him unhappily.

He sits down on the sofa and pushes his feet out of his shoes, puts them up on the stacks of magazines on the coffee table. "You're home early."

"So are you," she says, pausing for a moment. Now is the obvious time to mention the appointment with Lia Bates. To tell him how scared she is and have him hold her. "I was tired," she says, turning away. "I thought an early dinner sounded good. Want to help make supper?"

He nods and they head toward the kitchen. He slices vegetables for the salad while she tenderizes the steak, puncturing it in vicious, even rows with a two-tined fork. As is their ritual, they lean against the countertop and talk while the kitchen fills with the smell of broiling meat.

She watches his face while he makes them another drink and realizes how ashamed she is of having snooped in his desk. She is glad he came in when he did — before she could see more than the few facts that indicated she should definitely not be looking at this information.

Taking the glass he offers, she smiles at him. She is dying to read that file.

✍

Not as lucky as Alexis, Sy is still on the road on this Wednesday in October, two nights before Halloween; checking into the Mark Hopkins in San Francisco, he considers making a dinner reservation for himself but he really isn't interested in more fancy hotel food. He thinks longingly of a peanut butter and jelly sandwich and a good half-sour pickle. Upstairs in his room, after the bellboy leaves him in peace, he sets his overnight case on the bed and unpacks the photos of his family, setting them atop the television, which he turns on and mutes. He never carries more luggage than an overnighter, even when he is staying for a full week, with a few changes of shirts, socks, and underwear. His suit must last all week long. If he spills on his tie he sends out for a new one. He rationalizes that light packing eliminates the wait in the airport for baggage. (Carrying only the one suit means he can't be away from home for long.)

He changes into his running shorts and shoes, checks his watch, and decides to call home before going out for his daily five-miler. It's nine o'clock eastern time now, and by the time he gets back, cools down, and showers, Maggie may be asleep.

All the things he used to do to relax are gone now, whittled out of his life during the last few years by the ever-decreasing amount of free time. Running is the last pleasure left to him, and he refuses to give it up, even if it means going out late at night, in the middle of freezes, rain, dark streets. Running he must have. It has become a release for him, alone in strangely familiar cities night after night. No longer does he putter in the kitchen, cooking the big Sunday meal for the family as his father taught him: potato pancakes and brisket, honey chicken, all those parts of his past that he wanted his children to share and remember (ways of knowing his parents, who would never be knowable to Mikey or Kate); no longer does he mow his own lawn on a summer afternoon, his nose filled with the smell of sweat and fresh-cut green; it is too dark these days to throw a baseball with Mikey after supper; even grabbing the new Robert Parker novel as soon as it appears in the local B. Dalton on Central Avenue is beyond him. He is a traveling salesman who flies first-class, lives in luxury suites, eats out gourmet, and uses cellular telephones in taxis. When he comes home, he feels as if he is landing on another planet. But what right has he to complain?

He picks up the telephone and punches the Scarsdale number. It rings on the other end five times before the message machine picks up; he disconnects before the beep. Puzzled, he decides Maggie may be in the shower. He will wait five minutes and then try again.

But waiting for anything makes him tense. He wants to get out and run, forget about everything except the rhythm; feel the sweat begin across his chest and back; cleanse his mind. When he sits for too long with nothing to do he goes into overdrive. At such odd moments he often extracts his calculator from his briefcase and crunches numbers on the liquid crystal display, going over the home budget, figuring how much they've saved by now, planning for the future.

He idles his way around the room, picking things up and putting them down again. He stops and stares at the picture of Maggie on top of the television, crouched by the side of her garden, jeans stained with dirt. Below her, the news unspools: Reagan's face, then Tom Brokaw's, then the weather.

It's funny that although Maggie and he don't seem to fight anymore nothing between them feels any better. The peace (the quiet) that had been in the marriage is gone. Maggie acts as if he *enjoys* being away from them all. Though he does love his work, he'd much rather be sitting around the dinner table with his kids than be here alone, though Maggie would deride that idea. What does she want from his life anyway? he wonders. Is he supposed to quit now, after everything they've already sacrificed? Now, when he is only a few steps (a year, or at the most, two) away from partnership and everything for which he's been killing himself?

Oddly enough, Maggie no longer complains about his travel schedule, and though, at first, he found the lack of interference a relief, gradually, her silence has begun to puzzle him. He can't understand what has changed. The suspicion that she is happier when he is gone slouches toward certainty. He feels like a stranger who does nothing more than pay the bills.

Sometimes it seems he doesn't recognize the girl he married twelve years ago. He goes to the mirror. Can it really be twelve years? He stands there observing himself, bending close to the glass. He's a hell of a lot grayer. But not fatter, he thinks critically, turning sideways to pat his nonexistent stomach. He is still lean. Still has his hair. Still short.

Maggie used to like the fact that she was taller. It made them, as a couple, a bit eccentric. They used to joke about it, horse around. He thinks about how they used to go to theater in the evening, get out at ten, and then go right around the corner for a double feature. Supper on a weeknight with another couple. Drink too much and get sloppy together. He thinks about making love to Maggie and how it has changed (imperceptibly), in the last month. He feels as if she is not really *there* with him: as if she is off floating, somewhere else.

Now he breaks away from his reflection in the mirror and paces back and forth across the room. He fidgets at the mini bar, opens a bottle of sparkling water. This is the sort of hotel where they trust you to sign the chit for everything you drink. He does and stands, drinking directly from the bottle, in front of the dresser where he has set up the photos of Maggie and the kids. The travel folder was a Christmas present from Maggie his first year with First Boston. Red leather, it has twelve slots and each one is filled, the last with a photo taken this past June of his daughter, holding her new tennis racquet. Scanning the lineup, he realizes that he cannot remember exactly when or where each of these pictures was taken or how old the children were. He picks the folder up and pulls all the snapshots from behind the plastic covers, hoping that the backs are dated. Maggie (with typical attention to this sort of detail) has put a neat inscription on each one, as if she anticipated that he might need to do just this.

He sits on the edge of the bed and, holding the photos pinched along one edge like a book, he ruffles them with his thumb so that they flip past his gaze in a blur, his children's faces growing up right before his eyes. In this instant he sees a new possibility as clearly as if it is happening this very moment: himself, sitting here ten years from now, a new stack of pictures in his hand, Mikey with his first fishing rod, Kate in her first tennis tournament, on and on right up to caps and gowns at college graduation. With his hands shaking, he quickly returns each photo to its slot. He props the folder up again on the TV, and backs away from it fast.

There is something wrong, he thinks in despair. What is he doing here, in one more cold hotel room, while his children grow — unseen and untouched. What can it mean for them all? Now that Maggie has shut up, he hears his own answer in the silence. In the echo of their fading argument, he begins to see that he is more than a continent away from all three of them.

How had his father managed to work fifteen hours a day but still make his presence felt? Sy wonders. Maybe it was because Bernie Whitten was never away from home, or maybe because Sy spent almost every afternoon at the deli from the time he was old enough to reach the counters: clearing tables, emptying trash — Doris had weaned him on pickle brine instead of baby food. The three of them had been *family*, all pitching in toward the same goals: to pay the rent, to save for a good college, to buy a new dress for Doris at High Holidays. For Bernie, working long hours had nothing to do with wanting to work or loving what he did. He wanted more than that for Sy — he wanted his son to *love* his work. Now Sy does everything of which his father dreamed — except wear the family pocket watch and sleep in the family bed.

The thought of his father brings an ache to Sy's chest and he crosses to the bed and punches his home number again. He needs to talk with her. Where the hell is she? The answering machine again, Maggie's unreal voice. He leaves a short, irritated message. He picks up the newspaper and flips through it, throws it down. Then, in an attempt to blot out the anxious sensation, he takes up a yellow pad and forces himself to go over the details of the deal in his mind, making a few notes. When this preoccupation runs out, he thinks of a scotch, but vetoes the idea as it would ruin his run. He sits on the edge of the bed and reties his sneakers.

He is worried. About the distance, even when he is home. The way Maggie turned away from him on the stairs the weekend of Kate's operation. Maybe he had made a mistake in leaving town that weekend. He had felt he had no choice — but maybe he ought just to have said no. He shakes his head, confused. At one time in his life it had seemed there was always a *right* answer — if only you could find it. But now what is right for one part of his life is wrong for the rest of it.

He reaches over for the phone again. Five and then the canned Whitten line. A damn long shower, he decides angrily. He hangs up. He can't wait around anymore. He snaps off the light and slams the door behind him.

THIRTEEN

The Scorekeeper

Maggie pays the cabdriver through the front window, and looks up and down the dark street nervously. It is chilly and she shivers, wishing she had worn a coat; dry leaves scud over the sidewalk. There is no one in sight. Squinting under the dim street lamps, she locates the building and then climbs the stairs, clutching her purse against her stomach like a shield.

Chelsea is a charming area of Manhattan, and Nicolas's sublet is in an old brownstone. As she enters the foyer and scans the buzzers for his name, a couple comes out the door and she catches it on the backswing to avoid ringing. She has never been to his apartment before, and she likes the idea of surprising him. It took quite a bit of arranging (lying) to manage this trip into Manhattan: Sy is out of town; the children are spending the night at the Kirchenbaums', making Halloween costumes with Samantha and Joshua for Friday night. In the event that Sy calls from San Francisco, Maggie plans to say that she turned the answering machine on and went to bed early with a headache.

Before driving to the train station, she bathed, dried her hair so that it would float around her face, perfumed and powdered herself; she had even gone out that afternoon to buy new silk panties and bra. This break in their pattern — of afternoon trysts in the attic, where they do nothing but sex — is quite conscious on her part. His talk the other day about the two of them making a life together both intrigued and frightened her, and now there are many things she needs to know. She wants to see where Nicolas lives and what it would be like to spend an entire night together for once. To see on which side of the bed he sleeps, whether he reads the paper over breakfast — the inconsequential details that make up the patterns of a life.

In the dim hallway, she stops in front of number 3A. Takes a deep breath. She wonders why she is so nervous. A band of light glows beneath the door and, dimly audible, a radio plays, the music interrupted by an announcement. As she raises her hand to knock, she freezes. Two voices: he is not alone.

She stands there, indecisive. It had never occurred to her that someone else might be with him. She can't imagine walking away now, leaving without having had the chance to see him, getting a cab back to Grand Central. This evening has taken too much arranging. She stands, still, in front of the door. Yet, even as she is trying to decide what to do, she is simultaneously struggling to overhear what the voices say. To discover who it is. She hears his voice, deep, and then a response, lighter and higher-pitched. A woman. Anger moves through her body as water moves through a seine net, leaving behind detritus: envy.

The words come to her as a low murmur, a muffled stream of sound. When she was young she used to stand outside her father's home office just like this, ear to wood. Eavesdropping on his patients' sessions. She always had a pretext ready to explain her presence, should anyone come along and find her. Standing here now, remembering, she smiles to herself, bemused: how strange that one door is so interchangeable with another, that the streets of our adulthood so often merge into the hallways of our childhood homes. One moment overlaps the next thirty years later; the past, newly clothed, masquerades as the present.

But the voices at this door, in this time, grow louder; her attention refocuses on this moment as the others approach the entrance. Moving with haste, Maggie backs down the hall into the stairwell, where she stands, eye pressed against the crack of the door. Nicolas holds the door, dressed in jeans and a tennis shirt, smiling. A young woman exits, also smiling, carrying in her hand a can of coffee. Maggie relaxes a little: a neighbor on the borrow. But still, she notes (resentfully) as the other woman passes her hiding spot, a good-looking neighbor. Nicolas shuts his door. Maggie hears another slam, echoing his, from farther down the hall.

She emerges from behind the exit door, feeling silly and sticky around the armpits. She approaches once again and knocks.

When he opens it, a slow smile crosses his face. "Well, hello." He is clearly delighted.

"A little surprise," she says, suddenly shy.

"A big surprise!" He wraps his arms around her as he kicks the door shut and they kiss. Her tension simultaneously heightens and dissolves.

"A drink?" he asks, as they move apart.

She nods and looks around.

The place is astonishingly messy. She restrains the urge to walk around and pick up the newspapers that lie in drifts on the floor, the towel draped over the back of the leather sofa. Instead, she follows him to the kitchen. Nicolas looks up from putting ice into a glass.

"Not exactly Fifth Avenue," he says, following her gaze.

"It's not bad," she says, encouragingly. "Maybe a little too much of the modern bachelor for you."

He cocks his head. "That's what I am though."

They laugh.

"Well," she says, "this is just temporary anyway. Soon you'll be getting a place. With your own furniture, books, pictures."

"That depends."

"On what?"

"You." He looks at her and extends her glass.

She takes the drink and goes to sit in the living room, shoving the newspapers aside.

He sits down with her and begins to nuzzle her neck. "How did you manage to get into the city at night?"

"A little finesse," she says airily, preferring not to remember just how she had accomplished it. "I can stay, if you like."

"I like just fine," he says, stroking her hair. "Just fine."

"Who was it I saw leaving your place as I was coming up?"

His hand stops stroking midair. "A neighbor."

"You've never mentioned her," Maggie says casually, rummaging in her purse for a tissue.

He shrugs and smiles. "No reason to, I guess."

"No reason?"

He stops, looks at her hard, then catches on. A wide grin crosses his face. "You're jealous!" he says with plain delight.

"I am not! You're free to do whatever you want."

"True," he observes. "And I am."

"Am what?" she says, suddenly suspicious again.

He puts his head back and laughs. "Being with you!"

"Don't make fun of me, Nicolas," she says, a warning edge in her voice.

"Who's making fun?" He kisses her palm and smiles at her, knowingly. "I just love it when you're jealous."

She pulls her hand away sulkily. "Like I said — you're free."

"But I don't want to be," he replies. "I told you that."

She studies her shoes. "Forget I asked," she says now. "It's not important."

"It is to me," he says.

She gets up and paces. "Is that the bedroom?" she asks, nodding in the direction of the only other door. She looks at her watch. Time, she thinks with exasperation, is like a wayward child — bullheaded and slippery in the extreme — disappearing around all sorts of corners when you least expect it.

"You know," he says slowly, "sometimes it seems like all you want to do is go to bed. You don't like to talk anymore."

"That's not true!" she cries, stung. "It's just — we have so little time together." She crosses to nuzzle his neck but he remains cool.

"That's exactly what I mean," he says. "We used to talk all the time. Now we just screw."

"This must be a joke," she says with a short laugh. "Imagine a man complaining that a woman wants too much sex."

"I'm serious." He drinks from his glass and watches her.

She gets up and looks out the window. "Maybe it wasn't a good idea to come here."

"Why?"

"If I'd wanted to fight with someone I could have called Sy in San Francisco." Her voice quivers. "And you're making me feel ashamed — what's wrong with wanting you?" she asks, defiance mixing with tears. "Can't you understand that this is the first time for me?" She looks away and her voice drops to a whisper. "I used to feel so . . . so stunted. Shut out. With you it's been different."

He gets up and wraps his arms around her, smooths her hair. "I do understand. Why do you think it's that way?"

She shrugs. "I don't want to know. Knowing might change it."

He holds her, but he is very still against her. "I want more of you than just this," he says at last. "I don't want it to be just sexual."

"We've been friends too long for it to be 'just sexual,' " she says, pushing back so that she can look him, with an earnest intensity, right in the eye.

"I don't want to be 'just friends' either." He shakes his head. "I feel so much more than that."

"Nico," she entreats. "*You* gave me myself. No one else. That makes the bond between us unlike anything else. No matter what happens in the end."

He kisses the side of her neck. She puts her hand across his mouth, looks him in the face again. "I love you for it, Nicolas. I always will."

He takes her hand away, kisses her again, and slides his hands down her body. Hooking his thumbs on the hem of her skirt, he pulls it up. His eyes gleam. His palms cup her buttocks. He pulls her against him, hard, and squeezes.

"Too hard," she murmurs, quivering against him.

He senses in her words not a complaint, but an observation. Reading her, he does it again, firm flesh kneaded between his thumb and forefinger; harder and then, again, even a little harder. Now she groans and arches against him. He gets hard against the rough denim of his jeans.

He pushes her toward the bedroom. She complies, walking backward, hampered by her hiked-up skirt and heels. With a small shove, he topples her backward onto the bed, unmade, a tangle of sheets and the dirty clothes that he was gathering up to take out to the laundry. She falls softly, lands with her arms out by her sides. He stands above her, between her legs, smiling. He bends to kiss her while, over her head, he roots through the clothes. Pushing her arms up, he takes a tie and wraps it around her wrists.

Startled, eyes wide, she looks up at him. "What are you doing?"

He smiles as he knots her hands above her head. He doesn't answer. Instead, he takes something and puts it over her eyes.

As he ties the cloth, it scratches her eyelids. A little pulse of fear runs through her, then changes to excitement: not to be able to see where he will touch her next is like a return to infancy — now everything depends on sensation and nothing on knowledge.

"Who do you belong to?" he asks.

"No one," she answers defiantly. Blindfolded, still half dressed, she is getting wet with anticipation.

His hands check the knot around her wrists — make sure it is tight, but not too tight. "Who do you belong to?" he repeats.

"No one," she answers, more defiant still. She wriggles, pretending to try and free herself. This is a new game but without even thinking she knows all the rules.

"Naughty girl," Nicolas says, unbuttoning her blouse and fondling her breasts. "I'm going to have to punish you."

She starts to giggle. She can't believe they are doing this, but it excites her the way nothing ever has. She closes her eyes and pretends she is watching a movie. "No one," she says again, provocatively, daring him.

He slaps her then, softly but with sting, on the belly.

"Hey," she says, surprised.

Again, softly, on the breasts.

Her body is lighting up. The sting of the slap turns to warmth, then to heat. It matches the heat below.

"You have to let me go," she says.

"Not yet. Not until I'm finished." He pulls her skirt down over her hips.

A zipper rasps down. His weight tilts the bed. He pushes her legs apart and her inner thigh quivers, anticipating his touch. But he doesn't touch her there. He just leaves her, humiliated by the weight of her own desire, waiting until he decides what to do next.

She lies spread out, a sweetmeat on a pile of laundry. The

smell of sweat from the dirty clothes rises up around them, mixing with the smell of her perfume and her body. He starts to suck on one breast, nibbling and biting the nipple, harder and harder, while softly pinching the other. Then switches. In a minute, she is so excited that she comes, without his ever having touched her anywhere else.

"What do you want now?" he asks.

She feels she can't say it but her hips rise in silent appeal.

"Say it."

She is still silent.

He slaps her belly again: he is reading her the rules. She groans.

"Say it."

Now he does not touch her, and the absence of that touch burns. She needs to feel him, to be touched and so reassured — absence is hell. Torture in the purest black: the empty sky. "Touch me," she begs, at last. "Touch me there."

Satisfied by her submission, he at last begins to rub her through her panties. A light teasing touch that just brushes the tip of her clitoris, until she is so wet that the crotch of the panties is wet. He pulls them off and at last begins to insinuate his fingers into her, a little at a time, two fingers then three, burrowing, scooping into her as if she is a fertile garden, opening her up to be sowed.

She gasps, spreads herself wider, lifting her hips off the bed. His whole hand is inside her, stroking in and out, accelerating, he fucks her with his fist. One and two come in an instant, from his hand. He doesn't even let her recover, but, demanding, puts her through the paces, wanting to see what she can do. His tongue brings her to three and four, and a minute later to five and six. When she stops screaming with the pleasure of seven in a row, she realizes for the first time that her wrists hurt.

She waits. Her body glows all over. He leaves the room. She is out of breath, sweaty and hot. Her throat aches. He comes back into the room. He lies beside her on the bed. *Click, click,* something in a metal bowl.

"What are you doing?" she asks.

"You look so hot," he answers, pushing her legs apart again to put his fingers up inside her. Now she feels something else:

what is he doing? He sucks on her nipple and his mouth is cold. She gets erect again. Inside her, his fingers are still stroking and she is getting incredibly wet, there is the strange sensation of something trickling out of her; it is ice melting.

"I thought you might want to cool off," he whispers, taking another piece and beginning to stroke it across her stomach and breasts. It is melting on her, the water is dribbling off her breasts, out of her cunt, onto the sheets. He laps it up as it runs down her. "You know you are mine," he says now. "You belong to me."

"I belong to you," she says and the joy of it fills her. To be held, to be owned, to be joined and bound together makes her know that she is. The skin of her wrists burns from the tight cloth, aching, and that heat magnifies the cold below, the stripes he is painting on her body.

His tongue is on her now, warming and freezing, lapping, while the burning above intensifies and pain and pleasure fuse, and when he mounts her, his penis pushes the ice up inside higher and higher; as the ice melts, a little waterfall of cold spills from inside her. She is hot on the outside, iced on the inside, forced to the edge.

She is his slave, his thing to do with as he wills, his child; she builds, she raises, she is almost there; she screams as he pushes her over the edge, and she flings herself out, into the blackness, free because she knows he holds her. Bound with and by this emotion she names love, she goes under, somewhere dark, the center of the earth; he bites her neck softly, to mark her, to bring her back to this bed, this time, now.

Sometime later, he unties her and rubs her wrists, kisses the veins where they run, calm, beneath the surface; he worships her survival. They roll apart and lie side by side in the dark. They do not speak. In the immediate glow, she draws close by his side. Tears form at the corner of her eyes for their return to separateness, for the loss of the bond.

They fall asleep this way. Sometime in the middle of the night, Maggie wakes, needing to go to the bathroom. When she comes back to bed, she cannot get comfortable. Anxiety twitches. She keeps thinking about the children and wondering whether or not Sy has called. The room is strange to her, overheated, the sheets seem slick (she wonders when they were last washed), and Nicolas's form unfamiliar. They do not curl together the way she and Sy usually do. She had thought this would be a tender night, but now her mind is plagued with the image of her husband, asleep in his hotel bed by himself. Right now, the intimacy of sleeping together transcends the intimacy of sex, and guilt assaults her. She stares out into the darkness and at four, falls back to sleep at last.

In the morning, traffic noise wakes her. Six o'clock. Too little sleep has given her a headache. She is sore, especially her arms and shoulders. She groans as she rolls over.

Suddenly she wants to get up and away from that bed. Consciousness has returned, accompanied by shame. The dirt of what they did. She does not want to look at Nicolas's face.

"How about I make us something to eat?" she offers in a subdued voice. She intuits his assenting nod.

She borrows a shirt and goes hurriedly into the kitchen, rummaging in the refrigerator until she comes up with enough to turn out a couple of plain omelettes and some toast. As the butter melts in the skillet, she pours two small glasses of juice. Nicolas comes out of the bedroom, rubbing his eyes, and watches her as she cooks.

She puts two plates down on the table. She feels a little better, the distance she needed attained.

Nicolas butters his toast and chases the eggs around his plate. "Have you thought any more about Maine?"

"Have you?" she parries, unwilling to be trapped into talking about this. She busies herself spreading jam on the toast.

"I've been making inquiries. But it all depends on you."

The weight of everything descends on her. The eggs seem greasy and cold in her mouth. "I don't want it to depend on me," she says at last. "You need to do what's right for you."

"I want to be with you."

"I know." She is running from being put in a corner by his love. What does he mean to her? she wonders, as she stares across the table at his handsome face.

"Just think of the kind of life we could have," he goes on, ignoring her silence. "I keep picturing it — coming home to you every night, the kids playing checkers by the fire. All in a home we've made together."

His words echo across the table at her: what about all the

nights when Kate and Mikey are less than perfect; when they whine, or an earache interferes with the plans for dinner and a movie; what about the nights they are bored and restless, or the times they get themselves into trouble? With the exception of that one night with Mikey, Nicolas has a skewed picture of how easy children are. Not the sort of person from whom you can expect the practical, he wants to switch jobs at the drop of a hat, he wants to make love in the middle of the afternoon. On the other hand, she reminds herself, Sy, who had always seemed entirely dependable, has now become dependably undependable. She sighs and leans her head in her hands. She had thought that being here last night would provide the last link, the answer. It has not.

He watches her. "Don't you want us to be together?"

She has already made a home, ordered fabrics and furniture, planted a garden, renovated, and renewed. Had two children and raised them nearly by herself. One of the things she likes best about the affair with Nicolas is that in no way has she ever been responsible. Slowly she turns her head and looks around the apartment, at the stacks of dirty dishes, the signs of bachelor life.

"Don't you want to be with me?" he repeats insistently. His eyes allow her no escape.

"You know I do." She evades his gaze. "I love every minute we have together." She doesn't want what he offers her, but neither is she yet willing to relinquish that which she takes from him.

"That's not what I mean," he says, his voice stubborn. "I mean do you want to be with me every day?"

"It's not so easy as that for me," she says, getting up to pace with frustration. "I'm not divorced, or separated, like you. I have children depending on me — we're in entirely different situations."

"Do you still love him?"

"I don't know. I don't know what I feel."

"And what about the children?"

"What about them?"

"Supposing he fought you for custody? And won? Would you still come with me then?"

She simply stares at him, struck first with terror at the idea of Sy suing for control of her children's lives, and then with shock — for in asking this one simple question he has revealed how little he knows her. There is no man for whom she would leave her children. "I need time," she says. "There are a lot of people to think about here." She gets up and clears the table, then fills the sink with soapy water.

Nicolas goes into the living room and turns on the news. When she finishes the dishes, she heads back to the bedroom. He comes up behind her and catches her shoulder. He holds on. "Come back to bed," he urges.

"I want to take a shower."

"Maybe I should make you," he says suggestively, running his hands around her waist in a tight circle.

"Don't talk like that!" Mortified by the memory, she had hoped he wouldn't bring it up.

"Why not? You liked it a lot."

She freezes.

"Why not admit it? We both loved it." He strokes her back. "It was the best I've ever had."

"Liking it doesn't mean you have to repeat it."

"Who said anything about *having* to?"

"It doesn't mean you want to either." Something strikes her then. "Have you ever done that with anyone before?"

He shakes his head. "Never. I never trusted anyone enough."

"*You* never trusted?" she echoes, surprised.

He nods. "I didn't hurt you, did I?"

"It was bad," she says with a low voice, putting it in the past tense. "We should never do it again."

"My little Puritan." He laughs, amused now. "We'll do whatever you *want* to do."

"It wasn't my idea," she says, somewhat hotly.

"I didn't hear you objecting."

She pushes away from him and goes to the bathroom. The heat of the shower water scalds her skin. Taking up the soap, she scrubs and scrubs at her body, but the stain of new knowledge is permanent: it will never wash out and it cannot be forgotten. The simple fact is that she did like what they did: she did love it. The lure of it pulls at her even now, and for the first time she wonders whether her desire for Nicolas is really, in fact, something else. Her willingness — no, eagerness — to be subjugated by him scares her more than cheating on her husband, more than the idea of divorce. It was exciting, but is it what she wants to live with in the long run?

As she turns the shower off, she thinks that last night she rippled her fingers in a dark pond within herself; as in childhood fantasies, this pond has a resident monster lurking at the bottom. For the first time she sees that, if she stays with Nicolas, it will be hard to resist slipping in, late at night, naked and willing, to swim repeatedly with her own inner dangers.

ᔓ

Outside, it is close to dark. Inside, the children intensify as the daylight diminishes. Too impatient to wait any longer, Mikey and Kate struggle into the costumes they have made and pivot with excitement in front of their mother. They are showing off to their first audience. She claps her hands as they run, billowing in white sheets, back and forth in front of her.

"See how I did this part," Kate says, holding up the white wing of her costume. "Mrs. Kirchenbaum helped me make it so that it would look like I was *really* flying." She strokes it in the mirror, pleased.

Maggie smiles.

"Mom," Mikey asks, "could you put some black lines on? I want to look like there are spider webs on me."

Maggie gets her eye pencil and starts to sketch squiggly lines across his sheeted face. He wriggles. "Hey, that tickles!"

They laugh together and she thinks, with regret, that she missed something Wednesday night: this is the first year they have ever made their costumes, and she didn't get to watch them do it or to help. His brown eyes watch her, carefully, as she circles the very rim of his eyes with the liner; he does not even blink, trusting she will not let the sharp point slip.

They are costumed as spooks, in clear defiance of the superhero craze that has seized everyone under twelve. She had been certain that Mikey would insist on being a Ghostbuster. She leans back on her heels and looks at her handiwork critically. It's the best she can manage. "Take a look," she says.

He studies himself in the mirror and nods in approval. "Radical, Mom."

"Me, me!" Kate squeals, looking at her brother with delight. "Only make mine a different color — 'cause I'm a girl ghost. Do you have pink?"

"How about blue?"

"Pink's my favorite."

"These are my eyeliner pencils," Maggie retorts. "Do I look like I've got pink eyes?"

"Oh, Mom," Kate giggles. She puts her face up and Maggie goes to work with blue and green, getting artistic and even drawing in a few spiders and bees along the way.

"Coolo!" Kate declares when she checks it out in the mirror. "I love you, Mom." She gives her a big hug and then she and Mikey run down the stairs as the doorbell rings, announcing the arrival of the Kirchenbaums for supper. Maggie hears the commotion begin and smiles with pleasure at their excitement. Her heart lifts: this Friday she is glad she is nowhere else than right here with them.

An hour later, they twirl in front of the hall mirror, having eaten next to nothing, still admiring their reflections, still fiddling and adjusting, a rowdy crowd, stamping with impatience. Sy and Jerry have their cameras out — one 35 mm. and one video — with promises for an even exchange of snaps and tapes.

"Let's go! Let's go!" Mikey's voice is even louder than usual; Sy throws Maggie a look and smiles indulgently at his son's enthusiasm. Though she smiles back, sharing that pleasure, she feels as if he has tossed a live grenade into the fortress she has erected around herself over the past two months. Everything is happening at once: Nicolas, pressuring her to leave Sy, and Sy for once making good on a commitment and reminding Maggie that he can be a good parent when he tries.

"It's dark now, Mom, can't we leave?" Kate entreats.

"Come on, Mrs. Whitten," Samantha says in her most persuasive, most reasonable, voice, "or all the other kids will get there before us."

Maggie represses the urge to observe that the neighborhood won't run out of candy, and stoops instead to wipe the ring of spaghetti sauce off Mikey's mouth. He gives her a surprising hug, which fills her with warmth. "I guess it's time," she agrees.

Shrieks of joy. All six move toward the door in a wave,

tripping and jostling each other as the long white sheets tangle and get underfoot. They trundle out, each grabbing a pillow-case for a candy sack. Maggie waves as they go down the driveway, and then stands in the doorway to watch as Sy's flashlight bobs through the black night and Jerry herds the flock across the street. It has become tradition for the Whittens and the Kirchenbaums to go trick-or-treating as a group, with the fathers acting as the Sherpas. The sound of excited children's voices filters up and down the ordinarily quiet street, and Maggie stands there, remembering her own childhood, when she and her friends haunted the darkness, alone and safe. Not anymore, she thinks, not my kids.

The air is clean and cold against her cheeks, and she stands there for a minute, sniffing. Someone has lit a wood fire; it brings home the idea that winter is truly just around the corner. Up and down the street, lights flash like summer fireflies through trees that are now fully bare-branched. Maggie closes the door with regret, wishing she could go and sit on the glider, bundled up in her down vest, to watch the parade of children pass by. But soon they will storm her doorbell, giving her no peace, and she wants to get the dishes cleaned up first.

Back in the kitchen, Jan's dark head is already bent over a sink deep with soapy water. Biting the tip of her tongue in concentration, she diligently scrubs out the spaghetti pot.

Maggie picks up a dish towel and starts to dry; they work in companionable silence for a while. Jan is more like a sister to her than a sister could ever be; she refills their wineglasses.

"Nice supper." Jan takes a big sip, her large hands leaving soap suds on the wineglass. She resumes scrubbing, her body jiggling with earnest motion. "Halloween spaghetti here is turning into a real ritual."

"Does it seem like a weird thing to eat for Halloween?" Maggie laughs. "My family always had spaghetti and garlic bread. My mother hates to cook," she goes on, taking more plates from the table and loading them into the dishwasher. "But spaghetti is one thing she did really well. The whole house smelled of the sauce by the time I came home from school. I liked that spaghetti more than the candy that came later."

The doorbell rings. "Here we go," Maggie says, putting her towel down and heading toward the front hall.

"I still can't get over that the kids wanted to make their own costumes," Jan says when Maggie returns, and hands her a wet knife to dry.

"By next year we'll be in Big Top buying Dracula or Ghostbusters." Maggie slides the knife home into the block.

"Just a question of time," Jan agrees dryly. "And next year the girls will want one thing and the boys another. Did you see Josh had his pistols on under that sheet?"

Maggie laughs. "Mikey had his rubber knife." She sighs and takes a paper towel to wipe the fingerprints off the front of the refrigerator door. "I wish he'd outgrow this weapon-crazed phase."

"Martha Sullivan says her David is finally getting interested in something else."

"How old is he?"

"Eight. Maybe there's hope." She hands Maggie another load of wet utensils and the doorbell rings again. Maggie goes to answer it and returns a second later. "The Carters with fright wigs, the Weisses as the Three Stooges."

Jan laughs. "That's what they went as last year!"

"Ellie's pretty tired."

"Is her chemo finished?"

"For now, I guess," Maggie says, putting the Parmesan away in the refrigerator. "I drove her to her last treatment in July. It's not the sort of thing you can ask too many questions about."

They both fall silent.

"Hey," Maggie says after a minute, trying to restore a lighter note, "thanks again for taking the kids the other night."

"No trouble." Jan turns the water off. "Did you sleep off your headache?"

Maggie turns so that Jan will not see the flush on her cheeks, and busies herself with hanging the colander back on its hook. "It was much better when I woke up." She brings the last load of plates from the table and starts to stack them in the dishwasher. This time the doorbell provides a welcome distraction, and when she returns to the kitchen Jan seems to have forgotten the topic.

"I was surprised to see Sy home so early," she says, as she sips her wine.

"So was I," Maggie agrees. In fact, she had been shocked when he'd turned up, quite unexpectedly, in the early afternoon. "He said he was tired."

"Sy? Tired?" She starts to laugh. "That's a new one."

"Maybe all those red-eyes are catching up with him." Maggie had watched his shoulders as he went up the stairs and she'd thought of what might have happened, if this were a different day, if Nicolas and she had been here together, upstairs. Or the other night, that scene she is trying so hard to repress. Suddenly her entire life seems balanced on a precipice.

She had followed Sy upstairs, just to see what he was going to do. He lay down on the bed, saying he wanted to take a nap. She'd gone over and felt his forehead, but his skin was cool to her touch. He closed his eyes under her hand. She'd started to rub his head, as if he were a child. When she asked what was wrong, he mumbled again that he was tired and turned on his side; in an instant, he was asleep.

His fragility frightened her: Maggie always counted on Sy to be strong because he had always been strong. In all the years of their marriage, she could number on one hand the times she'd seen him take a nap. Surprised, she just sat on the end of the bed and watched him sleep. After a while, she went downstairs.

He'd slept for hours, and during that time she kept wondering if maybe he had suspected something. He had not even asked her where she was Wednesday night, though he had called around nine and left an irritated message on the machine.

"He took a long nap," she says now to Jan. "I guess he wanted to be awake enough to take the kids out tonight."

Jan pulls the plug in the sink and leans against the counter thoughtfully, her hands still covered with soapsuds. The dishwater gurgles noisily down the drain. "Don't you ever wonder what keeps these guys going?"

"When you got married," Maggie asks dreamily, looking out the back window to the round yellow moon, which hovers just above the treeline, "what did you think it would be like?"

"Like my parents," Jan answers promptly. "I thought Jerry would graduate from law school and we'd raise a family and be together every night."

"My mother was the one always taking off. I always wanted

to go one better than what she and Dad managed. Make a *real* family. Belong somewhere." She sighs. "I never thought I'd end up like this. This footrace is absurd." She sighs. "No one will win."

Jan sips her wine for a moment. "When I look at the women I'm working with down at the hospital, you know, who mostly have no husbands at all anymore, or never did — just too many kids and sick ones at that — I think, damn but I'm *lucky*."

"I'm too mad to be guilty these days." Maggie's voice rises. "It really galls me that Sy can make time for what he *wants* to do. Like the trick-or-treating tonight — I'm sure he had to do some fancy footwork to be sure he didn't have to stay an extra day in California. But when we're in a real crisis, like Kate's operation/or Mikey's experiment with the Dimetapp, where the hell is he?"

Jan lays a hand on Maggie's arm and her touch calms. Maggie laughs, a little self-consciously. "It seems to me," Jan says after a minute, "that you need to be doing something yourself. What happened to going back to work?"

"Sy didn't want me to."

Jan is silent, looks away. "That's just what the men are always doing," she says slowly after a minute, "blaming someone else for their own lack of priorities. Seems like if you want to go back to work, you will."

In silence they finish up. Maggie wipes the counters down as Jan scours out the sink. The doorbell rings again and they both go to answer it this time. Three Spidermen, Ernie, Bert, and a dinosaur leer for their candy. After buying off the horde, the two women sit down at the bottom of the staircase, so that the next time the doorbell summons them they won't have so far to walk. As mothers they are accustomed to doing their talking whenever and wherever they can.

"I watched Sy over dinner tonight," Jan says thoughtfully. "If you look at your kids' faces as they're near him, they are incredibly intense."

Maggie nods. "Maybe they're trying to woo him back into living with us." This thought makes her sad. And then her anger returns: if only he had been here, she wouldn't have turned to Nicolas. But, even as she thinks it, she knows this is not the whole truth. She might have turned to Nicolas regardless. Or she could have been stronger, she could have said no to him and dealt with Sy and their problems head-on. She could have left Sy first and found Nicolas second. The alternatives are endless. She sighs again.

"What is it?" Jan asks. "You seem so down tonight."

"I don't know. . . . The complications of life, I guess."

"For instance?"

"I'm wondering how much longer we can go on pretending to be a family."

Jan leans back against the stair above and sips her wine. "Pretending?"

"Pretending."

"What are you saying?"

"I'm saying neither one of us has our hearts in this anymore. We're not *together* anymore."

Jan tips her head to one side and looks speculatively at Maggie. "Does that mean you're with someone else?"

Maggie turns her face so she will not have to look at Jan.

"I didn't really think you were home with a headache."

Maggie doesn't answer. She rubs her thumb up and down the curve of her wineglass.

"I left Jerry once," Jan says into the long silence, thus giving Maggie an opportunity to confide her own guilty secret. "For about a month."

"Were you with someone else?"

Jan shakes her head, ruefully. "I'd just had enough of him, that's all."

"But you went back. Why?"

Jan shrugs. "Sometimes that old cliché about the kids is true. Then after I came back, we had the twins." She shakes her head. "It was the right decision. If I'd left Jerry for good, I just would have been moving my problems to a new stage."

Maggie looks at her thoughtfully. "Would you believe I was asked the other night whether I'd consider leaving the kids behind if Sy fought me for custody?" She laughs incredulously, short and sharp. "Sometimes you think you know someone so well, and they you. Maybe all that only comes with living for a person for a long time." Maggie falls silent. Her mind circles around to the sex she and Nicolas had Wednesday night, all limits blown: no handrails, no guardrails. Anything they do now will be anticlimactic. Sex with him has been addictive, and it was always moving, inexorably, to the single act of that night. There were seeds of it the first time they'd gone to bed, the way he'd made the responsibility for pleasure all his. It had suited her then; she is not sure that she can allow it to suit her now.

Jan gets up to answer the doorbell.

"Is he married?" Jan asks, breaking into her thoughts as she sits back down.

"About to be divorced."

"What're you going to do, and do you mind if I ask who it is?"

"I don't know yet, and yes I do mind." She shrugs with embarrassment. "Maybe I'm being silly."

Jan shakes her head. "Whatever . . . I admit I am insatiably curious."

"It's Nicolas Linden," Maggie says slowly, after a minute.

"Alexis Somers's ex? Does Alexis know?"

Maggie shakes her head. "It's sad, but we've really grown apart. When she left him, Nicolas seemed so lost. He just kept turning up on my doorstep."

"It must be hard, with him one of Sy's oldest friends."

Maggie looks away, sensing Jan's disapproval. "We've known each other a long time, too," she says defensively. "I've been so alone the last few years that I might as well have been separated. A single parent."

"Oh, Maggie, I know just how this scenario works," Jan says, putting her hand on her arm. "You see your best friends more than anybody else, and these little undercurrents develop." She sighs. "But it's complicated."

"He wants to change things — and I like everything just the way it is."

"What do you get from him that you can't get here?"

"Oh, not much except attention. Admiration. A little worship on the side. And, of course, exceptional sex." She blushes.

"Mmm," Jan says. "Hard to give up. Without a doubt."

"I'm not sure I'll have to give it up," she answers defiantly.

Jan looks at her quizzically. "How much of your unhappiness is just the situation? It's hard to like living with someone when they're never around."

Maggie stares at her, struck by this thought. "That's true," she says. "Separating out the problems is hard."

"If Sy were around every night — sharing it all — how would you feel then?"

Maggie is caught off balance, taken aback by the simplicity of the question. "I don't know," she answers slowly, "but it's an interesting idea."

"There's a difference between a bad marriage and a marriage that's going through a bad time," Jan reflects. "The fact that there are children involved ought to make you really consider hard. You've got to be damned sure you know what you're doing." She runs her fingers over her glass. "I wouldn't leave Jerry if he was the one cheating. I'd just get him to stop!"

They both laugh.

"What I really hate the most about all of it is that it's so *familiar!* I mean, didn't we have some ideals at one point? Didn't we say we'd never get married because marriage was a sham?"

Jan nods. "And then we said, well, we'll get married, but we'll do it better than our parents did because they didn't know the true meaning of commitment. Of being equals."

"And look where we end up: right here, in just exactly the same spot. Full of intrigue and lies." Maggie shakes her head in disgust. "I grew up in a house where my mother spent a lot of time with men other than my father." She stares off into space. "I always vowed I'd never be like her. I thought she was such a traitor."

"How do you feel about her now?" Jan asks, curiously.

"The same way!" Maggie exclaims, bursting into laughter. "Isn't that ridiculous! I make excuses for what I'm doing, of course — like my father was there for her every night — but in my heart I *know* those are just excuses." She sighs and drinks some more wine. "We just rationalize whatever we really want to do, so that we can go right ahead with it." She pauses. "Maybe I hate her less. Because now I see *how* it works."

"You've got to decide where the love is, Maggie. Do you realize you haven't said one word about loving Nicolas?"

Maggie drops her face down into her hands.

Jan puts her arm around her. "Everything will work out in

the end — whichever way you choose. Just don't jump into anything."

∽

Later, when Sy comes back and Jan leaves, Maggie watches everything he does very carefully, as if she is gathering facts upon which to base a decision. While he helps the children brush their teeth, reads each a story, and puts them to bed, she watches. Absorbed as he is in these tasks, she feels an aura of sadness clinging to him, as visible as the tired sag of his suit when he gets off the plane.

At last all the chores are done, the children asleep, the doorbell stilled, the lights out in an attempt to discourage anyone who might ring late. At nine-thirty, they get into bed together.

"What's wrong?" she asks. "You seem so sad."

"I've been feeling strange all week."

"Are you sick?"

He shakes his head and turns on his side to face her.

She finds it hard to meet his eyes, she sees so much trust there and she keeps thinking of all she has betrayed. The desire to blurt out the truth wells up in her: she imagines that he will forgive her and she will be cleansed — confession. But she suspects that anger is the motivation here, hidden and slippery, and so she controls herself.

"After I tried calling you and you didn't answer," he goes on, not having sensed her distraction, "I went out running and started thinking. I don't really belong here with you and the kids anymore."

Maggie sits very still against her pillows, heart pounding. "What do you mean?" For a minute she is overwhelmed with the fear that he is going to tell her he wants to leave her.

"There's this distance between us," he goes on, "all the time now."

"About three thousand miles," she answers, bitterly.

"I should have known you'd make some crappy comment. I used to be able to count on you to *listen*."

"Sorry," she mutters.

"We can't even talk straight. What's happening to us?"

"I don't know."

"You've shut me out. What in hell has changed so much?"

The truth is as close as he is. How easy (how pleasurable) it would be to say, "Yes, I got tired of waiting; yes, I went away; yes, I did find someone else." If she begins to make up some lie, some reassurance for his fear, she will start to sob or laugh hysterically. So she just sits there, without speaking, overwhelmed with the intensity of emotion.

"What's going on, Maggie?"

Anger rescues her, storming inside her body. "I didn't leave first, Sy," she says. "You did."

"But I didn't think I was going anywhere."

"The point is that you did! You walked off and told us to hang around until you felt like getting back. I've got news for you — people don't work that way. They can't just wait around while the world marches on."

"It wasn't the way you make it sound," he protests.

"No? How would *you* describe it?"

"I was working. It wasn't like I was off with some other woman."

"I could understand it better if you had been. Then at least you'd be real, instead of some windup toy they stick in front of a deal. The bell on the floor of the Exchange rings and you all start salivating like Pavlov's dog!"

"All I do is for you, for the kids," he says, defensively. "My family comes first."

"You don't do it for us! That's just what you like to pretend. You know, you used to tell me all these wonderful stories about your father, about how the family *was* the most important thing to him — so I don't understand why it's so different for you."

He looks down at the blanket. "My father worked to earn a living. I guess I wanted more than that. *He* wanted more for me than that."

"Of course he did. But he wouldn't have wanted you to work *without* living. And that's what you're doing, what you've required us to do."

They sit in silence for a time.

"I feel like we're not married anymore," he says slowly.

"Then what the hell are we?" she says angrily.

"Living in the same house. And that's all."

Again she is silent and the silence cuts at him. He wants her to deny that it is true; he wants her to tell him that they will be bonded together forever. He has not felt so lonely since his parents died. He closes his eyes but the tear slides out anyway, rolling down into the cup of his ear.

Maggie sees that first tear. She reaches out to touch it. Her finger comes away wet. Once again, he seems as fragile as a child, and once more she is frightened by that. She puts her hand on his shoulder and he turns to her; she holds him, rocking him across her lap, bending to kiss the top of his head. She is startled to see how gray his hair has become, to feel its wiry texture, to know that a few nights ago she held another man and he was different. Now she is the one who closes her eyes.

"I need you," he says now, fiercely, reaching up to pull her down into the bed with him, so moving her from comforter to partner.

She cannot avoid seeing his face now, this face she has loved for so many mornings and evenings, beside her with tenderness and devotion in front of the altar; with strength and tenacity through their two labors. Without thinking, she reaches out to kiss him; for the first time in a long while he is not tentative in response.

To her surprise, her body responds. This breaks something inside of her: if she had waited, she might have discovered these feelings with Sy. Now they will never share the elation of her discovery; instead, she will always remember Nicolas — the one who was there when she first let go. She holds Sy tightly and wonders at the treachery of her body (how can it be that she lies so easily with two different men?) and the treachery of her heart (how can it be that she loves both?).

Sy does not reach up to turn out the light: he is forcing her to see with whom she is making love. For the first time in a long time, she meets him with her body and does not close her eyes. And though their coupling is only quietly ecstatic, though it continues for minutes and not hours, though it is not perfect — it is enough for satisfaction and fulfillment and contentment.

Afterward, they hold each other. Now it is her turn to cry. "I miss you," she says, the admission torn from down deep inside her, an old scab picked free at last. "It hurts so much when you are gone."

"I know," he says. "It hurts me too."

"Soon there won't be anything left except the pain."

"I know." His voice is merely a whisper.

"What are we going to do?"

"I don't know."

Holding each other this way, they slip into exhausted sleep.

✌️ FOURTEEN

An Impossible Standard

Christa yawns, sleepy after one beer.

"Cheap date," Weldon observes, grinning and leaning on the bar with one elbow. They are packed in at Hurley's, a popular bar and restaurant that serves as a hangout for the midtown banking community.

"I was up half the night," she protests.

"That junk bond deal you were talking about in morning meeting yesterday?"

"Something else," she says, shaking her head and yawning again. "*Everything* else. I hate this rat's ass time of year."

"There's always a lot right before the holidays," he observes idly, eyeing some co-workers farther down the bar.

"It's not the work I hate — it's the pressure. . . . Promotion time. 'Tis the season to be greedy." This last is said in Cash's drawl, but of course, Weldon does not recognize it as such; nevertheless, he laughs.

"Why is it you insist on making sure everyone knows you're from Dixie?" he asks, still grinning. "Some of us wouldn't consider that an asset, you know."

"You can run but you can't hide," Christa grins. "I'd know you in a dark closet." She tilts her head to the side and pauses for a minute, thinking. "Kentucky probably."

"Hell," he grins, simultaneously pissed and pleased that she has been able to pin him down so accurately. "Little town in the western part of the state."

"You should hear my cat. He's the real southerner in the stew pot."

"You have a cat that talks?"

"You come on over some night," she says, lifting an eyebrow. "I'll make you gumbo and Cash'll wear your ears down a bit."

"I thought you'd never ask," he says, amused.

"Mmm," she answers, sipping her beer and thinking that she hadn't meant to. Still, maybe it is time to stop being so juvenile: maybe it is time, as Sy had pointed out, to admit how much she really enjoys this man and swallow the fact that he doesn't much resemble the Prince Charming she'd had in mind. *After all*, she says to herself, *I am hardly Sleeping Beauty myself.* "Weldon," she says.

He looks at her and waits.

"I know I did apologize about that night at the Ballroom, but still . . . I feel rotten about it."

He raises an eyebrow. "So you said."

"We just got involved in our squash game, then before I knew it he'd suggested supper . . ." Her voice trails off.

He looks at her, hard. "Why is it you have so much difficulty admitting you plain forgot?"

She sighs. "I forgot."

"Mr. Stratton is a formidable distraction."

"Not anymore."

"How's that?"

She runs her finger through a puddle on the bar top and frowns. "I got smarter, that's all. When he finished his supper he trotted right back to Alexis — just as if they were married."

"Maybe someday they will be."

"Just so." She nods and smiles. "Anyhow . . . I'm sorry about it all. Forgive me?"

"If I spent time worrying about what's behind me," Weldon says, "I wouldn't have time to enjoy what's right here on my plate." He raises his finger at the bartender and motions for two more beers. "One thing I've learned here in New York — there's no dearth of opportunity. For a deal or a date." He grins at her and reaches over to touch her hand, on the dark slate of the bar.

She looks down. His fingers are long, the clear nails bluntly trimmed; the color of his skin moves from pink on his warm palm to dark brown on the back of his hand. He strokes her finger with his. Embarrassed, she fixes her gaze on her lap.

"Glad to be going home tomorrow?" he asks, withdrawing his hand and restoring them to normalcy. Tomorrow is Wednesday, the day before Thanksgiving, and Christa is going home for the holiday for the first time in four years.

Smiling, she raises her head and sees clearly now, as if she is looking at a photo developing in a bath of fixative, how arrestingly, amazingly handsome he is. "Actually, I am," she answers after a minute, pausing to clear her throat. She can see from his expression that he is interested in her answer, in everything she is willing to reveal; how long it has been since anyone wanted to listen to her that way. "I haven't seen my family in over a year." She lifts her beer mug and swallows. "What about you?"

Before Weldon can answer, a hand descends on Christa's shoulder; she swivels on her stool under the unexpected touch. In the gloom of the bar, she peers up into Jon's face.

"Hey there, you two," he says.

Her pulse jolts. "Hey there, yourself."

He slides onto the stool next to them. "Mind if I join you?"

"Not at all," says Weldon. "We could use a little fresh conversation."

"Are you implying that mine is stale?" Christa exclaims indignantly, fluttering her hand out into the air.

They all laugh.

"What're you doing midtown, anyway?" Christa asks curiously.

"Taking care of business." He grins.

"What've you been up to, Jon?" asks Weldon.

"Not much," Jon says with a shrug as he signals the bartender with a glance. "I got back from Paris yesterday — I'm still pretty wiped out." He grins and orders a single malt scotch straight up. "How about you two?"

"Just the regular grind," says Christa. To her surprise, the initial flutter she'd felt at Jon's sudden appearance has cleared. Fiddling with her beer mug as the men talk about some deal of Weldon's, it rests easy with her that they are going to be friends and nothing more. *Sometimes your own strength comes up and takes you by surprise*, she thinks to herself. *Sometimes you manage better than you think you can.* "Work's crazy," she says, as Jon turns back to her, "and everybody's bonkers waiting to hear about promotions."

"I hear Alexis might be up early," Weldon says then, fluidly. Christa looks at him with surprise from the corner of her eye, realizing that under the guise of spreading a rumor he is pumping Jon. At this moment Weldon strikes her as downright clever: he has asked the question she would have loved to ask but could not without the risk of being obvious.

Jon smiles, with pride. "Well, you never know for sure. But among friends — I think it is a real possibility."

"Hewett is too set in its ways to promote a woman early," Christa observes. "Especially to partnership in mergers." Jealousy flashes through her despite all her good intentions.

Jon shrugs. "There are always exceptions for special cases."

"And she is most certainly a special case," Christa mutters, stirring the bowl of peanuts with her finger and then sucking off the salt. She may have accepted the relationship, but that doesn't mean she has to like or trust Alexis Somers.

"Pardon me?" Jon asks, tilting his head to indicate he didn't hear her.

"Nothing," she answers, looking up in time to see Weldon repress a grin.

"Is Aviation General one of your clients?" Jon asks, turning back to Weldon.

Weldon, startled, hesitates a minute, flagging the bartender for another round. Then, slowly, he says, "We took them public in 'seventy-six." His face is full of caution, Christa sees with surprise. She wonders why he feels he has to be careful.

"A few months back the military brass at the Paris Air Show couldn't stop buzzing about how hot AG's new avionics system is," Jon goes on, oblivious to Weldon's hesitation, sipping his scotch. "If I were their investment banker" — now a twinkle comes into his dark eyes — "I'd be in a hell of a hurry to get them some major shark repellent. I'd lay money on them getting the subcontract for the new bomber the Pentagon's raffling off this spring." He looks at Weldon over the rim of his scotch.

Weldon's face is now totally controlled and impassive. Christa knows him well enough to read that look: Weldon has a full stable of facial expressions — about five different smiles, two or three quiet stares, and a few kinds of laughter as well. This look means that he already knows about the contract Jon is mentioning, but does not want to discuss it.

"First that contract," Jon goes on now, "and then I discovered those hundred and seventy-five acres next to LAX that they're carrying on their books for the price they paid to acquire it in 1947." He shakes his head. "With stock that undervalued it's a natural takeover play. But I guess I don't need to tell you."

Weldon smiles, again quite noncommittally, still refusing to comment. "You know what an entrepreneurial C.E.O. can be like," he observes. "A headstrong guy and the cotton in his ears backs up to his brain."

"A real pisser," Jon agrees. "A little recapitalization and they'd be safe. It really bothers me when a virgin like AG gets raped by a raider."

"That's life," Christa points out.

Jon shakes his head. "Well, I still hate it. If you could lead that one, Weldon, *you'd* be promoted early."

Weldon smiles, a little more tension leaking out around the edges, Christa thinks.

"It's a good recommend, but I still hate it." Jon changes the subject. "What are you two doing for Thanksgiving?"

"Heading South," Christa says quickly. And then she gets a sudden impulse. "I haven't been back in a long time, and I thought Weldon might get a kick out of seeing my old hometown."

Jon's eyebrows stretch upward and she sees that she has scored: he is surprised to see her going somewhere with another man. Smothering a smile, she turns quickly to Weldon, to check out his reaction to this previously undiscussed offer of hospitality. A small smile plays at the corner of his mouth and she wonders, suddenly anxious, if he will give her away.

"Lex and I are headed up to Canada to ski for the weekend," Jon says. "We've both been working so hard we figured we deserved some kind of time off."

"Sounds like fun," Weldon says. "I usually get out to Sun Valley for the holiday." He smiles at Christa's discomfiture in amusement.

"Gotta hop," Jon says, shaking his head at the bartender's

offer of a refill. "I've got a deal that's doing the giant slalom downhill and the client's gone totally snowblind." He reaches for his wallet.

"My pleasure," says Weldon.

"Thanks." He nods. "Maybe the four of us could get together for dinner sometime?"

Weldon nods. "Sounds interesting."

Christa plays with her beer mug.

"You work on this one," Jon says with a laugh, giving her shoulder a gentle shove. "There's no love lost between these two women." He raises his hand and elbows his way toward the door.

As soon as he is out of sight, Weldon bursts into laughter. "What possessed you to do that?" he asks at last, when he regains control, wiping the corners of his eyes with his fingertip.

"Do what?" she growls, looking away.

"Pretend you'd invited me home for Thanksgiving."

"Well, I was going to but I hadn't gotten to it yet."

"Don't you bullshit me, Christa Brooke!" In anger, his face becomes intense. "You had no intention to invite me back to North Carolina." He hoots with laughter. "Your father would wet his pants."

"My father's quite liberal," she answers stiffly.

"It is my experience that fathers are rarely liberal when it comes to their daughters."

She falls silent. "Well, *I* would like it if you came with me," she says after a minute. "My father will just have to time-warp himself forward into 1986. If there's a problem, let him solve it for himself."

"Look, Christa," he says, pushing his glass around on the bar top. "I'd like to come home with you." He looks up at her reflectively. "But I really resent the way you put out your invitation: I resent being used as some kind of a tool in your game with Jon."

"I may have asked you when he was here because it occurred to me right then. But I *would* like you to come," she says quietly. "Let that be enough."

He searches her face. "All right then," he answers, slowly. "I *will* come."

"Good. And by the way," she goes on, changing the subject altogether and returning to another point of interest. "What did you think about his scuttlebutt on Av Gen?"

"What do I think?" Weldon snorts. "I think that information has round heels."

Christa raises an eyebrow, and looks over at him, puzzled. "I don't get it."

"That information has already been to bed with someone else." He crumples his napkin in disgust. "It's well-used."

"What are you talking about?" she demands.

"I lost the Av Gen account this morning."

"You're kidding!"

He shakes his head. "C.E.O. called me, said we're out. Two guesses who's in. Two guesses."

Christa shakes her head. "No," she says, not believing. "It can't be."

"Oh, yes it can. Yes, indeed." He nods. "They're moving over to Hewett, where Alexis Somers is dealer-manager for the recapitalization I proposed to them three months ago. *At least* three months."

"But why?"

"She sweet-talks better than I do," he says bitterly, with a shrug. "Roger Apbst listened to her when he wouldn't listen to me. It's damned obvious how she found out about the company to begin with, especially about the buyback based on the real estate sale. You couldn't know that without a lot of digging, and *why* would she have gone digging in just that spot? It's too much coincidence to swallow in one bite, don't you think?"

Christa nods. "I can't believe it. But if Jon had already set it up for *her*, why would he pass it on to you *now*?"

Weldon is very angry, his fist tight on the bar. "They're living together, aren't they? There must be a lot of stuff she could see, or overhear. He might not have *told* her."

"Maybe." Christa slides back on her stool. "And why would he reference you as their investment banker if he knew they were going over to Hewett?"

Weldon shrugs. "Maybe he knows they're moving. And maybe he doesn't know anything about it at all. About any of it."

"Well, why didn't you say something?" Christa asks, shaking her head. "If it'd been me, I'd have let him have it."

Weldon shrugs. "I figure there's a small chance he's totally in the dark. If he didn't give her the information and he really doesn't know anything about what's coming down, he will soon enough. And then he'll have to put it all together — have to see how she's used him. And that's a mighty big sting. I didn't feel like easing his pain any by warning him."

Christa laughs; despite her friendship with Jon she thinks he gets all he deserves with regard to Alexis. "I wonder if she could get fired for this," Christa says, slowly, finishing her beer. "If they ever found out."

"More likely promoted," Weldon retorts, finishing his.

⌢⌣

"Well, we did invite a few other people," Sy says, struggling with the poker and a heavy log in the fireplace. "But it ended up just family. Sometimes I think that's nicer, anyway." He smiles at Maggie's mother and wishes again that Vanessa didn't make him feel so clumsy. There is something about her (maybe it is the way she stretches out in front of the fire's warmth, long legs extended) that makes him uncomfortable. When Vanessa is in a room, she takes it over with her presence, no matter who else is around.

Mikey has finished setting up the checkers board on the game table by the sofa and Sy smiles. "Ready for me?"

Mikey pauses in his alignment of red and black. "But I promised Uncle Nico I'd play with him." He blinks at his father, as if he is uncertain of what he is meant to do in such a situation.

"I don't mind, Sy," Nicolas says, coming down the hall from the kitchen with a glass of wine in his hand. "I turned in my dish towel." He goes to sit beside Mikey and ruffles his hair.

"But I wanted —" Sy breaks off and stops, flushing as he sees Vanessa's knowing half smile.

"You took the last game," Nicolas is saying to the boy, consulting the small white pad they keep in the cardboard box, "so that makes it fifty-three games for you and forty-one for me."

"Whatever," Sy says to no one in particular, feeling disgruntled (displaced). He does not let his dismay show: he wants neither Mikey (who might feel guilty) nor Vanessa (who would positively gloat) to know how much it hurts him that Mikey would rather play with Nicolas.

Mikey bounces on the couch with barely contained excitement. "After tonight it'll be fifty-*four* to forty-one," he announces with relish.

"Don't get overconfident now," Nicolas cautions.

Sy leans against the mantelpiece and watches this interchange between his son and his best friend. He has been gone all week long and he was looking forward to spending today with his children. Somehow every time he has looked for them they've been off doing something else. It strikes him that they do not turn to him automatically anymore. Perhaps it is all due to the fact that they are growing up. (Or, chillingly, perhaps not.)

He wished they could have been alone today, without even Maggie's parents down from Boston. He wanted it to be just the four of them. But Vanessa and Turner had been planning this trip since June; and when he'd spoken to Nicolas on the phone late last week to give him a progress report on the buyers he'd found for Linden's, Nicolas had sounded so downcast about spending his first holiday since the separation alone that Sy had asked him to join them. Nevertheless, Sy had been a little bit pleased at Maggie's less than thrilled reaction to this invitation to Nicolas (though he had insisted they honor it) because it indicated to him that she, too, wished they could have some privacy today.

"Maggie says you've been traveling a lot," Vanessa says now, eyeing him where he stands. Never known for an abstinent nature, she sips a drink, her fourth of the evening.

He nods, and nervously smoothes his shirt down into the waist of his trousers. Vanessa's gaze penetrates. He never knows where to look at her, what part of her to focus on. When he looks at her eyes, they see too much; when he looks at her lips they seem too full; if he looks at her legs, her breasts, her lap — well . . . it all makes him uncomfortable. She is a woman radiant with her own power: despite her sixty-odd years, you notice her in a sexual way. There are some women you ought never to feel sexual towards, he thinks. Your mother-in-law is one. How relieved he has always been that Maggie does not resemble her mother in the least. "I've been traveling too much, really."

"Well, what do you plan to do about it?"

"I don't know yet," he evades, wanting to say, *MYOB, you old crow.* Vanessa is opinionated and he doesn't feel like discussing their problems with her. Volatile, she would not hesitate to argue in front of a roomful of people. "I'll have to see."

"If I were home night after night all alone, with these two kids — oh!" She gestures with her hand. "Loveable they may be — but a little adult conversation goes a long way. I'm sure you know what I mean."

He nods, but he is not at all sure.

"I would be so stir crazy!" She laughs. "We called it cabin fever when I was a girl." She purses her mouth. "And, of course, it's an impossible situation for the children."

Turner, who has walked into the room, just in time to catch the tail end of his wife's remark, comes to stand beside Sy at the fire. "What's impossible?" he asks mildly, rubbing his palms together in front of the warmth and then picking up his coffee again.

"Sy's traveling," Vanessa supplies, giving him a visual nudge.

Turner turns to his son-in-law and scrutinizes, deeply, but with kindness. While Sy has never felt close to Turner, he respects the older man, who has never tried to push their relationship. When Sy first met him, he had worried that a psychiatrist would be forever analyzing other people around him. To his pleasure, he found that if Turner did so, he kept his conclusions to himself. He is a gentle man with a fine sense of humor, overshadowed by his fiery, unpredictable wife. Sy has never fully understood Maggie's dissatisfaction with her father: it seems to Sy that his wife asks for more than it is reasonable to expect and so inevitably Turner comes up short. Perhaps, he muses, we are all fated to apply ourselves and those we love to such an impossible standard: husbands, wives, children, and parents alike. Perhaps it is part of our human condition: to strive and fail in these tests of love.

"I'm sure it is — for the children, and Maggie, and Sy himself," Turner observes, reaching over to touch the arrangement of white lilies and crimson orchids Maggie has placed on the

mantelpiece. He is a tall man of seventy-odd years, still handsome, with a hitch to his stride that has developed with age.
His hands are soft and lined, thickened at the pad of the fingertips; Sy is reminded of his own father's hands, wiry and
strong, chapped around the cuticles.

Sy gives him a shy, grateful smile. It is the first time that
anyone has alluded to the problems with which this situation
presents him. For the first time, Sy notices how large Turner's
ears have gotten, as out of proportion to his face as a baby's
head is to its body, and he wonders why it is that the body
seems to put this extra burst of energy into the nose, the feet,
the ears, as the years decline. For a moment he imagines them
all as potatoes, sprouting new buds in some ironic growth
spurt, all the while getting softer and more starchy.

"If it's so difficult for him," Vanessa continues, as if he were
not standing right there in front of her, "why do you suppose
he continues to do it?"

Turner regards his wife with a meditative smile and the
creases around his mouth deepen. He does not answer for a
moment and Sy realizes that his hesitation implies the question
to be worthy of consideration. Vanessa sports a triumphant
smile in this instant, but when Turner looks back to his son-
in-law he does not do what both Sy and Vanessa expect.

"I think Maggie and Sy will sort this out as best suits them,
my dear," he answers, quite mildly, instead. And, with that, he
turns, ending the conversation by crossing the room to sit beside his grandson and watch the checkers game.

It is into this tableau that Maggie walks a second later, with
the first load of dishes crammed into the dishwasher and the
roasting pan submerged in a sinkful of soapy water: Sy silent
by the fireplace, Vanessa sulking in the wing chair, Turner and
Nicolas and Mikey all engrossed in the checkers game, Kate
nowhere to be seen. Maggie settles into the chair opposite her
mother, thinking to herself that her daughter is probably upstairs trying on her grandmother's collection of vivid lipsticks.

She sighs. It has been a difficult day; but then again, when
do her parents ever come to visit that it is not difficult? The
family, reassembled once again, does not — cannot — replicate
or resurrect the outgrown, forsaken unit of childhood. All the
moments they spend this day are heady with intense pleasure

and difficulty: everything from disappointment to mistrust; expectation to disillusionment; pride occasionally; once in a while even a little acceptance and laughter.

As she watches her father oversee the checkers game with Mikey, pointing out the boy's mistakes as he makes them, she realizes that at one time she had thought children did all the leave-taking; now she sees quite clearly that even after all these years she is still fighting the natural separations her parents want to put between the three of them. It is hard to accept that parents can come and go as well as children.

The already-existing tensions were increased today, of course, by Nicolas's presence here: to look down the holiday table, loaded with roast goose and vegetables in silver dishes, the bright red stain of cranberry against the white damask, the glow of magenta cyclamen against the candlelight — only to feel her lover's eyes follow her every move. She wanted today to seem normal. But reality kept interfering and, for the first time in many months (perhaps her whole life), as much as she wants to pretend, she also wants to look, hard, at what is really going on.

Here they all sit, trying so hard to reach out and connect; they are crippled by their pasts, their personalities, *the way they are*. Here is her father, who professes to be so interested in her son, and yet can manage only a visit (a mere four-hour drive from Boston) once a year. Here is her mother, still happy to poke and prod and provoke, and never able to remember her granddaughter's dress size. Here is Nicolas, still flashing her his secret looks. And here is her husband, who continues to look away. It is all profoundly depressing.

"Sy's been complaining that his travel tires him," Vanessa says to Maggie; her tone is irritable.

"Vanessa! That's not what I said at all," Sy exclaims, his voice rising in exasperation now, to his mother-in-law.

Vanessa arches her eyebrows. "Defensive, aren't we?" she says.

Sy looks away, still unwilling to get into an argument over it. He and Maggie are strained enough with each other, without having to deal with parental interference, and he doesn't want Maggie to think he's been discussing private problems with Vanessa. Disgusted with his mother-in-law's eternal kibitzing (and with his own silence), he puts his glass down on the mantelpiece. "I'm going to find Kate," he says, and leaves the room.

Maggie watches him go and feels sorry for his retreating back. Her mother can be an exasperating adversary.

"She's probably upstairs sneaking my lipsticks," Vanessa observes.

Maggie, surprised, nods. "I thought the same."

"You *did* the same. At just her age." She looks back into the fire and sips her drink again. "Speaking of her age, Maggie — now that both kids are in school full-time, are you finally going back to work?"

"I've been thinking about doing something," Maggie admits, her stomach tightening. She doesn't really feel like talking about this with her mother, but once again she feels incapable of extricating herself. How many times has this happened before: like swimming down a river that has a waterfall midway, she keeps telling herself that it's time to get to the side, but somehow she just keeps drifting along in the middle of the stream; before she knows it she's heading out and over the falls, screaming to be saved.

"And what have you decided?"

"That it still isn't the right time to go back full-time in the city."

Vanessa's eyebrows go up another notch. "Why is that?"

"If the kids were sick, or had a half day, or even were on vacation, I'd have a problem." She hears herself explaining, rationalizing, defending.

Vanessa laughs, dryly, thinly. "I should think all that could be solved with a little live-in help. You should have had it from the start, in any case."

"Let's not go back into all that," Maggie answers shortly now. "I didn't want it then and I don't want it now," she says (continuing the argument she believes she does not want to have).

"No — what you're really saying is that you don't *want* to go back to work."

Maggie stares at her. From across the room she can feel both her father and Nicolas's attention divert from the checker game onto Vanessa and her.

"I just can't see killing myself to get us all up and out of the house in time for me to catch a train," she says at last, "and then dragging myself back at night totally burned out and not able to give my kids a damned thing. You know, with Sy traveling so much the situation is really quite different. You can pay someone to watch your kids — but not to raise them."

"Well," Vanessa says, sipping again, her expression fixed. "Other women seem to manage it. *I* managed it."

"You had Daddy — and even then —" She breaks off.

"Even then what?"

"Who do you suppose would pay the price in a situation like this?" She doesn't wait for an answer. "The children would, that's who."

Vanessa stares at her. "I wasn't aware there was a price."

"There's always a price, Mother!" She is quite suddenly furious and short of breath. As she says the words, to which she has never before really given much thought, she knows, without doubt, how true they are. Nicolas catches her eye and she flushes, remembering from whom she first heard them. "Look — the point is that I've never wanted to be like you or live my life the way you lived yours. Why can't you accept that?"

"Well, did I do so badly with my life? Was your childhood so impoverished?" Vanessa snaps sarcastically. "Tell me how you were shortchanged, Maggie." Their voices are raised now and Mikey watches with anxious interest.

Maggie's heart pounds. "That's not the point and you know it. Whatever my childhood was — it's in the past now, and it's my *children* I'm concerned with. What I do with my life isn't always a commentary on what you did with yours. Yours isn't the *only* way, you know, to be either a woman *or* a mother." And even as she says this, she flushes, feeling Nicolas's presence on the other side of the room, a presence giving lie to every word she utters.

"Well, then," Vanessa says crisply. "What are you planning to do with yourself? In a few more years even if they do come home sick they won't want you hovering over them!"

Stung by this (quite possibly the truth), Maggie replies, "Whatever I do, it will be something important to *me*." She flushes with anger and yet continues to respond. "Something to enjoy. In a place where I can set my own schedule."

"You sound like you're ready to sign up at the hospital candy shop." Vanessa is clearly amused.

"And if I did, so what!" This comment makes Maggie even more irritated. "I don't need to go back to work for the money. I've got the luxury of choosing what I *want* to do."

"But *why* would you choose something like that?"

"To get outside my own world for a while." Maggie pauses, struggling for the right words. "What a relief it would be to think of someone other than me and mine day after day."

"I don't understand that at all," Vanessa declares flatly. "It seems to me you have *never* thought of yourself. You've dedicated yourself to the kids, to Sy."

"It's still my own small, insulated world." She is frustrated at not being understood.

"And what *does* Sy say about this?"

Maggie rolls her eyes and looks over at her father, who sends her the slightest smile.

"Whatever she wants to do is fine with me," Sy says, from the doorway, where he has been standing for the last minute, unnoticed, watching.

Maggie looks up. Still uncertain of what to do next, she hasn't even broached the subject with him yet. She smiles at him, a long smile that comes from the heart.

Vanessa turns to look at him, stiffly bearing the weight of the motion on one arm, and suddenly she looks fragile; it is an impression of frailty she would loathe if she could see it. Maggie wonders if she is well.

"Maggie's been talking about going back to work since last spring," Sy goes on, coming into the room. "At first it seemed it might be hard for us, but over the last couple months I realized that we could cut her a little slack, after all the years she's been doing for us. I know how to run a washing machine." He sits on the arm of his wife's chair.

"That's preposterous, Sy," Vanessa says, indignantly. "You're never home."

"Maybe I'll have to be here more."

"You've never taken her seriously," Vanessa goes on, ignoring his last comment, now really steamed up. "That's why you've allowed her to make such a waste of her life. And now she'll go off and volunteer for something — fritter away more years."

Sy looks at her coolly. "I don't 'allow' her, as you say, anything at all. She decides what she wants. You know, you've really got some nerve — you pay us absolutely no attention all year long and then you make one quick trip down here and assume you have the right to run everybody's life. That's the real waste here: all this criticism and no acceptance."

The room is silent.

Vanessa's chin quivers. "I think I'll go put on a pot of coffee." She pushes herself up out of the chair and hurries into the kitchen.

Maggie gets up and starts after her.

"Don't," Sy says, putting his arm out. "I did it. I'll go." He gets up and follows Vanessa into the kitchen.

Maggie can't bear to sit there. She stands up and says, to no one in particular, "I'm going to check on Kate."

Once out in the dark hall, she leans against the staircase and tries to catch her breath. All her life she has hated arguments, all her life she has sat still for her mother's sniping. It hurts to know you cannot please your parent: her mother is always negative and her father never comments; just once she would like someone to tell her she has done a good job. And yet, it confuses her to feel this way, for she knows that as an adult she should not crave this sort of approval. What the hell, she thinks, and smiles to herself, remembering Sy's reaction. That moment when he looked at her, so strong, so *with* her, had given her a flash: an emotion from the past that, like a smelly old dog lying in front of a fire, raises its familiar, dear face, yawns, stretches, and looks around. In that instant, she remembered: the love and how it felt.

Nicolas finishes his game with Mikey quickly, making a stupid move on purpose so that he can get up and follow Maggie. When he excuses himself to go to the bathroom, he is certain Turner shoots him a knowing look, but he does not care.

The hall is dark. He goes into the bathroom and flushes

quickly for effect, then is about to go upstairs when he sees her on the window seat.

"Maggie?" His voice is an insistent whisper.

"Nico?" She strains to see in the dark.

Nicolas slides into the window seat beside her. "There you are," he says, settling in and putting his arm around her.

She draws back from his touch. "What if someone comes?" she asks.

"Can't I comfort you? Just two old friends."

She doesn't protest further, but sits passively, tolerating his touch.

He sighs. "I can see how much she upsets you. The two of you are so much alike."

"I don't think that's a compliment."

"You know it is." He kisses the back of her hand. "Why didn't you tell me about being restless, about wanting to find something new?" he asks after a minute, in a very quiet voice.

"I would have," she says. "When I had decided what the hell to do. My mother caught me by surprise."

"Really?" He hears his tone, which indicates that he plainly disbelieves her. He is trying to restrain himself from getting more sarcastic.

She nods in the dark.

"I thought you had decided not to go back to work."

"I did. But I also decided that I have to do more than just this. I need more."

"Why?"

"Isn't that obvious?" she asks with irritation.

"What's obvious is that you'll have much less free time."

"So?"

"So you won't be tempted now — and isn't that really the point?" Even as he says this, he knows it is unwise: he does not really want to hear what she will say if pushed. The last few weeks have been very difficult: waiting, without saying a word, to see if she would decide to leave Sy and come away with him. Waiting, and all the while quietly going about trying to sell Linden's. Keeping faith that she will feel so bound to him, as he does to her, that she will come and bring the children too. Tonight, having Thanksgiving here, has been excruciating.

Wanting her, knowing she really belongs to him, and yet having to see Sy lean over to give her a kiss, see Sy carve the bird and sit at the head of the table. But Mikey will always prefer to play checkers with Nicolas. It is a bond between them.

"Tempted how?" Maggie asks now, sounding confused.

"To spend more afternoons with me."

"That's not it at all! Why do you have to interpret it as having something to do with you? It's incredibly egotistical."

"All right," he says, putting his hands up in the air and backing down. "Sorry I brought it up."

They sit for a moment more in silence.

"When can I see you again?" he says after a while.

She fiddles with her watch, thinking. "I'll have to work it out," she says. "But we should go back in the other room now. They'll wonder where we are and I have to make sure my mother's all right."

"Fine," he says, his voice hardening. He aches all over with the desire to make her his, to have her put her arms around him right now. He wants to be held. But she slides off the seat and walks away from him, leaving him without so much as a squeeze of her hand.

He knows what I am thinking, she realizes, as she walks toward the light of the kitchen. Her entire family is gathered around her and yet here is this intrusion — some odd, other part of her life that she cannot manage to integrate with the rest. She feels like a conductor standing in front of an orchestra, the members of which stubbornly refuse to play in the same key: it occurs to her now that taking up with Nicolas had been an act of desperation, and one that threw everything out of balance. She turns in the darkness, to soften the distance between them, which she knows is painful to him. "I'll call you on Monday."

She can see his silhouette: he raises his hand. She turns and follows the whistle of the tea kettle to the kitchen.

Back in the family room, Sy has returned from making it up with Vanessa. The anger blown off in a burst of steam, apologizing turned out to be easy.

Sy discovers Mikey playing a new game of checkers with Turner. "Where's Nicolas?"

Turner gestures toward the hall. "He left a little while ago.

Gave me a chance to see what kind of checkers player Mikey is."

Mikey's face is anxious. "Is Grandma O.K.?" he appeals to Sy.

"She's all right," Sy says, sitting back in the chair. "We worked it out. Sometimes Grandma makes me mad — that's all."

Turner reaches out and puts his arm around his grandson. "People get angry," he explains, "and when they do, it's good if they can talk about it."

"But sometimes they can't?"

He nods. "Sometimes people don't like to talk about how they feel. Usually they end up yelling about something else then. Getting mad and doing stupid things they don't understand."

"But in a *family*," Mikey says, his chin quivering. "In a *family* people shouldn't get mad."

Turner smiles. "But they do," he says, ruffling Mikey's hair and giving Sy a wink. "*Especially* in a family."

FIFTEEN

Just Business

"Families can surprise you," Christa is saying to Sy that Monday morning, back in the office. "I was always so sure taking Weldon home would be a problem and then it turned out to be nothing. I think they were just happy I came at all."

Sy puts his feet up on his desk and leans back. "Sometimes parents can surprise you in a nice way," he says.

"Seeing my father accept him made me see the problem was my own. So, I guess sometimes you can surprise yourself," she adds, in a low voice.

"I surprised myself this weekend by thinking about surprising my wife," Sy says.

"You don't seem the type to do a new piece of jewelry," she observes with a grin.

He laughs. "I was thinking more along the lines of a new job."

"You're joking?"

"No."

"You've been here eight years! Next year you'll probably make M.D."

He smiles at her with sadness. "Look, I never said it wasn't going to hurt."

"You must love Maggie and the kids a lot — to step out of the race just before you've won."

He tilts back in his chair. "It's more complicated than that.

When I imagine myself as partner what I see is more prestige, more money, and more work. Sound about right?"

Christa nods, not sure of what he is driving at.

"And I know myself well enough to recognize that once I get to the place I've been itching toward for the last eight years, I'll look around and say 'so what's next?' I'll be looking for the next rung up."

"In all probability, you will."

"It's finally occurring to me that maybe I'm not willing to let the rest of my life swing in the breeze while I struggle to get to that next rung."

"A new job?" Christa muses. "Something totally different? Out of the industry?"

"Something absolutely different. *If* I can land something absolutely different."

Christa cocks her head and studies him. "My impression of you is that when you want something bad enough, you find it."

"I've got no experience with anything except this," he answers, his shoulders betraying his tension. "It won't be easy. I guess I'm a little scared about it."

She smiles at him and lays her hand on his. "How fortunate it is that easy and possible are two entirely different concepts."

～

"I wanted a moment alone with you," Waterston is saying, swiveling his desk chair to look out the windows over the harbor, a magnificent view. "To let you know how much we think of the job you've been doing."

Alexis feels a burgeoning wave of triumph: he has asked her into the inner sanctum to tell her personally that she is being promoted. She pictures herself behind such a desk, gazing from such a window.

"Bringing in Aviation General was a coup," he continues. "And everyone here knows it. Real applause from us to you, Alexis."

She smiles and waits, readying her face so that her reaction to his announcement will look modest. He looks out the window again and now the small silence extends. Into a middle-range silence. Alexis's smile begins to feel stretched too tight across her face. It is in this silence that she realizes what is to follow.

He clears his throat. "I wanted to tell you myself, before the partnership promotions are published later today, that we will be paying you by far the highest bonus of all the principals this year, $900,000, in recognition of the incredible job you've done. That will bring your total comp to almost a million one. However" — he clears his throat again — "though I tried, *personally*, to get you promoted to managing director, I wasn't able to push it through." He spreads his hands in front of him. "It is still a year early and some of the other partners just wouldn't go for it. Causes too many problems in their departments. I don't agree with the decision, and I wanted to tell you myself because I knew you would be hoping."

Alexis nods, dumbly, speechless under the tide of disappointment and fury. She feels she is shrinking, like Alice, smaller and smaller in her chair. Soon her voice will be too tiny to be heard. "I see."

"There will be no problem next year," he says, relieved that this obviously difficult interview will contain no confrontations or high emotions. "I'm certain of it. You've just got to hang on. In the meantime, there is the bonus for consolation."

How obtuse he is, to imagine that a large bonus will console her: this has nothing to do with money and everything to do with pride. Nevertheless, she nods and tries to muster a smile. There is no disgrace in being promoted next year, but to Alexis something enormous has been lost: this is not the way she had planned it would go. She had counted on rising above the others, being different. And there is the loss of her self-respect, as well. She feels like the biggest fool ever, having allowed her ambition to push her into a place she should never have ventured. "I understand," she says, smiling again tensely. "And thanks for your vote."

He smiles to see how well she takes it.

His relief makes her even angrier. Why should she be a good girl, take the company line, play for the team? She goes on now. "Actually, I'm glad we had this chance to talk by ourselves. I need to take a week's leave for some minor surgery," she says then. "Starting tomorrow. I hope it won't inconvenience anyone."

Just as he has boxed her into a corner of polite acceptance with his announcement, so she has retaliated. There is no way he can refuse a simple — but important — request such as this, especially from such a valued member of the team; nevertheless, it will be an extreme inconvenience, especially as they are about to begin work on the Av Gen deal, and Roger Apbst has made it a condition that Alexis head the recap. Watching Waterston's face, she fights down a smile. *Tough shit if it inconveniences you,* she says to him silently. *I'm going to schedule my surgery and get my life in order. Enough is enough.*

"Have you spoken with Chase?" He raises his eyebrows.

"My next stop," she says, rising. "I'll only be out a week. He shouldn't have any trouble handling things on his own for such a short time." With that she extends her hand, they shake quickly, and she gets out, closing the door behind her.

Fuck you, she thinks, striding quickly down the hall toward the elevator as tears thunder at the back of her eyes. *Just see how long it takes me to get out of your neat little box.*

⟍⟋

Alexis is muddled from the post-op medication the nurse has given her and she wants to cry. She is so alone, totally alone, and she wants to call Maggie but she can't manage the coordination required to dial the telephone. She puts her head back on the pillow and floats, a tear escaping down her cheek. Noises from the corridor wash through the room, the Demerol washes the pain from her body, but nothing washes the loneliness from her mind.

A knock on the door: she opens her eyes, thinking it is the nurse, back with the ice water she'd asked for a long time ago. Instead she sees Jon, hesitating on the threshold, his face dark, worried.

"Can I come in?"

"What are you doing here?" she asks thickly. She should be shocked but somehow she isn't. The room tilts from side to side but Jon just stands there.

"It's me who should be asking that."

"You're out of town," she says, trying to keep her eyes open. Her hands stray to her hair; she doesn't want to look like a waif, but the drug has drawn a haze, like fog, through the room. She gives up and lets her hands drop back by her side.

"You were counting on it, weren't you?" He comes to stand

beside her, throwing his overcoat on the chair beside the bed. "You just waited until I was out of town and then checked yourself into the hospital as if it were a hotel." His voice rises on the last word and he shakes his head in disbelief. "What the hell are you doing here?"

"It's nothing important," she says listlessly.

"Let's try this again." He takes a deep, even breath to control himself. "What are you doing here?"

"How did you find me?" she asks, stalling.

"Soolei."

"She promised!"

"So I twisted her arm," he says impatiently. "And actually it didn't take much — because she *likes* me. *She* thinks I'm good for you." He sighs. "Now stop putting me off. You scared the crap out of me."

She closes her eyes for a minute and tries to organize her mind. She is glad to see him, but she is so afraid for him to see her this way. She wants nothing more than for him to put his arms around her and hold her tight. "You know that pain I've been getting with my period every month?" She struggles to sit up higher in the bed so that she can see him better, be less flat on her back and out of control, but the incision hurts. She grimaces unintentionally.

"You didn't make much of it," he says, taking her arm and helping her slide up on the pillow. "I thought it was just cramps."

"Well, so did I." She takes a breath. "But my gynecologist decided it was time to take a look. Seems that it's actually endometriosis." Another breath and she blinks slowly. "Which is no big deal, but you've got to treat it. With a medication that will keep it in check. Or else get pregnant."

"I know what endometriosis is," Jon says. "My sister had it." He sits down, carefully, on the edge of the bed.

She is encouraged that he does not look shocked or repulsed or anything other than interested and concerned. The fuzzy feeling from the Demerol recedes a little. "Well, then, you know it's not serious. I'm just going to have to be on the medication for a while."

"Or get pregnant."

She laughs weakly. "Not much chance of that."

"Didn't it ever occur to you that it might be a good idea to talk this over with me?"

She shakes her head. "Why would I do that?"

"We could get married, you know. We could have kids."

She looks at him in absolute astonishment. "Is that what you want?"

"I don't know." He paces back and forth at the end of her bed. The nurse comes in and sets down a pitcher of water and a cup on the table. She looks at them and then leaves.

"What I do know," Jon goes on, coming over to pour her a glass of water, "is that we're practically living together — and then you shut me out like this. I should have been here the whole time, right here, when you went down to surgery and when you came back up."

"I managed it," she says, slowly picking up the glass and sipping it. The water is cool and fresh in her mouth.

"And that's really the point, isn't it?" He stares at her. "When are you going to let yourself *need* someone? *Depend* on someone? It hurts me that you didn't *want* me here."

She feels confused and nauseated. "Come on, Jon. We're *not* married. I couldn't expect you to act like a loyal husband."

"And if we were? Would you include me in these decisions then?"

She stares at him and sips again. "I didn't mean to hurt you." She cannot understand why he is so angry. Everything has always been loose between them. She'd thought he wanted it that way. "I was afraid to tell you."

"Afraid of what?" He is bewildered.

"That you'd feel pressured. That I'd feel pressured. We're at such a delicate place right now." She shrugs. "And of seeming weak, I guess." She stops and looks away for a minute. "I don't know. I was scared. Maybe it was just the easiest way to get through it. To sort of pretend it wasn't really happening."

"You can't be serious."

She smiles, halfway. "It didn't work very well," she admits. "Just before you came in I was feeling more alone than ever before in my whole life. Like a little kid. Maybe" — she pauses to take a breath — "once you've let someone in you can't just boot them out anytime."

"Don't you know how much I love you?"

She looks down, embarrassed. "I do know, but . . ." She hesitates. "Do you really want to get married and have a baby? The only time we ever talked about all this you said you hated all that."

He stops and stares at her. "True. But I could change my mind, you know. It's been known to happen."

"Yeah, but not now, not like this. It's the last thing we'd need right now. Be reasonable, Jon. We're still living in separate apartments." She shifts her arm and the intravenous line tugs on the back of her hand. Flinching, she readjusts the tubing. She looks up at him. "And *I'm* not ready for a baby." Here her voice wobbles a little. She feels tears at the back of her throat. "I'm too confused. The last thing I need is another big decision in my life right now." She turns her face away to stare at the blank white wall.

He takes her hand. "I guess I'm angry because you didn't tell me."

"I understand," she whispers. "I'm sorry."

"I want to be with you, Alexis," he says slowly. "But I can't be if you don't let me in. It hurts me." He looks over at her. "Is this what happened with Nicolas?"

She closes her eyes. She is too tired for this.

He stares at her. "You shut him out, didn't you?"

"Look, there were a lot of problems between Nicolas and me." She opens her eyes with an enormous effort. "You can't pin it on one thing like that. I suppose in the end I did shut him out. I had to — for survival's sake." She shakes her head. "But I certainly didn't mean to hurt *you*. I just thought —"

"You didn't think!" he interrupts. "If you had, you'd have known the answer. This was just one more way of pushing me away."

"What do you mean?"

He looks at her, his dark eyes carrying another message now. His expression pierces the drug-induced fog surrounding her. "Maybe this isn't the time to talk about that."

"To talk about what?" she answers with annoyance and fatigue. "Don't be coy."

"How do you suppose I felt when I saw *over the Broad tape*

that Aviation General had left First Boston to do a recap through Hewett."

"Well, that's just business," she says, uncomfortably, looking away now.

"*My* business! You took *my* information and used it."

"I have other sources besides you! And anyway what difference does it make now?"

"A lot of difference to *me!* And I *do* know it! I know it here —" He taps his chest. "And it makes me feel *lousy*."

She doesn't say anything. His reaction was something she had not thought about when she sneaked her look at the material in his desk. His reaction was not something she had considered when she'd called Roger Apbst and told him his time as C.E.O. of Av Gen was limited unless he listened to reason — her reason. She had made herself blind to all these ramifications because she had so desperately wanted to pull it off.

"To hear about it that way, sitting in the office with my ass hanging out in the breeze!" He shakes his head, angry, remembering the humiliation. "Even worse, I'd been talking about it last week with Weldon Robb, not knowing what you'd done even though *he* already did!"

"You talked about it with Weldon?"

"Sure I did. He's their investment banker."

"So you're saying you were willing to give him information about the company — but not me." Her voice is indignant.

"There's a huge difference between talking about it with him and talking about it with you, and you know it — I wasn't telling him anything he didn't already know. He's their investment banker."

"*Was* their investment banker," she retorts.

"You don't get it, do you?" He paces a little. "This is not some joke!" He stops at the foot of the bed and stares at her. "I thought you cared about what we have. I thought we were partners. I thought we were *together*. Then you do things like this . . . and that . . ." He lifts his hand in the air and shrugs. "I wonder if I know you at all."

She knows he has a right to be angry. She should have told him she was going to the hospital; she should never have looked inside the desk. "I'm sorry, I'm sorry for it all." She starts to cry.

"Don't you understand — I don't like us having all these secrets — they get between us." He comes back and sits down beside her. "If you'd just *told* me you'd looked at the file so we could have decided what the hell to do — it's an enormous conflict of interest."

"But no one will ever know."

"I do!"

"Well, you'll forgive me, won't you?"

"That isn't the point! How am I supposed to deal with this? How am I supposed to forget?"

She just looks at him.

"And more than that — this has to do with what's right and wrong. Look," he appeals to her now, "if my road show hadn't been canceled I'd never have known you were in the hospital, but the fact that you didn't tell me would still mean that you'd left me *out* of it. It would be a sign of the way things are between us. Just because you don't get caught doesn't mean it's the right thing to do! And the same is true of Av Gen."

"You're right," she agrees slowly. "I guess I just didn't think you'd want to know," she answers back, her voice small now as she gets close to the truth. "I was ashamed of my own desperation. I thought I was willing to do anything to make sure I got promoted."

"And was it worth it?" he asks bitterly.

"I didn't get the promotion, did I?"

"Are you saying it would have been worth it if you had?"

She stares at him. Blinks. "It wasn't worth it, regardless," she says slowly, shaking her head. She lifts her fist, lets it fall on the blanket, a weak gesture for her frustration. "And even though I know that now, even though I'd take it back in a minute, I *still* wish I could be managing director at Hewett before the year is out." She looks away from him and sighs. "I'm not willing to be just the same as everyone else. I'm not willing to run in that sort of track."

"When you do this sort of thing, you're not running in remotely the same kind of track." His voice is soft and weary now.

She puts her head back on the pillow. "I'm tired, Jon. I've got to sleep for a little while."

He looks at her for a minute. "I'll go then." He gets up and starts to walk toward the door.

"Jon?"

He turns. Her face seems very small and white against the pillow.

"Do you think you could stay for a while?"

"You said you wanted to rest."

"I do. But I want you to stay. Would you just sit with me while I sleep?"

He hesitates for a moment, his anger still plain. Then he turns, draws the chair up to the bed, and takes her hand. She closes her eyes.

✁ SIXTEEN

Loyalties

Snow hisses against the panes of Maggie's bedroom window. In the dark, she sweats and twists under her blanket. Anxiety is her bed partner tonight. It is only eleven o'clock, but she went to bed early, knowing that she would have to get up early to shovel out the driveway so that she could drive the kids to school. If indeed there is school. The snowstorm had moved into Westchester County this morning — the first week of December is atypically early for a blizzard in New York — and as she watched it begin sugaring itself down inch by relentless inch while she listened to school cancellations over the radio, she'd wondered with resignation how it was that Sy had, once again, managed to be out of town (in Boston) at just the right time. All flights out of Logan and into La Guardia had been canceled by noon.

Having spent the day amusing her housebound and cranky children with rounds of games and art projects, she is now too nerved-up to sleep. The question of Nicolas and Sy revolves like a carousel in her mind. She throws the blankets back and gets up to peer from the window in the dark. The snowfall has grown lazy now, she sees, just random flakes and the wind gusting drifts of what has already fallen.

Making up her mind, she pulls on her socks, puts a sweater on top of her flannel pajamas, and goes to check the children. Then, heading downstairs, she pulls on boots, parka, mittens, and hat, wraps a scarf around the back of her head and across her mouth. Outside, the still night is a moonscape. Her lungs ache at the first inhalation of frigid air — reminding her in an odd turn of seasons of the way the ocean numbs one's legs in spring.

Weighted by the snow, the double door of the garage is impossibly heavy; she tugs and at last it slides open. Squeezing past, she gropes in the dark for a shovel. Already her feet are cold; stomping against the hard cement, she tucks the pajama legs into the tops of her boots and wades back out into the white dark. Eager for physical labor, she attacks the worst part of the drive in a burst of energy, and buries her mind in the sweet rhythm of hefting shovelfuls of heavy, wet snow. It does not take long before the sweat of exercise begins to replace the sweat of anxiety. The muscles of her shoulders and back burn. After twenty minutes or so, Maggie stops shoveling and leans on the handle to catch her breath. She looks back over the ten-foot patch she has cleared, and thinks of her husband.

Despite his distance right now, when Sy is at home these days he is not quite so far away as he was, and his renewed energy toward her and the kids makes Maggie feel guilty. A few times since Thanksgiving he's come home in time for supper, and last weekend he took the kids to the zoo for a few hours to give her a break; her own reaction had surprised her. It is a lot easier to rationalize being with Nicolas when she and Sy are either fighting every minute or not speaking at all because he is never around. It is a lot easier to hate him, pure and simple, when there is nothing to remind her of the lost love or trust or enjoyment.

Right now, she does not know what she wants — from him or herself, for him or herself. But one question plagues her: does she love Nicolas enough to go off to Maine and make a life together with him? Once she would have seen the way he made her feel in bed and called that love, just as once she had seen the way Sy had made her feel safe in life and called it love. Now she knows the differences. She wonders if love always has to be just one emotion masquerading as another. In her heart, she does not believe that this is so: perhaps, with nurturing, love can grow beyond its original incarnation.

She exhales, a puff of smoke, and drags the toe of her boot across the snow-encrusted shovel. A sly question now intrudes (she has invited it in at last): *if* she no longer wants to be married to Sy, and *if* she does not love Nicolas enough to take the risk of uprooting herself and the children, what then is left?

She does not believe that she can raise the children alone; she does not believe that she can survive as a single woman and mother. She stands very still under the bitter wind, head bowed.

Around her, silence. A blister has risen on the web of tender skin between first finger and thumb, and she pulls her mitten off to suck at the sting and then goes back to shoveling. Suddenly she dreads the thought of the party they are giving next week, which will expose the crux of all the problems. For, of course, Nicolas will be at her party, just as he was at Thanksgiving dinner. Nicolas, his eyes asking her to remember their afternoons together. Nicolas and Maggie, spinning in their troubled pas de deux: Nicolas, who is not ready, it seems, to take no for an answer; and Maggie, who is not ready to say it. And Sy, who will not see any of it.

One of the things that she fears the most right now is Nicolas's unpredictability. She had never taken seriously the idea that he might sell Linden's, but he had gone ahead and done it, the letter of intent signed as he bailed out just in time. She had thought he was only rambling when he brought up real estate up in Maine, but last week he had negotiated on office space in Bath. Radical moves frighten her. It is one thing to go to bed with him, but another thing entirely to marry and depend on him. His quick decisions would not have bothered Alexis at all; in fact, Maggie thinks now, had Nicolas taken such decisive steps this time last year, Alexis might not have divorced him so impatiently.

Maggie had seen Alexis last week, for the first time in several months, at the hospital. When Alexis called and told Maggie about her surgery, Maggie had taken the train into the city immediately. Wary at first, they had both eventually broken down and admitted how much they missed each other. A few tears. A number of hugs. Sitting at the foot of her friend's bed, feeling guilty every time Nicolas's name surfaced, Maggie fought the strong compulsion to confess the affair and thus purge her guilt.

Alexis always said that smart people don't shit where they eat; in her mind, Maggie visualizes two birds, parakeets probably, captives in a wicker cage, vainly trying to keep their droppings as far as possible from the containers of seed and water. Even as she shovels, she berates herself: if only she had simply looked away from him that first time; if only she had let herself know that to use Nicolas as a retaliation (however pleasurable) for the problems with Sy was nothing short of obscene.

At the front steps, she sits down with a tired thump to survey her work, wiping her nose on her mitten. The driveway curves away into darkness, scraped clean enough for a single car to pass, the snow mounded in heaps along the sides. Two stories above her, the children sleep on in ignorance of her dilemma, trusting her to make all the right choices and so protect them. Ironically enough, though her marriage depends on giving Nicolas up, though the future depends on understanding what and why and how, she still wants him and the blanket of blindness she found with him: it will hurt to let him go. How can she lose the magic that has made her life so much less lonely? she wonders.

The moon comes out, a sudden glow of white that pushes back the breaking clouds; Maggie looks across the neighbor's yard, down the slope of woods. The train trails by; through the black limbs of trees, shivers of light come from its windows as it passes in the distance. It whistles as it nears the station, and then throws a big spark — illuminating the night for a moment, overpowering the moonlight on the snowbanks.

Quietly, she begins to cry. She mourns the loss of so much (all the years, all the trust, all the innocence between her and Sy), everything she has betrayed by being with Nicolas. And she cries, too, simply to consider losing him, and his hands on her face and on her body, the pleasure and connection they were able to share. She wonders if she will ever feel this way again, with any man.

The moon goes behind a cloud and the landscape around her darkens. She wipes her cheeks on the back of her mitten and shivers. Her backside feels as cold as the stone of the steps on which she is sitting. The moon slips back out, bright white, reflecting off the field of snow and illuminating her as she sits in the dark shadow of the house. She puts her face up into that light, as if it were the sun. With a drop of her head, she acknowledges she can delay no longer.

⤳

Inside the house, the phone is ringing, but Maggie does not hear it. Getting no answer, Nicolas puts the receiver back into the cradle with an angry click. He knows she is home, and is certain that she is avoiding him. Since Thanksgiving, he has begun to realize that by some means he does not understand he is losing her.

He pushes himself up from the armchair and goes to the kitchen to get another drink. The ice rattles against the glass as he loads it with scotch. He looks around him in disgust and shakes his head: soon he'll be out of here no matter what she decides. Packing to leave will require a single suitcase. In Maine, he will find a place with a view of the ocean. He stands in the kitchen, looking out the window onto the snow-covered fire escape, getting angrier by the minute and by the sip.

He trusted Maggie. All those long evenings when they'd talked their hearts out, speaking with a depth he had never before approached with any woman; he'd trusted her because she was equally vulnerable. Their partners had wandered from city to city, deal to deal, week after week like itinerant, over-paid peddlers, while he and Maggie found a new source of laughter in each other.

He cannot bear the idea that she might really choose to stay with Sy or that she would take a job just to avoid being with him. He is certain that only one reason exists for such choices, and that is security: Sy is the safe route; divorce will seem dangerous to Maggie.

He finishes his scotch and pours himself another; he begins thinking of what he can do next, other than just sit and wait. If she doesn't make time to see him soon, if she continues this charade of pretending everything is fine (when apparently it is not), he knows his opportunity will lie at the Christmas party. He hadn't been planning to go, as Maggie had said last week that Alexis might be there. But now he changes his mind. If he has to, he can approach her then, make his pitch, win her back. If he has to, he can confront Sy and precipitate a crisis.

He is a little drunk now, but not so far gone that he doesn't recognize the danger in this idea. He would lose his oldest friend and probably Maggie as well. He tries to discard the thought, but it shimmers in front of him: what pleasure there would be in letting Sy know just how passionate Maggie can really be. Nicolas grins out into the darkness.

He goes back to the living room and sits, again, in the armchair by the phone. He pulls a magazine into his lap and tries to read, but the motion of moving his eyes left to right makes him sleepy. He thinks of his father, dead over twelve years now, who came home each night to a chair not unlike this one, tired from arguing with housewives who were always trying to squeeze themselves into dresses a size too small. He wonders what his father would think of what he's made of his life (of selling Linden's). He shrugs.

✍

Maggie stands. As she goes down the steps to collect her shovel and return it to the garage, she hears a car spinning its tires as it labors up the hill at the bottom of Mardon Road. She cocks her head, wondering if the driver will make it and which neighbor is out so late on a night like this.

The headlights turn down her driveway. The vehicle approaches, brakes to stop in front of her. Maggie squints into the glare. She recognizes neither the car nor the driver behind the snow-encrusted black glass of the windshield.

She comes around the side and — still keeping her distance — tries to see who it is. The window rolls down.

"Didn't want you to be a snow widow," Sy says, his words visible as his breath plumes out into the frigid air. He douses the headlights, turns off the engine, rolls up the window. Stiffly he climbs out and stamps his feet.

"What the hell are you doing here?" she asks, stupefied.

"I found a rental car in Boston. This way at least I get to sleep in my own bed and see the kids for breakfast," he says, shrugging happily and rubbing his warm lips across her cheek. "We spend enough nights apart as it is — I wasn't willing to miss one we were supposed to have together."

"Oh."

He slips his arm around her. "I'd have taken care of this," he says, looking at the job she has done. "You must have been out here a long time."

She nods. "I couldn't sleep anyway. But I think tomorrow I'll call Mackie's and see if they can plow us from now on."

"Sounds good to me." He begins to move toward the house. "Come inside and I'll make a fire. You can pour us a couple scotches to warm up."

"It's late," she says dubiously.

"It's never too late for a scotch and a fire. Come on." And with that, he tugs her out of the moonlit night, up the front steps of the porch.

~

Alexis is still at the office. Thumbing through the merger agreement for Av Gen, she slugs one more time for hidden alterations in the boilerplate. Her attorneys at Wachtell Lipton provided her with a twenty-page commentary on the 150-page draft, and now she flips back and forth between the two documents, snorting with disgust as she pencils in her notes. There is no way she will allow her client to accept the "hell or high water" clause thrown in — predictably undiscussed — on page seventy.

Last night she was here late, keeping the deal patched together. Restless tonight, she taps her pencil on the blotter. The brief hospital stay has slowed her down and dragged her out and the firm's decision to pass her over makes her resentful about working into the early hours of the morning. In fact, only because she had been concerned about her client falling prey to Chase Porter's ineptitude had she forced herself out of bed and back into the office; it was good she had been so conscientious, because yesterday Av Gen began having trouble with its financing and only her ingenuity in mediating between the parties involved was now keeping the deal afloat. Chase had not been able to manage it despite his seniority — all of which gave her a kick.

She smiles to herself, wondering once again, and with vengeance, if Waterston has heard yet about the incredible offer Salomon Brothers made her today. This industry generates as much gossip as it does profit, and though Alexis has told no one of the offer (not even Jon, who is out of town; she hopes he will call), once a news item is in the pipeline there can be a leak anywhere. Right now she is just considering the possibility (and wondering if she leaves how she can manage to take Roger and her book of clients with her).

Her back aches and she pushes the papers away from her, checks her watch. She is surprised to find it near to midnight. She is irritable tonight; Lia warned her not to do too much too soon. She picks up her desk calendar to check her schedule for tomorrow as she crosses to the coffee pot and pours herself another cup. Reviewing the page, she sees it will be another full day and late night, and she sighs. No time for even a nap.

She riffles through the crammed pages of the calendar, and pauses at the blank on December 15. There is something she should have written in on the fifteenth, but hadn't; she thinks for a minute, and then it comes back: Maggie's party.

She hasn't seen Nicolas in months and she doesn't want to see him now, especially not in the fishbowl of the Whittens' party. Nevertheless, it is important that she go and convince Jon to accompany her: she needs to reconnect these separate parts of her life. In another few months, the divorce will be final, the marriage behind her. Then it will be easier — to run into Nicolas, to speak to each other without recrimination.

Alexis puts the calendar back on the desk and takes her coffee to the window, pressing her nose against the cold snow-spotted glass and looking down into the white crevasse below her. Her feelings for Jon have become deeper and she is scared. She feels so vulnerable. It had been wonderful to wake up in the hospital and find him dozing in the chair beside her bed, to allow him to help her home the next day and tuck her into the bed in her apartment. Nevertheless, she feels his distance and his hurt at her betrayal, and she knows, instinctively, that he needs time in which to recover.

Her office window looks uptown, and Alexis can just make out the seasonal red and green glow of the Empire State Building. The snow is definitely letting up; the streets are deserted, with not a taxi in sight. Right after lunch tomorrow she will do some Christmas shopping for Jon, she decides, maybe go up to Cartier or Hermes, and find a very small, expensive, extravagant present — maybe something that could be hidden under his pillow or his breakfast toast. Something to indulge him, even though she knows indulgence cannot heal the wound.

She exhales, long and slow, and stretches her arms over her head to clear her mind. The coffee has brightened her some, and she returns to the desk, beginning again on the paragraph she reread three times before taking the break. But after a few minutes, she finds herself drifting again, and this time starting to feel low.

She tries to reassure herself: the depression is surely just due to the hour, she thinks, looking down at her watch. It is past midnight, after all, and she needs to go home. She pictures herself unlocking the front door of her apartment, hears the echo as she walks to the hall closet to hang up her coat. It would be better to stay here than go back to that silence and emptiness. Pulling her suit jacket from the back of her chair, she goes to the closet to hang it up and takes out her makeup kit and towel at the same time. She'll run upstairs to the exercise room for a quick shower and then sack out on the couch. She stoops to pull her boots off, and as she does the phone rings shrilly, startling her. The large panel of her phone board lights up five times; she watches, knowing that a call at this hour cannot be good. Either a deal approaching disaster or a pervert.

She crosses to the desk and lifts the receiver, using her neutral business voice. Guarded. "Alexis Somers."

"Hi." It is Jon's gravelly voice that comes through the receiver.

"Hello," she says with a laugh of relief; so glad for the sound of him, she slumps to sit on the edge of the desk. How she wishes he were here, to put his arms around her, to hold her. Not just a voice across the wire. "When the phone rang I thought you were Av Gen about to crater."

"Why aren't you at home asleep?"

"Too much to do." She hesitates. "I'm glad you called — I'm feeling a little blue."

"Why?"

"Missing you."

He is silent for a minute. "I miss you, too."

"When will you be back?"

"I'm not sure. I may stop and visit a friend in D.C. on my way home."

Jealousy knots her stomach. She restrains herself: she will not ask whom he is visiting.

"Maggie and Sy's holiday party is next week." She has changed the subject deliberately. "I'd like it if you'd go with me."

"I'm not sure what my schedule is for next week."

"All right," she answers slowly. "I'll tell Maggie I'm coming and that you may."

"I was surprised when I rang the apartment and you weren't there. I thought you weren't going back to the office until Thursday."

"Well, they were letting Av Gen slide right down the tubes! Porter is such an ass and I'm tired of covering for him — I think Waterston is finally beginning to realize what a complete zero he is."

"If he hasn't seen it for the last five years why should he wake up now?"

She pauses. "Well, if I'm not here to cover for him, it might be a start."

"If you're not there?"

Her pulse quickens with excitement: to tell the secret at last. "I had a piece of interesting news today," she says, drawing it out as she gets up to walk around and sit behind the desk in her chair with a satisfied thump.

"Such as?"

"Such as Salomon wants me to come over to head up new business development in M&A."

"You're fucking kidding." For the first time, his voice regains its vitality.

"No, but it's kind of a good news, bad news joke."

"O.K. The good news first."

She laughs. "The good news is that they want me as a full partner, and it's a chance to make a mark for myself. Their department is in sad shape. Two mil a year guaranteed, with a two-year minimum on the deal."

"Alexis — that's major!" He laughs with delight. "And the bad news — that Solly's not one of the Big Four for M&A?"

"Well," she hesitates. "That is *one* reservation. It's not what I dreamed about — making partner here at Hewett. But, you know . . . what I'm most worried about is how much work it's going to be."

"Hard work never stopped you before."

"I was counting on being able to lean back just a little now." She laughs at the irony. For a moment the lamp seems glaringly bright. She reaches over and pulls the chain, sitting there in the dark. From the window comes the sound of the snow hissing against the glass. "It's a challenge to build a whole new department there, but it means I'll have to sink at least two more years of my life into it full-time."

"Meaning what?"

"Meaning I don't want to make the same mistake again." Suddenly shy, her voice drops, but she clears her throat and goes on with firmness. "Meaning I'd like it to be different with us."

There is silence from his end of the line for a minute. "Well, that all depends on the two of us. And it's going to take time." His voice is even, but reveals his hurt once again. "I'd like it to be different for us than it was with you and Nicolas." He sighs. "It seems to me the real point here is how you feel about leaving Hewett."

She is quiet for a minute. "Lousy. Making partner here is what I dreamed about for years. I guess I'm . . ." She searches for the word and surprises herself. "Sad."

"Are you over being pissed?"

"I may never be." She laughs. "I just feel both ways at once."

"Speaking of pissed, I ran into Christa today."

"That must have been rough," she says after a minute, feeling awkward.

"It wasn't pleasant. Weldon is still ripped. Think how bad he must look right now — I'm sure they're riding him for losing the account."

"Life in the big city." Her voice is defensive.

"Don't be so flip about it. I'm the one who has to deal with the flack. Christa is as high-minded as they come. I think she got a lot of pleasure watching me squirm."

Silenced, she does not even try to reply. How she wishes she could undo it all; she wonders when (or if) it will no longer

be an issue between them, and then is ashamed of herself for
not having more patience. When she speaks again, her voice is
small. "I'm sorry, Jon. I'm so sorry for the whole mess." They
talk a minute more, about other things, then hang up. She sits
in the dark, staring out into the remnants of the storm for a
long time.

✎

When Alexis dials voice mail the following morning, she
finds a message waiting for her from Lionel Edwards, the in-
house counsel at Hewett. Her body tightens: to be summoned
to Edwards's office first thing in the morning is ominous.

He gets right down to it, peering up at her over his half-
glasses with a noncommittal expression. "I'd like to talk to you
about the Av Gen deal you just brought in. As you are undoubtedly aware, this is precisely the sort of deal that sets the
SEC sniffing the wind these days, and I think the firm needs to
be prepared to answer some questions." He clears his throat
and pulls his heavy gold pen end-to-end through thick fingers.

She sits up straight in the slippery red leather chair. She
looks cool, even though her heart is pounding. (Secrets do not
become easier to live with over time.) Nevertheless, she knows
how to play this game. "Shoot."

"As I understand it, Av Gen originally was a client of First
Boston's?"

She smiles. "With what little First Boston was doing for Av
Gen, it's hard to imagine calling them a client." She shrugs and
smiles, briefly. "But yes, historically, First Boston was handling
the account."

"How did you come to be aware of Av Gen?"

She frowns, tries to recall. "I believe I finally met Roger
Apbst at a defense-industries conference last year. Of course,
Av Gen has been on our list of aerospace prospects for years."

"You are friends with Jon Stratton down at Keufel Ross, are
you not?"

She purses her mouth (how she dislikes his tight-assed
evasions). "I am." She waits, looking back into his pudgy face
quite openly.

"You are more than friends?"

"I'm sure you are already aware that Jon and I have been

seeing one another for some time now." She puts a spin of irritation on her tone.

"Were you aware that he was going to publish a report on Av Gen?"

"Jon does reports on all the aerospace companies. He's published on Av Gen before."

"Did you know that he was going to publish a new recommendation on the stock, highlighting the takeover opportunity, this month — just before your recapitalization plan made his prediction true?"

Her heart lurches, but she stares him straight in the eye. "Of course not."

"You don't find it an amazing coincidence that exactly three days before Apbst announces Av Gen will do a recap through us, your friend Stratton releases a report that proposes practically the exact same thing?"

"All the good aerospace companies are takeover bait these days — that's why our group was so successful last year. Besides, all of it is public information anyway — you only have to go look! What's amazing is that First Boston hadn't already convinced Roger Apbst to do the recap. Weldon Robb must have been aware of all these possibilities. He'd probably pitched Roger on a similar idea."

"So, how is it that you were able to convince Mr. Apbst when Mr. Robb was not?"

She smiles. "I just pointed out that if Av Gen were to be taken over — which was only a matter of time — he would undoubtedly be looking for work." She crosses her legs and leans back a bit in the chair. They are past the worst point: the lie. "You have to understand people's weaknesses, Lionel. Roger Apbst wants to remain C.E.O. of his company in a very big way. Instead of fighting that fact, I just used it." She relaxes. "Besides — I've handled three major takeovers in this industry, while Weldon hasn't. I convinced Roger Apbst that Hewett had the experience."

Edwards smiles. "Indeed. Well, Alexis, I see no obvious problem here — though the SEC may wish to dredge one up. But, I must also warn you that this kind of inquiry can also lead to a situation in which your interests and the firm's may diverge. If you feel that situation is developing I advise you to seek your own independent counsel. It's not always easy to say just what constitutes a breach anymore. There's always been a lot of loose information and now they want everything nailed down tight — as unrealistic as trying to make life fair."

Alexis smiles politely, even as the anger booms in her ears. The message he carries is one hundred percent clear: the firm is happy to take the new business she has brought in — but if there is any question (reasonable or otherwise) about *how* she obtained it, she will be on her own. This meeting with Edwards is designed to create a record: Legal inquired and was reassured with logical answers. By following through this way, they have cleared their name of responsibility. He probably has a tape recorder in his desk drawer.

There is no loyalty here, in either direction. They owe her nothing; she owes them nothing. This is a business transaction. It's not like family or marriage or any of the other relationships you enter into — where it is possible to make a mistake and be forgiven. Her mistake was ever expecting it to be otherwise. Here what counts is bringing in a deal that looks clean. There is no point in confessing to having stolen the idea for the recap from Jon, nor would it make amends to him or to Weldon Robb. It would only serve to ruin the rest of her career. No, she thinks, shaking her head as she goes down the hall to her office, her only regret about the entire fiasco is the breach of trust she has created between Jon and herself.

SEVENTEEN

A Christmas Party

Alexis pilots the twists and turns of the Hutchinson River Parkway, out of the city to Scarsdale. Three weeks have passed since she decided to resign from Hewett and join Salomon; one remains until her 1986 bonus check hits and clears her bank account. Only then will she tell Sam Waterston she is leaving.

Despite the challenges before her, Alexis is depressed. She feels she is fighting to bulldoze an invisible wall between Jon and her. To move past it requires forgiveness, and forgiveness itself requires both time and serendipity.

She looks out the windshield at the dark and barren roadside. Around her all is in flux; this sensation (unnerving) compels her to reach to people of mutual history, like Maggie and Sy. So, though Jon had quietly refused to accompany her tonight, she had made herself come alone. If anxiety over confronting her ex-husband proves to be the cost of this evening, then so be it. She will not turn her back on her past, present, or future.

Pulling onto Mardon Road, she parks and walks up the driveway. She is calculatedly late, not wanting to be among the first to arrive. It seems infinitely easier to ease herself into the waters of the party when it is busy, inebriated, loose.

The night is cold. Music filters out across the frozen lawn. A large wreath of silvery pine cones and branches hangs on the door, and through the front windows of the living room she can see people dancing.

Her hands sweat inside her gloves and she shivers. She takes a step backward, thinks — for a moment — of retreat.

"I'm going to this party," she says aloud and reaches out to ring the bell. But before she can do it, Maggie throws the door open. Taking Alexis's hand, she draws her into warmth, light, a babble of voices. From the hall spill the smells of a wood fire, balsa sap, expensive perfume. From a tall crystal vase on the foyer table, a profusion of leggy white roses unfurl, filling the air with the scent of raspberry and tea (Nicolas has remembered that Christmas is the only time of year Maggie enjoys roses, when her own garden is bare).

"I was beginning to think you weren't coming," Maggie says, smiling, as she slides Alexis's fur coat off her shoulders and onto a hanger. "I wouldn't have blamed you," she goes on, turning back from the coatrack, to give her a big hug, "but I'm so glad you did." They embrace for a moment; both of them feel the other tremble and they hold tight for an extra instant.

She ushers Alexis toward the bar, which is set up comfortingly near the fire. At the far end of the room, a Christmas tree glitters, its tinsel reflecting colored lights over the room and the dancers. Across the marble mantelpiece is woven a web of fragrant eucalyptus, dried white baby's breath, and violet statice from Maggie's summer garden; studded throughout are the flickering tongues of tiny candles.

Champagne in hand, they sip.

"How's Sy?" Alexis asks.

"Well, the 't' word is still a large part of our life — but I won't bore you with that refrain."

Alexis stares at Maggie, who seems to shine tonight with a new intensity. She has never seen her look more lit from within. It is not her clothes, or makeup, or hair. It is something else.

Maggie throws up her hands in a shrug and laughs. "Apart from that he's just fine. He's over there," she turns to scan the crowd, "talking to Christa."

Alexis smiles tightly and nods.

"You look great," Maggie says.

Alexis digs in her purse for a cigarette. "So do you. I don't think I've ever seen that dress before."

"Christa helped me pick it out," Maggie answers, smiling at

the compliment. She has tied her hair up with a ribbon the same deep green as the silk dress.

"I didn't know you and Christa were such good friends," Alexis says, feeling jealous.

"We've gotten to be," Maggie says, glancing away.

"I thought it might be easier to be late," Alexis says, looking around again. "But now I think nothing could make this any easier."

"Silly," Maggie scolds. "At least half a dozen people have asked for you."

"Is Nicolas here?"

Maggie nods.

"Did he bring a date?" Alexis asks bluntly.

"Actually he did," Maggie answers, a queer look crossing her face. "Rather unexpectedly, in fact." When she opened the front door earlier tonight, she had trouble concealing her reaction. Being near him tonight is making her intensely anxious, though the girl's presence does put off the confrontation she has been dreading.

People start to drift over to them; soon Alexis is swept up in several conversations. Everyone knows she and Nicolas are nearly divorced, and no one seems at all intrigued by this. They are more interested in gossiping about business, asking about the merger she's working on, hearing about her plans (the Av Gen merger had earned her a feature in *Corporate Finance Week*). Asked to dance, Alexis keeps looking out the corner of her eye, searching the room for Nicolas. Back at the bar a while later, breathless from a fast dance, she sees him at last. He is lounging against the window seat with a blonde who tosses her head and laughs in a hiccough. Quickly Alexis looks away, but it is too late. She has caught his eye. So acknowledged, she must now cross the room to speak to him or else appear a coward.

"Hello, Nico," she says, strolling over. He just looks at her for a minute. A beat passes, long enough for her to wonder what the hell he is thinking. She can't tell if he is glad to see her, or still angry, or just plain indifferent. (This idea galls her — better he should hate her.) It is strange to stand in front of him this way: here is the man with whom she lived for nearly thirteen years, all her young womanhood; now they eye each other, enemies in a war built on familiarity. In her mind, she had made him dead; she had extinguished her memory of the Nicolas she knew. Yet now, absurd and contradictory though it may feel, here he is. She smiles awkwardly. Her face flushes and she shoves her hands into the pockets of her black velvet trousers. "How have you been?"

He nods, finally, and looks at her with that superior half smile that used to seem so sexy and now strikes her as merely adolescent. "Lex, meet Lola."

There is something obscene about his tone, she thinks. As if he is saying, "past, meet future." Being reduced to a category — and one created solely in his mind — infuriates her. The fact that he has picked a woman in her twenties (and with a name like Lola) makes her want to laugh. She can tell from his voice that he's had a lot to drink.

"Lola," Nicolas goes on. "This is my ex-wife, Alexis Somers."

Lola's face doesn't change, her half smile locked into place. "A pleasure," she says, nodding at Alexis.

Alexis extends her hand. "Lola," she says smoothly. "I don't believe I caught your last name." And wants to smirk when she realizes that the girl is too brain-free to understand how Nicolas has reduced her by introducing her by her first name alone.

After a short and stilted conversation, Alexis leaves them and makes her way to the powder room in the hope of being by herself for a moment. She is taken by surprise by the depth of the sadness she feels at seeing Nicolas again — especially here, at Maggie and Sy's, where they once shared so many good times together. (Divorce has many stages, it appears: this sense of grief is yet another.) There is much about her marriage that she still misses, not the least being their old, comfortable place here.

The small lavatory off the foyer is occupied, and so Alexis goes upstairs to use the master, noticing as she hurries by that Maggie has woven red satin ribbon and white lilies on the banister this year. The children are asleep, so Alexis tiptoes up the stairs quietly, groping her way in the dark, into the dim light of the bedroom. Once inside, she closes the door with relief. Afraid that she is about to break down and cry, she doesn't want any witnesses. She takes several deep breaths, trying to regain her self-possession.

"Well, if it isn't the new partner from Salomon," drawls a voice, sarcastically, from inside the bathroom.

Alexis's eyes fly open; startled, she backs up against the door. Christa emerges and then hesitates a moment on the threshold. "Are you all right?"

Adrenaline surging through her body, Alexis exhales. "You scared me — I didn't know anyone was in here."

"Downstairs was busy."

"Yes," she murmurs, "it was."

They stand and stare at each other a minute more.

Then Christa makes a tight, disgusted moue with her mouth, as if she has something sour on her tongue. "You know, though I've never liked you, Alexis, I do have to admire the way you always manage to get exactly what you want."

"Why don't you like me?" Having caught her breath, Alexis is intrigued (but not upset) by this bit of candor (no one has ever told her they don't like her). Leaning back against the door, she fishes in her evening bag and pulls out her lighter and a cigarette.

"That should be obvious." Christa laughs with bitterness. "You made it impossible — impossible — for Jon and me to be friends."

"Is that what you tell yourself?" Alexis looks at her, very directly. "I think the truth is that I made it impossible for you and Jon to be *more* than friends." She lights up, and exhales. "That's your real problem."

Christa flushes. "True," she answers levelly. "But I always said you weren't good enough for him and I was right."

"How so?"

"You let your ambition pull him down. I once thought only a man would make that kind of choice."

"You have different standards for men and women?"

"I expect a woman to be more committed to what she knows is right." She stares at Alexis. "Passion sits a lot better on a woman's shoulders than greed."

Alexis smiles. "You're naive if you think women are different."

She shrugs and picks up her bag from the bed. "The whole thing is ironic."

"What is?"

"The way you trot around, your fist in the honey pot, licking your fingers for everyone to see. You took Jon's information and made hay." She shrugs. "Then you just up and move, get yourself a brand-new deal."

"Why don't you lay off?" Alexis says, a flash of anger showing now. "You haven't the least idea what you're talking about." She inhales harshly. "What right have you to judge me?"

"Sorry," Christa says indifferently, turning to the mirror to fix her lipstick.

They stare at each other for a moment in the glass, belligerently.

"You know, we're never going to like each other," Christa says at last.

"That's an accurate assessment."

Christa does not reply.

After a minute, Alexis turns and goes back down to the party.

✧

A few minutes later, Maggie, too, tries the powder room and finds it to be occupied. She, too, makes her way up the staircase and crosses through her dark bedroom. In the bathroom, she closes the door and fumbles for the light switch. Before she can turn it on, a hand covers hers, keeping the small room black.

"What are you doing?" she whispers, frightened, twisting away from his grasp.

"Waiting for you," Nicolas answers.

She can smell the scotch on his breath and knows he is not going to be reasonable. "Let's go downstairs," she says, trying to pull him toward the door, out into the light of the hall. "You haven't eaten, have you?"

But he crowds her with his body, putting his arm around her waist and pulling her up against him. "So feed me."

She puts both hands on his shoulders and tries to push away. "Someone might come up," she protests.

"Who cares." He bends his head and kisses the crook of her neck, where the edge of silk lies against her skin.

"I do!" she answers, pushing again.

He reaches up and pulls on the ribbon in her hair; she tries to stop him, but ineffectually, and it cascades down her back.

She attempts to retrieve the ribbon from his hand and fails. He is playing with her and this makes her angry. "What about Lola?" she demands.

"What about her?"

"You brought her, didn't you? I got the message."

"Not as big a message as the one you've been sending me. Nice to see I can still get you jealous."

"I am *not* jealous," she protests vehemently, fully aware that she most certainly is.

"Jealous *and* gorgeous," he says, smiling, and bending down to kiss her mouth.

She moves backward, but the sink is directly behind her and she is trapped between the edge of it and his body. His kiss is deep, beautiful, his mouth encircling hers: the rush between her legs leaves her no choice but to remember.

"We have to stop." She breaks off the embrace by twisting her head to the side. "It's wrong."

"Stop with the little girl moralizing," he says, pulling her chin with his hand so that she has to look at him. "You are a woman."

Words catch in her throat and she tries to slip past him now, out the door, but he has her by the shoulder and won't let go. He is demanding her answer: now. He pulls the neckline of her dress down and cups her breast. Her nipple points up into his palm. "A *woman*."

"A *married* woman." She tries again, unsuccessfully, to push him away, to keep his hands off, at least to readjust her dress so that she doesn't feel so vulnerable. She hates how much she still likes his touch.

"Married how?" he asks, crowding her backward, still fondling her breast. She hears a click as, behind him, he locks the door with his other hand. "In what way 'married'?" His voice sneers, faintly muddied with liquor. "I am the one you married — with your body." He kisses her again and she struggles to get away, harder now, because his touch is no longer pleasurable. "I'm not going to hang around waiting anymore," Nicolas murmurs into her hair. "I'll show you what you want."

"You just *think* you want me," she says, shoving him from her again, hard. "But you don't. Not really. It's only because you know you can't have me that you're so determined."

His eyes glint in the light from the street lamp outside. He is angry now, she sees. "Who says I can't have you?"

"I do." Her voice trembles and a tremendous rush of sadness and completion fills her. Here it is: one part of her answer. She had not known she could face it until right now. It feels good; it feels clean. "Can you understand?" she beseeches him, needing him to acquiesce. "Please, can you?"

But he doesn't answer her. Instead, he tugs her back to him with arms that encircle her smooth and strong as a snake.

"Nicolas!" She tries to push again, frightened now by the strength of his grip. "Stop it!"

He just keeps kissing her face. "Stop it!" she says again, louder now. But he straps his hand down across her mouth. She twists, fights for breath, pulls desperately on his hand, trying to free her voice. He tugs the dress up and shoves his fist between her legs, the force of it lifts her up onto the ledge of the sink. Her head bangs against the mirror. Panicked, she is afraid to call out and be caught in this incriminating situation, afraid that the children — so nearby — will hear. Silently she struggles to get free. Her panty hose rip as he shoves her underwear down. When he takes one hand off her to unzip his pants, she sees the momentary chance to escape, kicks out and tries to slide down.

He shoves her backward into the mirror again. The glass cracks against her skull. She tries to focus, but the room slips into blackness. She fights for breath as he forces himself between her legs and inserts himself like a weapon.

"No!" she says, still dizzy from pain in her head. "You're hurting me!"

She is very dry and his penis burns as he moves; he pays no attention to her protest. He pulls her back and forth, using her hips like a lever. The faucets of the sink cut into her back and her head bangs again against the medicine cabinet. Nicolas doesn't even look at her. He is using her body to declare his ownership.

"*Don't* make me remember it this way!" She is crying, choking on hate for his perfidy. She loathes every move of his once-exalted body and she hates herself as well, for having allowed this to happen. Through the wall, she hears Kate begin to cry, calling out for her mother.

"Nicolas!" Freeing her hand, she slaps his face. "I've got to go to Kate!"

He doesn't appear to register her words, he just goes on; the motion is savage. There is only the sound of her own crying, echoed by her daughter's in the distance. She slaps him again, harder. "Can't you hear Kate?"

"Kate?" he says now, seeming almost drugged. Uncertainly, he slows down. His fingers dig into her buttocks.

"Let me go!"

He loosens his grip, still inside her, not finished. The crying of the child is now clearly audible through the bathroom wall. He moves back and releases her.

She slides off the pedestal and pulls her skirt down. Her mind is numb, her body on fire. "You bastard!" She unlocks the door and flees.

Kate is sitting up in her bed, rubbing her eyes, sobbing.

"What is it, sweet girl?" Maggie puts her arm around her daughter.

"I dreamt an airplane crashed. Where's Daddy?" Her sobbing fades into a hiccough.

"He's downstairs. And I'm right here." Maggie wipes her face with a tissue.

"He'd never leave us, would he?"

"Never ever." Maggie kisses the top of her head and eases her back down between the sheets. "Now go back to sleep. We're both downstairs."

She sits and waits until Kate's eyes close, a gentle flutter, and her breathing eases back into slumber.

Maggie tiptoes from the room, leaving the door ajar.

She goes back into her bedroom. Nicolas is still there, waiting.

She stops short, not wanting to come near him.

"I'm sorry," he says. "I had too much to drink — and I just miss you so much."

"It's *over*, Nicolas!" she hisses at him, keeping her distance. "Let go. I *never* belonged to you. You *never* owned me."

He turns to the window. His voice is low. "I'm leaving for Maine next week. Are you coming with me or not?"

"I already gave you my answer. Stop torturing us with possibilities that can never be."

"You're staying with *him?*" Though he remains turned toward the window, his voice is harsh with disbelief.

"I am staying with *myself*. It is not a question of you or him anymore."

He doesn't answer. The silence extends.

"I need some privacy now. Please." Her voice is steady.

He turns and walks from the room, without looking back at her.

She sits on the bed and wraps both arms around herself to calm the shaking of her body. Then she stands up, goes into the bathroom to take care of the mechanics of getting clean. When she comes back out, the room is still empty. She leans her head against the wall and a sob escapes her, the dry rasp of loss.

✨

By midnight, everyone has gone home. The dishes are stacked in the sink and Sy wanders through the house, turning out the lights, feeling contented. He ambles upstairs and stops short. Maggie is throwing clothes into a heap on the bed. As he comes into the room, he sees that under the heap is a suitcase.

"What's going on?" he asks slowly, coming into the room.

"I'm packing."

"You going somewhere?"

"I need some time."

"What the hell are you talking about?" He is as incredulous as if he'd come up the stairs to discover her on a ladder painting the bedroom.

She makes herself speak evenly and calmly, hands still folding and stacking. "I need time to think, and I can't do it here." She doesn't look up: if he argues with her she will break down and blurt out everything. She is walking on the edge.

"Think about what?"

"About us," she says shortly, stuffing a pair of knee socks into one of her shoes. "About me."

"Don't do this, Maggie," he says softly, reaching out toward her, but she avoids his hands. "I thought things were better."

"They are enough better for me to know that I can't go on living like this."

"Would you just slow down for a minute?" he begs.

She shakes her head and clenches her teeth against the panic she feels inside. She is operating only on adrenaline.

"But I've got something to tell you."

She pauses for a moment, eyes him, but does not stop moving. "I'm listening."

"I wanted to make it a surprise celebration — not like this, in the middle of an argument," he says with despair. "I wanted it to be over champagne."

"Timing is all," she observes with bitterness.

"I got a job offer."

She stares at him and her expression hardens. "I hope you're not picking this moment to tell me you want to move to Siberia or Denmark or God knows where." She picks up a stack of underwear and throws it in the suitcase.

"No!" He shakes his head. "C.O.O. of a small company where I wouldn't have to travel at all."

She freezes, her hands arrest midair over the suitcase. "No travel?" The words sound strange in her mouth, as if she is repeating the news that she has just won a million-dollar lottery.

"None at all!" He nods, his face bright. "It's just what you always wanted."

"And what about what you want?" She stands still a minute more, curiosity moving in beside the anger. "Do *you* want to work for a small company where you won't have to travel?"

"I think I do," he says slowly. "Maybe I've been chasing something I didn't really want or understand. Or more to the point, maybe what I *do* want most has been right here all along."

She stares at him. *Too late*, the voice inside her whispers. "You can't be serious, Sy," she answers, sickened. "That's one of the oldest clichés around."

"I know, I know. But maybe it's true."

"Or maybe you just want to *think* it's true."

Now it is his turn to anger. "Look, what do you want? I'm offering to hang around in a small-time job so that I can be here with you, all of you, night after night."

"And listen to the way you see it! You might as well have said '*sell out*' to a small-time job!"

He stares at her. "Yeah . . . well."

"Why would you even consider it?"

"For Chrissakes, I know we can't go on like this."

"You'd better be damned sure of your motives — or in the end you'll wind up hating us for everything you decided to sacrifice."

"C'mon, Mag." His voice entreats her. "You know this is what you've been bugging me for for years."

He doesn't get it, she thinks. He doesn't have any conception of how far this has gone. "Too bad you didn't listen years ago," she remarks, wearily.

"What do you mean?"

"Too much has happened — feelings change. Time changes you, changes all of us. How can you not understand?" She is yelling at him in a whisper, her teeth clenched.

"What are you saying?" He looks confused.

"I'm saying I need some time to think, *by myself*, about what I want to do."

The realization that she intends to go and will not be dissuaded slowly crosses his face. "You're leaving?" he asks in a whisper. "You're really leaving?"

"I am going away for a while," she says slowly, enunciating carefully so that he cannot mistake her words. "To decide whether or not there's enough left between us to warrant trying to fix everything." She turns and zips the suitcase closed.

"You can't." His voice is panicky. "You can't just up and leave."

She doesn't answer.

"Well, where then?" he asks, dogging her steps, as she leaves the room and heads down the stairs. "You've got to tell me where you're going!"

"I can't tell you what I don't know."

"What if there's an emergency?"

"Get in touch with Alexis. She'll know where I am." She rubs her hand over her forehead and sets the suitcase down on the floor of the foyer. "I'm taking the car. I've left a note for the kids on your dresser, explaining that I went up to visit Grandma and Grandpa in Boston and that I'll be back inside of a week."

"You're going to Boston?" His voice is anxious, shrill.

"Are you kidding? With my mother doing her daily critique?"

"But what about Christmas?"

"Whatever I decide, I'll be here for Christmas."

"And who's supposed to take care of the kids this week?"

She smiles. "It'll give you a chance to see if you really want to be part of this family — before you go volunteering for something you're not absolutely interested in. Because that's what it takes to be a good parent, Sy — absolute interest. As for marriage —" She shrugs. "I don't know what that takes anymore. Maybe I'll figure it out."

"Don't go." He blinks against tears. "*Please* don't go."

"I have to," she says, through a set jaw.

He stares at her. His expression clears and something like understanding crosses his face. Uncertainly, slowly, he nods.

Maggie gets her coat from the closet, shoves her arms into the sleeves, and opens the front door. She stands there for a minute, feeling both courageous and sick: she wants to ease his pain, but the truth cannot be eased. How she pities him, his face so sad, so broken with the knowledge that his insight may have come too late; how she admires him, simply for the way he waits there on the stairs, alone and brave in the midst of his own fear and hurt, not protesting any longer, giving her the necessary room.

As she hesitates there, the wind around her ankles and the dark night waiting across the threshold of the door, she wants to run back into the warmth of this house and his arms, into the very same cocoon from which she has emerged. A bleak strength surges through her. She has grown up too much to return to such intrauterine blindness. If she returns here it will not be because she has nowhere else to go. Holding his face in her mind, she steps through the door and closes it behind her.

EIGHTEEN

Talking in the Dark

Christa lays the racquet across Kate's feet. "You can't afford to waste a good serve on a foot fault."

Kate looks down, her sneakers pinned under Christa's Prince. "But I won't be able to move, or swing, or anything." Her lower lip juts out in a pout.

"Sweetheart, I learned just like this. It's the only surefire way to keep your feet where they belong."

"But it's too hard!"

"Most things worth doing are hard, dear." She readjusts the racquet in Kate's hand. "Now, let's see your toss."

Maggie, sitting to the side of the court under the oak tree, Cash on her lap, smiles. It is the last Saturday in May. Memorial Day. The sky is a marvelous blue. Perhaps Christa will stay the night. She will cut some daisies and put them beside the bed in the guest room. And a lavender soap in the bath.

Sy, whose new job in Connecticut allows him to be home every night, had to go into the office this morning for an unusual last-minute problem. He threw a worried look at Maggie as he left this first morning of their long weekend, but she waved him off quite cheerfully. She does not mind if he has to put in occasional overtime: having him home so much makes her quite tolerant, generous really, of the occasional interruption in their home life.

"Think of your body as a spring," Christa coaches. "Coiling up and then snapping into the ball."

Kate groans. "You're a tough teacher, you know that?"

Christa nods, happily. "You're going to be a fine player someday, Kate. You'll look back and think of me then. I predict it."

Kate reaches up to give her a hug and Maggie can see Christa's face flush with pleasure. At the same time that Maggie feels a twinge of jealousy for the intimacy her daughter and Christa now share, she also feels the backwash of pride: she has raised a daughter who can give of herself.

"Hey!"

They all turn to see Sy stride across the side yard, still in his suit. Maggie thinks again how much snappier his step seems in the last few months. Sometimes he gets a wistful look in his eyes (when he thinks no one is looking), and it will be hard next winter to read the *Journal* announcements of those promoted to partnership at First Boston. *From my class*, he will think. But she is willing to bet that if asked, he'd answer that giving up Wall Street has been worth it.

He pulls his watch out of his pants pocket and checks the time. "An hour late," he groans. "Christa, I'm really sorry. Did you mind waiting?"

"I've been having a great time with Kate. We've got her feet on the ground and her arm in the air now. Why don't you hit with her for a while?"

"But what about our game?"

"We've got all day. Besides, Maggie said the Kirchenbaums might stop by and then we could play doubles instead."

"Want to, Maggie?" Sy raises his eyebrow.

"You bet." She smiles. "Jan said they'll come over after lunch."

"Great. I'll hurry up and change."

He is back in a minute, the tails of his shirt untucked. He runs out onto the court and Christa comes to sit down with Maggie.

Maggie hands Cash back to Christa. He stands on her thighs, kneading with his paws, rubbing his cheek against hers and drooling with love.

They watch father and daughter play for a while. Maggie passes Christa a glass of lemonade from the tray at her feet.

"Thanks. See how much better she's hitting?"

Maggie nods. "She's returning with a lot more spin."

"She wasn't getting her shoulder to net."

Maggie snorts. "Now why couldn't I show her that? It's so basic."

"You're her parent."

"I keep thinking we should get her lessons."

Christa shrugs. "Nothing could be better for her than playing with Sy."

"Now that it's staying light longer they've been rallying every night after supper."

"When you think where you were last year!" She shakes her head.

Maggie smiles. "The best thing he ever did was take this job," she says softly. "And I never thought he really would."

"Neither did I." Christa smiles. "What have you decided about staying on over at Sprainbrook versus going back to work in the city?"

"I made up my mind after the first day of work." Maggie leans back in her chair. "When I was realistic about what it meant to go back full-time. . . ." She shakes her head. "I had to admit that I didn't want it enough. But doing part-time sales work over at the nursery — in perennials, which I love — well, it was a good answer for a medium-sized itch." She smiles. "I'll work there through the summer. Then we'll see. The job is a kind of ballast, it keeps me in balance." She shifts in her chair.

Christa nods. "Maybe you can work your way back into New York later, if you decide that's what you want."

"Mmm. Maybe." Maggie sips her lemonade thoughtfully. "I've been spending a lot of my afternoons ruminating and writing. When I was rereading my journal last month I realized . . ." She hesitates then, suddenly shy.

"Go on, go on."

"I don't know." She laughs self-consciously. "Maybe just that writing in a journal is kind of like talking to yourself in the dark. Or," she adds, darkly, "eight years of analysis."

Christa laughs. "A shrink's daughter to the end."

"Very funny." Maggie waves her hand through the air. "I'm serious — it's a way of making sure you don't forget what you know. Writing it down makes it real."

"I never thought of it that way. I guess that's because I don't like to write things down."

Maggie nods. "I've discovered I do. I *like* to keep track of myself. So many things have changed over the last year. It seems as if I ought to be able to do something with it all. You know — a story, maybe a novel, set here, about people like all of us. . . ."

"Us?" Christa lifts an eyebrow doubtfully.

"About what it *feels* like to" — she hesitates, searching for the word — "compromise."

"Better not say thayat, or it won't sell!" Cash exclaims.

Maggie laughs and scratches the cat between his ears. "I wasn't thinking about it selling, Cash dear. Who knows, I probably won't even do it." She winks at Christa. "Anyway, what's up with you?" Maggie asks, switching the subject off this new idea. (She does not tell Christa that she has already written the first chapter and titled it *Mixed Doubles*.) "Every time you come out to visit you're a little more relaxed."

Christa shrugs. "I don't feel so pressured anymore. Maybe I don't care as much if I make partner — I might even want to do something else at some point." She laughs gaily and Cash reproaches her with his paw, shifting about in a disgruntled fashion on her bouncing diaphragm. "The idea of spending my life pulling taffy with other people's money has come to seem less than thrilling." Christa frowns and scratches Cash beneath his chin. "I played squash with Jon last week."

"He and Alexis have had a hard couple of months. She wants him to move in, but he says he's not ready."

"The gossip mill has it that she's really cleaned house over at Solly." Christa smiles, despite herself. "You have to admire her tenacity. And where is Nicolas?"

Maggie flushes at the mention of Nicolas, whom she has not seen for three months, but of whom she thinks nearly every day. "He's up in Maine, doing real estate deals."

"You guys must miss him."

Maggie smiles. "Actually, we've been pretty preoccupied with getting ourselves put back together this winter. He calls once in a while. Sy says he sounds good but lonely." She pushes from her mind the first picture that has come at the sound of his name: empty attic space, its dust undisturbed.

"And who isn't?"

Maggie smiles. "Seriously."

Christa shrugs. "Maybe I wouldn't have *picked* being alone. On the other hand, I have my work, friends, Cash, my tennis and squash. That's the way my life is." She stops with a grin. "Am I being incoherent?"

"I understand you." Maggie smiles. "Happiness — in spite of problems."

The two women are quiet now and turn to watch the action on the tennis court. Sy comes to the net to discuss a question Kate asks. They smile at one another and he ruffles her hair.

"I do love him," Maggie says aloud, forgetting herself for a minute at the sight of him touching Kate with such tenderness.

"Did you ever doubt it?"

Maggie nods. "I sure did." She grins. "When I came back at Christmas, the first thing Mikey did was fall down the stairs and slice his forehead open. Sy went for the Bactine and I went for the Band-Aids. By the time we got finished taping Mikey together I knew that I wasn't going to leave. There was still too much to find out about."

"Your kid's scraped head pulled you back together?" Christa says dubiously. "Much too simple."

"Some things are. We *just like* to make them complicated." Maggie shrugs.

Cash purrs and stretches in Christa's lap. She scratches him behind his ears. "I'm thinking of getting another cat," she says. "I've already got the name picked out."

Maggie grins expectantly.

"Credit."

"Cash and Credit!" Maggie laughs. "Male or female?"

"Female." Christa smiles. "My own family, of sorts. Maybe I'll even let them have a litter."

"And will this one talk too?"

"Everybody ought to have a voice, don't you think?"

"Indeed," she agrees dryly. "A voice for all."

The two women stand and cross the lawn to the house. It is time to make lunch. The afternoon waits, full of lazy promise. Sun circles their heads as they walk, arm in arm, and in the garden, Maggie sees, the ink blue iris have begun again, pushing up green to stretch toward the sky.